I0603922

storm seer

STEPHANIE A. CAIN

STORMSEER
Storms in Amethir: Book Three

This book is a work of fiction. Names, characters, and places are products of the author's imagination. Any resemblance to actual events or persons living or dead is purely coincidental.

Copyright 2015 Stephanie A. Cain
All Rights Reserved.
Cover art by Nicole Cardiff

ISBN: 978-0-9903758-5-2
First Print Edition, July 2015
Published by Cathartes Press

BOOKS BY STEPHANIE A. CAIN

STORMS IN AMETHIR
Stormsinger
Stormshadow
Stormseer

The Weather War (forthcoming)

FAITH AND FEALTY
Sow the Wind

DEDICATION

To Dacia Daniel,
who was a constant source of encouragement,
even if she didn't know it

ACKNOWLEDGEMENTS

I must offer my thanks first and foremost to Jessica Kemery Miller, who provided insight and early critiques, particularly on the character of Yarro. My thanks go also to my incomparable critique partners: Laura VanArendonk Baugh, J. Decker Payne, and Jillian Storm. Their input has been invaluable through the process of writing and revising this novel. Their willingness to accept panicked text messages and phone calls from me when I said, "I can't do this!" was nothing short of saintly, and I am incredibly grateful at how many times I was talked out of ditching this novel.

This novel was finished thanks to the support I received from my fellows at the Twitter Monthly Writing Challenge, particularly Kristy Acevedo, who started the challenge, Christina Ochs, Heather Jackson, Nina Lake, Amelia Lindsay, Sydney Strand, Michael Fedor, Claudia Blanton, Ginny Frey, and Natalie K. Never underestimate the power of finding your tribe on social media!

My ever-supportive parents gave me a love of words and story-telling. Dacia Daniel sent me a message on Facebook after she read *Stormshadow*, and a printout has been taped to the wall by my desk ever since. My cats Eowyn, Strider, and Eustace Clarence Scrubb were always more than willing to chew up manuscript pages or sit on my keyboard.

Thanks also to my fellow IndyScribes, who constantly challenge me to be a better writer. I am also grateful to the talented Nicole Cardiff, who created amazing cover art for this novel.

And most of all, I am grateful for my readers. You enable me to keep telling stories that are close to my heart, and I would love to hear from you.

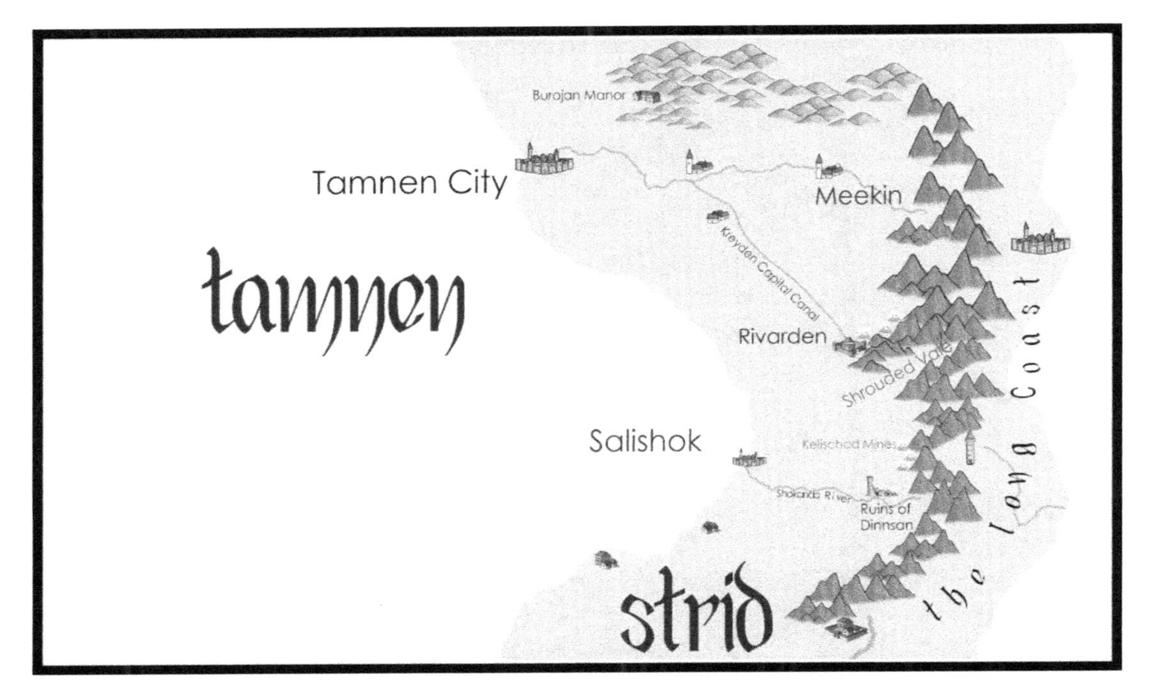
Burojan Manor
Tamnen City
Meekin
tamnen
Kreyden Capital Canal
Rivarden
Shrouded Vale
Salishok
Kelischad Mines
the long Coast
Shalant River
Ruins of Dinnsan
strid

PROLOGUE

Lord Arisanat Burojan stared down at the concentric terraces of the quarry, trying to gauge how much higher the water had risen since his last visit. At least fifteen feet. Perhaps twenty. The foreman had a crew manning the pumps during daylight hours now, diverting the water downhill to the manor and the village. It wasn't a long-term solution, but it bought time.

Time for what, Arisanat had not bothered to tell anyone. He had barely admitted it to himself, despite what he had already done. There were some lines no man ever intended to cross.

Then again, there were some things no man was meant to bear.

The water in the bottom of the quarry was stunningly blue. His sister, the sculptor, told him it had something to do with the color of the stone and how light reflected up through the water. Arisanat just thought it was deceptive, as so few things in nature were. Usually nature was forthright about its desire to destroy you. Stone crushed you. Cold stole the breath from your lungs. Avalanches buried you alive. But the quarry—the source of Burojan Family's wealth—the thing they had looked to for generations to supply all their needs—the quarry waited until they had nothing but it, and then it tore itself open and began to flood.

Of course, there were bogs north of here, up where the foothills gentled into flat moors before reaching the sea, where the ground seemed solid until a man or a horse had gotten far enough he would never escape. Then the surface of the ground opened up and swallowed you. Arisanat had never seen it, but he had heard stories from those who had.

Still, he had never expected to be betrayed by the thing he had loved most. Just as he had never expected to have the person he loved most stolen from him.

"How much?" he asked finally.

The man who stood next to him at the quarry rim had been waiting, perhaps not patiently, but in silence, for several minutes. The man looked nondescript: he was dressed in plain wool, neither too expensive nor too cheap; he was on the short side but sturdily built; he had a scruff of a beard but his hair was tidily cut. He did not look like he was here for a clandestine meeting.

"Five thousand," the man said. "In gold."

Arisanat raised an eyebrow. "I expect you to want it in mixed coins from varying kingdoms, so it won't be traceable."

The man barked a short laugh. "My master doesn't worry about people tracing things."

"Perhaps I do," Arisanat replied.

"You don't need to worry if you deal with my master." The man's words were confident rather than bragging. That ought to comfort Arisanat. He had, after all, decided he would hire only the best.

But a decision like this didn't come easily to a man like him. He had expected to spend his life in quiet non-brilliance, taking satisfaction in the fine grade of marble he shipped from his quarry to the palaces and manors of three kingdoms. He had expected the most difficult decisions ahead of him to be what addition he made to Burojan Manor using stone he had quarried with his own hands.

He had not expected his little brother, his brilliant strategist brother, to be swept away from him.

Venra had been twenty-six. He had been in command of the entire eastern Kreyden District. He had been everyone's darling. King Marsede, the generals, the soldiers, everyone had loved him. Even Princess Azmei and her brother had loved Venra. Arisanat's throat tightened. Or at least they had, until he died. Then they forgot him, just like everyone else.

"I will pay your master's price."

The man bowed. "It will be as you say, Lord Burojan." He paused. "You understand the high cost involved in what you propose?"

"Of course I do," he snapped. "I have already paid with the currency dearest to me. What your master demands is only gold."

Only gold, he said, as if the Burojan fortune was still what it once had been. As if the quarry were not nearing the end of its life. As if the ultimate price of this agreement would not be the life of a monarch.

The man bowed again. "It will be as you say," he repeated.

"When?"

"When the timing is right. Opportunities always present themselves."

"If no opportunity arises in the next month," Arisanat said, "create one. Razem has already lived to be older than my brother, and he must die after his father. I want them both dead by Longday."

The man opened his mouth. He may have meant to agree or protest, but Arisanat didn't care. He cut the man off before he could speak.

"Remember what fate befell the last assassin I sent."

The man cleared his throat. "My master will wish to know if this is revenge we are performing for you, or a coup."

Arisanat looked at the man with no expression. His face was as cold as the stone.

"Why not both?"

PART ONE
RUMBLINGS

CHAPTER ONE

Azmei Corrone, known to most now as Aevver Balearic, had long since realized she was a poor postulant to her chosen god.

She stared across the rooftops of the city, her throat clogged with memories and emotions. The setting sun made her wince, but she didn't turn away. This was her first daylight glimpse of her home in three years, and she would drink it in as long as she could.

She shouldn't be here. If she were truly the obedient apprentice she had tried to be, she would have stayed down below in their room on the inn's first floor. But to be in Tamnen City, within sight of the palace where she had grown up, and not see it—that was impossible. She had slipped away to the roof of the inn as soon as the inn staff brought Master Tanvel's bathwater.

It would be so easy to make her way to the palace and declare herself. She would be welcomed back with open arms. It was common knowledge that the princess' death had taxed the king's health. More troubling still were the rumors that Prince Razem still mourned his sister, going about dressed in dark clothes and snapping at people for no reason and drinking himself to sleep each night. She had not kept away for this.

Azmei swallowed with difficulty and pulled her knees up to her chest, resting her chin on them. The palace looked no different. The white stone walls soared gracefully over the city, towers proud and strong, banners flying to ensure the people of Tamnen City that their monarch was within and all was well in the world. If she squinted, she could picture herself and her brother, standing on one of the balconies.

There was no soft footfall to give her warning, but Azmei sensed the air shift around her a moment before Tanvel's hand came down on her shoulder. He squeezed gently. "I told you to stay in the common room," he said.

"I know. I'm sorry, Master Tanvel." Her voice was choked.

Tanvel sighed through his nose and sat next to her. "I would have spared you this, at least, Aevver. You are the most courageous young woman I have ever met, but it would be better if you did not seek pain needlessly."

"I failed them," she whispered.

"You did what you thought was best." His voice was sharp. "What I thought was best. For all our investigation, we are still uncertain who paid the Perslyn contract on your life."

"Perhaps we should have let my father decide what was best." Azmei closed her eyes. "Razem is out of control, they say."

"And your father ill." Tanvel's hand fell away from her shoulder, but he didn't move. "I have heard the stories. More even than you have." He was silent for a moment. "Would it comfort you to know that your father was apprised of *every* detail of your assassination—and how it failed?"

She jerked her head around to stare at him. "You—told him?" Hope bubbled inside her chest, mixing with relief and guilt.

"I thought it best that the world believe you dead. Your father, however, was owed the information that someone was attempting to destroy him, and that we could not determine who was behind it. He also deserved to know Razem was not his only heir." Tanvel's bearded face gave away little emotion, but he slanted a look at Azmei that warmed her. "I thought, too, that if I had a daughter such as you, I would want the truth of it, however hard. So I told him that you were sore wounded and thought it best to stay in hiding. He agreed."

"Then Razem also—"

But Tanvel was shaking his head before she finished the question. "Marsede meant to tell no one. Your brother is not skilled enough to portray this rage for so long. He would have recovered too quickly from your death. Everyone knew how close you were."

Her relief shriveled as quickly as it had grown inside her. "Razem will never forgive me," she murmured, and looked back at the sunset.

"Perhaps not. But he's a fool, if that's the choice he makes." Tanvel's voice was implacable.

"Have I lived up to your expectations so well, Master?" She didn't look at him. She didn't want him to know how badly she craved his approval. She knew she was only deceiving herself if she thought he didn't already know.

"You have done well, Aevver." They watched the sun sink slowly behind the city walls. Neither of them spoke again until it was nearly full dark. Then Tanvel cleared his throat.

"That is why we are here. The Shadow Council has received word that King Marsede treats with Strid, via an intermediary, and that a tentative truce is on the verge of being forged. Knowing of the matter's personal importance to you, they sent us here." He paused. "They have chosen your final test."

Azmei gulped. Her final test. The last hurdle she must pass before being accepted as a Dedicate to the god of peace. There had been times in the last three years when she could easily imagine living the rest of her life as a Shadow Diplomat. The fellowship she had found among the Aspirants was so very different from the largely isolated life she had led before. Yet she had made promises, and she was not one to break promises. When this test was over, Azmei would have to choose. And she had no idea what choice to make.

Could she truly live as the Shadow Diplomats did? She loved the freedom and strength she had found in herself over these past three years. But could she truly dedicate her entire life to anything other than the kingdom she had been born to serve?

Azmei had learned many things during the past three years on Ranarr. She had learned to like fish rolls and tepid tea. She had learned to be physically still and silent for hours at a time. She had learned her way around the sea passages under the towering limestone island.

She had never learned to enjoy communing with the god of peace. And if she could not worship the god she professed to follow, could she ever truly deserve her place among the Shadow Diplomats, who served him by delivering swift death when negotiations failed?

Was that what held her back? After months of soul-searching, she still wasn't sure. It might be that she was afraid of committing herself. It might be that she didn't truly believe the god of peace—or any of the gods—would ever wake from their slumber. It wasn't as if the god spoke to her. As far as Azmei knew, he spoke to no one. It could be that the god of peace slept just as deeply as all the others. She couldn't imagine how the world would shake if the gods ever woke from their slumber. Once upon a time, she had hoped to see it. Now, she wasn't so sure.

"Your thoughts are far from this moment." Tanvel's voice was vaguely reproving. Her tendency to lose herself in her thoughts was still her weak spot. She could spend hours trying to tease an answer out of a tricky situation.

"I'm sorry, Master," she murmured. She straightened her back and gazed out across the darkened city. "I am wondering what this test will mean for me. I am considering that after this test, I will have a decision to make. I am weighing the god's will in my heart."

"You aren't giving any thought at all to whether or not you will pass this test?"

She heard the amusement in Tanvel's voice, but she thought—she hoped—she also heard approval. It made her smile, though she still didn't look at him.

"I will pass this test, Master Tanvel."

He grunted. "Good."

It was true that he hadn't given her any of the specifics of the mission, but that didn't matter. She would always strive to do whatever her teacher required of her. She knew he would never require anything unreasonable or impossible. He had earned that trust, just as she had earned her confidence.

"What is my assignment?"

Instead of answering, Tanvel stood and motioned for her to precede him back inside the inn. Azmei stole a final glance at her city, then ducked back in the window. The hallway inside was deserted. It was a narrow servants' corridor, and at this time of night, when meals were being served in the common room and beds being turned down in the private rooms, there would be no one here.

"The time has come for you to finish what you started," Tanvel said softly as he led the way back down four flights of stairs. His hand hovered at her elbow, just barely touching the thin linen of her sleeve. "You must make your way to Meekin to deal with House Perslyn."

Azmei managed to not flinch. The Patriarch was one thing, but she didn't relish the idea of dealing with Yarro Perslyn. The descriptions she had heard from his sister Orya—the woman who had once been Azmei's friend and who had tried to kill her—made Yarro out to be a young man with severe needs. It was possible he was mad, though Orya's words made it sound rather more complicated than simple madness.

"And what will you be doing, Master?" she asked.

Tanvel glanced over at her, but he left the matter for her to think over. When they got to her room, she stopped just inside the door.

"You must have some errand here in the capital, or you would at least travel part of the way with me."

Tanvel rubbed a hand down his jaw. "I will be attempting to keep your father alive."

He refused to explain his statement until after she had bathed. She did so as quickly as possible. When she was dry, she dressed and combed her hair. It would dry wavy. It always did. But she clipped it out of her face before peeking out of the door. Tanvel was waiting, a tray of food balanced on one hand while the other clutched two mugs of ale.

"It's about time. I'm famished," she said, and stood aside so he could enter.

"And impertinent," he said, his lips curving in a rare

smile. "One can still see hints of Princess Azmei in Aevver Balearic, from time to time." He surprised her by bending to brush a kiss against her temple as he walked past. "Your father and brother might consider you much changed, if they were to see you now, but I daresay they would still recognize you. Now. Come. Sit and eat while I explain what we are both to do."

She obeyed as he unrolled a map of Tamnen across the table.

"I know it must be difficult being back here," he said, his voice even. "But you have been trained well, and your time in Tamnen City is nearly finished."

"I wish you weren't staying here alone," she said miserably.

"We cannot risk your being recognized, and I will need to infiltrate the palace if I wish to have any success at guarding your father."

"This is all too vague. If we knew for certain who contracted the assassination—"

"—or who was carrying out the contract, yes, I know," Tanvel broke in. It occurred to Azmei that he was treating her much more like an equal than a student. When had that changed? Sometime since their arrival in Tamnen, she was certain. "But the information is reliable. We know the Perslyn family bid on the contract, and we know they lost." He smiled grimly at her. "Partly thanks to our success in rooting out Perslyn operatives in Ranarr."

She knew he was right. Since her apprenticeship to Master Tanvel, they had been focused on discovering how deep the Perslyn network ran and how far it stretched. Certainly it was widespread in Tamnen, but Azmei had been shocked at how many tendrils of the network they had discovered in Ranarr. At least they were certain the assassination plot had not come from Strid. Tanvel had actually gone there as part of her father's peace negotiations, though her father had not known it. It had been too great an opportunity to pass up, and it had proved a worthwhile effort.

"Still. I don't like leaving you."

"Do you think you have gained so much skill in three years that you can head off any dangers that might threaten me, with my thirty years of experience?" Tanvel's voice was mocking, but he was still smiling at her. Azmei flushed at his teasing and ducked her head.

"No, but even you can't see what's sneaking up behind you."

"I have a friend or two here in Tamnen City. I will not be entirely alone, even if I will be without my apprentice." Tanvel pushed a bowl of soup across the table at her. "Eat up before it gets cold." He settled into a chair, holding his own soup bowl under his chin.

"Do you have any instructions for my task in Meekin?" Azmei asked, reluctant to let the subject drop but knowing she had pushed it as far as she could.

"Find out who paid the Perslyn to kill you. If you can, gather the evidence the king will need to deal with them legally. We know none of the Nine will go down without hard evidence."

"If it *is* one of the Nine," Azmei said, though they were almost certain it must be.

Tanvel pressed his lips together. "At the very least, satisfy your own curiosity." He sipped his soup. "Then kill the Patriarch."

Azmei swallowed. She had been preparing for three years to kill the Perslyn Patriarch, but there was still a part of her that was unsure she could manage it. "And then?"

Tanvel's smile turned sad. "Then you will have a decision to make, my young Aspirant. If you succeed in killing the Patriarch, the Shadow Council will accept you as a Dedicate. You will be allowed to work on peace missions without my constant supervision." He sipped his soup again. Azmei wondered how he did it without getting his beard wet.

"I confess," he went on, "I wish I had the liberty of overseeing your test. I would never be permitted to pass judgment, but I would take pleasure in seeing how well I had taught you."

"Don't you already know that, master?" she asked, holding his gaze. "All I have done these past three years is to be a credit to your teaching."

"And you have done it well," he assured her. He was silent for a moment before clearing his throat. "You will have no aid in Meekin. There will be an observer, of course, but you will not know who it is. Be certain, though, that whatever you do will be noted."

Azmei drained her soup. "You said I had a decision to make," she said, and the words echoed back to her from their first meeting, when he had told her she must decide whether to publicly survive the assassination or go into hiding and play dead. He had always left the difficult decisions to her. It was one of many reasons that she loved him—he never treated her as if she were incapable of making those decisions, even if she made the wrong choice.

"I did indeed." Tanvel set his bowl aside and took a long pull from a tankard. "You may return to Ranarr as a Dedicate to the god of peace. Or you may return to Tamnen as her princess. Once we have destroyed the Perslyn brood in its den and uncovered its patron, there will be no more reason for you to remain in hiding. You will be free to live the life you had planned for yourself."

Azmei stared at him, almost wishing he hadn't said it. Of course it had occurred to her, but wishful thinking was one thing. Tanvel presenting it as an option was another thing entirely.

"The life my father had planned for me, you mean," she murmured.

"Perhaps so, but it was the life you were prepared to live, before you met me." Tanvel was watching her. Azmei couldn't identify the strange gleam in his eyes. Did he want her to remain a Shadow Diplomat? Did he think she should return to her old life? And if she did, should she marry Vistaren as planned? Would it truly make any difference in the war now?

Azmei lifted her own tankard. "What do you think I should do, master?"

She saw the surprise bloom in his eyes. She had asked his opinion many times in the past three years, but it was obvious he hadn't anticipated the question. He turned his gaze down into the depths of his tankard, jaw working.

"I do not know," he said finally. His voice was low. "You are the finest student I have ever trained. True, you have stronger motivation to learn than any of the rest of my students. But you have an aptitude for intrigue and understanding people. It would serve you well as a Shadow Diplomat, even though you lack faith in the peace god." He licked his lips. "And yet..." He studied her face. "And yet, I think the world could use a queen such as you would be. You were already well on the path to being a fine queen for the Amethirian Empire. You won Vistaren's loyalty and the loyalty of two of his finest servants. You charmed the Ranarri people, who are seldom impressed by outsiders. I believe you would be good for this world."

Azmei stared at him. Never had he spoken to her like this before. She felt her throat tighten and fought against a sudden upswelling of emotion.

"And there is this: as queen, you might be in a position to end the war between Tamnen and Strid. As Shadow Diplomat, you almost certainly never would."

Having spoken his piece, Tanvel sucked down the rest of his tankard of ale and stood. "Do not think on it overmuch, Aevver. Get through the test. Things may look much different after you have had your justice."

CHAPTER TWO

Prince Razem Corrone had been angry, off and on, for most of the past four years, since the Dinnsan Massacre. His favorite cousin Venra had been killed in the final defense of Dinnsan, along with nearly two thousand of Tamnen's best-trained warriors.

Razem had simmered with anger through Venra's funeral, barely able to meet his cousin Arisanat's red-rimmed eyes as the man wept for his younger brother. It had been Azmei who had comforted Arisanat. It had been Azmei who had spoken so eloquently of Venra's generous spirit and kind sense of humor that all the other hardened warriors at the funeral had wept along with her. It had been Azmei who spent the next month with Venra's family, ensuring they wanted for nothing that she could provide. Razem had served as a poor representative for his father at the funeral, then pushed his horses all the way back to Tamnen City, where he had urged his father to mount a counter-offensive that would retake Dinnsan and push the Strid out of the Kreyden District forever.

When Azmei had come home and agreed to a marriage treaty with the Amethirian Empire, Razem's anger had burst out at her as well. They had argued almost until the day she set sail to meet the boy she had agreed to marry. Razem didn't know what grace had led him to make his peace with her before she left, but he was grateful for it. It had been the last time he saw his sister.

He heard someone knock on the door to his chambers, but he ignored it. His head was throbbing, and though he'd meant to be up before dawn, he'd let himself linger in bed. It had been a mistake, as it always was. Whenever he slept past sunrise, his dreams turned foul. Ra'zem didn't bother listening to the lowered conversation. Gendo would tell him if it were important.

The door closed. Gendo's footsteps were soft on the marble floor. "Prince Razem? His Majesty requires your presence in the council chambers."

Curiosity flickered to life in the back of Razem's mind. That was new, at least. His father hadn't had much use for him lately. "Did he say what the matter is?"

"I'm sorry, highness. I told the messenger you would attend the king with all speed."

With a groan, Razem climbed from his bed. He rushed through his ablutions and let Gendo dress him in clothes appropriate for the council. Twenty minutes later, he presented himself.

"My lord father, you summoned me." He hoped that had been a pleasant tone of voice. He didn't actually wish to be obstreperous. But when he glanced up at his father, he saw that Marsede looked troubled, but not angry.

"I did, Razem. Thank you for your promptness." The king was not an old man. He was not yet sixty. And yet he looked older than his years. The war with Strid had aged him, Razem thought, and Azmei's death had been yet another blow to his health. Life had not been kind to Marsede Corrone.

Life did not seem to be in the business of kindness.

"How may I serve, Father?"

Marsede gestured for Razem to take a seat at the council table. Razem obeyed, glancing around at the assembled faces. Lady Riman of the Second Family, Lord Birona of the Third Family, Lady Tel of the Fourth Family, those were all expected. Lord Belnat of the Sixth Family was less so, though he was pleasant and well liked. Arisanat should have been there, as the head of the First Family, yet he was absent. The Fifth Family had no representative currently on the council, though they were ever in the king's heart, since Queen Izbel had been of the Fifth.

"I have just finished explaining to the council that I have been negotiating with the Strid this season," Marsede said. "Not for peace, as that would please none of our people and solve no problems, but yet for common ground, from which we may eventually reach some truce that would end the fighting while we attempt true peace talks."

"What?" Razem bounced back out of his seat, mouth open, but his father was already gesturing for him to sit down and be silent. Razem swallowed his protests but remained standing, glaring defiantly at his father.

"Sit you down, son." Marsede's voice was harder than it had been a moment before. "You will hear me before I listen to your diatribe against the Strid. I am weary of war. My council is weary of war. My people are weary of war. It would not surprise me were the gods themselves weary of this war. The only people gaining from this war are those who supply the army with weapons and armor and food." Lord Birona shifted in his seat, but didn't speak.

"And Azmei's murderers!" Razem burst out. "Have you forgotten about your murdered daughter?"

"How could I?" Marsede's voice crackled harshly. "Did I not raise her? Did I not dandle her upon my knee? Do not lecture me about your sister, boy!"

Around the table, several of the assembled counselors shifted in place. Razem swallowed the accusations he had been ready to spew. His face grew hot. His father had never spoken to him thus in front of the council. They had exchanged plenty of heated words in private, but never in public. Suddenly he wished very much to be in the practice ring with Emran Kho, as he usually was in the morning, instead of here in the council chamber. He dropped back into his chair without a word.

"I have weighed all these things in my heart, and I have come to believe that Azmei would wish us peace. She went to Ranarr in the name of peace. She accepted Vistaren of Amethir's marriage proposal in the name of peace. And yes, she even died in the name of peace. Why would she then wish war upon us, when she made the ultimate sacrifice attempting to bring us peace?" Marsede rose from his chair and paced slowly along the length of the table.

Razem didn't know if his father was expecting him to respond. He wasn't sure what he would say. Azmei might counsel peace if she were here. But if she were here, Razem would have no need to argue.

"I have sent emissaries in secret to speak with the Strid. One of the Diplomats who traveled here after Azmei's death was willing to negotiate on our behalf. He has been half a year in Lindira, and finally he has accomplished at least one of the objectives we gave him." Marsede stopped pacing and placed his hands on the table, leaning in to look at each of them in turn.

Razem wondered if he was supposed to ask. He didn't. His father had told him to be silent, as if he were a small boy. Very well, he would be silent.

Marsede leaned forward still further. "The Strid have agreed to give us Jacin Hawk."

For a stunned moment no one spoke. The counselors looked around at each other, mouths open but silent. Razem stared at his father, wondering why Emran Kho wasn't here. Hawk had been Kho's commander until he was captured.

The silence dragged on so long it was becoming uncomfortable. Razem could see that Lady Tel wished to speak, but she only stared at the king. Lord Belnat was gnawing on his lower lip with such fervor that Razem wondered if it would be bloody when he left the council chambers. Lord Birona's shrewd gaze was turned, not on Marsede, but on Razem.

Razem cleared his throat and stood again. "At what price?" he bit out.

Marsede met his gaze. "We are returning their Duke Oler."

"The Deranged Duke!" Razem burst out. "Father, have you gone mad? Duke Oler slaughtered women and children! He put the aged to the sword and spared no nursing mother!

How can you—"

"Because he has no health left to him, and we would let him die in his homeland," Marsede interrupted. "He is a frail old man himself, now, and I will take any advantage I have that might yield me a temporary truce. If they will give us our Hawk in exchange for their dying Duke, I will take that trade."

"Damn you," Razem growled. "You are not the father I thought I had."

"And you are not the son I would wish for!" Marsede snapped. "But you will go to Salishok, and you will exchange their damned duke for our war hero Jacin Hawk, and that is final!" He slapped his palm against the wooden table with a crack that made Lord Belnat jump.

Razem drew himself up until he felt as if his spine were a sword. His gaze locked with his father's and his heart begin pounding in his chest. But he had never seen his father so implacable before. Even when he sent Azmei off to the highest bidder in Amethir, he had been apologetic rather than authoritarian. Today there was a light in his golden eyes that made them seem as if they could burn right through Razem. He dared no further protest.

"I will serve as I am ordered," he gritted out, "but I will not like it."

"I do not ask you to." Marsede's gaze was steely. "Bring Jacin Hawk home in one piece. Shower him with all honor and glory. Give him every courtesy. Flaunt him as a hero in Salishok and every city and village and hamlet between there and Tamnen City." He drew himself up to his full height. "And when you have done that, you may beg my forgiveness and all may yet be well."

Razem could feel his teeth cutting into his lips, but he refused to show his father any expression besides defiance. Who, he wondered, would tell Lord Arisanat? It wouldn't be Razem, that much he would swear to. "If that is all," he said.

Marsede made him wait for an answer. He looked around at the group of nobles shifting in their seats and refusing to meet anyone's gaze. He lowered himself into his seat and tapped his fingers on the carved wooden arm. Finally, when Razem thought he would burst, Marsede said, "The lord-general will accompany you. Speak to General Kho about your escort."

Razem forced himself to bow, his gaze never leaving Marsede's face. He left the council chambers without looking at any of the other members of the king's council. He hoped he could eventually forget everyone who had witnessed this confrontation. He wouldn't like to hold it against them for being present when his father provoked the argument.

As he strode through the vast stone corridors of the palace, he considered and discarded a dozen things he should have said to his father in response to his cowardly pacifism. Nothing was sufficient to convey the depth of his rage, though. No words could capture the gut-twisting hatred he felt for the Strid. He wanted to march all the way to the Strid capital and raze it. He wanted to leave nothing but a path of ashes from the border of their kingdoms to the lavish palace where Prince Anderlin lived his depraved, debauched life.

"You could set the building alight with your eyes, I believe, Prince Razem." Emran Kho himself, dressed in his characteristic linen and wool, breeches tucked neatly into his boot tops, shirt buttoned to the neck. He was a tall man with black skin and broad shoulders, and Razem had always privately thought he had the most wistful smile in the world. Their relationship had always been distant, but polite.

Razem's rage boiled over. "Did you know what the king was planning?"

Kho straightened, his hands loose at his sides. "I knew I would receive orders today, highness, if that is what you mean. But I did not—still do not—know what those orders may be."

His forthright address soothed the roughest of Razem's temper, though it did not make him any more patient. Razem scowled and folded his arms across his chest.

"My father, in his infinite wisdom, has agreed to a prisoner exchange with Strid. You and I are to travel to Salishok with Duke Anyet Oler so we can get the Hawk back from his

Strid prison cell."

The effect these words had on Kho disappointed Razem. The general didn't even blink. He merely said, "So that is the king's will. When shall we leave?"

Razem opened his mouth to respond, then drew in a long breath. He was going to have to travel halfway across the kingdom with Kho, and he had always liked the man. He didn't need to be at odds with him. "The king didn't see fit to inform me," he said, only a hint of acid in his voice. He took another breath, feeling his heartbeat slow infinitesimally. "But I imagine we leave at our earliest possible convenience."

Kho nodded. "Am I to attend the king?"

"He told me to consult with you about the escort." Razem finally mastered himself enough to smile crookedly at Kho. "I assume that means you and I are to plan all the particulars, subject to his approval."

"Very good, highness. Shall I accompany you to your quarters? We shall begin planning at once."

***

"—and that's for Da when he gets back from the quarry!"

Arisanat paused in the passageway and glanced at a passing servant. The man moved closer. "The Lady Rija is within, my lord," he murmured. "She and Master Variden have a...project, I believe they are calling it."

Arisanat raised an eyebrow and tiptoed to the archway into his son's rooms.

"I think he'll like it," Rija was saying. "You got her hair and eyes right. Will you give it to him now? I think I heard his carriage in the courtyard."

"Not until it's done. I haven't got Uncle Venra in it yet."

Arisanat's throat tightened. Variden had only been four when Venra was killed. He couldn't possibly remember much about his uncle, but Arisanat and Rija talked about him to Variden. He drew in a long breath and stepped back from the archway.

"By the winds, I come home after a long journey and the only one to greet me is the chamberlain? Don't I have a son, or did the horse traders finally steal him away?"

"Da!" There was a clatter inside the room and then Variden ran out to the passage. He launched himself into Arisanat's arms.

"Oof—you're too big, I'll drop you," Arisanat teased, pretending to lose his grip. Variden shrieked with laughter and wrapped his arms and legs around his father. Arisanat kissed his son's temple. "Did you miss your da, Vari?"

"I did! Aunt Rija wouldn't let me ride my pony or play in the courtyard fountain or *anything*!"

Arisanat glanced over Variden's head at his sister, who had come out of the room and was leaning on the door frame. "Aunt Rija, that's dreadful."

"I know, I'm horrible. I made him do all his lessons and practice his singing, *and* I even made him help the chambermaid tidy his room, since he'd thrown his building set all over." She was grinning as she complained, though, her eyes twinkling.

"Thank you for taking time to correct his hoydenish ways," Arisanat said. "I suppose this is what comes of a man trying to raise a child all by himself." He tickled Variden, and the sound of his son's giggle made his eyes sting. Gods, he loved the boy. He was nothing like Arisanat, but he shared Rija's artistic bent, and Arisanat thought him the spitting image of Venra at eight.

"Now you must go away, Da," Variden said. "I'm making you a gift, but I have to finish it." He squirmed. "Put me down."

Arisanat kissed him once more and set him gently down. Variden darted back into his room. When Rija didn't follow, Arisanat glanced questioningly at her.

"Don't worry, Kala's in there. She'll watch over him." Rija took his arm and turned him back towards the front rooms. "So. Tell me about your journey."

Arisanat cleared his throat. "Journey itself was

uneventful. The quarry's filling faster than it was, though. If you need any more of that heartstone marble, you'd best send the orders up at once. I think the vein will be under water before Longday."

"Gods have mercy, Aris," she whispered. Her brows drew together as she stared up at him.

"Never mind. Fenla's a genius, and his apprentice is nearly as skilled. Fenla has him up scouting for a new location." Arisanat straightened his shoulders; she didn't need to know how worried he was. "Your husband did request your presence at the estate."

She waved a hand. "As soon as this commission is finished. Another fortnight, at most." She pressed her lips together in something that was trying to be a smile. "We'll figure something out, Aris."

"Of course we will. We're House Burojan." He hoped his smile was more convincing than hers. "Now I could use a hot bath, and perhaps a massage. The roads are not smooth, this early in spring. I'll join you for dinner later."

"And Variden?"

"Tonight, of course." He paused. "Rija? When you go back to the estate, take Vari with you. I think he would be better away from the city, just now."

He smiled vaguely at her and headed for his bath. He opted to skip the massage, though, when his chamberlain knocked as he was drying off.

"Beg pardon, my lord. Councilman Birona is here to speak to you. I told him you are just returned from the country, but he insists. He says he must apprise you of developments within the council."

"Ah, well, let me finish dressing, then bring him in." Birona was head of the Third Family, and he had been a welcome voice of reason on the council this last year. Known as a moderate until then, he had been less than enamored of King Marsede's peace plans. "And send in wine and refreshments. My head is aching."

"My lord." The chamberlain bowed and withdrew.

Five minutes later, Lord Birona strode in. He was bulky without quite being fat, but his small eyes and broad forehead pushed him across the line into ugly. Nevertheless he was one of the shrewdest men Arisanat knew, as well as one of the richest. In recent years, with the slow failing of Arisanat's quarry, Birona's wealth was likely creeping up even on him. Best of all, for Arisanat's purposes, was that Birona's fortune had been made on supplying the army and rebuilding Rivarden. Marsede's peace had threatened that.

"Burojan," Birona said, sitting without preamble or courtesies. "Trouble in the countryside, or was that a pretext to get away from the endless council meetings?"

Arisanat snorted and straightened in his chair. He removed a cinnamon shard from the little box at his elbow and stuck it between his teeth. "Neither. Just a bit of business that couldn't be done without me."

Birona merely grunted. He was studying Arisanat. The chamberlain entered with his tray of refreshments, poured silently, and vanished again. Arisanat sipped his drink and met Birona's gaze.

"Well, I hate to trouble you so soon after you returned home, but I might as well tell you what trouble the council has caused while you were away."

"Please do. Coffee or wine?"

"Need you ask? Wine." Birona took the proffered goblet and leaned back in his chair. "There's been some unrest regarding the new tax on coffee. Ridiculous. It isn't as if we can transport it from the Long Coast at no cost."

Arisanat rolled his eyes. "It could be worse. The council could have decided to tax salt."

Birona chuckled. "The king seems uneasy about the Amethirian ambassador's long absence. They keep making excuses about storm season, but I wonder... You don't suppose that Vistaren fellow is upset about the treaty being broken? Perhaps he'd rather have had Razem to begin with, anyway?"

Arisanat laughed with Birona. With Azmei's betrothal to the prince, interest had been piqued. It had gotten around

Tamnen City, at least in the Families, that Vistaren of Amethir was a same-lover. It didn't much matter now, Arisanat supposed, but the Azmei he had known would have wanted true love and an epic romance like those in the story books. She must have been bitterly disappointed to learn her betrothed's affection ran towards men.

"Just as well the plans fell through, then," Arisanat remarked. Birona gave him an odd look, but didn't protest. Arisanat bit back a smile. If Birona had recoiled, Arisanat could have blamed his long journey for the gauche words. As it was, he clearly needed no apology.

"But back to council business." Birona sighed. "I might as well warn you, since you'll no doubt hear it tomorrow. The king has had someone negotiating behind our backs."

Arisanat went cold. "What?"

Birona scrunched up his beady eyes. "There's been a Diplomat in Lindira. They've agreed to a prisoner exchange."

"Damn them," Arisanat whispered. His pulse began pounding in his temple. He had known something like this was coming, but it still hurt to have his suspicions proven. He darted a glance at Birona, hoping the man hadn't heard his incautious words, but of course he had.

"Damnation seems unlikely, but there will certainly be more loss of profits—and of life, of course." Birona drummed his fingers on the arm of his chair and took a long sip of his wine. "There are too many of us who stand to lose in this proposition." His voice was grim. "I have poured a great deal of my own purse into the rebuilding of Rivarden."

Arisanat gulped his wine, trying to push down his temper. "Why did you do that? I've always wondered."

Birona shrugged. "After the Push, I put certain plans in motion. There were quite a few loyal Tamnese citizens volunteering for the war after that, tensions running high and all. My agents had all they could do to keep up with demand. My father always invested safely, but I prefer to invest only when there is a chance of great reward."

Arisanat offered him a faint smile, though his mouth had

gone dry. Perhaps Marsede's foolish actions had given him the opportunity he had been seeking. If Birona would back his claim, Arisanat should have more than enough resources to act as soon as Marsede was dead. He licked his lips and fished for another sliver of cinnamon to freshen his mouth. "No wonder your reception of the peace talks has been so...lackluster."

"I am sick to death of this whimpering after peace," Birona said baldly. "Particularly when we have the resources to win the war outright, should someone have the balls to commit them."

"Were I on the throne, there would be none of this whimpering after peace," Arisanat promised. It was the first time he had spoken those words—*were I on the throne*—and they stung his lips. But he didn't try to recall them.

"Would that we could see that day, Arisanat," Birona replied. "Alas, I suspect the prince will not oblige."

"Certainly he will not. As much reason as Razem has to hate the Strid, he lacks the audacity to defy his father."

"Then you believe we will come to terms with Strid?"

Arisanat narrowed his eyes. "You know Marsede's thoughts. He might even entertain the notion of a treaty marriage."

"Gods forbid!"

Arisanat allowed a little silence, then he tipped his head to one side and smiled faintly. "*I* forbid, Birona. The gods sleep, but I will stop it, if I may."

Birona licked his lips. "And you would have my help, I assume."

Arisanat tilted his head and smiled. "Who else but the head of the Third Family? We all know Lady Tel supports Marsede, but there are others who would ally with us to prevent a treaty."

"Through purely legal channels, of course," Birona agreed. He leaned forward in his chair, his bulk making it look like a mountain moving. "But who else would have the courage to move a bit...outside the bounds of the law?"

Arisanat bit back the smile that wanted to creep across his face. "Who can say? For now, let us agree that we will vote against any treaty Marsede proposes."

Birona held out a meaty hand for Arisanat to clasp. "So it is agreed."

***

Razem half-feared he would hear shouting as he approached Emran Kho's office. It had been four days since his father had swept his feet out from under him with the news of the prisoner exchange, and he still hadn't fully accepted it himself. He dreaded seeing how Arisanat was taking the news.

Arisanat had not been in the council because he had been called away to Burojan Manor, some sixty leagues northeast of Tamnen City, to deal with a crisis at his main quarry. Razem hadn't asked for details, but even three years ago, when Razem and Arisanat had been on speaking terms, his cousin had been worried about the lifespan of the quarry. The marble supply couldn't go on forever, and that quarry had been the mainstay of Burojan income for nearly two centuries.

There were raised voices in Kho's office, as he had expected, but Razem had not expected to see Destar Thorne doing the shouting. Razem eased himself up to the doorway, hoping to avoid Thorne's notice, but Kho saw him and cut Thorne off.

"While I appreciate your concerns, Prince Razem is here to consult with me and Lord Burojan. If you have nothing to add to the discussion about the prisoner exchange, I must ask you to go."

Thorne swung around to glare at Razem. "And you! You should have known better."

Razem raised his hands in a show of innocence. "I don't know what you're angry about, and I don't want to know. It isn't my fault."

Thorne's eyes narrowed. "You should have told your father this was a matter for warriors and ambassadors, not princes. Look what happened to your sister."

Razem's stomach tightened. "I had nothing to do with this, Thorne. My father acted without my knowledge, and he didn't see fit to *ask* me if I would go. He *ordered* me. And I, being a dutiful son, obeyed." Damn Thorne. Arisanat wasn't even here yet and already they were arguing.

"Being a dutiful son, your goal ought to be not getting yourself killed," Thorne snapped.

Razem made his voice cool. He liked Thorne, and he knew Thorne and Azmei had been close. But this was going too far. "As your purview is the sea, I fail to understand why you are even here."

Thorne's eyes narrowed even further, but he didn't reply. Instead, Kho spoke from his seat at the desk.

"I asked Destar to be here, your highness. I welcome input from those who have different outlooks than I, and Thorne is a brilliant strategist. I am certain he will have wise counsel on this matter." He slanted a glance over at the sea captain. "Once he gets past his temper."

Thorne sputtered but subsided, glowering at both of them. Without speaking, he stomped over to a chair that had been crammed into the office.

Razem leaned against the wall, folding his arms across his chest. "Who else is coming?"

"Captain Ysdra, my second here in the capital," Kho said. "I want him to know our plans, and, as I said, I value input from others, if it is well-considered."

Arisanat appeared just moments after Kho had finished speaking. He tapped on the doorframe, then bowed properly to Razem before acknowledging Kho. Smiling a welcome, Kho gestured him to a seat.

Arisanat was a tall man with broad shoulders. From a distance, he and Razem, six years younger, had been taken for brothers. They both had the brown skin and black hair of the ruling family, though up close an observer would see that Razem's eyes were truly golden, while Arisanat's were light brown flecked with gold. The purple godsmark on his left temple was the only thing that marred his looks, though Razem had always thought if Arisanat would let his hair grow out from its severe cut, that would hide it.

"Prince Razem," Arisanat said now. "Lord-General Kho. Lord-Captain Thorne." He sat in his chair with economical movements, not quite looking at Razem. "I apologize for my tardiness. I was waylaid by Lady Talt in the hall, and you know how she likes to talk."

Kho's smile was easy. "Well do we all know it, I think," he said. "But you are not late. We await Ysdra still."

Arisanat nodded and fell silent. Razem probably shouldn't speak. They had been stiffly polite with each other since Azmei died. They were certainly not as close as they had been, which was never as close as each of them had been to Venra. But Razem still cared for his cousin, and after a moment he couldn't resist.

"I hope your business at Burojan Manor fared well."

Arisanat's gaze wandered over to him. He seemed astonished that Razem would speak to him. "It went tolerably well, your highness. I thank you."

"And your sisters are all well?"

A pause. "They are as well as may be. Rija continues her work on your sculpture of Princess Azmei."

Razem nodded. "I am glad to hear it. And how fares the quarry?"

It was perhaps a small mercy that Captain Ysdra arrived at that moment. He bowed to the prince and lords, saluted to Kho, and took a seat.

"Very good," Kho said. "Does everyone know why we are here?"

"Aye," Thorne growled as Razem nodded.

"Yes, sir," said Ysdra.

Arisanat's jaw tightened. "I am not aware." His voice, which had already been cool, was icy now. He glanced over at Razem. "Perhaps your highness will enlighten me."

Winds take him. No one had told Arisanat? Razem swallowed. What would be the best way to break the news? If only he'd had time to plan this out—but then, Father hadn't given him time to plan what he would say, because his father knew him too well. If Razem had known he was expected to break the news to Arisanat, Razem would simply have skipped the meeting.

"Spit it out." For the first time in months, Arisanat didn't speak formally to him.

"It isn't easy news," Razem cautioned. He cleared his throat. "My father has arranged to trade a prisoner with Strid. He hopes it will further the peace talks."

Arisanat lifted his chin, nostrils flaring, and his face drained of color, but that was the only indication of his temper. He didn't blow up or lash out. If anything, he drew into himself, tightening. He met Razem's gaze for a long moment that was so cold it burned. Razem was aware of Ysdra and Thorne and Kho waiting for his reaction, but no one spoke.

"Does his majesty explain why he offers me this insult?" Arisanat asked finally. His voice froze the whole room.

Razem knew he had to thaw the situation somehow, but he had no idea what to say. He floundered for words and grasped the first ones that came to mind. "Not insult, Aris. His majesty honors the sacrifice Venra made for our kingdom. He deems it too high a sacrifice to allow anyone else to make." It was a bald-faced lie; many more people had died after Venra, and if they weren't of the highest echelon of families, they were still *someone's* family. But if it appeased Arisanat—

"Your highness will forgive me if I do not take it thus." Arisanat was drawn so tightly into himself that he seemed almost a statue. "No good can be had by appeasing the Strid dogs. They are honorless. Every concession Marsede makes shows his weakness in the face of their barbarity."

Razem agreed with Arisanat more than he did Marsede, but he couldn't admit that, not even in as private a setting as this, after his outburst in the council chamber. Nor could he bring himself to defend his father's actions. He met Arisanat's gaze unhappily.

"And you summoned me here to tell me this? Why?"

Arisanat gestured at the others. "So you would have witnesses to see me speak treachery? Is Lord-General Kho here to arrest me?"

"No!" Razem exclaimed, shocked. "How could you think so? My father has not suppressed the speech of those who are against the war. Nor would he suppress the speech of those who support escalation. You are here because my father wishes you to travel to Salishok with us."

Arisanat stood so abruptly his chair scraped back against the stone floor. "Your father would have me watch yet again as someone returns from the war when my brother never will?"

"Damn it, Aris, do you think you are the only one who mourns Venra?" Razem flared. "My father grieved for his nephew before he grieved for his daughter. I lost a man who was as close to me as a brother! You do not have sole possession of his memory!"

That was probably the wrong thing to say, but Razem had lost two people now—his best friend and his sister. Arisanat had never been close to Azmei.

"If you had truly loved Venra, you would not have agreed to give your sister to Amethir in exchange for peace talks," Arisanat spat.

"I did not agree. I protested! But Azmei herself agreed, and she was right to do so."

"Then she got what she deserved." Arisanat's voice was ugly.

Razem punched him. His fist connected solidly with his cousin's nose, sending a shock of pain all the way up his wrist. He heard Kho and Thorne shouting, but he was too focused on the sight of bright red blood erupting from Arisanat's nose to pay attention. Arisanat rocked back in his chair, eyes wide. Apparently he hadn't expected Razem to hit him. For that matter, Razem hadn't expected to hit him, either. His body had acted before his mind caught up with it.

There were hands on his arms, grasping so tightly it almost hurt. Arisanat's face was flushed as Captain Ysdra flung an arm across his chest to keep him from throwing himself at the prince. Ysdra was getting blood down his uniform front, but he didn't seem to notice.

"What the hell was that?" Thorne was shouting in Razem's ear. "Are you a prince or a mewling brat who squabbles and settles things with his fists? Grow up, lad! Your sister wouldn't have wanted this."

Razem tried to shake him off. He stared at Arisanat, who still hadn't checked the blood flowing from his nostrils. Kho was talking angrily in Arisanat's ear, a wad of cloth gripped in one hand. Razem closed his eyes. He was such a fool. He wanted to punch Arisanat again. It had felt good to make his cousin feel the pain Razem was experiencing. But he knew he had just ruined everything. There would be no hope of settling things amicably between them now. He slumped back in Thorne's grasp.

"Ysdra." The captain jumped to help Kho convey Arisanat from the room. Razem's cousin looked furious, but said nothing.

Thorne shook Razem. "Little fool." He directed Razem back into a chair. "What would you have done if he'd struck back? He could be flogged for such an offense. Were you trying to provoke that?"

"What? No!" Razem stared at him. "I would never—"

"Good. That's meaner than I thought you were." Thorne shook his head. Razem wished he could see past him to his cousin. "I'm disappointed in you. I thought you had better sense."

"You heard what he—"

"I did," Thorne interrupted. "And I also know that Kho just the other morning gave you a lecture on self-control." He made a wry face. "I know that because he had to give me the same lecture this morning." He sighed and sat in Arisanat's vacated chair.

"My father's going to kill me."

"He can't. You're the only heir he has." Thorne didn't make that sound like a compliment. "But he might wish he could. You fool, I thought you understood Arisanat was the sticking point in all this."

Razem rubbed a hand through his hair. "I thought I was the sticking point."

"No, you're just being a little shit. Arisanat has a serious grievance against the crown, and he is of the First Family. He has enough clout to make things very difficult for your father, especially if he talks Birona around to his way of thinking." Thorne glared at him. "Have you been so wrapped up in yourself that you honestly didn't know all this?"

"I—You mean—I—" Razem broke off and leaned back heavily in his chair, the breath whooshing out of him. "Do you think Aris *will* make things difficult?"

"Damned if I know." Thorne rolled his eyes up to glare at the ceiling. "Sleeping gods, if I had known taking the promotion to Lord-Captain would mean I had to wrangle wayward, willful, royal brats, I would have refused the title and run off to Amethir. Marrying one of their stormwitches would have brought me less trouble than this has."

Razem suppressed a flash of resentment and stared at the floor, trying to look properly cowed. He didn't have any right to resent Thorne's words. They were true. He'd been a complete and utter fool. For several minutes he sat and listened to Thorne's breathing while he tried to regulate his own. Finally he murmured, "What should I do, Destar?"

"I haven't a clue, your highness. I don't know Lord Arisanat well. What do *you* think you should do?"

"Ugh. Apologize to him." Razem groaned. He rubbed his hands over his face. "Beg his forgiveness. Perhaps I could be honest with him about my own reaction to Father's decision."

"Honesty usually is the best choice, as long as you think you can manage it with tact." Thorne slanted his gaze over at him. "And without any more punching."

"He'll probably need some time to cool off," Razem said hopefully, but Thorne snorted.

"When has putting off a foul task ever made it more palatable? Nay, if I am the one giving counsel, I say you should apologize quickly, before this becomes a stone lodged in Lord Arisanat's heart. You and he were close once, weren't you? Closer, at least, when his lordship's brother was alive."

Razem nodded. "We went there every year for Longnight. My sister loved the snow they get in the hills." He swallowed against a sudden thickness in his throat. "I never cared for the cold, but it pleased her so." He shivered.

Thorne rested a hand on his shoulder. "I miss her, too, lad."

Not knowing how to respond to that, Razem simply nodded and went.

***

Arisanat was—for good or ill—easy enough to find. He and Emran Kho were sitting on a bench at the edge of the practice rings. Arisanat still held a red-stained wad of cloth to his nose. The two men did not appear to be speaking. Razem let his steps slow as soon as he saw them.

He was almost more ashamed to face Kho than Arisanat. Kho's lecture about discipline should have stuck in his mind more this morning. Instead Razem had allowed his temper to overrule his thoughts and had made an already difficult situation worse. It was tempting to wait here and watch to see what sort of mood Arisanat might be in before approaching. But no, that was cowardly. Razem may be a fool, but he was not a coward.

He took a deep breath, steeling himself for the humiliation to come, and stepped forward. Kho saw him coming at once. He stood, resting a hand briefly on Arisanat's shoulder, and bowed to Razem.

"Lord-General," Razem said, pitching his voice low and trying to sound humble, "I would speak with Lord Arisanat alone."

Kho bowed again silently and took his leave.

Razem walked closer to his cousin but did not sit. He felt as if he should ask Arisanat's permission before sitting, and besides, he didn't think it wise for them to be too close to each other just now. He couldn't guarantee his cousin wouldn't swing for him, and Razem truly didn't want him flogged.

"I must beg your forgiveness, cousin," he said after several long moments of silence. Arisanat had not even turned to look at him or acknowledged him in any way.

"Must you?" his voice was rough. Razem felt a fresh pang of guilt. His thoughtless reaction had just scraped a blade across Arisanat's still-oozing grief. And it was true that Arisanat had poked at Razem's own sore spot, but that was no excuse.

"Yes, I must." He made his voice firm. "We have always been friends, cousin, and I would not be the one who destroyed that friendship. I have many fond memories of the time we spent together as children. And I was thoughtless in my own grief, unmindful of the grief that is yours, that needs must always be sharper than mine, for the love of a brother. I have felt that grief myself. I was wrong to slight it."

"You were." A simple statement of agreement, nothing more. But the fact that Arisanat was responding to him made Razem breathe a bit easier.

"I must confess something to you as well," he went on. "My reaction, when my father told me of the impending prisoner exchange, was not so eloquent or graceful as yours. I raised my voice to my father in his council chambers. I defied the king to his face. He had been well within his rights to rebuke me then and there. But even with more cause, he did not strike me, as I most shamefully struck you."

Arisanat's shoulders heaved twice. He straightened up, lowering the bloody cloth. "Sit down, you maundering lump. Anyone who looks at us will know we have quarreled, else." There was impatience but no affection in the words. Still, Razem took another deep breath and sat obediently down, and valiantly ignored being called a maundering lump.

"For my part, I apologize for what I said of Azmei," Arisanat said. "I knew it would wound you before I said it." His throat moved as he swallowed. "I wanted to give you some of the pain I have carried all these months."

Razem nodded. "We have both suffered great losses. Perhaps they were not quite the same, but they were both terrible." He licked his lips. "Aris, I need you with me. I do not think I can go to Salishok and accept Jacin Hawk back to our kingdom unless you are by my side." He looked over at his cousin, seeing that behind the dried blood his cousin's face was drawn with grief. "I must have your blessing, or I must defy my father."

It was even almost true. He hated what his father had done. He hated the thought of carrying on with peace talks when the talks were tearing their kingdom apart. If Venra's brother were truly poised to act against the king, Razem must know. And if Arisanat decreed that Razem should defy the king...well, as much as it might pain Razem, he would know what he must do. He would not enjoy arresting his cousin, but inciting the prince to civil war would be treachery of the highest order.

"Don't be a fool." Arisanat's voice was harsh as his fingers closed around Razem's wrist. "You cannot defy your father, and I would not ask you to."

"But will you grant me your blessing?" Razem whispered. "Will you come with me?"

Arisanat's fingers tightened until they gripped hard enough that Razem's wrist bones creaked against each other. "You know I will, lump." His voice caught as he said the words, but while there was still no affection, there was also no cold formality in them, either.

Razem swallowed hard against a sudden rush of emotion. He had never been as close to Arisanat as he was to Venra, but then the four years Arisanat had on Razem meant he was there to teach the young prince how to pack snow best for building a fort wall and which way to lean to steer a sled the way it should go. Razem was grateful his hasty reaction hadn't ruined all of those good memories in a single instant.

"Thank you, Aris. That means more to me than I can say."

"You'd best think of a few things to say before your father hears about this." Arisanat's voice was dry as he released Razem's wrist and stood up. "Come. If we are going to the desert, I expect we have some planning to do."

CHAPTER THREE

"Get up."

Jacin Hawk looked up from the book he had been reading. It was an old one, predating the current Tamnen-Strid crisis by at least a century, and it was a love story, which wasn't his usual preferred reading, but it was better than the zealot poetry he'd been given last month. "What?" he grunted.

The guard standing outside his cell door was probably a decade younger than he was, if not more. Certainly no older than twenty-five. He shifted his weight and rested a hand on the doorframe. "The king has sent someone to see you. You ought to be presentable."

"As if I give a damn." Hawk turned his gaze back to the book, licked his thumb, and carefully turned the page. He knew it would anger the guard. It was meant to. Though he had been left here to rot for six long years, he had taken care to never become a tractable prisoner. He might not be the Tamnese Hawk any more, leading a line of charging swordsmen against the thieving Strid, but he would not be meek under the threat of confinement. Not when he had faced down death and laughed.

"Get up, damn you!" the boy snapped. "Commander Ayowir will be here in just a few minutes, and I won't have you disrespectful or dirty."

Hawk didn't look up. "Come in and make me, then." He had to fight to suppress the smirk that wanted to crawl across his lips. The younger ones always had less self-control. Hawk almost enjoyed the company of a few of the older guards. The ones who remembered the days before the invasion, who had grown up without constant warfare. Hawk himself had been sixteen when the Strid attacked the Kelischad Mines, and it had been another three years before he went off to war after that. This boy, though, had grown up in a country constantly at war. What did he know of real life?

"Winds take you," the boy growled, and the clank of keys told Hawk that he *was* coming in. Was this audience truly all that important, then? What made it different from the hundreds of other encounters he had had with Commander Ayowir over the years? She was a hard woman, but she'd always seemed fair.

With an exaggerated sigh, Hawk closed the book and set it aside. He hadn't been enjoying it, anyway. It was just something to pass the time. He had a lot of time that needed passing, these days.

"Very well, what is it you want me to do? I only have the one set of clothes. I had a bath two days ago and I've hardly exerted myself since then." Hawk stood. "Is she such a delicate lady she'll swoon at the sight of my unshaven face? I haven't held a blade in six years, by her orders, so she'll have to excuse it."

It was an exaggeration. He'd been given knives with his dinner for the past three years, ever since they decided he wasn't going to escape. And once a month they tied him to a chair and shaved him. He supposed they were afraid he would slit his own throat if they let him shave himself.

He'd given it thought, actually, but his nature had never been one inclined to despair, and he had calculated that his maintenance would cost the Strid more than burying him would. He liked the idea of inconveniencing the enemy by simply continuing to draw breath.

"Tamnese scum," the boy spat, and cuffed at him. "You will stand out of respect and give the Commander your attention."

Hawk caught the boy's wrist in one hand. Not tightly—he didn't want to frighten the boy into drawing his sword. He just wanted to remind him that Jacin Hawk was not someone to toy with. "Watch yourself, boy," he muttered, making his voice hard. "I have known the Commander longer than you've been out of swaddling. She and I have come to our own understanding."

"That's enough, Hawk," said a calm female voice. Ayowir was a tall, rangy, rawboned woman with a ruddy complexion. She wore her long blonde hair plaited back from her face, exposing an ear with a chunk missing. Hawk had been forced, grudgingly, to respect her, first as they faced each other across the disputed leagues of the Kreyden District, and then as her captive. She had never been friendly with him, and never would, but they had each other's measure, and there was, as Hawk had said, an understanding between them. "You've embarrassed him. I'll have to assign him somewhere away from prisoners now." She didn't look at the boy as she spoke of him. Hawk did, just long enough to see the boy flush red as a battle flag.

"Just doing my patriotic duty to inconvenience you a little bit every day," Hawk said lightly. He released the guard's wrist and the boy pulled it back, rubbing it with his free hand. "What are you here for?"

Ayowir's lips quirked in something that was nothing like a smile, but wasn't quite a grimace. To Hawk's surprise, she didn't answer him at once. "Go back to the duty station and see that we aren't interrupted," she told the guard.

The boy didn't manage to meet his commander's gaze as he saluted her, but he did have time for a venomous look at Hawk. Hawk bared his teeth at the boy.

When they were alone, he repeated his inquiry. "What is this about, Ayowir?"

She pursed her lips, and now that she met his gaze, Hawk could see the confusion in her gray eyes. "Freedom, Hawk. Is that sufficient to catch your interest?"

She sat in the single chair in his cell. In truth, it would have been an actual room, had the door been solid wood instead of an iron grille. He had a small fire pit, a table and chair, a chamber pot and washbasin, and an actual bed. Hawk could complain about many things since his capture by the Strid, but he could not complain of his treatment.

Hawk remained standing, though his leg was beginning to ache.

"Freedom," he said, when he thought he had let enough time pass that he wouldn't sound overeager. "That's a broad concept."

Ayowir shifted back in the chair, her knees settling apart, one foot back in case she had to stand suddenly. Her eyes roved frankly across his features, and Hawk pictured himself as she must see him: a broken warrior with a bad leg, paler than he had been since birth, thinner than he should be, his light brown face half covered in three weeks' worth of black whiskers that were, these days, more liberally sprinkled with white than he would like. Thirty-six was not so old as all that, he thought, but his captivity had aged him. He wondered if Ayowir still saw the warrior in him. His heart was still a warrior's heart, he wanted to say. But it was not her business what Hawk thought of himself.

"Freedom," she said. "Your freedom, in particular." Her gray eyes were considering.

Hawk stiffened. "I won't betray my country," he spat. They had been over this too many times to count, early on. Why would she return to it now?

"Did I ask you to?" Then she made a wry face. "Recently, anyway. No, Hawk, I confess, I'm being mysterious only partly by choice. The truth is, I know little more than you. But here it is: My king and yours have seen fit to communicate through an intermediary, and the upshot is that Anyet Oler is to be released to us, conditional upon our returning you home in more or less the condition we found you." She did smile then, her thin lips pulling to the right thanks to a scar from her partly-missing ear. "Though I rather think we did a fair job of patching you up, all things considered."

He would have lost the leg—if not his life—if the Strid battlefield combers hadn't found him when they did, and he and Ayowir both knew it. As it was, he was lucky to have kept the use of it. He had not had the opportunity to discover if he would limp over long distances, but in his cell, he had only been troubled by it when the rains were coming.

"They would give back the Deranged Duke," he

murmured, and was rewarded with a flash of ire in her expression. Anyet Oler was Ayowir's uncle, or something like that. But she didn't speak her reply aloud. Hawk wondered what she would have said. There could be no denying that Oler had waged systematic genocide against the Tamnese people of the Kreyden District. Never mind that half of them had Strid blood in them somewhere, even if it was mostly long generations ago. Things had been tense enough, thirty-six years ago, that Hawk was one of the few half-bloods of his generation.

"Anyet is dying, Hawk," she said finally. Her voice and expression were wiped of any emotion. "To my thoughts, Tamnen is getting a better deal. But we will take him back, if only to bury him among his ancestors so he may rest peacefully."

Gods grant his spirit never rest, Hawk thought. But something stayed his tongue. He wouldn't want to be buried in the land of his captivity. He could hardly blame the duke for that, even if he blamed him for much else.

"What are the particulars, then?" he asked after it became apparent Ayowir was not going to speak again.

She frowned, returning from wherever her thoughts had taken her, and Hawk reflected that he could have murdered the Strid commander just then. Six years ago, he would have. Just two years ago, he would probably have tried. What had happened to him lately?

"We will go to Salishok. Your Prince Razem and whoever they replaced you with will meet us there, under flag of parlay, and I suppose you will go home a grand hero." She tipped her head to one side, watching him. "I will have someone come in tomorrow to shave you. And I will speak to the watch commander about giving you time alone in the yard. I won't have the Tamnese bureaucrats say we mistreated you."

He smirked at her. "Most kind, Commander."

Commander Ayowir was as good as her word. The next morning a barber came in and not only shaved Hawk but trimmed his hair until it was chin-length. Hawk stopped him then. He liked it long enough to pull into a stubby tail if necessary. The man sniffed and scrubbed his hair with a harsh, astringent-smelling soap, not once, but twice. Hawk's eyes watered at the strength of it, but he hoped it meant his scalp would quit crawling and itching. Apparently the commander wished to return him to Tamnen free of lice as well as any other ailments.

After the barber finished with him, Hawk was given a heartier breakfast than he'd seen since his recovery from the leg wound. And then the watch commander appeared and conducted Hawk to his appointed exercise time in the yard. Hawk wasn't sure what to make of it all, but he wouldn't look a gift horse in the mouth. He had done what he could to keep his muscles strong in his cell, but you could only manage so much in a small space. He centered himself in the yard and began moving through the slow forms of his discipline. When no one stopped him from that, he gradually increased his speed until no one could believe his exercise was anything other than martial in nature.

Still no one came to stop him or send him back to his cell. With a shrug, Hawk lost himself in the forms until he felt his muscles begin to shake. It took less time than he would wish, and that brought him back to himself with the grim reminder of all the strength and speed he had lost. He slowed to a stop and then began stretching so his muscles wouldn't protest as much the next day. Only when he had finished did one of the guards collect him and take him back to his cell.

His lunch was larger than he was used to as well. Hawk finished what he could, then tucked a crust of bread away for later. He spent the rest of the afternoon reading. After a supper that had actual meat in the stew, he went to bed, which was when he noticed they had swapped out the old pallet for a softer one with cleaner blankets. Hawk raised his eyebrows, but after a moment he decided they wouldn't want him picking up the lice again from his bedding. With a shrug, he went to bed.

The next several days followed the same pattern. Hawk was measured and given two extra sets of new clothes. A cobbler came to trace his feet and returned the next day with a pair of boots that was only slightly too large. One of the guards brought him a pipe and a pouch of tobacco. Another pressed a small wooden carving into his hand when she collected his supper dish.

He lit the pipe and examined the little carved hawk. It had intricate feathers and cleverly cut wings that looked graceful without being in danger of breaking off. He had seen that guard carving when she sat outside his door, but they had rarely talked.

He could understand why the Strid administrators might want to soften him towards his captors, since they had agreed to set him free. He could even see why they would want everyone to believe he had been treated well during his captivity. But he could not parse the reasons behind the guards giving him gifts. He had never been a compliant prisoner. But then again, he had also never tried to kill any of them. Perhaps that was reason enough.

***

Hawk squinted up at the hot, desert sky and wondered what he was going home to. He had no family left to welcome him home. His friends had all been in the army. Were they still even alive? He couldn't expect everything to be the same as he had left it six years ago. Who would even care that Commander Hawk was home?

You're feeling sorry for yourself, he thought, giving himself a mental shake. *You're old enough to know better. Gird your loins and get over it.*

"Deep thoughts, Hawk? You look troubled." Commander Ayowir had come alongside him on her gray gelding. She was watching his face curiously.

They had been traveling at a relaxed pace, starting after the sun was well up and stopping for lunch. Upon reaching the more arid foothills surrounding Salishok, though, Ayowir had decided they should begin earlier in the morning so they could rest during the hottest part of the day. For the last three days of their journey, they had been up before the sun and on the march as soon as a thin line of pink warmed the eastern sky. They marched until noon and then set up tents and rested in the shade until early evening, when they packed up for another three hours of marching.

Hawk had been allowed to ride with no bonds on his wrists. He had a guard posted at his tent, though he was not bound with even an ankle shackle. If he had truly wished, he could have escaped with little effort. At this point, however, he saw no reason to escape.

He gave her a rueful smile. "This still seems less than half real. I suppose I won't believe it until I wake up in Salishok again."

Her lips curled slightly—not quite a smile, but an acknowledgement. "It's real. I'll actually sort of miss you, you know." She slanted a look at him. "You've tested my patience often enough, but I suppose I've grown used to you."

"What a heart-warming compliment." He didn't suppose it was politic to admit he liked her. The enemy was supposed to be faceless and emotionless. He couldn't see her that way, not after six years of constant exposure to her. Then again, he'd never really seen the Strid that way. He had hated them, but he had always known they were people, not faceless monsters. Didn't their blood run through his own veins? Hadn't his father been Strid?

His mother, who had been of no particular family in Tamnen, had fallen in love with a Strid tanner who lived on the outskirts of town. Hawk's father had been skilled at his craft, and he had provided well for his wife and only child, but there had been a certain divide between their family and the rest of the town. A few other children straddled the Tamnese and Strid communities in town. But the relative peace into which they had all been born had only been a shaky pause in the centuries-long hostilities; tensions had been heating up again in the decade leading up to Hawk's birth. Losing both parents in the Strid invasion when he was young had cast the divide in stone.

Still, It wasn't the Strid people he hated, but the Strid army and the king who sent that army time and again into the Kreyden District, trying to seize the diamond mines and the natural resources that by rights belonged to Tamnen. Hawk wondered if Prince Anderlin or King Harkai would be there at the prisoner exchange. He might be willing to sacrifice himself if he could take Anderlin or Harkai with him.

"Don't think about it too much," Ayowir said, her voice startling him from his memories. "We'll be there tomorrow, and you'll see for yourself it's real."

Hawk wrenched himself back to the present conversation. "I suppose I'll believe it then," he said, giving her a vague smile.

Indeed, it wasn't until the next day, when he saw the hulking brown stone walls of Salishok looming up from the foothills surrounding the Shokanda River, that it truly felt this exchange would actually happen. A group of soldiers from the Tamnese Army rode out to meet them while they were still at least an hour from the city. The Tamnese exchange party had not yet arrived in Salishok, and until that happened, the Strid party must camp here. Commander Ayowir seemed unhappy about it, but not surprised.

That night, Hawk was shackled to his cot.

CHAPTER FOUR

Razem had been to Salishok once before. Three years ago, the day after his sister sailed off to marry the Amethirian prince, he had ridden for Salishok at the head of his father's army. Princes of Tamnen always proved their worth on the battlefield, and Razem had been no exception. He had taken command of the Kreyden District, headquartered out of Salishok.

He had been guided by several more experienced counselors, of course. Lord-General Kho had not accompanied him to Salishok last time; he had had his hands full in the capital. But Baron Arkad, whose ancestral home was in the Kreyden northeast of Salishok, had been on hand to advise him. And Colonel Tropas, an officer with ten years in the Kreyden, had been his second-in-command. Tropas had taken over as the district commander after Razem's melancholy homecoming to the capital.

He was very much dreading his return to the Embattled City.

Salishok had been on the front edge of the war with Strid fifteen years ago. Over the years, however, the Tamnese army had pushed the Strid back forty miles from the city walls. It meant the city was not literally besieged, but there was the constant threat of it. Food was strictly rationed to maintain a six-month supply in the crown storehouses. The Salishok Reservoir was guarded day and night to prevent sabotage or poisoning of the water supply. Trade caravans were accompanied by army detachments, rather than the mercenary caravan guards that plied their trade further north away from the district.

As a consequence of the tense situation, when Razem, Arisanat, Emran Kho, and their soldiers traveled to Salishok, they took with them a long, winding caravan of merchant wagons. The merchants slowed them, of course. Veteran soldiers could easily march twenty miles a day, but the gargantuan horses pulling the merchant wagons could not be pushed, and Kho had advised letting the horses graze at least an hour each day to supplement the supply they had brought with them.

"The more we conserve on feed, the more they'll have to sell when we reach Salishok, and that earns you a great deal of currency in the current political situation there." Kho was riding next to him on an immense black gelding, his eyes constantly roving across the ranks of soldiers and to the dry plains beyond.

Razem knew better than to utter what he was thinking. *I'm the crown prince. I shouldn't need political currency.* After assessing the situation with Arisanat and learning how much clout his cousin had gained in the council recently, Razem was reevaluating everything about the crown and how the kingdom actually worked. He had been given lessons in statecraft and policy all his life, but he was finally beginning to actually understand it. Upon reflection, he rather thought Azmei had understood the situation much better three years ago than he ever had.

These new revelations didn't exactly curb his temper, but they did make him bite his tongue against quick retorts.

"I hadn't thought of that," he admitted instead. "I am grateful for your guidance, General Kho. Although I spent a year out here in the Embattled City, I never came to know all its nuances as you do."

To his pleasure, Kho smiled. "My prince flatters me."

"No, your prince speaks the truth. I am coming to understand that I have much yet to learn. I could do much worse than to learn from you, Emran."

Kho turned to study him, still smiling, though his eyes were searching Razem's. For his part, the prince tried to hide any resentment he might feel at having his ignorance on display. He wasn't at all certain he had succeeded, but he hoped Kho would at least credit him for attempting to keep a humble attitude. He lifted one shoulder in a self-deprecating shrug.

Kho laughed, a low, rich chuckle that relaxed the tense muscles in Razem's back. He hadn't realized how desperately he wanted to please Kho. He wanted peace with his cousin, of course, and he wanted to do what was required of him in Salishok, but more than either of those things, he wanted Kho to like him, to approve of him. He wanted the Lord-General of his father's army to believe Razem would one day be a king worth serving.

"I am honored that you wish to learn from me, Prince Razem." Kho held his gaze for a few moments longer, then returned to his relentless scanning of their surroundings. "I will be happy to serve in any way I can."

Razem nodded gratefully and allowed the conversation to lapse into silence.

***

The day before they reached the Salishok Plains, a courier from the city met them. She had dark circles under her eyes from riding through the night. She told them the Strid party had arrived two days ago. She had been dispatched to inform the prince's party while the Tamnese army invited the Strid to camp at least an hour's ride from the city walls.

The remainder of that day was spent in a traveling conference with Kho and Arisanat. Razem's cousin was of the opinion that the Strid party should be made to wait even longer for the prince's arrival. Kho disagreed, pointing out that the purpose of the prisoner exchange was to improve relations with Strid, not to increase the hostility.

"The crown prince of Tamnen will not bow and scrape to whatever ambassador the Strid have sent!" Arisanat said hotly. "It is not seemly, and we already do them more courtesy than they do us. We know they have not sent Prince Anderlin to make the exchange."

"Thank the gods for small mercies," Razem muttered. "Aris, I don't intend to bow and scrape, but I don't see any sense in lording things over the Strid. There is no point in embarrassing whatever lord the king has sent in place of his uncontrollable son."

"And if we receive the Strid party with more ceremony than is required," Kho added, "it will be a less obvious show of Prince Razem's position of authority. Only the man who has much has the ability to be generous."

Arisanat didn't look happy, but he managed a grudging, "Well said. I am content."

Razem nodded for Kho to set about giving the orders for a small but adequate force to be assembled for accompanying the prince's party, while the bulk of the soldiers were left behind with the merchant caravan. He waited until Kho was out of earshot before commenting, "You're not content. Nor am I. But we will make the best of this situation."

Arisanat was silent for so long Razem glanced over at him. His cousin was frowning down at his horse's mane. "I believe you are a more forgiving man than I could ever be, Razem. I still wish for Anderlin's bloody head to be hung on the Salishok city gates."

"As do I." Razem's voice was hard. "For my sister's sake as well as for Venra's. But I will bide my time yet."

"Do you truly believe Anderlin was behind the assassin who struck down Princess Azmei?" Arisanat still did not look at him. His voice was low.

"I cannot prove it. But ultimately I place the blame at his feet, even if he was not the man who paid the contract." Razem scanned their surroundings, a habit he had picked up over the past several days of riding next to Emran Kho. "We were assured the assassins had traveled to Ranarr at the same time Az did. That means they weren't hired by the Amethirians to prevent the marriage. We know the Ranarri wouldn't assassinate Azmei. They were the ones who brokered the marriage treaty."

"At your father's urging," Arisanat pointed out.

"True, but they pride themselves on being peacemakers. Murdering a princess in cold blood does not exactly strike me as an act of peace."

"A good point."

Razem sighed. "I have gone round and round in my mind over this matter, Aris. I cannot believe it was anyone other than the prince of Strid."

"There are those in our kingdom who do not wish for peace." Arisanat made a wry face. "For that matter, I am among them, as you must know."

"You've made no secret of that! But anyone who would commit such a heinous act might not speak out openly against the peace." Razem shook his head. "And what would killing Azmei accomplish, anyway? The peace might be halted temporarily. Or permanently, I suppose, if the killer convinced us Strid was responsible for the attack. But there has never been any evidence that Strid was behind it."

"Isn't it odd that Strid wouldn't claim the kill?" Arisanat asked.

"I don't know. Perhaps they realized that they had crossed a line." Razem rubbed his thumb across his fist. "Perhaps it was Anderlin acting alone, rather than on King Harkai's orders. They would have kept that quiet, were it the case."

"Perhaps." Arisanat didn't sound convinced.

"Azmei was loved by everyone. Even if someone didn't approve of the peace, most of the common folk wouldn't have the resources."

"And the nobility? The Nine may have open access to your father, but the lesser nobles have no such recourse. They would have to file a petition to see your father, and even then he would have the power to deny their request. Perhaps one of them grew impatient."

"It can't be inexpensive to have a princess assassinated," Razem objected. "No, I cannot believe it of any of ours."

From the corner of his eye, he saw Arisanat's shoulders relax. "I am glad to hear it. I would hate to think any of us had lost your confidence."

Razem smiled. "You never could, Aris. You know I love you. For your own sake, as well as for Venra's. We have had many pleasant times together, have we not? Of all the places I have seen in our great kingdom, the hill region around Burojan Manor is my favorite."

Arisanat smiled back and reached over to clap a hand against Razem's shoulder. Though they rode in silence the rest of the morning, Razem felt a weight lifted that he had not realized he carried.

By lunch time, Kho had given all the orders necessary to separate their force in two. He explained it as they ate. When they set out again, the force that was to ride with the prince had separated itself from the merchant caravan. Razem, Kho, and Arisanat joined them, along with Duke Oler's medical wagon. They traveled at a much faster pace that afternoon. As the sun was setting, they could see the squat walls of Salishok in the distance.

Razem gave the messenger letters to carry to both the military and civilian authorities, as well as one for her superior that commended her for her service. Razem and Kho had questioned her during the afternoon about the mood in Salishok, and the prince had found her informed and well-spoken.

The next morning they rose early. Razem had his usual morning status report on Duke Oler's health—he was in good spirits now that they were within a day of their destination, but he had weakened considerably over the course of the journey. They ate breakfast on the march. Razem wanted to arrive at the city by noon. He had given orders that the Strid party should be allowed to arrive in Salishok once the prince's party was inside the gates. There would be rooms prepared for them, though they would be required to leave the majority of their soldiers outside the walls.

The first thing they did when they arrived in Salishok was endure an official welcome from the city leaders. Razem put on his most cordial expression and did his best to convey that he was pleased to be in Salishok again, and that he was looking forward to enjoying all the delights the city had to offer. It was partly true, at least. He enjoyed the dry heat of the Kreyden

District, and he was looking forward to the unique fruits that grew in this region. After diamonds, the largest exports of the Kreyden District were fruit and fruit wine.

"I am honored to have you here, Prince Razem," Baron Arkad said as they made their way to the palace. "We have set aside the most luxurious accommodations for you and your honored companions." He wiped a finger along his thin mustache. "I was not certain what you intended for Duke Oler, so we have prepared a comfortable and secure room for him. I have heard that he is in ill health."

Razem nodded. "He is very weak. His mind is still as healthy as it ever was—which I realize is not saying much. But the healers who have treated him for the past year of his illness know best what he needs. I will have Rendon, the head healer, speak with your chamberlain."

"Very good, very good." Arkad was a solid man who had once been a warrior of some note. His muscle had largely run to fat in recent years. He was at least sixty and possibly older; his son led their soldiers now. He smiled at Razem. "You are looking well, your highness. It truly is a joy to see you again."

Razem felt a rush of affection for his old advisor. "And you, Arkad. You look hale and happy."

"I am a grandfather now! Rasha's wife gave us twins this past Autumn Evener. Twins! Bless her, a girl and a boy. It has brought new joy to my life, having the babes." Arkad beamed. "I confess, I have not been as attentive to matters of state as I should have since they were born."

Razem chuckled. "I congratulate you and Rasha's wife both. And Rasha, I suppose, though I wonder if he has any time to spend with his children, if he is taking up the slack you leave in the rope."

"Insolence," Arkad said happily. "Rasha and Jemi are here in the city. I summoned them when I learned you would be coming with the Deranged Duke. I could not have you here without seeing them again."

"I am glad to hear it." Razem's pleasure had dimmed somewhat at the mention of Duke Oler, though. He pursed his lips. "Arkad, what is the mood here in Salishok? What do people think about Duke Oler's imminent release?"

Arkad frowned, scratching at his beard. "Well, it has been...a rather mixed reaction, I suppose I should say. There are those who see this as a step towards peace, and plenty of us here in the Kreyden would like to see that. Goodness knows, I had hoped Rasha would inherit my lands in a time of peace, and now here I am twenty years later hoping that perhaps my grandchildren at least will see peace." He shook his head. "But there are others who... Well, they aren't so optimistic, I suppose you might say. And it is hard for me to fault them. This city alone has six or eight score who lost family or property to Oler's depredations. When you look out at the region as a whole, there are probably hundreds of orphans who were made by the Deranged Duke and his men. And that's not counting Dinnsan, which I know was particularly painful for you." He glanced over his shoulder, where the rest of the prince's party walked some distance behind. "Not to mention poor Burojan there. I can't believe he came with you."

Razem clenched his jaw, but after a moment he managed to relax enough to speak. "Venra's death was a blow to all of us, it is true. I told Aris that I couldn't come to Salishok if he didn't come with me, to give his blessing." He met Arkad's gray eyes and was pleased to see a light of respect there. "I don't know if I handled it well, but he agreed to come. Though I confess, I had choice words for my father after he put *me* in the position to break the news to Aris."

Arkad grunted. "I imagine your father was not terribly impressed."

"My father rarely is." Razem sighed. "He loved Azmei so much, Arkad. I have difficulty living up to the standards she set me. Not only did she offer to live in a foreign country away from all our people, but then she died because of her desire for peace. Father sees only that, and he doesn't understand that I desire peace, too—but peace without conciliations. Is that so difficult to understand?"

"Mmm. It is often difficult for the young to understand

the old, as much as it is difficult for the old to understand the young. But I think your father understands you very well, Prince Razem. My suspicion is that he simply disagrees with you. Perhaps it is that, having lost one child to the war, he fears even more mightily the thought of losing the other child to the same war." Arkad squeezed Razem's shoulder.

Could that be true? Was it possible that Marsede's stubbornness over this whole matter was him trying to protect Razem? Razem stared at the baron, trying to form a coherent response. To his mixed embarrassment and relief, Arkad chuckled.

"I see this is a novel suggestion. Well, think on it, young man, as wisdom from this particular old man." He patted Razem's shoulder and let him go. When he spoke next, he raised his voice. "Here we are, then. My chamberlain Risia will show the others to their rooms. I myself shall accompany you and Lord Burojan."

CHAPTER FIVE

"Hawk! Get up! We're moving into Salishok today."

Hawk sat up on his cot, rubbing his eyes. His reflexes were rusty; the guard's approach hadn't wakened him. For that matter, he hadn't been in the habit of sleeping in the middle of the day when he was a Tamnese warrior. And that thought brought on its heels another thought: When had he stopped thinking of himself as a Tamnese warrior?

"Prince Razem's party has arrived, then?" he asked.

"Duke Oler has reached the Embattled City," the guard replied. She was a mahogany-skinned woman with wide lips that were currently flattened in disapproval. "I assume that means your prince is with them."

Hawk nodded, not bothering to argue with her. Let her have her zealotry. He would settle for swinging his legs over the side of his cot and searching for his boots.

"Commander Ayowir has ordered that we ride within the hour. You have little to pack, but be certain you are ready." The guard turned to go.

"I don't suppose you'd be kind enough to release the shackle on my leg?" Hawk made his voice as mild as possible. "I have no desire to run away and destroy the peace process. I merely wish to have my boots on before the last minute."

She snorted, but turned back and knelt to unlock the shackle. "There will be no peace. Don't delude yourself. We are exchanging one prisoner for another, but that does not mean the war will end."

Hawk shook his head. "Do you not wish to learn what peace was like? You must be too young to remember it. I am not."

"Silence! I will not hear your seditious talk. There can be no peace while you Tamnese dogs live in our Kreyden." She stood and strode out of the tent.

Since when was talk of peace seditious? Hawk wondered. He didn't bother with being offended over being called a Tamnese dog. He'd heard it often enough over the past six years.

He was washed, shaved, and dressed when the next guard arrived to take him to Commander Ayowir's tent. As he walked away from his own tent, he saw servants already disassembling it. The guard he followed this time was a slender man about his own age. Hawk wondered if this man would also consider peace talk to be dangerous. He decided not to try him, but the thought continued to trouble him as he greeted Ayowir.

She was dressed in her full uniform despite the heat, her sword resting on her hip and a dozen medals decorating her sash. Her hair was braided in a crown about her brow, which was furrowed. "He looks shabby," she said to someone over her shoulder. "Let's put him in nicer clothes."

To Hawk's astonishment, the two people who bustled up to him were tailors, a man and a woman. They measured him and studied his complexion and within minutes were coaxing him out of his clothes. He shrugged out of his tunic and shirt, then glanced meaningfully at Ayowir.

"I have my modesty," he said, and was rewarded with her sharp bark of a laugh.

"If you had modesty, it was lost to me years ago when I first had you deloused," she said. "But to please you, I'll turn my back." She did so and the tailors gestured again for Hawk to remove his breeches. "I know we just gave you new clothes, but with Prince Razem's greeting, I will not have you returning home looking shabby. Your uniform was burned long ago—not that it would fit you now, I suppose—but we'll at least deck you out properly."

As Ayowir spoke, the tailors draped him in silk and linen, the trousers so thin he almost felt he had none on. He had to admit they draped nicely when tucked into his boots, but he wished they had more substance. The silk shirt was fine, but the bright blue tunic they put over it made him feel like a court dandy. Warriors in the desert wore light-colored clothing, both to serve as camouflage against the dusty landscape and to protect them from the sun's heat. Blue seemed ridiculous, and he said so.

Ayowir turned around and put her hands on her hips. "Just wait until we're finished with you, then," she said, and Hawk flinched as the woman tailor draped a scarlet cloak around his shoulders. His reaction made Ayowir laugh again. She dismissed the tailors with quick praise and then beckoned Hawk to come over to the table.

"Have a glass of wine. I think you'll need it for the afternoon to come." She made a face. "I could do without all this ceremony, and honestly, I share your opinion of the clothes. But I have my instructions, and I am going to give the people of Salishok the best damn show they could ask for when their war hero returns."

"I'm no war hero," Hawk muttered. He had been a captive for six years. What kind of hero was that?

Ayowir's eyebrows shot up. "I think you'll see differently when we get to the city." She poured a glass of wine for him and one for herself. "Drink up," she added, and followed her own instructions.

When Hawk got to the bottom of his goblet, he saw that she had one last piece to complete his outfit. He nearly dropped the beaten copper vessel when he realized what it was.

"I know you thought this lost on the battlefield," Ayowir said, holding the scabbard across her palms. "I couldn't let you have it, but I wouldn't let it be destroyed. Talon was almost as iconic as The Hawk, you know." She gave him a crooked smile. "I think this is all a mighty mistake, but as I said, I have my instructions. And if I have to give you back to the Tamnese, I'm damned if I give you back less than what you were."

Talon. Hawk felt his throat tighten. He *had* thought his sword lost on the battlefield, and he had mourned the loss of the sword as much as the loss of his honor. Having the sword back would not make him again the man he had been, but it was the next best thing. He rested his hand on the pommel of the sword, fingers tracing every swirling detail. "I thank you," he choked out.

Ayowir's figure was suddenly blurry as she stood back from him. Hawk blinked, hoping his tears would not spill over. But when his vision cleared, the commander's face held no judgment.

"I know as well as you do what a sword means to a warrior," she said softly. "As I said, I won't return you to Tamnen as less a man than you were."

***

They rode into Salishok with barely two-score men accompanying them. Ayowir rode at the head of the column with Hawk at her side. When he remarked on the small force, she shrugged and said it was a necessary concession. And, she pointed out, if the Tamnese intended to take her captive, they would do it regardless of how many soldiers she brought with her.

What shocked him even more than their small party was the flourish of trumpets when the city gates opened. A crowd lined the street on either side, their voices raised in cheers and song. Hawk straightened in the saddle, his back stiff with surprise. His horse felt his unease and began prancing. Distracted, Hawk took the opportunity to gather himself as well as the reins. By the time his horse was under control, he had pushed away his emotions and stared straight ahead.

They took a circuitous route through the city, and everywhere they went, the street was lined with cheering citizens. Hawk began to wonder if anyone was left to run the shops or guard the city walls. There were plenty of children, to be sure, many of them throwing flower petals and dancing alongside the horses, but even so, the city away from their parade route must be completely empty.

"And you thought you weren't a war hero," Ayowir said to him, just loudly enough for him to hear over the shouting.

But I'm not, Hawk wanted to protest. Why did they cheer

for him? He had been good at leading soldiers, but he had also been wounded badly enough to be captured. He had spent years living among their enemies. He had gotten very bad at hating those enemies over the past six years. And he had been replaced by competent commanders after his capture. It wasn't as if his return to Tamnen would mean anything. There would be no place in the new army for an old veteran with a bad leg.

He wanted to stare at the crowd, but he was also afraid to look at them. Why did they celebrate his return? What could he mean to them? The children couldn't understand what they were cheering for, of course, but their parents knew. Did they expect Hawk to take command of the army again and lead Tamnen to victory? Did they believe he would return Salishok to the prosperity it had known twenty years ago?

I am not the person you think I am, Hawk wanted to scream at them. *I am not a miracle. I am not a hero.*

He had to keep swallowing against a swell of anxiety. The longer they rode, the more afraid he grew. With this set up, the prince must be planning something elaborate once they arrived at the palace. What would he say? What would he demand of Hawk? And what would be the price for all this later?

It was every bit as bad as Hawk had feared. Prince Razem made a great show of his deep affection for Commander Jacin Hawk, proclaiming him a national hero and declaring that babes yet in their cradles would grow to adulthood on stories of his gallantry and daring. He made a great deal of noise about this unique moment in history, where Strid and Tamnen were able to put aside their long hostilities to allow the dying Duke Anyet Oler to return to his home. Commander Ayowir, who appeared to be the highest-ranking person Strid had sent, gave a short but eloquent speech about the value of having learned from each other during the six years they had spent together, and how she hoped this could signal the beginning of a new, international understanding. Hawk, standing at Prince Razem's left hand, heard someone to the other side of the prince snort at this. He glanced over, curious who could be willing to show his skepticism so brazenly in front of the prince and was left feeling as if he'd been punched in the gut when he recognized the unmistakable features of his former superior, Venra Burojan.

After a moment, he realized it couldn't be Venra—he was older, for one thing, even older than six years would have made him. And Venra had never worn his hair so short, nor had he carried a prominent godsmark on his temple. But this must be his brother, then, the Lord Burojan. Hawk couldn't remember his name, but he swallowed hard against a sudden tightness in his throat. If he were here instead of Venra, who should by rights be standing in that place of honor next to the prince...

Prince Razem cleared his throat and Hawk realized his attention had been drawn away from the ceremony. He made a mental check of his facial expression and was satisfied he had shown none of his shock and grief, but his inattentiveness must have been obvious. He took a deep breath and straightened his shoulders, directing his gaze back to Commander Ayowir.

When she was finished, Razem glanced over at Hawk. "A few words from you would be good, Commander Hawk." His voice was gentle, but his gaze was implacable. Hawk realized it was not a request.

He cleared his throat and nodded once. What could he say that would be appropriate? What could he say at all?

Speak in Tamnese, he reminded himself. *Don't panic.* He had spoken nothing but Strid for so long now that his own native tongue felt odd on his lips. He stepped forward to the spot Ayowir had vacated, and was nearly bowled over by the wall of sound that crashed against him. The people cheered and whistled with such fervor he couldn't believe it was for him alone. Did they think this was a true peace?

He looked down into the first few ranks of faces. A woman about his age was clutching a young boy to her, tears streaming down her cheeks. His gut gave another horrible lurch. Did she think that Hawk was only the first of many?

Did she have a husband she thought would be coming home? But no power on earth could return the dead to life.

"My cherished countrymen," Hawk began, and his voice cracked. Fortunately it was masked by the ongoing cheers. He swallowed. What could he possibly say that would not be a deception? He lifted his hands, wishing they would shut up. He was not deserving of this accolade. He had done nothing but eat Strid food and read Strid books for six years.

"My cherished countrymen," he began again, when the applause had dropped away to a muted whisper of sound. "I cannot fully express all of my deep emotions at being among you again." Applause. Good. That seemed sincere enough, and grateful enough.

He took a deep breath. "I am proud to have served Tamnen in the past, and I shall be proud to serve Tamnen in the future. You all honor me with your presence here." He looked over his shoulder and sketched a bow, keeping his voice raised.

"Crown Prince Razem honors me with his presence here." His eyes found Lord Burojan's and he was momentarily breathless at the depths of the hatred in the man's eyes. "My Lord Burojan honors me, as does—" He glanced around again. "Baron Arkad. I am a humble man, my cherished people. I am not deserving of these honors. But I am deeply grateful for them. My heart soars at once again breathing the air of my beloved Tamnen."

His throat closed. That would have to be enough. A few words, Prince Razem had said. They would have to do. He stepped back from the railing of the balcony as the crowd cheered once again. Hawk's bad leg twinged and he stumbled. Just a little, but the vigilant Prince Razem noticed it. The prince caught him, both hands coming up to grasp Hawk's forearms, almost as if he were greeting him anew rather than supporting his weight. "Just a moment longer," Razem murmured, his voice loud enough for only Hawk to hear. He waited until Hawk had regained his balance and nodded his head slightly. Then he stepped back to the railing.

"And now, dear people, I urge you to go forth and celebrate our honored hero's return home!" the prince cried, his voice ringing out over the noise. "Celebrate freedom!"

He stepped back again and met Hawk's eyes. "You will join us, of course, Commander Hawk," he said. Again, it was not a request. Hawk didn't bother to nod acquiescence as Razem went to Ayowir and began speaking with her.

"I would not have had you back," Burojan said. He had come close without Hawk's noticing it. Hawk chastised himself; he could be complacent no longer. "My brother died at Dinnsan, and it was not your fault or the prince's, but I would not have had this trade." The man's gold-flecked eyes reminded Hawk that he was—as Venra had been—the king's first cousin. It had been easy to forget, with Venra; he'd been a superb commander and easy-going, never one to stand on rank. Hawk feared this Lord Burojan was not like Venra.

"I am grieved to learn of Lord Venra's death," Hawk said. He choked on the words, and perhaps the man read the sincerity in him, for the chilling hatred in his eyes lessened somewhat.

"So was I. But grief does not bring back the dead." He gave Hawk a hard smile. "Nor does a prisoner exchange make peace."

Hawk bowed his head. Could he and this man ever be friends? Venra had admired his brother.

Prince Razem looked over his shoulder. "Arisanat, Commander Hawk. Come. We have much to discuss."

CHAPTER SIX

Razem had spent weeks thinking of little else besides getting Jacin Hawk in his custody and surrendering the Deranged Duke. He had written and rewritten the florid speech he'd given to the people of Salishok. He had jotted down a list of questions to ask the man about the Strid and his treatment, as well as more mundane questions about his life before the war and his desires now that he was free. He had read the file on Hawk, such as it was, but that told him nothing about who the man actually was.

Of course, before he managed all of that, he had to actually offload the duke. Commander Ayowir—who had turned out to be a woman, and what a shock that was—had brought a full complement of healers with her, prepared for whatever condition the duke might be in. Razem had agreed to accompany her to the duke's chambers, though he had to summon Baron Arkad's chamberlain to lead the way. In the meantime, he gave orders for Hawk to be given refreshments and shown to the sitting room that separated his chambers from Razem's.

The duke was sitting up in bed when they arrived at his room, which was a distinct relief. Razem had been more than half afraid the duke would up and die on him before the Strid officially took custody, and he could only imagine the horror of war that would follow *that* particular tragedy. But the duke looked as hale as he ever did these days, his pale skin almost gray and looking like onion skin, it hung so loosely around his face. His blue eyes were keen, though, and he turned them to his visitors the moment they entered.

"Ah, Prince Razem. What new torture do you have in

store for me today?" the duke asked. Razem swore mentally as he felt Ayowir tense beside him. She relaxed at the duke's next words, though. "Removing alcohol from my diet, perhaps? Or do you plan to have someone clean my bedsores while we chat?"

"Duke Anyet," Commander Ayowir said, going to both knees in front of him. Razem tried to hide his surprise. That was more respect than any duke should command.

"Ah. My apologies. I did not realize Razem had—" The duke broke off and stared at her. His eyes wrinkled at the corners and his lips trembled. "Elin, I think, isn't it? Sasha's girl Elin Ayowir."

Ayowir's voice was even. "Yes, Uncle. I was given the honor of conveying you home."

"Am I no longer in disgrace, then?" the duke asked dryly. "I was under the impression that Harkai was displeased with me."

"He was displeased with you and his son both, Uncle. But it is clear that the gods have punished you far more harshly than the king would have." Ayowir spoke briskly, though both of her hands closed around the duke's thin, age-spotted one on the coverlet. "My mother died two years ago. She never gave up hoping to see you return."

The duke coughed so harshly it shook his entire frame. He lifted his free hand to cover his mouth. Razem didn't miss the fact that the palm was red as he lowered it. He thought, however, that Ayowir hadn't noticed. Strangely, he found himself hoping she hadn't. And why should he give a damn about this Strid soldier who spoke so familiarly to a man who had massacred women and children?

Angry with himself, Razem turned away. He would let them continue their reunion in private.

"Prince Razem." The duke's voice was rough and wet, as if the coughing had torn his throat.

Razem hesitated for a moment and then turned.

"I would have you hear this from me. Once only, but I feel I may say it, as I shall likely not live to see the consequences." Ayowir was staring up at her uncle in confusion. Razem jerked his chin in an upward nod, watching the duke's face.

Duke Anyet looked down at his niece long enough to cup her cheek in his palm. Then he turned his gaze back to meet Razem's. "I was wrong. I served as the tool of Anderlin's hatred. I knew there was no honor in killing civilians and infants. But I mistakenly allowed myself to believe that any disgrace would fall solely on the head of the one who ordered the atrocity." His thin lips curved in a humorless smile. "I failed to recognize that *I*, not Anderlin, was the one who ordered that atrocity. For that, Prince Razem, I am most heartily sorry."

Razem stared at the man. He couldn't forgive him. There was no way under the sun that he could forgive the Deranged Duke for his murderous rampage. But he could at least appreciate the apology. It would have little effect here, spoken in private with only the three of them to witness it. The duke would certainly die before word got out, and no one would believe Razem if he and a Strid commander were the only living witnesses. Ayowir would likely deny it, anyway. But the fact remained that the Deranged Duke had recanted his position. He had apologized for the massacre.

It meant very little in light of the hundreds of lives that could never be returned.

But to Razem, it was a balm of sorts. He could not forgive the man, but he could at least rest easy knowing they were not sending the duke home so he could share all of his strategy with others.

Razem nodded shortly. Then, with nothing further to say, he turned and walked out of the duke's rooms. He waved a hand at the guards standing outside. They knew the duke was to be handed over to the Strid. They would handle the details from here.

***

Of course Razem could have no peace to puzzle out the meaning of that last encounter with the duke. He still had Jacin Hawk to deal with. And from the way the man had handled today's ceremony, Razem knew he wouldn't enjoy most of what the prince had to tell him.

His first impression of The Hawk was of a shadow. The man didn't seem to want to be in front of a crowd. He didn't seem to enjoy the celebratory atmosphere. He certainly was only a shadow of his former self. Razem hadn't known him even to speak to, but he had seen him in the palace from time to time before his capture. He would not have recognized this lean, underweight man who favored his left leg ever-so-slightly as the vaunted military commander who had been in the habit of striding everywhere he went, cloak streaming out behind him, head held high and gaze sharp.

And having to catch the man after his speech had certainly been unexpected. Razem went through his mental list of questions and added a few to the list while subtracting a few others. Somehow he didn't think asking The Hawk about Strid culture was as important as making sure the Strid hadn't starved or tortured him—and making sure of that fact before they left the palace and escaped Razem's vengeance, if they had.

He shoved open the door to the large sitting room where he had directed The Hawk and General Kho to wait. Kho was standing by a table against one wall, picking over a selection of fruits, meats, and cheeses. The Hawk was sitting on a low couch against the opposite wall. His head was back, his eyes closed. He had his fingers curled around a wine goblet so tightly his knuckles were white. Kho glanced over at Razem when the prince walked in. The Hawk jerked upright, wine slopping over the edge of the goblet. A moment later he was on his feet, his gaze hooded and watchful.

This was a man who had been exposed to too much, Razem thought. He didn't know what he meant by it, but the thought prompted in him a mixture of sympathy and regret that made it difficult to speak.

"Lord-General Kho, Commander Hawk," he said, nodding. "Be at ease. Hawk, have you eaten?"

"The commander will not eat," Kho said, biting off each word. "It seems our good Tamnese food is too rich for him now."

Razem saw Hawk's shoulders slump for a moment before the man straightened and said, "I apologize, your highness. My diet has consisted of a great deal of bland grains and cheese, with the occasional goat or chicken. I fear I shall have to reacquaint myself with our better range of spices."

The man seemed to think before each sentence. His words came out with a faint lilt, not quite an accent. Something in the thoughtful crease between Hawk's eyebrows reminded Razem that the man had probably spoken nothing but Strid for the past six years. Razem's own command of the language was barely passable, but many of the Kreyden officers spoke it fluently, and Hawk's file said he was a half-blood. He might have grown up speaking both languages in equal amounts.

"Of course. I should have thought of it myself." Razem snapped his fingers for a servant. "Have the kitchen send up some rice and a mild flatbread." Before the servant could do more than bow, Razem added, "And send one of our healers."

"I thank you, your highness, but I am quite well." Hawk's voice was pleasant. Razem wondered what it would sound like raised in command on the battlefield. "I was not mistreated."

"Nevertheless, I should have had a healer waiting here to speak with you. Perhaps they will have some advice for readjusting to our cuisine." Razem smiled, hoping to put the man at ease and wishing Kho would relax, too. If nothing else, it would provide a good example for Hawk.

Razem turned to the table, where another servant was waiting with a plate filled with his favorite sharp cheese and spicy meat. Razem nodded over the selection and accepted a glass of wine. Then he went to sit on the couch nearest Hawk's.

"Sit, Commander Hawk. We shall be informal tonight. I

think we have all had enough ceremony to last at least a week, have we not?" He tried a brilliant smile, which got him a faint one in response. It wasn't what Razem had been hoping for, but it would do for now.

"Again, I thank you, your highness." Hawk lowered himself to the couch more carefully than he had stood. He did not spill his wine.

"Perhaps we should also have a language tutor for the commander," Kho said. There was an edge to his voice. So he'd noticed Hawk's lilt as well. Razem wondered why it sat so ill with Kho. The man was usually so easy-going and slow to show his temper that his reaction made the prince even more curious than he would normally have been.

"I think that will not be necessary, Emran," Razem said, injecting a note of humor to his voice. He looked at Hawk. "So, Commander. Let me officially welcome you home."

Hawk gave him another faint smile. "Thank you, your highness. It hardly feels real, yet. Seeing familiar faces...helps." He didn't look at Kho as he said this, but Razem did, and was gratified to see the general wince.

"I assume your possessions were placed in storage in Rivarden after your capture was confirmed," Razem said, "but regardless, I hope you shall rest assured that you shall not be left to want for anything. My father and I are both cognizant of the service you have rendered to the crown."

"Again, I thank your highness."

Razem gestured. "I said we are informal today, did I not? You may call me Razem in this room."

He saw Hawk's throat move when he swallowed. "As you wish...Razem. Please call me Hawk, then. It is what I am used to."

Razem nodded. "If you were given unlimited choice and resources, Hawk, what would you do now? You are home. What is the desire of your heart?"

Hawk looked bewildered by the question. He stared at his wine goblet, but Razem wasn't sure if he even saw it. "I...I hardly know."

"You have no family left, I believe," Razem pressed. "Is there a sweetheart? A girl—oh, or boy, I suppose—who waits for your return?"

"I—no, your—Razem. I have never been in love." Hawk blinked, frowning. "I did promise myself that I would return to Rivarden someday, were it possible." He looked up, dark eyes searching out Razem's. "I promised only to myself, no other, but—"

"Then you shall return to Rivarden," Razem interrupted, relieved that the man had asked for something he could grant. "My father gave me instructions to parade you through the cities and towns of Tamnen, celebrating you as a war hero and your recovery as a victory for our side. Rivarden, where you were taken, is certainly the most important of those cities."

"Your Highness," Kho protested.

"We will go to Rivarden. Make the plans, Kho. We will escort Baron Arkad and his family back to their holdings and proceed from there into the desert."

"Sir, the desert is not a safe place," Kho said. "There are bandits. And this close to the Shokanda, it is likely we will encounter Strid irregulars."

"Is it?" Razem asked, momentarily diverted. "Well, good, then. We will be able to demonstrate to them as well as our own citizenry that The Hawk is back."

"Is that it?" Hawk said, his voice soft. "Am I to be returned to military duty?" His quiet tone gave no clue about his feelings on the matter.

"Does that not suit you?"

"I am happy to serve in any way I can," Hawk replied. "But the army has not operated all these years with a hole where my rank once was."

"Of course not, but you may be certain we will find a place for you. Perhaps I shall knight you. We haven't had a Glorious Knight of the Crown for several years. You might make a very good candidate." Razem's smile felt like it was full of teeth, but he wasn't sure if his annoyance was for Hawk's reluctance or Kho's obvious displeasure. Perhaps both. "I understand knights must undergo a good amount of suffering before they are found worthy."

Hawk subsided under that, but Kho did not. "Prince Razem, I must heartily object. Your father charged me first and foremost with protecting you and Lord Burojan and the duke, until we arrived here. And after, I was to extend that protection to Hawk. I cannot see any reason for us to venture away from the regular trade routes."

"Perhaps you cannot, Emran, but I can." Razem let his smile fade; he was gritting his teeth, anyway, so that it felt more like a grimace than a smile. He straightened in his seat and met Kho's gaze directly. "My father ordered me to show Hawk every honor, to display our gratitude and affection for Hawk before every major settlement in Tamnen. We will ride to Rivarden, and from there we will take the Kreyden Capital Canal up to Lishan. When we reach Lishan, I will decide whether we turn west for the capital or east for Meekin." He flashed a hard smile at Kho. "I will not have anyone accuse me of shirking the duties my father has laid on my shoulders."

Kho didn't like it. Razem could tell by the way the large man shuffled his feet and gave only a curt nod in response. But at least the general didn't protest again.

Razem turned to face Hawk. The commander was staring into his wine glass, but Razem couldn't tell if his head was bowed in acquiescence or merely in the hope that Razem would leave him alone. Unfortunately, neither of them had the luxury of being left alone. Razem drew in a long breath. He was about to speak when a tap on the door heralded the arrival of servants bearing two trays of bland food, followed by a healer in blue.

Razem corrected his posture so he would seem languid and relaxed rather than tense and impatient. Then he waved a hand to the servants.

"Bring the tray over here to the commander. He will tell you what to fill his plate with." Razem turned his attention to the healer, a walnut-skinned woman with cropped white hair who wore loose trousers and a thigh-length, wraparound tunic. He beckoned her over, smiling.

The bow she gave him was exact and polite. "Your highness," she murmured.

"Commander Hawk is concerned about his reintroduction to our cuisine," Razem told her. "As well, I am concerned about his physical condition and if there is anything we should provide to ease his transition home."

The healer looked startled, but the cool gray eyes that met his were appraising. "Very good, your highness. Have you any specific concerns? Torture? Starvation?" From the corner of his eye, Razem saw Hawk's head snap up, but the prince ignored it.

"No, no, nothing like that, I hope," he said briskly. "But you might look at that leg of his, see if there's anything that can be done. And take a look at what he eats. Stop him if anything is too rich or spicy for him." He paused and lowered his voice. "And you might check him—discreetly—for lice."

He hadn't spoken quietly enough. He saw Hawk flinch, though Kho and the servants didn't seem to have heard. The healer frowned at him, but nodded and moved away to begin her inspection.

Thinking to give them some privacy, Razem ambled to where Kho stood by the table again, staring down at the selection of food. Kho tensed as Razem approached, though he didn't look up. Razem had planned to ask what problem Kho had with Hawk, but thought better of the idea. Instead he selected a glazed berry and popped it in his mouth.

"I understand you are displeased with me, Emran," he said softly. "But I do feel it my duty to obey my father."

"A fine time for that, your highness," Kho muttered, but he looked over at him, one side of his mouth curling up.

Razem gave him a matching half-smile in return. "You may be right, Kho. But that's as may be. We go to Rivarden."

PART TWO
VOICES

CHAPTER SEVEN

The air smelled of sweet coffee, cherry blossoms, and blood.

Yar's stomach quivered, but he didn't respond to the question his eldest brother had just asked him. It wouldn't do any good to answer, even if he wanted to. Rith never understood the words Yar said, or the way he said them.

"Answer me, boy!" A sharp cuff to the back of the head interrupted Yar's rocking, but he kept his gaze lowered and unfocused. He didn't know the answer, anyway. His sister's friends meant well, but they didn't speak to him, except to give him directions in a tone of voice reserved for simpletons.

The scent of cherry blossoms tickled his nose, and he couldn't suppress the sneeze that burst out of him. Who had opened the window to the courtyard?

A chortle in the back of his head made him shake it violently, attempting to dislodge the sound. Rith's open hand came down on his shoulder, throwing Yar to the ground.

"Don't bother," said a tired voice. "He probably doesn't know." Yar didn't allow himself to feel relieved, but he did venture to push himself up on one elbow. It was his middle brother. Kesh had given up on him years ago, but it was a relief compared to the way Rith still tried to beat the weirdness out of Yar.

"You know what they're saying," Rith snarled. Yar didn't look up at either of his brothers. He sat up and resumed his rocking even as that same Voice in the back of his head made singsong mockery of Rith's anger. Yar didn't smile. Yar had never smiled easily, and his smiles had grown even rarer in the years since his sister's disappearance.

"And they've been saying it for three years now." Kesh pulled Yar to his feet and let go before Yar was quite steady. Even so, it left Yar's skin creeping and prickling. He shivered.

"Ungrateful cur," Rith snapped, and cuffed Yar again.

Yar hunched his shoulders and tapped his fingers against his thumb, one-two-three-four-three-two-one, one-two-three-four-three-two-one. *Let me alone*, he thought. He didn't speak. He tried never to speak to Rith. He hoped Rith had forgotten what his voice sounded like. Rith's ears made Yar's voice feel scratchy like uncarded wool.

"Stop being such an idiot. It isn't as if Yarro would have understood, even if she had told him anything. You know what he's like. It's like you're beating a cat. It's not only pointless, but makes you look a fool."

And cruel, Yar added. The Voice at the very back cackled in his head again. Yar's lips twitched, but he let his mouth fall slack. Did that one want to talk to him today? It didn't always, but it seemed to hate Rith.

"Fine." Rith stomped away. Yar didn't look up. He could sense Kesh still hovering nearby. He tapped his finger sequence against his thumb again.

Kesh sighed. "You could show a bit of gratitude. Thankfulness." He fell silent. Maybe he was waiting for Yar to answer, but Yar's vision was graying out. He ignored Kesh.

Was it foggy or was it just growing dark? Yar couldn't tell through the haze of smoke. *Why show me this?* he wondered. None of the Voices answered, though he heard Kesh mutter, "I don't know why I bother," just before he, too, stomped away.

Smoke. The sound of rushing wind. Rumbling, crackling laughter that vibrated his bones. Yar stared slack-jawed at a dark shape swooping and circling through the smoke clouds. He couldn't tell what it was. His eyes followed the patterns of its flight but the smoke was too thick.

SEE US. FIND US.

"How do you see a Voice?" he asked.

"I don't know, boy. How do you?"

Yar's heart leapt and fluttered like a rabbit caught in a basket. He had forgotten about his grandfather's presence. The Patriarch made Rith look kind, except he did it so quietly maybe people didn't notice.

Yar was startled into making eye contact with his grandfather, mouth gaping open to catch air and sunshine.

"I have always thought voices were things you heard, not things you saw. But seeing a voice would be useful, especially in our line of work, wouldn't it?" Grandfather's tone was cheery and kind. It turned Yar's stomach. His gaze dropped to focus on the corner of his grandfather's mouth. Looking straight into someone burned his eyes after only a few seconds. Looking straight into his grandfather might kill him.

"Ah, I see you have no answers for me. It was, perhaps, a purely hypothetical question?" The false sympathy in his grandfather's voice made Yar pull himself inward. "Your sister was very good at dealing in hypotheticals. Let's see if you have any aptitude for it."

EAT HIM, said one of the Voices in Yar's head. He exhaled a tiny breath that could pass for a laugh. He was rarely surprised by anything the Voices said, but what kind of creatures were these Voices, that they thought a human man would be tasty? Especially one as skinny as the Patriarch.

"If your sister left here, having decided to fake her own death, what would she have done? Would she have abandoned you as she has?" The old man clicked his tongue in sadness. "Such a shame. She always pretended to care for you. It is certainly what I thought."

She *had* cared for him. It was no pretense. "You said she was dead," Yar said, flicking a glance up at his grandfather. He wouldn't be able to tell if the old man were lying, but he had to see his eyes again, for just a moment.

As Yar's gaze dropped again, he saw the thin, wrinkled lips curl in a smile. "I did say that, didn't I? But it is not what others are saying."

"Did you lie to me?" Yar blurted. As if he couldn't imagine it. As if he trusted his grandfather with all his being. But then, his grandfather didn't realize how much Yar really understood. None of them did. They thought him a simpleton. That was fine, since it meant he didn't have to learn to kill. But it was just the Voices that made him seem unaware of the world.

"I didn't lie, Yarro, I merely told you the information we had at the time." The old man sighed and patted Yar's head. "I wonder now if I was wrong to do so."

Yar scratched his scalp. *Don't touch me*, he wanted to say. *Don't infect me.* But he just stared into the middle distance, wishing the Voices would send something to help him understand this. What were people saying, then? Why wouldn't Orya have come back for him if she was still alive?

"What are you thinking inside that locked up head of yours, I wonder," his grandfather said. "I think your brothers underestimate you. Your sister never did." Suddenly the old man's face was very close to his, iron fingers seizing his chin in a vise-like grip. "What do you know of Orya's plans, Yarro? Tell me! I am your Patriarch!" A fleck of spit hit Yarro's lips.

EAT HIM. BLIND HIM. LICK HIS EYEBALLS. Yar shuddered. He didn't really like that one. That Voice was always hungry, and if Rith brought out that Voice's temper, Yar's grandfather brought out its cruelty.

"Tell me!" His grandfather shook him so hard Yar's neck ached. "What did she tell you before she left?"

LIE TO HIM, whispered another Voice. It was sly, more subtle than the first. THE PATRIARCH WILL USE YOU IF HE KNOWS THE TRUTH. Yar blinked up at his grandfather. His lips were mushed together by the old man's grip, but he still said, "Goodbye."

Evidently his grandfather understood, for he shoved Yar away, letting go of his chin and making Yar stumble backwards.

BE INNOCENT. BE FOOLISH, said the second Voice, and Yar let himself fall down.

Underestimate me, he thought at his grandfather. An image of a dove fighting a serpent flashed before his eyes. His jaw went slack as he stared, rapt, at it. That was what he wished to be. A dove.

"Fool. Worthless fool." The old man's voice dripped contempt. Yar didn't care. He stared at the dove as it flapped its wings. Its beak was closed on the serpent's head. Yar wondered if it would win. How could it? Doves were peaceful birds. But if they were attacked, they would fight back. Anything would fight back when it was attacked.

He stared at the struggle in his mind's eye until he heard his grandfather stride away. The boot heels were loud on their tiled floor. He ought to get up, scamper away, hide. But the vision was taking root. Yar stared and stared, wishing the dove's beak were strong enough to bite down and crush the serpent's head. Why did the dove not fly away?

Then he saw the dove was on its nest. Of course. It couldn't fly away because it had eggs there. The serpent wanted the eggs and the dove refused to leave them.

Orya would never have left him. Never. Yar rocked back and forth, eyes unblinking, seeing not the lavishly appointed room around him but the serpent twining around the dove, trying to secure its grip. Orya was no dove, though. Orya was a serpent that nestled right against the breast. You knew she might bite you, might poison you, but you loved her anyway.

The dove beat its wings furiously, lifting itself off the ground with the serpent still attached. As Yar watched, the dove flew from its nest and crashed into a stone wall. The serpent, stunned, dropped from around the dove. But the dove, hindered by the extra weight it had carried, crashed into the stone again. It, too, fell dazed to the ground.

"Why?" Yar whispered. "Why whywhywhy?"

The dove rose first. It went to the dazed serpent and pecked out its eyes. Then she returned to her nest. Did Orya stay away from him because she was pecking out the dangers to him? But that made no sense. Yar had never been in danger. Not from anything or anyone except Rith and their grandfather. So if she had left to protect him, she would have taken him with her.

Why would Orya leave and not come back?

She wouldn't. She was dead.

***

Yar remembered the curl of his sister's dark hair, the cruel edge of her laughter that softened only for him, the shoes she discarded the moment she walked into his room. He remembered how she read aloud to him, making different voices for each of the characters. No one would ever have believed she did that.

But Yar was different. Their grandfather used him as leverage to manipulate Orya. Their eldest brother tried to beat it out of him. Their middle brother washed his hands of him. Only Orya had seen Yar for how he truly was. Only Orya had allowed him to be that way without placing demands on him. Perhaps it was why she had been so hard with others.

Orya spent so much compassion on Yar, she had none left for anyone else.

But she left me, he thought. *She promised to come back and said goodbye and never came back. She broke her promise.*

Yet if that were the end of it, why would his grandfather and brothers be trying to find out...whatever they had been trying to find out? They had never really said. Grandfather had hinted that perhaps Orya was only pretending to be dead. Yar wasn't sure why she would do that. More than that, he wondered why Grandfather thought she was.

It was something to figure out. Yar was good at figuring things out, if he wasn't interrupted by one of the Voices. Sometimes they helped him, but just as often, their whispers had nothing to do with anything going on around him.

SUN HEAT. He felt a flash of contentment, then realized it was not his own feeling. Frowning at the window, where he saw the lowering sun and a cooling world, Yar wondered for the thousandth, millionth, time what the Voices were.

He turned his thoughts back to Orya and all those questions Rith had asked about her. He wondered if he could ask Kesh. Kesh knew, that was obvious. But would he tell Yar? That was harder. He didn't think Yar understood things, so Yar would have to be careful about how he asked. And if Kesh even answered, it might not be an answer Yar could use.

But it was all he could do.

He wandered down the hall. He was still barefoot, and the tile floor was warm under his feet. His toes were grubby. Before Orya left, she had told him he wasn't a little boy any more. He ought to wear shoes. Yar's lips twisted and pursed. He meant to wear shoes. He just forgot. Sometimes one of the visions would take him and make him forget what he had been doing before it. Not always, but often enough.

His gaze wandered to the next window. Where had the in between hours gone? He had spent some time remembering Orya. He had drawn a picture, trying to capture the dove and serpent that had been in his visions more often. He had listened to the Voices talking about a war that was happening somewhere. He didn't think the Voices were part of the war. He thought they were just bored.

"What are you doing out of your quarters?" asked a kind female voice. Yar looked over to see one of Orya's friends watching him. He didn't meet her gaze, but he smiled. Tish was nice to him, even if she didn't understand him the way Orya did.

"Kesh wants me to come see him," he confided. Tish wasn't all that much older than he was, only a few years, but she still treated him like he was a little boy instead of seventeen. When Orya was seventeen, she'd already killed time and time again. Tish wasn't an assassin. She was a scribe for the family. When word came that Orya was dead, Tish had been the one who let him hug her when he needed, but didn't hold on to him so he could pull away when he had to.

Yar had fallen in love with Tish three years ago, but two years ago he'd realized she saw him as a child. It still stung to be around her, but he didn't like being away from her, either.

Tish's face melted into an expression he didn't quite understand. Did she feel sorry for him or was she just glad she wouldn't have to spend time with him today? "Well," she said, "you'd better not keep him waiting." She tilted her head. "At least it isn't Rith."

"I know," he said, making his voice happy, and he turned and left her standing there. He didn't know if she realized Rith beat him. Kesh knew and did nothing most of the time, but Kesh was the only one who really could do anything. Tish would lose her place in the house if she spoke out. Yar chose to believe she didn't know, but he had a feeling he was just lying to himself.

When Yar reached Kesh's quarters, he let himself in. If he knocked, Kesh might not let him in. This way, his brother would have to at least talk to him. There were others in Kesh's quarters. The room smelled of cloying smoke and tangy drink. Four men were gathered around Kesh's table along with two women. They were playing cards. Yar liked to play cards, especially Queens and Ship's Trades, which were Orya's favorites, but no one ever asked him to play cards anymore.

He couldn't really blame them. He and Orya had played often, but even with Orya, he would sometimes come back to himself and realize a vision had taken him in the middle of the game. He would be clutching his cards so tightly they had creased his palm, and Orya would be asleep or reading a book or simply gone.

"It's the freak," someone said. "Kesh, you ought to lock your door."

Yar felt a shiver down his back, but he was glad the others were there. If he acted out enough, Kesh might answer his question just to calm him down and get rid of him. It was a good plan.

"Kesh, why did they ask about Orya?" he asked.

He saw his brother go still, cards lowering to the table. One of the people snickered. "Go away, Yarro."

The visions could be an advantage. If people thought you were a simpleton, they expected you to act wrong. They were almost disappointed if you held a normal conversation with them. Yar opened his mouth and eyes wide.

"Why did they ask about Orya?" he repeated.

"Get him out of here so we can play," said one of the women. "If this is a ploy to keep from paying your debt—"

"Go on, Yarro." Kesh's voice was stern, but the hint of kindness was still there.

"Why did they ask about Orya?" Yar said again. "Is Orya coming home? Is Orya coming home? Is Orya coming home?" He let his voice fall into a singsong. "Orya, Orya, Orya, home, home, home."

Kesh's chair scraped across the tile as he pushed it back. "*You* need to go home, Yarro." He stood and came towards Yar. He was going to touch him. Yar steeled himself for it.

"Orya's coming home? Tell me, Kesh! Tell me! Tell!"

Kesh didn't really want to touch him. He paused, hands hovering close to Yar's shoulders. "There's someone operating who is as good as Orya. People think she must have been pretending to be dead." He gripped Yar's shoulders with both hands and ducked his head until Yar would meet his eyes. "But Orya's dead, Yarro. She's not coming back. Never."

Yar let his face crumble into disappointment, mouth open, tears leaking from his eyes, even as he turned the new information over in his mind. There were people who thought Orya was alive just because someone killed people as well as she had? It wasn't logical. But not many people needed logic. They believed what they wanted to believe.

He shook his shoulders until Kesh's hands dropped to his sides.

"Go on," Kesh said. His voice was soft. "Tell Tish I said you could have a fruit ice. She shouldn't have let you out."

"I told her you wanted me to." Yar spoke with no inflection. He let his thoughts roll on. Logical or no, could there be truth to the idea that Orya had faked her own death? To what end, though? Why would she need to get away from here and stay away?

Well, to get away from Grandfather. That made sense.

Why else?

To get away from their brothers? Probably.

Why else?

To get away from Yar?

He let his brother push him towards the door. He

stubbed his toe on the threshold but ignored the pain. As the door closed behind him, he heard someone say, "He didn't even have shoes on. What a freak."

It didn't bother him. He *was* a freak. Even though he had lived like this his whole life, he knew it wasn't normal for people to have visions all the time. He knew from Orya that most people didn't hear Voices in their heads. If they did, it wasn't polite to talk about them.

Yar was fine with not talking about them. But sometimes the Voices weren't fine with it. Sometimes they made him speak. That was usually when he got in trouble.

The passage back to his room was long. The house was built out of golden stone, and the sun slanted into this passage through the western windows. It felt good on his left cheek, so he turned his head to face the sun. He went to the window and leaned on the ledge, staring out into the sunset. Flat roofs and domed ones mingled along the canals and alley walkways. Meekin was a good city, he thought. They were nestled into the foothills by the Scarim Mountains, with plenty of trade. There was a school for musicians and bards, which he had heard about but never seen.

And there were fountains everywhere. In every square, every plaza, every courtyard, there were fountains. The foothills were dry, but Meekin had been built in a low, wet spot where two rivers came together. However many hundreds of years ago it was, Meekin's founders had deepened the low spot into a lake and channeled the water right around the buildings to create the canals. Orya had hated the canals, but Yar loved them, and he loved the fountains even more. The fountains seemed to sing at him, and if he were close enough, they sometimes even drowned out the sound of the Voices.

So what now?

He ought to go back to his rooms, but he didn't want to have a fruit ice with Tish. He didn't want to sit on one of the low couches with his doubts and questions. He took a deep breath.

So what did he want?

To find Orya.

SHE'S DEAD, said one of the Voices.

What if she isn't? he asked. *What if the rumors are true?*

But it was illogical. He knew it was. He just wanted to believe it himself, so he let himself be seduced by the hope. The truth was usually the simplest thing, and the simplest thing was that Orya had been killed while assassinating Princess Azmei. No one had ever told Yar why they had taken a contract to assassinate their own princess. Yar had never wanted to know anything about the killing business. That changed after Orya didn't come back, but by then it was too late. Orya was the only one who might have told him, and she was gone.

He traced his finger in circles on the rough windowsill. He liked the feel of sandstone. It scraped the pad of his finger as he drew letters and numbers in no order. Orya was probably dead, but there was an assassin good enough to be mistaken for Orya. Then who was it, if not Orya? Why did it matter to Yar? Because anyone as good as Orya might have met her? Or was it more than that?

YOU DON'T WANT TO KNOW.

He turned his head, humming to try to drown out the Voice in his head. Maybe he didn't want to know. Maybe he did. But the Voice couldn't tell him.

What would be the best way to find this other assassin?

FIND US. WE ARE WHAT MATTER.

He scoffed and turned away from the window, scuffing his heels along the stone floor as he walked. Why would he want to find the Voices? And how could you find a Voice? Would *they* help him find out the truth about Orya?

FIND US.

But perhaps they would. What if they knew what had happened? What if they had Orya with them somehow? What if they could answer all his questions?

But how did you find a Voice?

FOLLOW.

Yar shoved his fingers into his hair and gripped. He was

so *tired* of the Voices. Tired of having them in his head, tired of sharing his life with them, tired of being ruled by them. He was tired of how they could force visions on him without his desire or consent, how crippling the visions were. He wanted a real life, not this half-imaginary one.

He wanted to not be a freak.

"If I follow, if I find, will you help me?" he whispered. "Help me find Orya."

FOLLOW. FIND.

That wasn't an answer. Nor did it illuminate how he would be expected to follow or find. He groaned and headed for his rooms. It was ridiculous for him to believe he could make any difference, even if he did find them. What would it accomplish? Free him? More likely the Voices, once he was in their grasp, would enslave him utterly.

And how is that any different from how you live now? he asked himself.

He had no answer.

CHAPTER EIGHT

Azmei frowned at the off-white buildings of Meekin. Her journey from Tamnen City had been an uneventful one, punctuated by brief stops in towns along the canal to drop off merchandise shipments or take on new cargo bound for the east end of the line. She had spent much of the journey brooding over things she could not control, such as the as-yet unidentified threat against her father's life that Tanvel was attempting to puzzle out, and planning her approach to the task ahead of her.

Now she was here, in the city Orya had once described as a clean trade town with little crime, with a spring trade fair and fountains and beautiful parks. At the time, Azmei had wished that she had taken the time when she was younger to travel her home kingdom and appreciate all its many facets. She had not expected she would have a chance to visit it after marrying Vistaren. Then again, she hadn't married Vistaren, had she?

She paid the captain and stepped off the canal boat, pushing back her hood to gaze at the bustling docks. The Spring Evener had come and gone while she was traveling, so she hadn't had a chance to enjoy the bonfires and dancing, even as an anonymous visitor rather than a participant. It was probably for the best, though she had a hard time acknowledging the fact. All the same, it meant the town's population was swelling for the spring trade fair. That would be good. Plenty of outsiders, so no one would pay as much attention to one woman traveling alone.

"Is there a direction I can point you, my lady?" the

captain asked. He'd been watching her take in the sights. Azmei should have walked away if she didn't want to be disturbed.

"What is your favorite inn?" she asked.

"The Laughing Dog, m'lady," he answered, "but it caters mostly to a merchant crowd. Not to tell you your business, but you might be better pleased with the Owl's Nest. They're closer to the university, so the people who stay there are a bit more varied."

Azmei raised an eyebrow. "And a woman alone might not stand out as much, you mean," she observed. It occurred to her that, while she knew her people well, she had never had the opportunity to travel much, so she had no idea how women usually traveled.

"It isn't that you're without a chaperone, m'lady, so much as that you're without a guard. Women usually have a couple of those." The captain looked away from her. "And since you seem to wish to pretend you don't know how to use a blade, it would seem more natural to stay there."

"Ah." Azmei settled her bag on her shoulder. "And if I were to go looking for the horse market?"

"You'd find it inland from the canals, by what's called the Dry Gate." The captain looked back at her. "And you might wish to let it be a bit more obvious that you know the sword."

She smiled at him, hoping it looked genuine. "Let us hope that you forget I know the sword, Captain Farruth." She handed him another gold piece, which was a generous tip beyond her standard fare. "I mean no trouble to you or your boat."

"For which I'm grateful." He made the coin disappear. "Fare you well, Mistress Baelaric."

It was a clear dismissal, and Azmei was amused at how easily it fell from his lips. She had grown up a princess, and yet no lord or king she had ever met had spoken with any more assurance than a captain on his vessel. She nodded to him and began walking up the dock. In the distance she could see several towers, which she had already learned were the university buildings. She didn't want to stay at the Owl's Nest, since the captain would be able to name it, if he were asked. But she would at least see if there were other inns around the university. She glanced up, judging the time by the sun. Still at least two hours until dusk, she thought, which meant she would have time to take a room and then locate the Perslyn House.

An hour later, she had managed the first, but not the second. She had learned where the trade quarter was, where most of the guilds had their shops and guild halls. She knew where to look for the more expensive houses in the city. But she had not been able to force herself to actually go to the Perslyn cloth shop and follow someone back to the Perslyn family home.

Instead she had wandered through the university quarter and into the city's main park, watching the shadows grow longer and the crowds grow thinner. Though canals formed the main avenues through the city, there were narrow stone walks built along either side of the canals, and the city was dotted with several large squares built on more solid portions. The main city park was one such square, with paved pathways winding through groves of trees, bushes, and flowering plants. An immense fountain portraying an ancient battle between Tam and the Wyrm of Wynra created a watery playground that Azmei imagined must tempt children in the hotter months.

You're weak, she berated herself. *You are here for one purpose only—to destroy the Perslyn power structure and rescue Yarro from that family. If you can't even bring yourself to embark on this purpose, what will you do? What would Tanvel think of you?*

She shook her head.

What would Guira think?

Her nurse Guira was fresher in her memory than her mother, whom Guira had served first. She had taken Azmei under her wing in their shared grief over Queen Izbel's untimely death. Guira had served as nursemaid, counselor, aunt, older sister, mentor, and maidservant over the years. She had had much of the shaping of Azmei into the idealistic young woman who had agreed to marry a stranger in order to end the war that was tearing her country apart.

She had also hidden a playful side that rarely showed itself; one of the best days in Azmei's life had been the day in Ranarr when Guira had agreed that the princess deserved one final day of carefree happiness. They had wandered the Ranarri market, tasting of its delights and exploring its novelties and wonders. Azmei had purchased a sea-dragon bone comb for Guira as a present, and after Guira died saving Azmei from an assassin's blade, Azmei carried that comb with her everywhere, even though her hair was too short for it.

Azmei sat on the edge of one of the great fountain's smaller pools and trailed her fingers in the cold water. What *would* Guira think of Azmei's hesitance? She had been a peaceful, decorous woman for the most part, but she had fought fiercely at the last, and had sacrificed her own life to save the princess she had reared. Guira might dislike that Azmei had grown so familiar with killing. She might disapprove of the way she had walked away from statecraft. She might counsel against revenge for its own sake.

But Guira would approve of removing any threat to the throne of Tamnen. She would urge Azmei to do her duty, as she had always urged before. She would advise caution but firmness.

Azmei drew in a long, slow breath, enjoying the smell of cherry blossoms and honeysuckle. The day was drawing down into evening. The shadows had lengthened to the point that, were she dressed in dark clothing, she might pass unnoticed under the trees. She was still in her unbleached linen robe, which blended into the pale stone of Meekin in the light of day, but would serve her ill tonight. But under her robe she wore fine wool trousers and a silk shirt in shades of brown-gray. Boy's clothes, because she had preferred them even as a princess and had no reason not to wear them now. With her jaw-length hair in the dim light, it would probably pass unremarked.

She glanced up at the sky. The evening bell would ring

soon, and most of the shops would close, the clerks hurrying home to dinner and family. Azmei stood from the fountain and made her way, unhurried, out of the park and towards the trade quarter. She would see if anyone was in the Perslyn shop. If they were still there, she would follow them home. Master Tanvel had discovered early on that no one without the Perslyn name was allowed to work in any of the shops. He was certain that many of the cloth merchant Perslyns were unaware of the shadowy work their brothers and cousins did behind the scenes.

The pale flagstones of the park pathways gave way to rough-cut stone as she stepped from the park into an alley between two buildings bordering the park. She wanted to give her eyes time to adjust to the shadows before picking up the pace. She tugged off her robe and folded it into the small pack at her waist. Then she leaned her shoulders back against the wall, closing her eyes and concentrating on hearing everything that was going on around her.

Footsteps slapped past on the street she had just left, someone already running late, judging by the pace. A dog barked somewhere at least two streets over. Two people laughed in the park she had left behind, one male and one female; lovers, perhaps, but certainly two people who enjoyed each other's company. Ahead, someone shouted, the voice too distant for her to discern emotion. Overhead, the wing beats of a flock of birds. Doves, probably, from the soft whis-tle of the air through feathers. Azmei smiled. It had been far too long since she heard dove wings on a regular basis.

She opened her eyes and was able to see the distinct out-lines of doors and windows in the alley. She could distinguish each individual cobble as she set out again, her pace quicker now.

She was perhaps five minutes' walk from the trade quar-ter, even at a pace that gave no indication of the urgency of her mission. She met no gazes of the people she passed, but she smiled impersonally at each of them, pleased when most of them smiled impersonally back. People didn't remember those who behaved normally. Azmei looked like a boy walking from his apprenticeship to his parents' shop, and that was what people would probably remember of her, if they remembered seeing her at all.

When she reached the square where the Perslyn shop was located, she paused several shops away, dropping to one knee and pretending to fuss with her boot. There were four other people in the square: three men and one woman. The woman and one man were walking together, conversing but not close enough to each other that they were anything but colleagues. One of the men was gathering wares from a display table outside an ink and quill shop. Many years ago, Azmei would have yearned to go into that shop and browsed through the inks until she found a color that suited her perfectly. Now she felt a vague wistfulness as she saw the sign, but she pushed it away. The last man was walking towards her.

His eyes were focused on the ground in front of him. His shoulders were slumped and his steps were slow. Probably he was a discouraged worker who saw no future at the shop where he was employed, or perhaps he had been reprimanded by his master that day. But it was equally possible that he was a cutpurse trying to give off as harmless an air as possible. Azmei stood and angled away from him as if she'd seen a shop she wanted to visit before they closed. When she ducked around the corner of a building and glanced back, she saw that he had continued on without looking at her. The first, then. She smiled ruefully and shook her head.

The Perslyn fabric shop was a large building with wide glass windows in front. Vividly colored fabrics were displayed in the window, draped to show the flow and texture of the fabric as well as the color. Many lamps were still lit inside the shop and the door stood open to let in the night breeze. With a satisfied smile, Azmei settled in to wait.

She wasn't as patient as some of her fellow Aspirants with the Shadow Diplomats. She had never grown to enjoy the peace of the half-trance that allowed her fellows to commune with the peace god while being somehow aware of everything around them. Master Tanvel had described it as resting assured that any disturbance of the peace would break the communion and bring him back to full awareness. Azmei had finally admitted to herself that she didn't have as much faith as the others; she opened herself to the god but also watched her surroundings.

Yet another way she was a poor servant of her chosen god.

Despite this, though, the Shadow Council had agreed that she should be tested. They judged her ready to pit herself against her selected mission and prove her worth.

*Or un*worth, she thought wryly. *Perhaps they are just waiting for me to fall on my face.*

She shook her head. Be that as it may, she still had a task here, and the god of peace would welcome her if she opened herself to him.

Cease this mental chattering, she chided herself. She let her gaze scan from one side of the square to the other, seeing that only two shops were still open. Casting her thoughts back, she didn't remember hearing the bell, but she must have been hidden here for the better part of an hour. She looked back at the Perslyn shop.

Finally! As she watched, another lamp went out. Whoever was within had finished their closing tasks and was extinguishing the lamps. Only a few more minutes. Azmei rose from where she had been crouched and began moving to limber herself after the wait. She touched the hilts of each dagger in turn, making certain they were all there and ready. She did another scan to be sure no one had noticed her.

When she looked again, a man of about twenty was locking the door of the Perslyn shop. He had already closed the shutters over the wide panes of glass. He wore what appeared to be an expensive cape, a jaunty cap on his head. He didn't look around him as he stepped away from the shop at a lively pace. Azmei waited until he had a good lead, and then started after him.

She followed him out of the trade quarter and out to the

canals. He hired a boat, but Azmei had no trouble following his progress from the walkways. He had the boat stop twice to pick up others about his age, another man and three women. All were dressed for a social gathering, if not an actual ball or party. Soon a merry crowd floated along the canal. Their boatman made the last stop without direction from anyone. Here three more men joined the party. Azmei judged from the ease with which they arranged themselves that they had done this many times.

When the boat finally arrived at the private quarter, the Perslyn paid the boatman and the entire party shuffled off, laughing and chattering gaily. Whoever this Perslyn was, he was a popular one. Orya had seemed much more of a loner, though it was possible that had been cultivated to appeal to Azmei. All the same, Azmei found herself wondering if this Perslyn was limited only to the shop-keeping and textiles portion of the family business.

She began ducking into alleys and garden gates as the party made its noisy way along increasingly empty streets. The lights were on in most houses along this route, showing the occupants going about their nightly routines of dinner, devotions, and discussion. Azmei had to duck suddenly once when two of the party stopped to share a passionate embrace. She found herself nose to nose with a ghostly gray cat, who blinked and began to purr. Azmei smiled and petted it until the embrace was finished and it was safe to continue.

"Kesh! You took your time!" shouted a man's voice from the house as the party arrived at their destination. "I was about to begin without you."

"Don't worry, Rith, the betting doesn't start until we reach the house," replied the Perslyn who had led the way from the shop. His voice was good-natured where the other man's had been pettish and impatient. "And you'd best have a spread of food and wine waiting for me, or the betting won't start even then."

Their voices grew muffled as the entire party entered the house. The door thudded closed and Azmei was on the outside.

But she knew now which house was the Perslyn home. She knew that the man she had followed home was Orya's next elder brother, Kesh. He was one of the assassins, by all reports, though not said to be as brutish or vicious as Rith, the eldest.

And where in all this house was Yarro?

She smiled. Tomorrow, she would find out.

***

The next day, Azmei dressed carefully in clothes that would blend in while she was on the streets as well as when she took to the rooftops. Since she learned the tricks to climbing walls and leaping from building to building, rooftops had become her favorite place. Humans weren't made to fly, but running across the rooftops was the next best thing. Few people thought to look up, so traveling that way was good for avoiding notice. And on the rooftops, nothing kept you from basking in the sun.

She traveled using more conventional methods until she reached an area of the private quarter away from the Perslyn house. She had noted when she was here last night that the houses were built close together, many of them with walls surrounding them to form courtyards and family complexes. She would be able to travel via rooftop most of the way to the Perslyn house.

Azmei had a small pack holding enough food for her to spend the day watching the house, as well as various supplies she might need, like a small grappling hook, a lightweight rope, and a small bag of pekur, a gel that could be spread on the fingertips to help grip small projections or crevices in stone. She preferred to climb without it, but it was never smart to leave it at home. She found a spot where two walls met at an angle that hid her from the street and quickly unfastened the front of her robe. She needed her legs free, but wanted to keep the robe on to disguise her shape. Then she launched herself up the wall, fingers and toes catching at the smallest handholds. Within the space of a few moments, she was twenty feet up on the roof, crouched and looking down to make certain she hadn't been spotted.

No one raised an alarm and she didn't see anyone staring up at her hiding place. She settled in to wait for a few minutes to be sure. When she was satisfied she hadn't been seen, she set out across the rooftops towards the Perslyn house complex.

Five minutes later, she was studying the house and wondering where she might be most likely to find Yarro. Orya had talked about him as if he were a small boy, though she had said he was fourteen. Orya had said the boy was not to be trained as an assassin because he was different. She had described him as delicate, with poor eyesight and almost entirely deaf. Azmei had no idea if this were true or a carefully crafted lie to win sympathy, but she had judged Orya's affection for her brother to be real enough. Orya's last word as she died had been her brother's name.

She settled in on the rooftop of the neighboring house, tucked in against a chimney and wrapped loosely with her robe, cowl pulled up so she would blend in with the stone. From here she had a good view of the smaller of the two courtyards. This courtyard had a fountain and several small trees. A table and chairs sat in the middle of the courtyard. It was unoccupied, but Azmei thought there was a good chance someone would come out and she could learn more about the inhabitants of the house.

***

Waiting was Azmei's least favorite part of her new life. While she enjoyed time spent alone, she preferred to have a book to read or sword exercises to practice. She shoved the day's food into her pack and slipped it onto her belt. She had expected to have to watch the Perslyn house for a day or two after her arrival in Meekin. She had not anticipated it taking nearly a week for her to get her first glimpse of Yarro Perslyn.

Yesterday she had finally seen the boy. Boy! She laughed grimly and shook her head. Orya hadn't lied about his age, at least. He was old enough to shave, though he was also apparently "special" enough that he forgot to do so. Yarro had wandered into the area of the house she was watching—the bigger courtyard, yesterday, where Rith and Kesh had hosted their friends the first night she had watched them. He had been barefoot, his jaw a mess of three-day whiskers. He had come into the sunlight and sat on the edge of a shallow pool filled with golden fish. He paddled his fingers in the water and appeared to be having a conversation with the fish.

Trying to figure out what Yarro was about made Azmei think about her own observer. Several times over the course of the past week, she had wondered what he or she thought of her. The Shadow Council's observer must know she had arrived. Did they see her doing surveillance on the house? Would they be impressed or disappointed with the pace of her work?

And the question that weighed most heavily on her mind: were they responsible for whatever made the Perslyn family think Orya might be back from the dead?

Orya's body had not been returned to her family. She had been placed, along with her cousin and colleague Wenda, in a catacomb owned by the Shadow Council in Ranarr. Azmei had not mourned for her, though her feelings were still, three years later, in a muddle. She had genuinely liked Orya, though she had been cognizant of the woman's faults. And knowing how Orya worried for her brother, she had even been able to understand why Orya would do anything—even kill a princess—to take care of him. But she had not been able to forgive her for that, either, brother or no. Azmei would do anything for her own brother, but there were some things she probably should not be forgiven for, either.

She went through her morning routine quickly, her series of stretches, washing, dressing, and eating. Today, provided nothing went wrong, she would enter the Perslyn house and finalize her plans. Once she had seen the inside, she would know how to proceed.

The Patriarch must die, of course. Rith, the eldest grandson, would also need to be removed. He was cruel, and Azmei had seen in Tish's reactions yesterday that she was afraid of him. Kesh, Azmei wasn't certain about. She had already decided it might be possible to reason with him, if he were placed at the head of the entire family. Azmei had overheard someone say he tried to shield Yarro from their elder brother; it had convinced Azmei that Kesh was at heart a decent human being.

As much as anyone who spent their lives killing other people for pay could be a decent human being. But then again, Azmei had precious little room to judge on that point.

She stood. She had circled around this very idea for the past three years. The Shadow Council only accepted contracts that were in the interest of peace. If removing a single person was a more peaceful solution than a war, the Shadow Council approved it. In Azmei's case, her guardian Destar Thorne had hired the Shadow Council to protect her from assassins. Because the Ranarri Diplomats had brokered the marriage treaty, the Shadow Council agreed the marriage was in the best interest of peace, and they had protected Azmei from other assassins. Azmei had occasionally wondered if Tanvel had agreed to take her on as a student because he felt guilty for almost failing. It was good to know he was proud of her.

She hoped he survived protecting her father.

She pushed the thought resolutely from her mind. She had work to do. She strapped all of her daggers in place and took up her pack.

It was time to enter the Perslyn house. There were plenty of ways to gain access to a closed house. She could pretend to be a messenger. If she had more time, she could infiltrate the household. She could hire on with one of the groups who provided a service, whether it was ice delivery or repair work. But Azmei was tired of wasting time. She had decided to do this hard and fast.

She would go over the wall and sneak.

As she picked her way across the roof of Perslyn House, she wondered if her chosen method of ingress would gain her points for bravery with the Shadow Council's observer, or if she would be docked points for her reckless impatience. Either way, she told herself, it didn't matter. Tanvel had put his life on the line over this conflict. She could do no less.

There must be something here that would identify the person who had hired the Perslyns to kill Azmei. She and Tanvel had searched Perslyn offices in other cities, or had them searched, and they had found precious little of any value. It was why Tanvel had determined they must travel to Tamnen City at last. Azmei hoped he had found the proof he needed there, but she would search here anyway.

They knew the contract had originated in Tamnen. They knew the Perslyns had not acted on behalf of the Strid. They knew the assassins had no clue their attempt had failed.

Azmei eased up to a corner sheltered from anyone in the rooms above or the courtyard below and shrugged out of her robed camouflage. She would have to take care that the fountain didn't mask anyone's footsteps but her own. She swept her gaze across her surroundings once more, then eased over the edge of the roof.

Her feet whispered against the sandstone of the courtyard floor. She retreated to one wall and listened. In the distance, she heard the quiet murmur of voices. Nothing inside the rooms she meant to enter. She drew a slender lockpick from a pocket and let herself into the first room.

It had the look of a leisure space, with a cushioned reclining platform and a low table that held a stack of books. A taller table was placed next to the reclining platform—probably to hold trays of delicacies and beverages. Azmei slipped her fingers under the cushion, but found nothing. Neither table had a drawer, but she knelt to look at the underside of each. Still nothing. Perhaps this room was just as it appeared.

She had chosen her entry point to the house carefully. This room was outside the Patriarch's study. It was the room where he entertained the majority of his visitors. Azmei drew her lockpicks and let herself into the Patriarch's study.

She had waited until she saw the Patriarch and his grandson Rith leave the house, but there was no guarantee how long they would be gone, and it was possible someone else could discover her here. She doubted Kesh was allowed in the Patriarch's study unless his grandfather was present, but she could be wrong. In addition, she would have to be careful not to leave anything out of place after she was finished. The Patriarch would surely notice.

Her first task was to find a ledger. Any good businessman had to track his income and expenses, and the Patriarch was, by all accounts, a very good businessman. The ledgers of the cloth business were in the shop; Azmei had already ascertained that. But the assassination ledgers, those would have to be somewhere here in the house. The Patriarch's study was the most likely of places, though she wouldn't rule out the Patriarch's bedchambers.

A quick search of the desk turned up nothing. Azmei turned her attention to a cabinet under a painting of a pastoral scene populated only by grass, rolling hills, and sheep. She smirked at the painting. Trust a cloth merchant to think sheep were nice to look at. Kneeling in front of the cabinet, she made short work of the lock. Inside were records of a more incriminating sort. Apparently Orya had spent some time in the unified cities of the Long Coast before she returned to Tamnen in time to try to murder the princess.

Azmei noted down several of the names, wondering if any of the assassinations there would have ramifications in Tamnen. There was trade between Tamnen and the Long Coast, but the unified cities had never been a political threat. They were interested mainly in being left alone, and Tamnen—on the other side of a rugged mountain range from them—had been more than happy to oblige.

Azmei dug through the rest of the papers in the cabinet without finding much of interest. She replaced them all carefully as she had found them and relocked the cabinet. A quick glance at the lattice at the top of the room told her the sun's angle had shifted. She must have been in here nearly an hour. She couldn't afford much more time.

Was what she'd found proof enough that the Patriarch and his grandchildren were involved in Orya's attack on her? Azmei scowled at the papers she had scribbled her notes on. Yes. It was enough. But it got her no closer to knowing which of the Nine Families was plotting against the throne. She went back to the desk and performed a more thorough search, and this time she found what she'd missed the first time.

The middle drawer of the desk was too short. Azmei removed it entirely and set it aside, then ducked under the desk. There, looking secure, was the second, secret drawer the desk had been hiding. Azmei smiled grimly and tugged it open. There. Folded packets, encased in parchment and tied with black string. She started to open it, then jerked. Were those footsteps?

She settled the secret drawer carefully back and replaced the middle drawer. Tucking the packets into her shirt, she eased away from the desk, straining her ears. He would miss the papers, she knew that. But whatever information was in these packets, she needed it.

Rith Perslyn had a party scheduled tomorrow. There would be plenty of comings and goings in the house, and presumably the Patriarch would make an appearance. There would be enough alcohol consumed that no one would notice her slipping into the house and doing away with the Patriarch, hopefully before the man had a chance to miss his stolen papers. If that went smoothly, she could take out Rith as well.

Azmei listened at the door for a moment, then let herself out of the Patriarch's study. Tomorrow would end it.

CHAPTER NINE

The hot sun felt good on Yar's shoulders. The Voices had been arguing amongst themselves today, barely sparing him any notice. It was a nice change. He had wandered out to the bigger courtyard, where Rith and Kesh usually hosted their parties. The warm stones were pleasantly rough under his feet. The courtyard was filled with the fragrance of honeysuckle and jasmine mixed with the slightly fishy smell of the fountain.

Yar scratched his jaw and wondered when he'd last remembered to shave. Shaving always made him feel fond of Kesh. Maybe he ought to do it more often. Yar sat on the edge of the shallow pool filled with golden fish, enjoying the tinkle and splash of the fountain. He paddled his fingers in the water and remembered Kesh teaching him how to shave.

"You'll have to be careful not to cut yourself." Kesh's hand grasped Yar's, both of them wrapped around the razor's handle. "You don't want the smell to make you sick."

Yar would have nodded, but the razor was pressed to his cheek as Kesh showed him how to stroke it up his skin. He liked the scraping noise of the blade. It made him think of the lizards that lived in the courtyard, their scales rasping against the stone. A flash of light from the razor blade caught his eye and Yar blinked and stared.

A big, golden eye stared back at him, the scrape of the razor becoming the rasps of scales. Yar jerked.

"Careful, Yar!" Kesh tightened his grip on the razor and held it away from his skin. He turned to face Yar, ducking his head until Yar couldn't avoid his gaze. To Yar's surprise, Kesh's gaze didn't burn him or make his skin prickle. It was warm and worried.

Kesh licked his own thumb and pressed it against Yar's jaw, and only then did Yar smell the blood. "I know you don't like being touched," Kesh murmured, "but once you learn to do this yourself, I won't have to help you. Won't that be better?"

Yar lowered his gaze. He didn't know what to say to make Kesh stay like this. His brother seemed gentle when they were alone, but Yar knew that gentleness could change to impatience if he said the wrong thing. Or if he didn't say anything soon enough.

"I'm sorry," he muttered. "I'll learn soon."

Kesh sighed. "I don't mind, Yar. It isn't like Orya could have taught you this, anyway. Girls don't have to do this."

A hand tugged at Yar's sleeve, jolting him from his memories. He didn't have to look to know it was Tish. She was good about not touching his skin unless she had to.

"Yarro! I've been looking all over for you. Your brother doesn't want you wandering around today."

Yar kept patting the water, but he lifted his head to look at Tish. "He just doesn't like me having a good day."

"Be charitable. He is looking out for you in his way. It is hard for him to stand between you and the others. Your sister did it better."

"I miss Orya," Yar said. "Do you miss Orya?"

"Of course I do. I miss her every day." Tish's voice caught. Yar felt bad for asking. He knew she missed Orya. Yar had never seen Orya hug anyone except him and Tish.

"Do you think she will come back?"

Tish sat down facing him on the edge of the pool. "Yar, we talked about this. Orya is dead. She was killed three years ago." She lifted a hand as if she would touch him, but hesitated and pulled away at the last moment. "Don't you remember?"

He straightened up and glared at her. "I'm not stupid, Tish. I remember. You were the one who told me. But Rith and Grandfather said—"

"You shouldn't talk about this to me," she interrupted

hastily.

He ignored her. "Someone is hurting people in our family." His smile felt vicious. He wondered if that was because the Hungry Voice had heard him say that.

"And they think it's Orya?" Tish leaned in, her gaze intent on Yar's, but he couldn't meet her gaze long. What if she could tell how pretty he thought her? He shrugged and turned away from her.

SHE WANTS IT TO BE ORYA, said the Hungry Voice. SHE WANTS ORYA BACK.

So she doesn't have to take care of me anymore, Yar thought bitterly.

SHE'S LONELY.

Yar began rocking in place. Finally Tish sighed and took him by both hands. She tugged him to his feet and led him inside. Yar didn't bother struggling. He didn't want to leave the sunlight, but if Kesh said not to wander, he might have a party planned. He didn't like showing Yar to his friends, but Yar didn't care. He didn't like seeing Kesh's friends. He just wanted Tish and Orya. He wanted to go back in time.

I'm lonely too.

***

Usually Yar's sleep was peaceful, the only time he could be free of the Voices and their visions. He dreamed so much in his waking life that he never dreamed when asleep. At least he never remembered them. But that night, he woke repeatedly with the echoes of the word FOLLOW in his mind.

Finally he threw aside his blankets and rolled out of bed. It was dark in his room, but here on the western side of the house, he had no way of knowing if there were any edge of dawn to the eastern sky. It could be anywhere from midnight to dawn without his knowing it.

Yar fumbled a candle alight and padded barefoot to the door of his quarters. When he peered out at the main residence hall, he saw no one. It must be very early still. He had slept for at least a few hours, he thought, unless the Voices were waking him after shorter intervals than he thought. But it must still be closer to midnight than dawn, or the corridors would be awake with servants preparing for breakfast.

He eased the door shut again and considered. If tonight was anything to judge by, the Voices had decided they wanted him. He would go truly insane if they began waking him every hour of every night with that command booming in his ears.

What had he to lose if he obeyed? Orya had been the only one here who loved him. While Tish was kind, she would never think of him as a man. The rest of his family was reason to go, not reason to stay. Especially after Grandfather heard him talking to the Voices. What if he remembered what Yar said about seeing Voices and tried to learn how to use it for his killing business?

Yar went back to his bed and knelt in the middle of it. "All right," he said aloud. "I'll follow. I'll come." He took a deep breath. *I will follow.*

At once his mind was filled with images. They flew at him in a blur, faster than he could process them. He whimpered and clutched his head with both hands. The images didn't slow, but they did begin repeating themselves. He focused on each as it came at him.

A desert land with sweeping sand dunes and harsh cliffs; a hidden valley with sweet water and rich soil; a red horse looking straight at him; a copper-skinned woman with short hair and a sword on her hip; a beautiful magic-user with green eyes and long brown hair streaked prematurely with white.

The next time they cycled through, he noticed the desert cliffs seemed to have homes carved into them, the red horse had a black mane and tail, and the swordswoman also wore at least half a dozen daggers. Then there were more, a dove and serpent, a hawk, clouds of sand...

Yar whimpered again, feeling his bed tilt under him. They were too much. He couldn't process them all. The images would fill his mind, taking it over until there was nothing left of him. They would overwhelm him. They would erase him.

ENOUGH. The mental onslaught lessened immediately. HE HAS SAID HE WILL FOLLOW.

"Yes, and I'm only mortal," Yar whispered aloud. "Give me time to get about it."

There was the reverberation of laughter in his head, and then the Voices were gone.

For the first time in months, perhaps years, Yar felt alone inside his head. He thought about his grandfather, but there was no answer urging Yar to eat him. Greatly daring, he imagined Tish in her bath, water streaming from naked shoulders as she lifted up, showing him perfectly rounded breasts. No admiring Voice, nor even the Voice that mocked him for feeling desire.

With a gasp, Yar loosed the rein on his imagination. He thought of himself climbing naked into the bath with Tish, placing his hands on her breasts, pressing his lips against hers. He imagined the way she would feel against him, how their wet skin would slide together. He pictured himself slipping a hand beneath the water. No Voice commented on his fantasies or mocked him for wishing for them. Yar stuck a hand inside his sleeping pants and gripped himself, falling back onto the bed and losing himself entirely in fantasy.

When he'd finished, he wiped his hand on the bedclothes and sat up, feeling vaguely ashamed. The first time he felt alone in his head, and what did he do? He pleasured himself. Shoving aside the disgust, he got out of bed and went to the washbasin. When he was washed and dressed, he sat down to think.

Who knew how long the Voices would leave him alone? He needed to concentrate for as long as he possibly could.

He had agreed to follow. He was committed. Where was he going? The desert, apparently. How was he going? Perhaps that red horse would guide him? He wasn't sure where the desert was, except that it was south, towards Strid somewhere. He would have to pack for a long journey. He didn't know how far he would be able to travel every day. And if the visions came back along the way...

He shook himself. *Don't get discouraged. For now, you can think properly. Take advantage of that.* How much did he eat in a day? He wasn't sure, but he thought it was about half a loaf of bread a day, plus meat and fruits and vegetables. And he would need to carry water with him, especially since he was going to the desert. What else? Blankets to sleep. A cloak or robe. Good shoes. He wouldn't be able to forget to put shoes on if he was walking around outside.

What else? Think, what else?

Weapons. He shook his head. He hated violence. The smell of blood made him gag. But he would need weapons. Something to hunt with, something to defend himself with. There was a war going on somewhere out there, after all, and the Voices talked about it sometimes. It might cause him problems. Best to be prepared to defend himself.

Oh, of course. Money. He would need money. Yar frowned. He had been to the market with Orya sometimes. There had been a period of perhaps six months when she thought getting him outside their house and visiting places that were new to him would keep his attention better. Her theory had been that he might not get caught by the visions if there were enough things to catch and keep his visual attention.

It hadn't worked. Nothing had, until tonight. But he had loved her for trying, even as he resented the attempts.

Still, it served a purpose now. He could remember how money worked, with the copper bits and silver sovs. He thought about Orya haggling with merchants, insulting the quality of their wares to bring the price down. He wasn't sure if he could do it as well as she had, but he thought he could do it.

The money was the easy part. Orya had not given him any secret messages or told him any secret plans, but she *had* saved a large purse for him. He had never spent any of it. Orya's friends had taken care of him since she left.

Very well. He had a mental list of what he would need. He ran through the list again, deciding an extra pair of clothes, or perhaps even two, would be good to have. Then he got up and began collecting all the supplies he had deemed necessary.

When he was finished packing, Yar was still alone inside his head. It was amazing. He stared around his rooms, feeling as if his soul were uncurling and stretching its arms. Wings. Whatever souls had. He took several long breaths, holding them before releasing.

Then he sat down and pulled on his boots. They would make more noise on the stone floor than bare feet, but he thought it was more important to put them on now, while he knew he could remember them, than to wait until he had sneaked out. What if a vision came on him after he left the house, and he forgot to put them on at all? He would end up with bloody feet, and that would do him no good.

When he was ready, daggers on his belt and pack slung over his shoulder, he drew up the hood of his robe and slipped out of his rooms. He was alone in the first corridor. When he turned into the next one, a white-robed servant was walking towards him. Yar held his breath, but the servant merely bowed as he passed. How conveniently servants had been trained, Yar thought. They didn't meet one's eyes. Of course, Yar didn't usually meet one's eyes either, but he had never re-alized before how it limited him.

He reached one of the house's side gates without being stopped. He paused there in the guttering torchlight, looking down at the water just two feet below the gate. Would he have to steal a boat? But no, there was a stone walkway outside. Yar hitched his pack up over his shoulder and set off as briskly as he could. He would get well away from here and wait for the sun to come up. After dawn, he could find his way to the trade market, and there he would decide what he should do.

CHAPTER TEN

Arisanat wished he had never come on this journey to the desert.

He had never had any real choice in the matter. From the moment King Marsede had decided Arisanat's presence was necessary, it had been almost a foregone conclusion that Arisanat would go. He had grounds to refuse. He had enough support in the council that he could have gotten away with refusing. He would have been spared the torture of revisiting the Kreyden without his brother if he had refused. But refusal would have created a rift between Arisanat and the king.

No, it would have *revealed* the rift between Arisanat and the king.

He huffed and flopped over in his blankets, wishing violently for his comfortable down-filled bed and the soft silk sheets and fine wool blankets that he was used to. These bulky cushions they had brought with them from Tamnen City were considered the pinnacle of comfort in travel, but Arisanat could still tell he was less than a foot off the ground, where anything could crawl up into bed with him. The desert was home to vermin of all sorts, from four-legged to eight-legged to no-legged, and Arisanat was not overfond of any of them.

This had all been a colossal mistake.

Spending time near Razem was reminding him of all the pleasant times he had spent with his cousin in the past. It reminded him of a childhood spend sledding in the winter and berrying in the summer, of Longnights spent singing the fire to bed and Longdays spent dancing around the Lifetree and searching for fireflowers. It reminded him of a time when neither Razem nor Arisanat were angry men who had lost those they held most dear. Most of all, it reminded him that Razem was grieving, too.

He didn't want to feel compassion for the cousin he had

vowed to kill.

With a huff, Arisanat threw back his wool blanket and rose from his cushion. He left the tent and took a deep breath of crisp night air, untainted with the smell of banked fire or men's night farts. He stared up at the sky, wishing he'd grabbed his cloak from the trunk by the foot of his cushion. It was colder here than up north at his home. The desert was only hot in the daytime. He remembered his first time visiting the desert. He'd come to the Kreyden to see Venra, about a year after Venra had left Rivarden to take command in Dinnsan.

Dinnsan was a fortified city at the eastern end of the Salishok River. It was at least three hundred years old, and peopled by a mix of Strid and Tamnese, with a handful of people from the Long Coast on the other side of the mountains. It had been held by the Tamnese for the past hundred and fifty years, but the Strid had held it for eighteen years before that. Dinnsan's civilian authorities were almost entirely of Tamnese descent, and Arisanat had been surprised by the relative peace of the city, since it was at the bleeding edge of the Strid-Tamnese Conflict.

Venra had laughed at his naïveté. "Everyone here knows they're better off with Tamnen City in control, Aris," he'd said. "We have laws that provide for the least fortunate among us. We allow no religious zealots to control our policy. We have good tools for educating children regardless of class."

"Are the Strid really as bad as that?" Arisanat had asked.

"The Strid people are at the mercy of the Strid king's whim. I had an entire clan cross the river asking for asylum because King Harkai had decided the maker god's followers were trying to wrest power. This clan, some thirty people, left because Harkai had outlawed worship of the maker god."

Arisanat snorted. "How do you outlaw worship of a god? A faithful man would never renounce his god, no matter what you threatened him with."

"But in Strid, you can now be executed for worshiping the maker god." Venra shook his head. "I wonder how many blacksmiths and carpenters they'll have left in the kingdom before Harkai comes to his senses."

"I thought the prince was the dangerous one."

Venra shrugged. "He's reckless and arrogant, not mad. Harkai is said to be afflicted with madness that comes and goes. He'll come around eventually and probably repeal half of the edicts he issued during this period. But that will be too late for too many of his people. So they come to Dinnsan." Venra grinned, dimples making him look even younger than his twenty-three years. "And I welcome them and put them to work and tax them, so King Marsede is happy about them coming here."

Arisanat laughed and they had moved on to another topic. But the conversation had stayed with him. They did have a good system of government in Tamnen. The king ruled, but he ruled by the good will of the Nine Families. If any of his policies were deemed unwise by a majority of the Nine, there would be mediation and compromise. It was a good system, but after Venra's death, Arisanat had realized its limitations.

There was no mechanism for replacing a king who had gone too far down a faulty path. Dynasties changed, of course. There had been times when a king died without issue, so the rule went to the First Family, and then the entire ranks of the Nine were shifted. Once, three hundred and twenty years ago, three of the Nine changed completely because families Four, Six, and Nine were related to the old king, but not to the head of the First Family who succeeded. That was when the Corrone family moved up to First Family instead of Second. Eighty years later the Corrone family succeeded to the throne, and they had remained there ever since.

But now, Arisanat thought, shivering in the cold night air, it was time for a change.

Behind him, he heard rustling as someone put back the tent flap. Whoever it was made an insulted noise, presumably at the chill, and there was a bit more rustling before footsteps approached Arisanat where he stood. He glanced over as the person reached him.

Razem was shrugging into a cloak. "H'lo, Aris. Can't you sleep either?" he mumbled. He sounded sleepier than his words suggested.

Arisanat shrugged.

Razem wasn't discouraged by his silence. "We'll be at Baron Arkad's estate in a week or so. At least we'll have real beds to sleep in there."

"And it'll be warmer, I hope," Arisanat said dryly.

Razem laughed. "You know, I'd forgotten just how cold the nights can be in the desert. Funny how the memory tricks you, isn't it?"

Arisanat grunted. He didn't really feel like talking. He would just as soon not have company. Somewhere in the distance, a fox yipped and another one answered it. He tilted his head back and looked up at the stars. Somehow they looked closer out here, away from the city, looming over him as if they knew his secrets.

He began counting the days. How long was it before Longday? That was the deadline he'd imposed on the Problem Solver. Both of them dead by Longday, he'd said. Had the assassin struck at Marsede yet? Perhaps the king was dead even now, the couriers searching all over for Prince Razem. When would Arisanat have news?

And Birona—he should be working to bring the city guard over to their side. It was a delicate task, but Arisanat had no doubt Birona was up to it. The man dealt primarily in war materiel, it was true, but he also helped supply the city guard. He had influence and contacts that would prove invaluable to Arisanat's plans. Guiltily, Arisanat glanced over at his cousin, who had been unusually quiet.

Razem must have seen the glance. He turned his head. "Aris, is there trouble between you and Hawk?"

That was not the question Arisanat had been expecting, though he wasn't sure what he *had* expected. He hesitated. "I don't trust him." He drew the words out, as if reluctant to say them. "He is mild and agreeable, certainly, but he has spent six years among the enemy. Who knows what changes could have been wrought in that time? And is that agreeable person he presents himself as true, or is it a ploy?" Even in the light of the banked fire, Arisanat could see Razem's frown. "How do you mean?"

"To gain your trust," Arisanat said. "To learn our secrets. You're too trusting, Raz. By the gods, after what happened to Azmei, I'd expect more caution from you!"

As soon as the words fell from his lips, he wondered if he'd gone too far. But Razem didn't recoil. He merely stood, staring at the glowing embers. Arisanat drew a breath.

"I worry for you, cousin. Here we are in the middle of nowhere, with only a handful of guards compared to what you ought to have." He paused. "What if Hawk intends to guide our enemies here to kill you?"

Razem shook his head slowly. "I don't believe that Commander Ayowir would fight that way."

"Perhaps not, but she has the damned Deranged Duke now."

Razem pursed his lips, frowning out into the darkness. His arms were folded across his chest, and Arisanat saw his fingers tapping against his elbows. "I will take you in my confidence, Aris. But this must go no further. There is no way to prove it, for one thing. But when last I saw the duke, he all but begged my forgiveness. He knows he was—that what he did was evil. He knows he deserves damnation for it. I believe he would undo it, if he could."

"And if wishes were fishes, we'd dine well each night!" Arisanat snapped.

"Aris—"

"You're a trusting fool, Razem," he muttered. "Someday I fear that will turn on you."

There was a long silence. Sleeping gods, that had been ill said. What if Razem took that as a confession? What if—

"Well, *now* I'll be able to sleep," Razem said wryly.

Arisanat let out a long sigh of mixed relief and annoyance. "I beg your pardon, cousin. You know I do not like what we are about here. It makes me churlish."

"I had noticed." Razem's tone was mild.

"Razem—"

"Oh, let it go, you maundering lump," Razem said, and he flashed a grin at Arisanat. Arisanat's chest squeezed painfully. How could Razem still look at him with such affection? "I'll take your words under advisement and try not to be too trusting," Razem continued. "But for now, I think I could use a privy and a warm blanket."

Arisanat swallowed. "Sleep well, then."

"Good night."

Razem's footsteps faded as he returned to his tent, but Arisanat didn't move.

He was doing the right thing. Tamnen deserved a better ruler, a stronger ruler, than the Corrone family could provide. Arisanat had already proven to himself that he was capable of doing the hard things, making the difficult decisions and taking action on them. He would be able to take the war to the Strid and make them pay for all they had done.

If only it didn't involve killing one of his friends to accomplish it.

"If wishes were fishes," Arisanat reminded himself, and went back to his own tent, where he lay awake until morning.

CHAPTER ELEVEN

Hawk stared at the dusty village square. There couldn't be more than twenty houses in the entire village, plus a storehouse and a handful of buildings to serve as blacksmith, healer, and common hall. The village elder's house would be the closest thing to an inn. What could the prince expect to do with his entourage here? They would be lucky if the village had enough water for all the horses, let alone room to put them all. He glanced helplessly at Lord Arisanat, who was glowering at the village elder.

Hawk wasn't sure why Arisanat was blaming the elder. It was Prince Razem who was being unreasonable. Razem wanted every single person in the village called away from work to witness their arrival. Hawk couldn't exactly blame the elder for being irritated by the demand. The village had a spring and a small stream that provided enough water for a few fields of crops. Not much, certainly not enough to trade with other villages, let alone feed an army company. But enough to sustain the village. If the field workers were called in before the sun set, would they get enough planted today?

The village elder was going through all that again, his strident mishmash of Tamnese, Strid, and Kreydeni dialect doing nothing to move the obstinate Razem. Kho obviously found it astonishing that the man would speak in such a manner to his prince, but Razem hadn't even blinked when the man began his harangue, and Baron Arkad, who had counseled against the prince's order, was biting his cheeks to keep from laughing.

Arkad was obviously known to these villages between his

home and Salishok; when the elder's diatribe failed to move the prince, he turned his accusatory gaze on the baron. The baron held up his hands and spoke in the same patois.

"Perhaps, Elder Miran, if we discussed this all under the shade of your roof, with some fruit juice and salt, we could come to an agreement." He glanced at Razem, then added, "The prince commanded in Salishok, but as you know, he was never at liberty to enjoy your hospitality while he was here, since his command was cut so tragically short by his sister's death."

Hawk watched the prince as Arkad spoke, growing more and more certain that Razem didn't understand much of the Strid, let alone the Kreydeni dialect. When the prince didn't react to the baron's last statement, he was sure of it. The words had an instant effect on Elder Miran, however. The man's strident tone dropped to a more normal level as he said, "Ah, blessed daughter, I had forgotten why he never visited us. The gods forgive me for my pride."

Hawk turned his gaze back to Elder Miran in time to see the man straighten and bow deeply to the prince. "Prince Razem, forgive the foolishness of an old man. Please enter my house and share fruit juice and salt with me. Then when we have rested and talked, I will show to you the bounty that is Derdan."

Hawk had to suppress a smile as Baron Arkad translated the invitation for the prince. It would be better if the prince spoke at least a little Kreydeni, but Hawk knew why he didn't. For all the vaunted value of the Kreyden District, both to the rulers of Tamnen and those of Strid, both countries thought the Kreydeni were provincial at best, or primitive at worst. Not all of them, and certainly not most of those Tamnese who ended up serving in Salishok, but enough that the official language of the Kreyden District was Tamnese and anyone who didn't speak Tamnese was held in contempt.

Prince Razem considered the baron's words for a moment, and then nodded. He dismounted, handing over the reins to a waiting soldier. Hawk waited until Arkad, Kho, and

Arisanat followed suit before doing likewise. Despite three days spent largely in the prince's company, Hawk was still uncertain what his place was. Not to mention the fact that he was still regaining his footing in this country again.

He fell in step several paces behind the prince, letting the others go before him. He probably knew the customs here better than any of them, with the possible exception of Arkad, who seemed to be of the breed of nobleman who spent time getting to know the people he had power over. Hawk liked Arkad. Not only did the man respect even those who were lower than he, but he also seemed quite adept at handling the prince. Razem seemed a decent sort, but he was entirely unconscious of the privilege of his status. Kho—well, Hawk and Kho had once been very close. Since Kho's less than warm reception in Salishok, Hawk had no idea what to expect from the man. They had not spoken more than a handful of words to each other since that first day, and every time Hawk tried to approach, Kho abruptly found something else to be doing.

As soon as Hawk stepped inside the elder's house, he drew his sword and placed it next to the door. He saw that Elder Miran and Baron Arkad had done the same, but the others were staring in confusion—or, in Kho's case, consternation—at those who were disarming.

"It's customary to leave your main weapon at the door," Hawk told them in Tamnese. "As a show of good faith. Keep your dagger. It's expected you'll need that to eat."

"To eat salt?" Razem said, staring at Hawk but nevertheless drawing his sword and holding it out for Hawk to place next to Talon.

"The salt is just the important part," Hawk explained. "It'll be salted bread, usually. And sometimes meat, if the hunt has done well this week."

Arkad was smiling at him. Hawk wasn't sure what he had done that pleased the baron, but he gave him a brief smile in return. When Elder Miran gestured for them to sit, Kho and Arisanat were still lingering by the door, taking their time about drawing their swords and leaving them. When Razem realized this, he scowled at Kho.

"Go on, Kho. I hardly think Elder Miran is going to murder me in his own house, especially considering he's already placed his own sword there."

"My prince is kind to trust me," Miran said in heavily accented Tamnese. As Hawk had half expected, he spoke and understood the language perfectly. He had merely been giving himself time to take Razem's measure.

Razem bowed from his sitting position. "And the elder is kind to welcome me," he replied. "I apologize that I am not more fluent with your language. I understand some of it, but I regret that I have been unable to spend much time yet in the Kreyden District."

Miran shrugged and held out a leather flask. "Prince Razem is always welcome in the Kreyden. Share fruit juice with me, your highness, that you may properly be my guest."

"Thank you," Razem said, taking the flask and drinking from it. He offered it back to Miran, who drank and passed it to Baron Arkad. By the time the flask came around to Hawk, Kho and Arisanat had taken their places on the cushions as well.

"You already know Baron Arkad," Razem said. "Also with me are my dear cousin Arisanat Burojan, Lord of the First Family, Lord-General Emran Kho of the Tamnese Army, and Commander Hawk." He indicated each man as he introduced them.

Miran's eyes widened as he looked back at Hawk. "I knew of a Commander Hawk many years ago," he said. "Is it possible that you are he?"

"One and the same," Hawk replied. "I am fortunate to have been released from my captivity in Strid, thanks to King Marsede's generosity and Prince Razem's gracious welcome."

"Ahh. Then perhaps we will see hostilities diminish somewhat," Miran said. He brought out a loaf of bread and an ornate salt box. "Will you share salt with me, Commander Hawk?"

Hawk swallowed. Razem might not realize it, but Miran

was honoring Hawk ahead of him. Would the prince take offense? He glanced over at Razem, but the prince was smiling indulgently. "By all means," he said. "We are on a progress to honor Commander Hawk for the great sacrifices he has made in the name of his kingdom. You are right to show him respect, Elder Miran."

So he did understand. Hawk took the offered hunk of bread and bit deeply, pleased by the tang of salt on his tongue. The sharing of salt was not a custom the Strid had, nor as far as he knew was it practiced outside the Kreyden. But Hawk had always enjoyed it. He nodded at Miran, who passed the bread around to the others.

"So the purpose of your visit to Derdan is to show off Commander Hawk," Miran said. "Is it that we are finally engaging in peace? Or is it that we will see a return of The Desert Hawk and a return to victory?"

Beside him, Kho stiffened. Damn. Hawk could kick himself for being so slow to understand. The prince was going to use him to drum up support for the war, wasn't he? And in so doing, he demonstrated a lack of confidence in Kho's ability to lead the war to victory. No wonder Kho was so cool with Hawk! *Though if he gave me a chance to speak, he might understand that I have no interest in returning to command over the war,* Hawk thought bitterly.

"My father wishes to ease relations with Strid," Razem said smoothly. He drank from the flask and passed it to Kho, who unbent enough to take it and drink. Hawk watched him from the corner of his eye, wondering if Kho would be willing to share it with him. He was surprised when Kho did, in fact, pass the flask to him. Hawk gave Kho an apologetic smile as he took it, but Kho turned away.

With a sigh, Hawk drank deeply and passed the flask back to Miran. "I vowed that I would return to Rivarden to see her restored," he told Miran. "Prince Razem is kind enough to see that vow made good. He accompanies me to my home city. From there we have not discussed any plans."

Miran nodded slowly. "It is good," he said finally. "I offer you all shelter in my home for this night. Your men will need to camp outside the village. We have water enough in our cisterns to provide for them and the horses, but though I would wish to throw a feast in honor of the prince's visit, our storehouses are nearly empty. We are planting now, as you have seen, and are forced to rely on hunting to feed ourselves until the harvest comes in."

Razem nodded. "As a token of my well-wishing, I have brought supplies with me to feed not only my own men, but also your village," he said. "I would not like to burden your village overmuch."

Miran smiled. "Then tonight we shall feast!" He stood. "Would Prince Razem like to see the bounty of Darden? You may view the farmers at their work and see how diligent they are."

Hawk hid a smile. Miran had learned a great deal about the prince in a short time. Razem was already standing, smiling in anticipation.

"Come!" Miran said. "I shall show you my village."

***

The village of Darden was only the first in a long line of ceremonies Hawk had to endure. Hawk managed to wear a smile through the first night of singing songs about the war and Tamnen's fighting prowess. He even let himself be persuaded by Elder Miran to tell the story of his capture, though it was not a story he was fond of. The second village had more Tamnese culture than Strid; someone there even dug out the "Lament for Rivarden" and "Hawk's Rest," which had apparently been written in a frenzy of grief before it became common knowledge that Hawk had been captured rather than killed at Rivarden.

Baron Arkad explained all this to a horrified Hawk in a low voice as the singer—a sweet-faced boy whose clear soprano hadn't broken yet—managed to look soulful and earnest while mouthing rhymes about death simultaneously being a well-earned rest and a dire horror that must be avenged.

Hawk managed to sit still through the entire six verses, though he wasn't sure he had disguised his disgust. He applauded at the right moments, attempting to look humble instead of resentful. As soon as he could, though, he stole away from the firelight, muttering about finding a privy. Once he stood up, he decided he might as well actually find one.

When he came back from that errand, he paused outside the bright ring of firelight, watching the earnest faces and wondering if they believed the songs. How could they? But he remembered when he had believed the songs about Tam and the dragons and the making of the world. There was probably some kernel of truth to even those old songs, but he had never in his life stood ten feet tall or let his eyes glow with the force of his wrath, let alone leaped over men to get to his enemy. With a sigh, he tilted his head back and stared up at the stars.

"I gather you'd never heard that one," said the kind voice of Baron Arkad.

Hawk turned. He had lost his edge. Once upon a time, he would have been aware of Arkad as he approached.

"Gods, no. And it seems a bit maudlin to enjoy your own funeral lament." Hawk rubbed the back of his neck.

Arkad chuckled. "Ah, why not? There are plenty of kings who hired theirs written before they had need of it. Precious few of us get to see how people would mourn us."

"Mourning I could accept, if the man they mourned had ever actually existed," Hawk said. "But this call to vengeance... I am not a man anyone should die to avenge. If I must die, let my death truly serve the kingdom, not spur her into more wasteful spending of lives."

"Well spoken." Arkad sighed. "I think this current task must be little to your liking."

The boy soprano switched to a Kreydeni lament for the fallen. Hawk was surprised; he hadn't expected to hear the dialect in this most Tamnese village.

"I do not object to seeing my home again, or to serving my kingdom," Hawk said slowly, choosing words he hoped wouldn't offend the baron. "But I am uncertain of what the prince truly wishes of me."

"So, I think, is he." Arkad was not looking at Hawk. "Razem still mourns his sister. She was assassinated nigh on three years ago—you heard about that?"

Hawk nodded.

"Well. They were close, and the prince blames his father, Prince Anderlin, the Strid nation—everyone, really—for her death. And himself most of all, perhaps. He tried to persuade her not to go, to persuade their father not to send her. When he came to me as commander of the Kreyden forces, he hadn't yet accepted her leaving the kingdom to marry. And then to lose her as he did—" He shook his head. "He would like nothing better than to march all the way to Lindira and slaughter Anderlin and Harkai. But King Marsede urges peace, and he has ordered Razem to make a celebration of your return."

Hawk glanced over at the baron. The singing was loud enough that their conversation was private, though they could be interrupted at any moment. Arkad's expression, though, was troubled without being furtive; he must not care who might overhear them.

"I wonder if the prince misunderstood his father's intent," Hawk ventured. It wasn't exactly a criticism. Hopefully Arkad would understand.

"Just as likely," Arkad agreed. "Grief does not clarify one's thoughts."

Hawk's heart sank. If Razem had willfully misinterpreted his father's orders, that made Hawk's position more difficult. Arkad had made him aware of the king's will, but Hawk could not disobey the prince's orders.

Wonderful, he thought dismally. *So it is to be like this all the way to Rivarden.* And once they reached Rivarden, what then? Razem had not asked Hawk why he vowed to return, nor had Hawk volunteered the reason. Would the prince understand that Hawk felt his duty lay there?

"Don't look so glum, lad," Arkad said. "Razem is a smart man. He'll learn from you, if you're willing to teach."

"Given anyone else, perhaps I could." Hawk rubbed a hand over his jaw. "But if he is still so angry over his sister's death three years later, I am not sure. And he is in the position of giving me orders."

"As he was when I served him," Arkad pointed out. "Though," he added reluctantly, "that was before Azmei's death."

Hawk folded his arms across his chest, suddenly aware of the chill of the evening around them. They were climbing the season into summer, but this far from the fire, his thin shirt and light cloak were not enough to warm him. Or perhaps that was just his frame of mind.

"How many more villages do we have?" he asked. "Hedron and Issla and Milbarton..." He cast his mind back to the years he had spent riding between Rivarden and Salishok. "Haess."

"And Undra and Herew," Arkad finished. "Though as Milbarton is my village, I can do somewhat to lighten the burden there. I can pass the word that the singers will have a throat complaint this week—a nasty cough, perhaps."

"Have mercy," Hawk said, grinning faintly. "The prince might order the soldiers to take up the slack, and that would punish us all the more."

CHAPTER TWELVE

The party on the main floor of Perslyn House was in full swing. The first course of dinner was being served, and Azmei had already seen that the alcohol was flowing freely. She had observed long enough that she knew the Patriarch was in attendance and that he was not indulging. She hadn't expected him to drink much. After all, a drunkard wouldn't last long in charge of the Perslyn Family.

Everything was in place. Finally Azmei was ready to exact justice—which was yet more proof that she was a poor disciple of the god of peace. It was not in her religious code to mete out justice. That dictate came from her blood.

I am still a princess of Tamnen, she reminded herself. *I cannot let stand any threat to my father's rule. And once this mission is over...*

She didn't finish the thought. She still wasn't prepared to think beyond the Patriarch's death.

Instead, she drew her dagger and let herself into the darkened bedroom. A single lamp burned in a globe hanging over the bed. Azmei glanced at the level of the oil and filed it in her memory.

Time to check the room for the Patriarch's safeguards, to locate every trap and remove every weapon. He should notice nothing amiss, but he would have no escape. She began at the right of the door and made a methodical sweep of the room. From behind the wardrobe she withdrew a longsword, while from underneath the wardrobe she removed a loaded crossbow. She removed the bolt, tucking it into her belt next to a dagger sheath. The curtains around one bedpost hid a long knife. The pillow covered a sheathed dagger. She was surprised to see no obvious weapons inside the small writing desk, until she realized what looked like bottled inks were likely poisons instead. Smiling grimly, she swept them, along with the dagger and knife, into the leather sack she had brought with her.

A large urn near the window hid a stiletto and a pouch of throwing stars. Azmei tucked those into her sack as well. She completed her circuit of the room, checked the level of oil in the lamp again; she'd been here approximately half an hour. She should have time for another search. This time she did a quick grid search, which turned up another stiletto strapped to the bottom of the bed, but nothing else. That had taken another twenty minutes at least. Time for her to remove the weapons and take up her post.

She carried the leather sack to the window and the rope she had left in place before entering the house. The top end was tied to a chimney protruding from the roof. She threaded the bottom end of the rope through specially sewn loops at the top of the sack and tied it up high enough that the sack wouldn't show through the window. That would keep the weapons out of the way until she was ready to leave. As she checked the knot a final time, an odd shadow on the wall caught her eyes. She squinted and slid her hand up to touch it.

It was a crevice just large enough to provide a handhold. *So, the Patriarch has an escape route*, she thought. The rope would have been unnecessary. Then again, he might have cut them at a distance spaced too far for her to reach. She was a petite woman, and most men towered over her.

With a shrug, Azmei eased the window closed again. The handholds changed nothing, unless the Patriarch made a break for the window when she attacked. She would just have to make certain he didn't have the chance. Azmei slipped behind the curtains that hung around the bed. She fit easily between the wardrobe and the headboard, where she settled her shoulders against the wall, pushing herself into the aware state of half-meditation.

Carrying out justice is not a part of your teachings, O god of peace, she thought, *but your followers believe that injustice can be anathema to peace. If you could see my actions as bringing peace to Meekin, to the Perslyn family, perhaps even to Tamnen, would it be wrong?*

This mission was what Master Tanvel had decreed for her final passage. Azmei felt no sense of guilt or misgiving. She merely wished it to be finished.

Outside the house, the bell rang the warning for evening curfew—half an hour for honest citizens to return to their homes. Azmei lifted her head and drew in a long breath. Soon now, the party would be breaking up. The guests who planned to return home would leave. Those who planned to stay overnight would retire to more private gatherings in their rooms. What would the Patriarch do?

Footsteps hurried past the door to the bedchamber. Laughing voices reached her ears. A young woman shrieked in amusement or excitement. A deeper voice teased. Azmei couldn't hear his words, but she recognized the sounds of flirtation. That would be the middle son—Kesh. From what Azmei had seen, he was fond of women, wine, and cards. He was a trained killer as much as the others—as much as Orya had been—but he seemed to have no cruelty to him. The Patriarch and the eldest son, Rith, thought Kesh weak and lazy. Azmei hadn't formed an opinion yet, but she suspected he was strong enough to surprise them all. She just hoped he could be reasoned with. She didn't want to have to kill them all.

Assured footsteps strode to the door and stopped. Azmei adjusted her grip on her dagger. Here was the man she had been waiting for.

The doorknob turned and light spilled into the bedchamber from the passage beyond.

"You're sure you won't join us, sir?" The low, grating voice belonged to Rith.

The Patriarch laughed. "I have had enough of dancing in my life. At my age, I am more interested in warm wine than a willing woman."

Rith barked a laugh. "As you say, sir. I'll send a servant up with a drink."

"Never mind. I've already given the kitchen my orders. Go enjoy your party, Rith."

The door closed and the Patriarch's footsteps approached the bed, then paused. Azmei blinked slowly, praying that the god would protect her, hoping that at least her meditation had centered her.

She heard the Patriarch shuffling things around on top of the chest of drawers. He yawned loudly and glass clinked against glass as he poured himself a drink. He took a few steps towards the wardrobe, then stopped.

"You might as well come out," he said. "I know you're here."

Damn. What had given her away? Azmei shifted her dagger hand so her sleeve would hide the blade. She stepped out from behind the curtain.

The Patriarch looked amused, curse him. He was rapier-thin, his eyes steel mirrors that reflected her own inadequacy. "A veil and a hood both? You must not want me to recognize you. I already know you aren't Orya, despite what you seem to wish everyone else to think."

Azmei blinked. Why would they think she was Orya? They had been informed that Orya was dead. "Of course not," she murmured.

"I am the Patriarch of the Perslyn family," he said. "But you already knew that. And your name?"

"You do not need it."

"Ah, then I already know you," he mused. "I simply don't realize I know you."

Azmei inclined her head, keeping her gaze on his face. Her peripheral vision would tell her if he made any move. She would have to be careful of the wine glass he held. It could sting the eyes and blind her long enough for him to escape— or kill her.

"It might be easier if you removed your veil."

"I doubt it," Azmei said. "You have likely never seen my face." She smirked behind the veil. She didn't want him to see her face. It was an honor he didn't deserve.

"You wear kohl around your eyes. Is it because you are vain?"

She rolled her eyes. "It cuts the glare of the sun."

"Ah, so you believe yourself a practical person."

"Enough," she snapped. "I have no time for your guessing games. You don't need to know my name. It is enough for you to know that tonight I am your death."

"Do you think so?" He threw the wine cup. Azmei ducked and turned her head. She raised her dagger to deflect the cup, and as soon as it was past, she lunged at the Patriarch.

The Patriarch turned and threw himself towards the large urn standing in the corner. Azmei smiled at his choice. His having to turn gave her time to close the distance between them.

The Patriarch thrust his arm shoulder deep into the urn. A moment later he tensed. But he wouldn't be defeated by such a small thing as a missing stiletto. Any good assassin knew how to make a weapon out of anything. True to expectation, he tipped the urn over with a crash and rolled it at her so Azmei had to leap over it. She drew her sword with her right hand while she was still in the air.

She landed lightly, teeth bared. He was cornered. He'd chosen the wrong direction unless he wanted to retreat out the window, but Azmei was close enough she thought he wouldn't risk it. He would have to turn away from her, at least part way, to unlatch the window. That would expose him to a lunge, and he wouldn't want to take that chance. Still, someone had to have heard the urn fall, which meant Azmei was running short on time. She paced closer.

"You have more skill than I expected," he grunted. His hands were reaching behind him, scrabbling for anything that might be a weapon. "You searched the room before I arrived."

"I had a good teacher." Azmei smiled. "Necessity."

"Who are you?" he demanded. He threw an ash collector at her.

Azmei deflected it with her elbow. "Someone you tried to have killed." Her smile hardened. "The attempt failed, but it made me angry."

The Patriarch was out of options. He folded his hands in front of him in seeming acquiescence. "Please tell me. I am at your mercy. What have you to lose?"

Azmei's sword flashed out. It sliced his throat. The Patriarch's eyes widened. He staggered and fell against the wall. As he did, his hands flew apart, scattering a coarse dust into the air and across Azmei's face. Most of it was deflected by her veil, but her eyes instantly began to burn. Shit.

She kicked his feet out from under him and stepped on his wrist as she drew near. "Princess Azmei Reera Corrone," she said, and stabbed him in the heart.

Her eyes were streaming. She swore and wiped her blade on his robe, then sheathed it. She could hear footsteps pounding along the passage. Thank the gods she had prepared her escape route before entering the house. She ran to the window and pushed it open.

Azmei swung out onto the rope and pushed the window closed. She couldn't latch it, but at least it would take them a moment to figure out how she had escaped. With any luck, the first person into the room would think the Patriarch's attacker had fled through the halls.

She sheathed her dagger and climbed the rope. Upon reaching the rooftop, she pulled the rope, leather sack attached, up after her, coiling it around her waist like a belt. Now to reach the safe spot she chose yesterday. There she should be able to wait and watch. She wanted to see what the household did when the Patriarch's death was discovered.

She would have to return for Rith. But she didn't enjoy killing, no matter how good she had become at it over the past three years. Followers of her path did not kill without reason. Lawless killing never served peace. Judicious killing, such as this one tonight, often did. But any attempt to reach Rith tonight would almost certainly require her to slice her way through the rest of the household. She couldn't think of a single instance when killing house servants served peace.

When she reached her safe spot, nestled snugly against a

chimney, she crouched and wiped her eyes. They were still burning. The chimney funneled raised voices up to her, but she only caught a few: "Murder!" Then there was a lot of arguing, and someone shouted, "Orya—"

Azmei shook her head. How could any of them truly believe Orya had survived her attack on Princess Azmei? Not only survived, but escaped and gone into hiding? The royal family would never have allowed the princess' assassin to go free. Why would anyone think it possible? And yet if Azmei judged by the Patriarch's words, some did. Had the Patriarch encouraged that? But why would he do that?

Someone shouted orders. People spilled into the courtyard below. Azmei listened to the voice shouting. She thought it was Rith, though she wasn't sure. Then he bellowed, "Get Yarro here now!" and she knew it was Rith. Who else would think to involve Yarro in this? The man seemed to hate his little brother, for no reason she could discern.

Doors banged inside the house. They were doing a systematic search. She strained her ears. Running footsteps in the courtyards told her they were searching them as well. Good. Would they search the roof?

No. There was shouting from the courtyard where the Patriarch's windows opened. They'd found the grappling hook she'd left driven into mortar of the windowsill. The rope dangled to the ground, and they would follow the false trail she had laid for them.

Excellent.

What she heard next shocked her, though. Yarro couldn't be found.

"What do you mean, you can't find him?" Rith snarled. His voice carried so far she imagined their neighbors would hear it. Azmei crept from her hiding spot, scanning the rooftop to be sure she was still alone up here.

"He's not in his rooms. He's not in my rooms. He's not anywhere I usually find him." That was Kesh's voice.

"Ask Tish, then! She was supposed to be taking care of him."

"I can't find her, either. Perhaps she's looking for Yarro."

The conversation lulled. Azmei crept closer to the court-yard where Rith and Kesh spoke. She listened to the measured tread of footsteps leaving the household. Rith apparently believed the curfew didn't apply to his family. Azmei suspected he was right; the city guard wouldn't interfere with Perslyn family business.

"I want Yarro. See if he knows anything about this. If it *is* Orya—"

"You can't think it's her," Kesh interrupted. "She's dead, Rith. We got her personal effects back. Everyone said the Diplomats confirmed it. Her death and Wenda's."

She heard an explosive sigh. "Damn it, who else could it be? Who else could have ferreted out so much information about the family network? Kesh, we've lost too many operatives in the past six months. This morning, Grandfather was furious about some missing papers. Missing from his office *here*. Someone is waging war on this family."

"No one can say we don't deserve it." Kesh's voice was so quiet, Azmei had to strain to hear.

Rith growled. "Forget about that. Find Yarro. Bring him to me. He'll tell me what he knows or I'll beat it out of him."

"You can't possibly believe he knows anything about this. Leave him alone, Rith."

Azmei scowled and wiped her eyes again. The times she had seen Yarro, he'd been in a world all his own. He seemed unaware of what passed around him. His eyes focused inward, and he responded to very little of what Tish said to him. How could Rith think he knew anything?

"Just find him," Rith snarled.

Azmei shook her head. He was impatient, arrogant, and cruel. It was plain that Kesh recognized his older brother's failings. But how would Kesh react if he were confronted with the woman who had killed his grandfather and older brother? Would he accept Azmei's judgment as just, or would he try to fight back? She felt strangely reluctant about killing the man who, however weakly, tried to stand up for his little brother.

She squeezed her eyes shut for a moment and then stood. Crossing the roofs with blurry vision wasn't the safest thing to do, but she needed to get away from House Perslyn for now. She would be back all too soon.

***

The market was more crowded than Yarro remembered. The sun was high overhead before he'd managed to thread his careful way through the busy streets to make his purchases. Each elbow that bumped his made him jump. Every casual brush of skin or cloth sent his hair crawling.

He hated being touched. And here in the market it seemed impossible to avoid it.

The smell of sweat and cookfires clung in his nostrils despite all the market threw at him. Kazhin spice lingered in a cloud that made his lips tingle and overripe fruit cloyed the air, but always the smell of sweat made him want to snort. And the noise was no better. Vendors shouted all the fine points of their wares or shoved them under his nose, chattering so fast he couldn't follow them.

Yar had managed to buy a map, some food, and two water skins. Between transactions, he'd had to withdraw a space and hide in a dim alley, but he couldn't deny a feeling of accomplishment.

Of course, the most difficult task was still ahead of him. Yar needed a horse.

HORSES? YOU BRING US FOOD!

Yar groaned aloud. It had been foolish to hope the Voices were gone for good, and yet. *Not food*, he thought. *Don't distract me.*

Talking back to the Voices rarely made any difference, but he had never been able to break the habit.

YOU HAVEN'T FOUND US YET. The Voice took on a pouting quality.

"Are you close by?" Yar demanded. Then he glanced around. The alley walls towered above him, but they didn't deaden the market noise. A man in a hooded tunic had heard him speak. He shied away.

NOT CLOSE AT ALL. AGES AND AGES AWAY. The Voice had turned gleeful. HIDDEN FROM EVERY-ONE.

Yar snorted. *That's why I need a horse. Not to eat. To ride.*

FIND US! FIND FIND FIND—

Yar crouched, clutching his ears and squeezing his eyes shut. This couldn't happen here. Not before he'd acquired a horse. Not before he'd found a place to hide from his brothers tonight. He rocked a little, pushing against his temples. *Leave me alone. Just stop,* he pleaded.

A golden chuckle rippled through his head. LEAVE THE LITTLE BROTHER ALONE, said a warm Voice he loved. HE IS COMING TO US.

The hungry Voice whined, but they faded away from his thoughts. Yar cracked one eye to see the man in the hooded tunic peering at him again.

"You all right, lad?"

Yar shuddered and stood up. "My head hurt." He shrugged, trying to loosen the tension in his shoulders. "It's all right now."

The man looked unconvinced, but he moved on. Yar didn't really care if the man believed him. He was no one. It was the traders Yar would have to convince. If they didn't believe he had the gold to buy a horse, he would be in trouble.

He straightened up and made himself stand tall. Orya had always carried herself like the gods themselves owed her their attention. Yar knew he couldn't pull that off, but he could at least imitate her. He thought he heard one of the Voices chortling in the back of his head as he strutted out of the alley.

Most people didn't use horses inside the city walls. The canals made it unnecessary as well as inconvenient. The horse market, therefore, was located at the far edge of the market, close to the inns and the Dry Gate, which led out to the foot-hills. Yar had hoped to leave Meekin today, but he could tell from the sun's angle that he'd lost some time arguing with the Voices. He scowled as he threaded his way between stalls. Tomorrow, then, but that meant he would have to find a place to spend the night. Probably no one had realized yet that he was missing, but eventually one of his brothers would look for him. He wanted to be far from Meekin when that happened.

He heard the snorts and whinnies a few moments before the smell of horse reached him. Yar wrinkled his nose and followed the fence around to where the traders had set up their awnings. Only two horse pens were full. Yar looked from one to the other, shrugged, and went to the closest one.

"Good day, young master! I can see you are in need of a fine mount." The man bustling towards him had a thick mustache and beady eyes. Yar didn't want to look at him, but he forced himself to meet the man's shiny gaze.

"I need a good, hardy horse," he said, pushing his shoulders back. "A beast that can carry me and my pack a long distance."

"Ah, a journey, is it?" The man's smile showed a missing tooth. Yar wondered if he'd been kicked by one of his horses. "Traveling north? Or does the young sir merely dislike the crowding on the boats to the capital?"

Yar didn't want to answer. What if his brothers looked for him here? The trader might talk. But how to get out of it? What would Orya say? He lifted his chin. "I hardly see that it matters, so long as I have the gold."

The trader was already coiling a lead rope around his hand. He didn't even look back at Yar. "Quite right, young sir. I was only making conversation." He let himself into the horse pen, Yar following at a distance. "Let's see, the brown mare might do. She's sweet-natured and calm." The man gestured to a sway-backed mare.

"Sweet, perhaps," Yar said, "but hardy, she is not. Not with that back." He knew little about horses, but he knew what they should look like. He knew their backs and feet were the most important parts to watch.

"Ah, keen eyes, young sir. It's true she has seen better

days. What about this bay stallion, then? He's strong, right enough, and spirited enough for two." The trader disappeared around the mare. When he came back, he was leading a red horse that had its ears pinned back.

A charge bolted down Yar's spine as he and the horse locked eyes. *A red horse with a black mane and tail looking straight at him.* Yar sucked in a breath and stared back. The horse snorted, one foot stomping the ground. It was the horse from his vision. This must be a sign. He reached for the lead rope.

From behind him came the sound of a woman's laughter. "Not that one, boy. See the set of those ears? He's mean as a scorpion."

Yar ignored her and took the rope. "Hello, you," he whispered to the stallion. "Do you know me?"

The stallion snapped his teeth together, ears still pinned. Yar twitched, but he was proud he hadn't jerked away. Why wouldn't the horse from his vision recognize him? But he lifted his hand, palm up and flat, for the stallion to sniff. The horse eyed Yar for a long moment, then lowered his head until his muzzle tickled Yar's palm. Just as Yar's lips broke into a smile, the horse seized his hand between its teeth. Yar yelped.

"Narda, tell the boy no," the woman said. "Can't you see he'd eat the lad alive?" Her voice was nearer. As Yar fought to remain still, gaze locked on the horse's, a slim, brown hand entered his vision and flicked the stallion on the nose. The stallion released Yar's hand and backed up a step, shaking his head. Yar backed up a step, too, pressing his mistreated fingers to his chest.

"I like the look of this one," he told the woman without looking at her.

"I like the *look* of him myself," she agreed. "Just not his behavior. You couldn't even ride him. Hells, I'm not sure I could." She took the lead rope from Yar's fingers. "Trust me. Narda's just in it for the profit. He won't care if the horse kills you tomorrow, as long as he gets his gold."

He frowned, pursing his lips. The vision was clear, he was certain. He must have this horse. Or had it just been *that*

One, wanting a handsome horse to eat? Before he had formed an argument, the stallion reared.

It didn't get very high, but the woman was short. The stallion dragged her off her feet. As she swore and fought to regain her balance, her hood slipped down, uncovering wavy black hair that didn't even touch her shoulders.

"Damn it, help me, horse trader!" she snapped.

Yar moved before the trader could. He didn't know why the Voices wanted him to bring a horse that didn't like him, but he wouldn't disobey. He helped the woman calm the horse enough that he could unsnap the lead rope from his halter. The stallion trotted off, shaking his head and snorting.

Yar sighed as he watched him go. "I want that horse," he said. "You just made him uncomfortable." He turned to face the woman, who grinned wryly at him and shook her head.

"You're crazy, boy. He'll have that hand off next time."

"Your pardon, mistress," Narda broke in, "but you already said you aren't interested in buying the bay yourself, so—"

"He could have broken it this time and didn't," Yar said. "He just wanted to get my attention." The woman's smile faded and she studied him, her gaze sharpening. Finding himself the focus of an uncomfortable amount of attention, Yar made himself stare back at her. What he saw made him feel as if he'd been struck by lightning.

She had tawny golden eyes and brown skin. A hairswidth line of white kissed her left cheekbone. She was a head shorter than he, and fine-boned with a muscular build. A sword and dagger rode on her hips. Not just her hips, he realized, as his vision grayed out for a moment. *The swordswoman also wore at least half a dozen daggers.*

First the bay stallion and then the swordswoman! Was the stallion *her* horse, then? But no, she'd said she wasn't sure she could ride him.

"Are you my guide?" he blurted.

Her tawny eyes widened, the focus of her regard relaxing. She laughed. "Well, you seem to need one, especially when it comes to horseflesh." She put her hands on her hips, which only emphasized the blades. "Can you even ride at all?"

Yar hunched his shoulders. "A little." He'd gone riding with Orya from time to time. She didn't care about horses, but she was required to know how to ride, and she'd wanted to see if they would help him.

They hadn't, but it hadn't been awful, either. He liked the smell of horses, and the warm satin of their skin. It was why he'd decided to buy a horse instead of traveling on foot.

"Hmm." The woman strode into the herd, ignoring the horse trader's complaints. Did she work for him? Maybe she was his guard? But he'd said something about her not wanting to buy the bay. Maybe she was just a nosy customer.

"Come on!" the woman called to Yar. "This lad might do. Let's see you on him."

She'd selected a smallish dun gelding, which turned its head to watch Yar pick his way between the herd.

"Here, put your foot in my hands," she said, but he ignored her. Yar put a hand on the dun's withers, winding his fingers in his mane, and swung himself up onto its back. He collected himself, squinting down at her.

To her credit, she didn't mind his showing off. She laughed. "You look all right with him. Walk him around a bit. Oh, shut up, Narda," she added to the protesting trader. "If he can ruin the dun right in your pen, the dun isn't much to begin on." She turned back to Yar, tilting her head back to give him a conspiratorial grin. "And if you can ride the dun, we'll let you have another crack at the bay."

Yar shuttered his gaze and turned the dun, riding him in circles around the pen. After two circuits, at a walk and then a trot, he pulled up in front of the swordswoman and slid off the horse's back. Handing her the lead rope, he went back to the trader.

"I want to see the bay." Without waiting for a response, Yar went across the pen to where the bay stallion stood watching him. He'd been watching the whole time Yar was on the dun. Maybe he'd recognized Yar after all.

Yar fished in his pocket. He'd bought a twist of candied nuts before lunch, and there were one or two left. He shook one out onto his palm and offered it to the bay. "My name's Yarro," he whispered. "I think you know me, even if you don't want to admit it."

The bay snuffled the nut, lipped at it, and then took it. His teeth grazed Yar's palm, but didn't actually bite. That was progress, wasn't it? Yar smiled at him.

"There you are. Shall I take that halter off? You're a proud fellow, aren't you? You don't like the halter, I can see that. It's rubbing your ears, isn't it?" While he murmured to the horse, Yar worked his fingers up around the stallion's ears and loosened the halter, then slipped it off the horse's head.

"What are you doing, idiot boy?" the swordswoman called. Yar ignored her. He put his hand through the halter and pushed it up on his shoulder.

The stallion pressed its head against Yar's chest as he stroked carefully around its ears. The right one was raw. "Do you mind if I ride you?" Yar whispered. "Just a couple of times around the ring?"

The stallion didn't answer. He didn't really expect him to. Horses couldn't talk or anything, could they? Then again, just because the horses he'd known in the past didn't talk, that didn't mean none of them ever could. This horse seemed very intelligent. And after all, Yar had Voices in his head. Maybe horses could talk, and just chose not to most of the time.

Yar couldn't mount this horse like he had the dun. He coaxed the bay over to the fence, where he was able to clamber up and get a leg over. The bay snorted, his head coming up. His legs locked in place, his muscles rigid. One ear swiveled around towards Yar, who crooned nonsense sounds at him.

Yar wasn't sure how long he sang-talked to the bay, but he felt him gradually relaxing the longer he did. Yar wasn't really a patient man, but he'd lived his life without any sense of time passing. What was an hour if you lost it to listening to the Voices, after all? So what was an hour spent singing to a horse? Still, he relaxed himself when he felt the stallion's legs unlock.

"Come on," Yar murmured. "Just twice around the pen?" He tightened his legs and the stallion moved forward instantly, too fast. Yar rocked backwards, but kept his seat. He let the stallion do it his way, though. They went around the pen at a fast trot, every step jouncing Yar's backside. When the stallion was resigned to the fact Yar wasn't going to fall off, he slowed to a more comfortable, rambly trot. Two more circles later, he was walking. Yar guided him with leg nudges and shifting weight, and when they came to a stop in front of the horse trader and the swordswoman, both of them were watching, mouths hanging open.

The woman whistled. "I'd never have thought you could get him to go without reins or even a halter."

Yar shrugged and slid down, his boots raising puffs of dust when he landed. The stallion whuffled and rested its nose against his hair. Yar suspected he would find horse slobbers there later, but he did his best to ignore it for the moment.

"You're bossy," he told the woman. "What's your name?"

She propped her hands on her hips again. She dressed like a boy, in wide, unbleached linen trousers tucked into her boots and a silk blouse under a brown vest. "Aevver," she said. "What's yours?"

He swallowed. He didn't want the trader to know, but he wasn't going to lie to the swordswoman from his vision. "I'm Yar," he said. "And this is Firefoot. He's my horse now." He gave the trader a hard look. The trader shut his mouth with an audible click. Firefoot—where had that come from? But it felt right.

Aevver smiled. "Well met, Yar. Narda, I think you've got a bargain to seal."

***

Azmei watched from the paddock as Yarro Perslyn and

Narda dickered over the price of the bay hellion. She wouldn't have thought the boy could ride anything as strong and spirited as the bay, but then she had based her impression of Yarro mostly on what Orya had said of him. There was probably a lesson in that—perhaps it was a bad idea to believe anything you were told by a woman who was trying to kill you.

She glanced back at the horses milling about in the paddock. She had liked Firefoot herself, when she first spotted him. Then she'd seen him flatten his ears at another horse that was a little too close for his liking. And then she'd tried to reach for his halter, with Narda smiling and urging her on. The bay had bared his teeth, and if Azmei hadn't been quicker than the horse, she might be an eight-fingered ex-princess right now.

Narda had been all apologies and oozed compliments about how he'd thought she would like his spirit and he'd been just sure she could handle him, but Azmei had given him a few sharp words about warning a person next time they got within ten paces of that horse, and he'd subsided.

But Yarro had done something that got the horse's attention, and even when the boy had been trying out the dun gelding, that bay horse had watched him like a hen with its first chick. Magic, Azmei would have said if she were more superstitious. Whatever it was, Yarro had set his heart on that bay horse, and the bay horse had, apparently, set his horse on the tall, skinny boy.

"Firefoot," she muttered, and shook her head. She had once been as fanciful as this boy. Not so long ago, some might say, but to Azmei it felt like a lifetime. When was the last time she'd had time to read an adventure story? Then again, she'd lived an adventure herself, and found it a bit less to her liking than she'd always expected.

She wondered if she could ever live up to the Amethirian name she'd chosen for herself when she left her life as Princess Azmei Corrone behind. Aevver had been one of the Four Daughters of the Storm, she and her sisters among the most famous and powerful women in all of Amethir's history. The stories Azmei had read about Aevver while studying her be-trothed's culture had been moving and exhilarating. The sto-ries she read after her life was turned upside down in Ranarr had been equally moving, but somehow less exhilarating.

It was hard to be thrilled about a powerful woman de-feating and humiliating her enemies when you were having a difficult time doing that same thing yourself.

Behind her, hooves thumped gently against the packed dirt of the corral. Azmei turned and watched the dun gelding approach. When he got close enough, he dipped his head for a scratch, which Azmei obligingly provided. "We've both been forgotten, I think," she told him, rubbing the soft edges of his ears and pressing the palm of her hand against his huge, flat cheek. The gelding shoved his nose against her chest and Azmei laughed and looked back at the horsetrader's shelter.

Yarro was handing over some coin, though from this dis-tance Azmei couldn't see how much. They'd agreed on a price, and after that he might have no business left in Meekin. Would he leave right away or wait until morning? The sun was low in the western sky. The Dry Gate would still be open, but would Yarro want to travel in the dark? Azmei wouldn't, in this unfamiliar territory. Yarro, though, probably had little or no experience with traveling. He could hardly help but make a few stupid mistakes while he was running away from home.

Did he know his grandfather was dead? But then, how could he? There might be turmoil inside the Perslyn house, but none of it was yet showing from the outside. He would probably wish to get as far from Meekin as quickly as he could, fearing the Patriarch would be after him. Or did he think the Patriarch wouldn't miss him? But if Azmei could find him, Kesh could find him.

Azmei ran a frustrated hand through her chin-length hair. There were just too many unknowns! Where was Yarro running to? Why had he chosen to run now? Would he leave town immediately? What sort of supplies had he put in that pack of his?

And, she wondered, how long would he be coherent?

"Still here? I hope you aren't angry about my selling the bay to the lad. He was so keen on him, and you didn't seem to be interested." Narda's voice turned self-deprecating at that last.

Azmei laughed against her will. He was a merchant first and foremost, no arguing that, but he had a sense of humor that invited others to laugh with him, and that made her like him despite his motivation to earn coin. "He hurt my pride by scorning my suggestion," she said, "and I think he hurt the dun's feelings as well. I'd like to give this fellow a try myself."

The dun gelding really was a beauty. He followed her knee signals and picked up on her slightest cues. She liked his coloring for traveling unnoticed, and he was big enough to earn her some respect without being too large for her to ride comfortably. She was not a tall woman. Her instinct as a child had been to gravitate immediately to the tallest horse in sight, but she had learned how much better it was to have a comfortable one.

She tried a brown mare and another gelding, but she quickly settled on the dun. He was the best behaved, and after all, her pride *was* hurt. She'd picked him for the boy and he'd scorned her choice. Now she had to prove to herself that the dun was a good horse.

"Will you take him with you tonight?" Narda asked after they had settled on a price that was lower than he'd wished and higher than she had wished.

"It's late in the day for that. Are there inns that might take him? I know the inn I've been staying at by the university isn't equipped for horses."

Narda laughed. "Good luck even getting him there. Horses don't like the walkways much."

"I had noticed you don't see many of them deeper in the city."

"We're happiest out here where the air is a bit better and the hills a bit closer," Narda said. "And where there are inns with stables." He smiled at her. "I just sent your new friend down towards the street with his best chance of finding one.

You might follow him there."

Azmei made a show of considering it, then shrugged and shook her head. "Perhaps you would keep the dun one night for me? I'd consider it a concession to the fact that you grossly overcharged me." Her grumbling was just for show, but it seemed to please Narda.

"I'll be happy to keep him one more night. You'll be back first thing in the morning? I'd hate to get confused and sell him to someone else." He winked.

"Ah, but then you'd have to replace him with another of your stock," she pointed out, "and I might choose that big black next time." She pointed at a horse that was clearly too big for her, and clearly of better stock than her pleasant but undistinguished new horse.

Narda laughed and waved her out of his stall. Azmei went on her way pleased with the day's work. She had found Yarro and purchased a horse, and she now knew he would be one more day in the city, since he'd asked Narda about an inn. She was reasonably confident that Yarro wasn't sophisticated enough at subterfuge to realize he should only ask about an inn if he didn't mean to stay there.

She would come back early tomorrow and keep an eye on the gate. For tonight, she had a job to finish.

CHAPTER THIRTEEN

The first two inns Yar tried had no stables for horses. Finally he found the One-Eyed Pony. The inn was on a side street almost to the gate. From the side street an alley ran east, dead-ending against the city wall. Yar wasn't sure about it; there were weeds growing up between the paving stones of the alley, and one of the shutters on the inn hung cockeyed. But there was a stable, and two noses stuck out of the horse pen.

He led Firefoot to the flagged stable yard and paused. He looked around, shifting his weight from one foot to the other. He didn't have to wait long, though. At the first sight of Firefoot, one of the inn's ponies whinnied a greeting. A skinny child about ten years old came out of the inn. She took one look at Yar and Firefoot and darted back inside, yelling for her Ma.

The woman who came out wore a patch on one eye. She dusted flour from her hands.

"A real horse, indeed. Effa's not big enough to groom that brute."

"He doesn't need it. We'll only be here one night." Yar tried on a smile, though it pulled his lips too tight.

"Well, you can stable 'im yourself, once you've paid for yer room. I'm the landlady, Sertis. We've black soup for supper and bread and dark ale. Laundry's extra. We send it out."

"No laundry," he said. "I'll eat in my rooms."

Her eyebrows flew upwards. "Only if you pay for an unshared room. They're three sovs."

"That's a lot of silver for one night."

She shrugged. "You don't have to stay here. There's the Dancing Rat close, if you'd rather, and they're a sight cheaper, but you don't get hot supper."

"I didn't mean that," Yar protested. "I have the coin. I just expected it to be more—affordable." He glanced at the cockeyed shutter.

"My hired man's gone to be with his wife and their new baby." Sertis crossed her arms. "Will you stay or will you go?"

The sun would set soon, and Yar didn't relish the thought of wandering the alleys of Meekin after dark. He had always been safe when he was with Orya, but he knew there was a harder side to the city. He might as well spend the money. He had no idea how far he would have to travel to find the Voices, but he would just have to trust that they would guide him there, money or no money.

Yar fished through his coin purse until he had the exact coins. As he handed them over, her good eye narrowed. He wondered if he'd made a mistake. Had she seen how much money he had? Maybe he should have paid in copper instead of silver.

"Effa will show you around the stable." Sertis turned and went inside, while the little girl danced in front of him.

"This way," she said. "The ponies will like the company."

Yar followed her into the stable. Effa carried buckets of water and a scoop of feed while Yar unsaddled Firefoot and brushed him. He frowned down at his pack, wondering if he should take it into the inn with him. A private room should be secure, and after all, he wasn't planning on leaving it. Then again, if Firefoot had been as difficult as Azmei and the horse trader had said, he wouldn't let anyone into his stall except Yar. The pack and saddle could stay out here, bundled into the corner furthest from the door. The coin purse would stay on Yar's belt.

When he went into the common room of the inn, Yar had to pause. The gloomy interior made it difficult to see where he might find an open table. Once his eyes adjusted, he realized he didn't have to worry. Most of the tables were empty. Two men played cards in the corner, and a group of men and women sat laughing around a large table in front of the fireplace. Aside from that, the room held only Sertis. She nodded to him and gathered a tray of food.

Yar followed her as she carried the tray upstairs and showed him his room. "There's no lock on the door, but you can bar it from the inside. Privy's down the end of the alley. No chamber pots." She set the tray on the tiny table in his room and tramped off. Yar listened to the wooden stairs thump under her feet.

He sighed and slumped onto the bed. "What am I doing?" he muttered. How could he have thought it a good idea to leave home? At least there he had good food to eat regularly, and nice clothes. His grandfather had threatened to put him in assassin training, but he'd never actually gone through with it. Why couldn't he accept that Orya was gone?

But then there were the Voices. They would never leave him alone if he didn't come to find them as bidden. They might not leave him alone if he did obey, but at least he would know. Orya wasn't coming back for him. He would accept that, and he would go forward with his own life. Whatever it became.

He ate quickly, sopping up the black bean soup with his bread and washing it all down with the ale. Stronger than any he'd had before, the ale made his eyes water. It was good, though, and soon his tray was empty.

He was tired, but he needed the privy before he tried to sleep. He wish he'd known there were no chamber pots. He would have gone before coming up to his room. With a sigh, he picked up the tray and carried it back downstairs with him. Sertis raised an eyebrow when she saw him, but he set the tray on the nearest table and ignored her. He just wanted to have a piss and go to sleep. He was exhausted. He'd spent too much time talking to people all day. He needed a few hours of oblivion.

The alley was dark. The sun had set while he was inside. A single lamp burned on a free-standing post near the stable entrance. That would have to do. He headed for the privy.

After he'd finished his business, he started for the inn. A whinny from the stable caught his attention, though. Was that shrill scream Firefoot? Why would he be upset? Yar ran to the stable door and peered in. Two men were at Firefoot's stall, one of them nursing a hand.

"Demon beast bit me!" he snarled. "Kill it so we can get the pack."

Yar's eyes widened as the second man unsheathed a short sword. They would actually kill his horse just to steal from him? "No!" he shouted, before he'd thought it through. As both men turned to face him, he realized he had no weapon. Maybe someone would come from the inn if he shouted for help. He reached out and grabbed a hay fork just in case.

"You going to stop us, boy?" said the man with the injured hand. "Your demon beast ought to be put down. Safer that way, like." His companion walked towards Yar. Yar lifted the hay fork.

"Leave him alone. He's done nothing you didn't ask for." Yar's voice was shaking. What did he think he could do to stop them?

"And you'll get nothing you didn't ask for, either."

YOU COULD ASK US FOR HELP, whispered a Voice in his mind. Yar shuddered.

"That's right, boy, you should be scared," said the first man, misunderstanding. "Puit here has the thief mark, and I've killed men for looking at me crossways. But if you give us your gold, we won't kill you."

"You won't kill me anyway," Yar said. He wished he sounded brave, but to his own ears, it sounded more pleading than anything. "Firefoot won't let you."

"Ooh, Firefoot is it? A dead horse is no protection, fire or no," Puit turned towards the horse, but Firefoot knew a threat when he saw it. He reared, hooves flashing as they drove through the air. Cursing, Puit ducked, and then Yar had to quit watching because the man with the injured hand was swinging a club at him.

Yar ducked, lifting the hay fork to block the man's swing. Wood crashed together, jolting his arm to the shoulder and stinging his palm. He cried out, but swallowed it and poked at the man with the tines. Sneering, the man dodged and swung at him again.

"Little fool! I'll cut you into ribbons for a girl to braid!"

CALL ON US, growled a Voice. WE WILL HELP.

"No!" Yar hissed.

The man thought Yar was talking to him. He laughed and swung his club, striking Yar's shoulder. Yar's arm went numb. "You must have piles of gold to fight this hard for it," he said, and swung the club overhand at Yar's head.

ACCEPT OUR AID! thundered a Voice in Yar's head, and his vision grayed out. Panicked at his sudden blindness, Yar tightened his grip on the hay fork. He felt something jolt against his hands. The man shouted and wood smashed against Yar's knuckles. He tried to let go of the fork handle as pain exploded in his hands. Instead his fingers tightened around it and he jerked his arms back. The man screamed.

He was the dove, stabbing his beak at the eyes of the serpent. He stabbed and stabbed, trying to put the serpent's eyes out and protect his nest. His wings flapped and thrashed. His vision went red and then black again.

Yar's ears were filled with growling and the rumble of thunder, almost so loud it drowned out everything else around him. But he heard Firefoot's angry neigh and the horrible wet thud of hooves against flesh. Then wood squealed as the horse threw himself against it.

Yar's arms jerked back and thrust. The man in front of him grunted. Something wet spilled across Yar's hands. He tried to let go of the hay fork, but his fingers were locked around the wooden handle. The man was coughing, so close Yar felt the breath hit his face.

Through the grayness, black smoke roiled up, flooding his vision. Then slowly, piercing the darkness, two burning golden eyes, each of them bigger than Yar was tall, stared through the smoke at him. He could see nothing but those eyes, feel nothing but the heat of their gaze. His skin felt like it would crack and peel off his face. His arms were moving again. He stepped forward again and again. The fork swung in his grasp. Yar stumbled over something and went sprawling headlong onto his stomach.

His breath whooshed out of him at the impact. His hands flew open and he heard the hay fork skitter away from him across the dirt floor of the stable. Yar sucked in a breath and sucked in dust and hay and horse muck with it. He choked, coughing into the dirt until he could get his hands and knees under him and shove himself up. When he did, he felt himself tipping, reeling, and then his vision cleared and he realized it had been his interior world, not the actual one, that tipped around him.

Then he realized what he was staring at, and he screamed.

***

Azmei didn't waste any time when she got back to Perslyn House from the horse market. She slipped past half a dozen guards with little effort. Inside the house she knocked out a guard who was *almost* as short as she was. Wrapped in the guard's cloak, she walked confidently through the halls.

She found Rith in his room. He was passed out in a chair, the floor around him littered with empty wine bottles. The bed was unmade, one of the blankets trailing down to the floor. There was blood on the sheets—not much, but enough that Azmei could tell Rith had been celebrating his ascent to power in more ways than one.

She stepped past the bed, lip curling in disgust. He was a boor, and worse, he was cruel. There would be no negotiating with Rith. He didn't stir as she catfooted to stand in front of him. She watched him sleep for several heartbeats, one hand on her hip and the other on her dagger. Then she shook her head, let out a regretful breath, and slit his throat.

She wiped her dagger on the sheets. No sense in creating

more work for the servants than necessary.

From Rith's room, she made her way back outside, but she wasn't finished with Perslyn House. She climbed back to the roof, and when she reached Kesh's rooms, she let herself in a window in the darkest corner of the antechamber.

She wasn't surprised that Kesh had company—she had wondered if Kesh would be upset about the missing Yarro, and Kesh seemed the sort to comfort himself with physical intimacy. But it very quickly became clear there was nothing like that between Kesh and his companion. At least not tonight.

He was sitting on a low couch, facing the window where Azmei had come in. If she hadn't discarded the guard's cloak, he probably would have seen her, but her dark clothes and hood hid her well.

"I'm not sure why I'm sorry," Kesh was saying. His voice had the softening around the edges that told Azmei he'd had something to drink, but was still coherent—possibly more coherent than he would like to be. "He was a cruel, manipulative jackal."

Tish was sitting next to him. She watched him with compassion in her eyes, but she sat straight, without touching him. "He was still your grandfather."

"For whatever that's worth," Kesh said. He slumped forward, resting his face in his hands.

"Orya would have grieved, I think." Tish's voice was soft and sober. "She tried to please him, to earn his approval, even though she feared him."

Kesh snorted. "Orya wasn't afraid of anyone."

"Not for herself. But he threatened Yarro."

Kesh hunched his shoulders. "See? A jackal. I ought to hate him." He rubbed his hands over his face a few times and sat up. "Father was nothing like him."

Tish put her hand on his shoulder, but she still held herself apart. Azmei didn't think there was anything between them besides the affection a sister might have for a brother. Which might be for the best, considering what she suspected of Rith. At least he wouldn't be a problem for Tish any longer.

Kesh sighed. "Maybe that's why Father never came back."

Azmei reached behind her and pushed the window open again, letting a draft in. Then she took a single, deliberate step forward into the light. Tish saw her first and cried out, her voice choking on the cry. Kesh leapt to his feet at the sound, his gaze finding Azmei instantly. He jumped between Azmei and Tish, drawing his dagger smoothly.

"Who are you?" he demanded.

Azmei smiled behind her veil. "Not Orya."

Kesh narrowed his eyes. "That much is obvious. She was taller."

Azmei chuckled.

"Are you here to kill me?"

Tish gave a little gasp at Kesh's question. Azmei ignored her. "Not unless I have to. I have hope that the new Patriarch will be more inclined to...negotiation."

Tish said, bitterly, "Not likely."

Azmei didn't look at her. She was holding Kesh's gaze, and she saw the moment he understood what had happened. He looked steadily at Azmei as he said, "You killed Rith."

Azmei inclined her head slowly. "Congratulations, Patriarch."

Tish shifted to the front of her seat. "You...killed Rith too?"

Azmei could see the woman's hope in the way her hands clasped each other, wrists turned up. It was almost a plea. How horrible had it been for Tish, living in this house with Rith? He couldn't have been kind to her. Why had she stayed? Was it only for Yarro?

"Did you take Yarro?" Kesh demanded.

Azmei flicked a glance at him. "I did not."

"Did you *hurt* him?" His knuckles whitened on the hilt of his dagger.

Azmei held out an empty hand. "Peace, Patriarch. Your little brother is safe."

"He...he could come back," Tish said. Her voice was thick, as if with unshed tears. "I swear he's no trouble, not really." She gulped. "He's sweet."

Azmei lifted one shoulder in a shrug. "I think Yarro can make that choice himself."

"Why do you care?" Kesh asked. The question was genuinely curious rather than belligerent.

Azmei considered this. Why *did* she care? She had been curious about the boy who could inspire so much love and loyalty from Orya. She felt bad for him after seeing the way he lived. She admired the way he had struck out on his own despite his obvious handicaps.

"I'm not Orya, but I did know her," Azmei said at last. Tish cried out, but Azmei didn't stop. "I knew how she loved Yarro."

"Who are you?" Kesh asked again.

Azmei smiled. "You know I can't tell you that, Kesh."

There was a brief silence. The breeze from the window ruffled Tish's long hair. Kesh sheathed his dagger.

"What now?"

"That remains to be seen," Azmei said. "I did not kill the old Patriarch to put you in power. I came to mete out justice, for his part in Princess Azmei's assassination. No," she said as she saw Tish begin to rise. "I did not kill Orya. Wenda killed Orya. But the royal family must have justice from the Patriarch as well as his assassin."

Kesh's voice was quiet. "Rith wasn't involved in that."

Azmei arched an eyebrow at him. "I didn't kill Karsch to put you in power. I *did* kill Rith for that reason."

She saw Kesh's throat bob as he swallowed. "What do you want from me?"

Azmei relaxed the tiniest bit. She had hoped he would be reasonable. "Who wanted the Princess dead?"

"One of the Nine," Kesh said, shaking his head. "That's all I know. A man, but that doesn't rule out many."

Azmei nodded slowly. One of the Nine. Six of them had been men, three years ago. It didn't rule out many, but at least she knew it hadn't been Ladies Tel or Talt. She had already known it couldn't be Ilzi. Six families. Surely it hadn't been Arisanat, she thought. So that left five. It was more than she had known yesterday.

"It is possible you will yet make a good Patriarch," she told Kesh. "You will have to be shrewder than you have been, but make sure you remember how to be kind."

Tish sank back into her seat. "You won't kill us?"

Azmei tilted her head. "What will you do if Yarro doesn't come back?" she asked curiously.

Tish opened her mouth, but didn't appear to have an answer. Kesh said, quickly, "She'll always have a home here. For Orya's sake as much as Yarro's."

"I won't kill you, Tish," Azmei said. "Or you, Kesh, as long as you are careful to never again accept a contract on a Corrone."

"There's one out now on King Marsede," Kesh said. He flushed. "We didn't get it. But since you're so interested...someone called the Problem Solver took it. He's a Long Coaster, I think. I don't know any more than that. He never operated in Tamnen until last year." He lifted his chin. "When you declared war on us and eliminated so many of our operatives."

Azmei inclined her head, both in thanks and in acknowledgement of his last statement. She half turned, preparing to leave the room the way she had come.

"Justice, wait," Kesh blurted.

Justice? Azmei's eyebrows were raised as she turned back.

"Take good care of my little brother. In another family, he would have been treated better. Taken to the priests, maybe, or seen a healer. We didn't do well by him, but...tell him I love him."

Azmei didn't have a response to that. She left the house without looking back.

CHAPTER FOURTEEN

Never in Yarro's life would he remember how he managed to get out of the stable of the One-Eyed Pony. Perhaps the Voices took over him again. Perhaps Firefoot managed to splinter the stall enough to get to him. Perhaps his body simply knew what he had to do.

However he managed it, at some point Yarro became aware that he was crouched at the edge of a canal backwater, puking into the water. His throat was raw. He must have vomited several times already. The taste of bile was acrid in his throat, but overpowering even that was a bitter, metallic tang. He'd been hit enough times by Rith to recognize the taste of blood.

A hulking shadow loomed over him. Yar yelped and overbalanced. He fell into the water he had just fouled and came up sputtering. The water was cold and slimy, but at least it brought him to full alertness. Blinking water out of his eyes, he peered up at the shadow until it grew clearer and he could discern the shape of Firefoot.

The horse was studying him as if uncertain whether he was a foal in need of nursing or a snake that deserved trampling. Yarro hunched his shoulders and did his best to look unthreatening. He splayed his hands in front of his face and peered at them. They were crusted with blood. So, he saw, were his clothes, where they weren't smeared with mud or horse muck. Yar grimaced and wiped his hands down his front.

Then he looked at the canal water. The canals were clean, for the most part, though this was the tail-end of one of them.

He had no idea where he was in the larger city, but just here was a pitted stone wall with a grate, through which trickled water out of the city. The bile and blood Yar had vomited was already shifting that way on a nearly imperceptible current. Well enough; he was already soaked, so he might as well wash.

He preferred his baths to be hot water in a steamy room with thick towels waiting for him, but this would have to do. He ducked under the water and scrubbed his hands through his hair. When he came up, spluttering, for air, Firefoot snorted and danced a few steps back from the canal edge. But he lowered his head to snort at Yarro, so perhaps the horse thought his smell improved. Yar certainly did. He hated the smell of blood.

His mind shivered, his control fracturing.

Yar carefully steered his thoughts away from the smell of blood. Cherry blossoms, he told himself, thinking of the very best scent he could imagine. Honeysuckle. Chocolate.

He crouched in the water until he was shoulder deep. Then he scraped his fingernails over his tunic. He would have to wash them more carefully once he was out of the city, but in the meantime he could try to make himself as presentable as possible.

"You're soaked to the skin and probably bloody as well as dirty, idiot," he muttered aloud. Then he looked up at Firefoot. "Did anyone see me?"

The horse just watched him. Yar climbed out of the water to stand, shivering, next to the horse. The night air was cool. Yar peered up at the sky. It must be very late. How many hours had he lost to the—the—

CALL IT A VISION.

All right then, how many hours had he lost to the vision? He had been out of control and unaware of his surroundings. But Firefoot had come with him. And the pack was tied to the saddle. That was good, since Yar'd apparently slaughtered two grown men to keep them from stealing it from him.

His mind quivered and he shoved the thought away.

BE STILL, LITTLE MOUSE, slithered a Voice into his

thoughts. YOU COULD LET ME GUIDE YOU AS I HAVE BEEN.

"No!" Yar exclaimed, horrified.

THEN BE STILL. YOU PROMISED TO FIND US. WE WILL ALLOW NOTHING TO HINDER THAT. WE WILL ALLOW NOTHING TO HARM YOU. COME TO US.

Yar swallowed. "I'm a monster," he whispered. Firefoot nickered and Yar reached up automatically to rub his velvety nose. "A monster."

But whether or not the horse agreed, he allowed Yar to lean against his flank, drawing comforting heat from his skin. Yar let himself sob into the horse's mane for a few minutes, but when he choked on the snot and began gagging, he told himself he had to regain control.

"Me, not the Voices," he rasped. "Me."

He put his pack on, shuddering at the way it pressed his clammy clothes against his back. Then he grabbed at Firefoot's mane and swung up onto the horse's back. He might as well ride; if no one had noticed him wandering around bloody and dazed, surely they would overlook him riding.

Not knowing where he was, he allowed Firefoot to have his head. The horse wouldn't go back to the One-Eyed Pony, he thought, since it had been such a frightening place for them both. It might take him back to Narda's corral at the horse market, since it had spent so many days there. That would be fine. Yar could find his way to the Dry Gate from the market.

And eventually that was where they ended up. Twice Yar nudged Firefoot into the shadows to avoid being seen by a guard, but soon enough he recognized that the horse was taking him to the horse market. He got his bearings then and redirected Firefoot to take a more direct route to the Dry Gate. It would probably be closed, this late, but they could hide in the shadows nearby and slip out at first light.

Yar wanted nothing more than to be away from Meekin, away from this city where he had spent his life in a dream world, where he had murdered people to obey the commands of the mysterious Voices that ruled him.

He found a place that was sheltered. Then he stripped off his outer clothes and hunched against Firefoot's body, shivering for a long time. When he was warm enough to lie down, he dropped into an uneasy doze.

The Voices woke him. He jerked upright and awake in the same instant, staring around him. His heart was pounding, but he saw nothing except a few shadows moving through the dim predawn light. The traders were beginning to trickle towards the market, and travelers were drifting towards the gate, where the guards were preparing to change shifts.

Yarro watched as the new roster reported for duty and the old rotated out. Words were exchanged, news and gossip shared, and the night shift wandered home, yawning and rubbing sore limbs. "Wake up," Yarro whispered to Firefoot, who was already awake. Yar stood and stepped back to give Firefoot room to get himself up. The horse rose with a lurch. He whuffled at Yarro's hair and shook himself all over. Yar wondered if Firefoot's stomach was rumbling the way Yar's was.

With a clank and a groan, the Dry Gate heaved open. Guards took up their positions on either side of it. Yar could see the shanties outside the walls. Smoke drifted in through the open gates, and the smell of frying bread and fish wafted to his nose. He pushed a fist against his stomach, hoping he hadn't lost his coins. No, there was the purse, shoved down inside his breeches.

The first of those leaving the city had come to the gates now. Yar swung up onto Firefoot's back and nudged the horse in that direction. A few people looked at him, but they turned their attention away again, so he supposed he either looked normal enough that they weren't curious, or he looked dangerous enough they didn't want to ask. He hoped it was normal. He didn't think the guards would let a dangerous-looking person pass through.

"Fall off your horse?" one of the guards greeted him, laughing, as he reached them.

Yarro gave what he hoped was a rueful smile. "He's mean

as a scorpion. But my uncle says we deserve one another." He had no idea where the lie had come from, but it fell naturally off his lips.

The two guards hooted with laughter. "I'd say you need either a new horse or a new uncle, boy," said the woman on the left.

"Or both," said the dark-haired man on the right. "Be careful out there, lad. Joking aside, if you can't handle the horse—"

"I can, honestly," Yar interrupted. He wondered at himself. He would never have dared interrupt at his grandfather's house. "I was sleepy and Firefoot knew it. I got what I deserved."

The woman grinned at him. "At least you learn from your mistakes. All right, then. There's been reports of bandits to the south of the pass road. If you're heading that way, find some others to travel with."

"Thank you," Yarro said. "Give you good day."

"And you, young sir," said the man with a bow that looked teasing. Yarro wasn't sure what to make of it, but he closed his legs around Firefoot's flanks and let the horse carry him out of the city.

He didn't look back.

***

The morning after she met Yarro, Azmei rose early. She watched the Dry Gate until she saw Yarro join the line of people waiting to get out of the city. She quickly settled her bill with Narda, swung into the saddle, and joined the line some distance behind Yarro.

The road outside the gate took her between shanties and a few market stalls whose owners didn't want to pay the city's trading fees. She paused once to buy fry bread and honey, which she licked from her fingertips as she rode. When she judged she had gone far enough that the guard had forgotten her entirely, she guided the dun off the road and looked around.

It wasn't difficult to find a hiding place from which she could watch Yarro choose his direction away from the city. Avoiding notice wasn't much trouble either. People who lived in the shanty towns outside the walls might look out for each other, but they also didn't seem to care about minding other people's business, so long as it didn't mean trouble. Azmei didn't make eye contact with anyone and carefully ignored everything about her surroundings except the boy on the bright bay stallion.

As soon as Yarro had vanished from sight, Azmei guided her dun after him. She waited until some of the traffic had dropped away, turning towards the mountain trade route. Then she stopped to eat lunch and let Yarro get ahead of her. She would wait until this evening to catch up with him. Hopefully it wouldn't look as suspicious if a fellow traveler asked to share a fire. She spent the rest of the day traveling at a leisurely pace, stopping to look at a flower if it caught her attention, or watching the little stripey brown birds flitting in the bushes along the track.

What had made Yarro choose this trail? It was barely more than a single horse wide, threading its way southward through the low bushes and trees that dotted the dry landscape. But where did it lead? She had purchased a good map of the region during her stay in Meekin, and she was certain there was nothing of note between here and Rivarden, down in the desert. Could Yarro be heading there? But why? Did he know someone there? Was he just trying to run away to a place where no one would look for him? Azmei sighed and looked around her.

It was pretty country, if a bit desolate. The rolling terrain meant the walls of Meekin were soon out of sight behind her. To her left the Scarim Mountains loomed, seeming close enough to touch, though she was certain she had read it was several days' ride to reach the pass that led through the mountains east of Meekin to the Long Coast on the other side. With spring stretching out ahead of her, the day was pleasant and sunny, though she suspected the night would be cold out here away from city walls.

Midway through the afternoon, Azmei stopped to give the dun a rest and practice her sword forms. She didn't want to alarm Yarro by practicing in front of him, but she couldn't let her skills drop by not practicing at all. If she got in some practice now, she could skip tomorrow in the interest of building rapport with him. Then the day after she would be able to practice without scaring him. Hopefully.

Provided he agreed they could travel together for a while. She hoped he would tell her where he was going so she could tailor her own destination to his. It would be inconvenient to follow him without his permission when she could be traveling alongside him and getting to know him better. She was a better judge of character now than she had been when she met Orya, or at least she hoped so.

As she ran through the various swings, thrusts, parries, and blocks that formed the basis of all her other sword work, Azmei wondered if she should tell him who she was, or at least that she and Orya had once been friends. Her instinct was to keep that a secret until it was most advantageous to reveal it. But she also sensed that everyone around Yarro had probably operated with that same philosophy. Perhaps it would be better to be open with him. Then again, perhaps it was better to go with what he was used to. Then again, he was running away from what he was used to, so perhaps it would be best to...

She abandoned the circular thought process and focused on her form. She had more room here in the wilderness than she had had in her room at the inn in Meekin. She threw in a few leaps and tumbles, envisioning what her imaginary opponent might be doing to provoke such moves. If he thrust low, she could block it and sweep his sword down as she leapt closer to him. If he swung wide, she could duck under it and roll closer, coming up inside his reach and stabbing just so.

When she was breathless and felt her heart racing in her chest, she slowed her movements until she was moving fluidly through each stance in turn. It was a slow form of the moves she had been doing, but Master Tanvel had taught her using these forms, making her master the form before showing her how each stance could be used against an opponent. He had ignored the skills she already had with sword and dagger until she had mastered what he taught her. Then, in a lesson that had shattered her preconceived notions, he had shown her how to tie all of her skills together to become a whirlwind of death and defense.

At last her heart and breathing slowed to their normal rhythm. Azmei bowed in respect to her imaginary opponent and sheathed her blades. She was not good at communing with the god of peace, but she had learned to channel all of herself into the sword forms. She could take any emotion, any confusion, any doubt, and give it all to the form dance. When she finished, she might not have an answer to the question that was plaguing her, but she inevitably felt better for it. It was, in her opinion, better than prayer.

I am a horrible Aspirant, she thought, going to tighten the dun's girth. *Perhaps Tanvel was right to suggest I marry Vistaren after all. It can't have escaped his notice that I've never communed properly with the god.*

She vaulted into the saddle and guided the dun back to Yarro's trail. "I ought to give you a name," she told him. "What suits you? Sand? We're surrounded by enough of it, for certain. Sandy, maybe. What about that?" The horse made no response, but she decided it was a good name for him. It wasn't fancy like Firefoot, but it was a solid, dependable name for a horse that was shaping up to be a solid, dependable mount.

Master Tanvel had told her about the desert, but of course neither of them had known she would actually be traveling through it and into the foothills. She hadn't realized how very bleak and beautiful it would be. Harsh, she had expected; Tanvel had called the desert unforgiving. Azmei had known there was little water in the desert, but this utter lack of moisture, where even the plant life was tough and sharp-edged, was hard on the body.

They rode for perhaps another hour at a comfortable

walk, Sandy picking his footing through the scrub and Azmei content to let him. Yarro's tracks were plain ahead of them, and she didn't think the boy would stop until it was dark. Tanvel had taught her about traveling in the wilderness, but the first time they had done so, he had allowed her to make the decisions. That first night, still a princess used to having a handful of servants always within call, she had traveled until it was too dark to see the road clearly. She had ended up setting up camp single-handedly in the dark, while Tanvel sat by the fire and waited for her to finish. She had learned then to stop while there was still light to set up camp, but she didn't expect Yarro to know enough to do that. Soon enough, she would catch up with him.

***

Yarro let Firefoot pick their pace once they were out of Meekin. The Voices whispered in the back of his head, urging him on, but he wasn't inclined to listen closely to them after what they'd made him do in the stable of the One-Eyed Pony. Besides, he knew enough to realize he would have a sore butt at the end of today's ride. He didn't think there was any reason to make it worse by trying to trot or even canter on their first day. There were a lot of things he didn't know, but he wasn't stupid.

ARE YOU SURE? asked the hissy, sibilant Voice he liked least. PERHAPS YOU ARE JUST STUPID ENOUGH TO NOT KNOW HOW STUPID YOU REALLY ARE.

"Maybe so," Yar said aloud. "I'm stupid enough to listen to you lot."

UNGRATEFUL BOY. WE SAVED YOUR LIFE.

"Maybe. But maybe you just like killing. I could have run away." But Yar knew that was oversimplifying things. He couldn't have run away without letting Firefoot be killed by those thieves. He had fought to save his horse as much as to save his possessions or his own life. He had bought Firefoot, but he was under no illusions that he owned the horse. This was not a creature to be possessed. He was a companion who allowed Yarro to ride along with him, nothing less.

They traveled at a slow pace, the Voices working harder and harder to get his attention. Yarro stubbornly pushed them away, focusing on Firefoot's ears, his mane, the gentle sway of his walking gait. He tried to enjoy the warmth of the sun on his right side, the light breeze that ruffled his hair. But eventually it became too insistent to ignore. Yar drew Firefoot to a halt, but before he could dismount, the vision was on him.

The woman from yesterday, with her golden eyes and daggers and wry grin, was staring at him. She had her hands on her hips and a look on her face that he couldn't read. She turned and shouted at Firefoot, who turned and ran away. When Yarro tried to intervene, the woman drew her dagger and her sword and shouted at him, too. Yarro tried to get away, but he tripped over his own feet and fell. She came towards him, her sword lifted above her head. She was going to kill him!

But she darted past him, her blades raised against some threat he couldn't see. Was she defending him? Or had she invited the attack? Yar craned around, trying to see what she was fighting.

Yarro's body outside the vision lost its balance and fell off the horse. He didn't come back to himself until the ground jolted him back. He lay staring up at Firefoot's belly and the darkening sky beyond, unable to breathe in or out, his eyes wide as he struggled for air that wasn't there. Finally he managed to suck in a short breath. He took another breath and another and rolled over onto his belly, away from Firefoot's huge hooves. The horse wasn't moving, but Yar didn't want to risk it.

What were the Voices trying to tell him? Was the woman going to kill him? Or was she part of the war the Voices talked about? Yarro shivered. Either way, she was dangerous. He was glad he had gotten away from Meekin when he had. Wherever the Voices were leading him, he was at least away from her.

Leg muscles screaming, Yar managed to climb to his feet. It was almost completely dark now. He should have stopped sooner so he would be able to see where he was sleeping. He must have lost hours to that vision. Cursing himself, he wound his fingers in Firefoot's mane and started looking for a good place to spend the night.

He stubbed his toe and yelped in surprise. Only his grip on Firefoot's mane kept him upright, though he had to scramble for his footing. The horse didn't seem to appreciate being used as a prop; he snorted and shifted away from Yar, which made him lose his balance entirely and fall to his knees. He stayed there for a while, feeling tears sting his eyes. It wasn't fair. He hadn't asked to be different. Why couldn't he have just been like his brothers? Why did he have to hear Voices? If he'd been normal, he wouldn't be out here stumbling around in the dark like a blind man.

ISN'T THAT WHAT YOU ARE? hissed the most slithery of the Voices. A BLIND MAN WHO CAN'T SEE ANYTHING CLEARLY, EVEN IN HIS OWN MIND.

"Shut up," Yarro choked. Was that really one of the Voices, or was it his own thought? Did it matter? "I hate you."

He pushed himself to his feet and stretched his hands out in front of him. He transferred his weight to the back foot and slid the other forward slowly, sweeping it from side to side until he was sure the way was clear. Then he stepped onto that foot and repeated the process with the back foot, bringing it forward in a tentative step. After a few halting steps like that, the movement got easier. He still couldn't see much, but at least he didn't think he was going to fall over something.

He almost jumped out of his skin when his fingers felt something. He realized before shouting in terror that it was his horse. He swallowed his alarm and said, "Hello, Firefoot."

The horse whickered at him and stayed there, letting him touch without actually supporting him. That was okay. Yarro was just glad the horse hadn't run away and left him all alone.

NOT *ALL* ALONE, whispered the Voice. YOU HAVE US.

"Some comfort," he muttered to it. He closed his eyes, just to see if it made any difference. He quickly opened them again. There wasn't much light, but there was some. A glow in the east told him the moon was beginning to rise. He looked around, trying to see if he could tell what was nearby.

Firefoot walked into his hand, pressing him away from the direction he'd been going. Yarro let the horse nudge him about twenty paces. Then the horse quit walking. Yarro took a couple more steps on his own, then realized he couldn't feel the horse's shoulder under his fingers any more. He stopped and turned around.

Firefoot's bright hide gleamed faintly in the moonlight. The horse was standing still, watching him. Yarro wondered if horses could see better in the dark than people.

"You want to stop?" he asked the horse.

The horse didn't answer, but Yarro shrugged and walked back to him. "Here, then?" The horse snorted and lowered his nose to touch the ground. Yarro leaned down to peer at whatever had caught Firefoot's attention. It was a few wisps of grass. He ought to take the horse's saddle off, he supposed. He hadn't bothered replacing the halter that had chafed at Firefoot's ears, but he'd thought he needed a saddle to hold onto. Not to mention he needed to tie his pack to something.

"All right, hold still," Yarro mumbled. He got the saddle off Firefoot's back and dropped it to the ground, wrinkling his nose in disgust. It was wet underneath. He yawned and fumbled a piece of bread out of his pack. "Do you have enough grass?" he asked Firefoot, who still didn't answer. But he thought he heard the sound of grass ripping in the horse's teeth.

Yar sat down next to the saddle. It smelled of leather and horse. He wrinkled his nose again but didn't move away from it. He could use the saddle as a pillow, maybe. He wrapped himself in his cloak and tore off a bite of bread. After a few more minutes, he was fighting off yawns between every bite. He washed down his last bite with a gulp of water and curled up, tucking his hands and feet inside the thick wool of his cloak.

The longer he lay there, the colder he felt. He hadn't realized how much heat Firefoot had provided while Yarro was on his back. And just moving must have kept him warmer, too. He shivered, his body wracked with yawns so deep they shook him, but too cold to fall asleep. A single almost-sob escaped him, and then he remembered that he'd brought a blanket too. He fished it out of the pack and wrapped it around him, cloak and all. It eased the worst of the cold. He wasn't completely warm, but he was able to stop shivering.

Yarro at last closed his eyes and slept.

***

If Azmei hadn't been watching for the boy and his horse, she would have missed them in the dark. As it was, she might have anyway, if not for Firefoot's greeting whicker. She stopped walking, shortening Sandy's lead and bringing his head down.

"Hello?" she said softly, but there was no response. She peered through the darkness and finally made out the huddled shape of Yarro sleeping on the ground, curled tightly into a ball. If the idiot boy was so cold, why hadn't he built a fire? Shaking her head, Azmei led Sandy off some distance and found a camping spot for herself.

By the time she'd scraped together some kindling, she had familiarized herself with the makeshift camp Yarro had claimed. Camp, she thought, was too generous a word for it. The spot itself was fine—off the road by about thirty paces and sheltered by a rise in the ground and several bushes. But what had he been thinking, to simply curl up on the ground without bothering to tether his horse? She shook her head and bent to breathe life into her fire.

Perhaps the guards at the gate hadn't given Yar the same lecture they had given Azmei about bandits and the dangers of the wild. She wondered idly if it was because he wasn't female. But no, she'd heard them start in on the man behind her as she was riding away from the city. Perhaps he just hadn't paid attention. It was more than possible, considering the day-dreamy way he seemed to go through life.

Once she had gathered more sticks for later and started

boiling water to brew some tea, Azmei found a good stone to prop her pack against. She spread her blanket on the ground and sat on it, keeping her cloak on and pulling the blanket up to cover her legs. She was far enough away from Yarro's camp that he probably wouldn't even notice her in the morning, in the unlikely event he should be up and moving before she was. She doubted he would be. He couldn't possibly be used to traveling as far as they had come. They were only two leagues or so outside the city, but it was enough that he would be feeling it tomorrow.

The water was beginning to spit and hiss, so she dropped in a ball of compressed tea leaves and took the pot of water away from the heat. She would nestle it in near the fire to keep the liquid warm and it should last her most of the night. She hadn't had much chance to sleep late into the day these past three years, but she had discovered she didn't mind that so much as long as she had at least a few gulps of hot tea to start her morning.

She poured some tea into a heavy clay cup and settled back against her pack. She would sleep for two hours or so, then wake to check the fire and her surroundings. In the meantime, she let the heat of the fire lull her into a doze.

She woke again to the sound of screaming.

"Sleeping gods!" she swore, jerking to attention. It was Yarro, and he sounded like he was being murdered. She struggled out of her blankets and ran towards his camp, drawing her sword. As she approached, she couldn't see the source of danger. She dropped into a half-crouch, slowing her pace to give herself time to find the boy's attacker. But there was nothing.

His horse snorted and shifted away as she got to the camp, but the only thing disturbing the horse was Yarro's screams. He was tangled in his blankets, flailing as if struggling against an unseen enemy. His eyes were closed.

Azmei sheathed her sword in annoyance. A nightmare, that was all. But what should she do now? Should she wake him? It probably wasn't the best idea to let him keep screaming, since there might be other ears out there to hear. But she didn't want their next encounter to be colored by fear.

Still. It was cruel to let him keep suffering. With a sigh, Azmei crouched an arm's length from his feet and grabbed one to shake it. "Yarro!" she called softly. "Wake up, friend! Wake up!"

It took longer than she'd expected for him to rouse from his dream. When he did, he went still except for his heaving chest, staring up into the dark sky.

"It was just a dream," Azmei told him.

"It's never just a dream," he mumbled. Then he seemed to realize he was talking to someone else. He pushed himself to his elbows, staring at her for a moment and then jerking his gaze down. Azmei glanced down to see what he was looking at—her hands, which were propped on her thighs. "Who are you? What are you doing?" he demanded.

"I'm Aevver Balearic," she said. "We met yesterday, remember, friend? At the horse market. I'm camped not far away. You woke me with your screams."

"Aevver Balearic," he repeated. He shuddered and stared at her hands a moment longer. "Horse market. I remember." He wouldn't meet her gaze.

"Would you like to come share my fire, friend?" she asked, making her voice as gentle as possible. "I have tea. It might soothe you after your nightmare."

"No," he muttered. "Leave me alone."

Perhaps it was too much to expect manners from a boy who'd been mistreated as Yarro evidently had. "Very well. I'll leave you alone," she said, and rose from her crouch.

"Are you following me?" he blurted.

Azmei raised an eyebrow. "Do you want me to answer the question, or leave you alone?"

"Answer."

"I am traveling to Rivarden," she said, deciding on her story at the last moment. "I don't like boats. They make me sick. So I'm not taking the canal."

Yarro looked over towards his horse. "Where's

Rivarden?"

Was it possible the boy was traveling on his own with no knowledge of geography? "South of here some distance. In the desert. There are fewer people there than Meekin, but it's an important place. Have you heard of the Rivarden Push?"

His face closed. "No. Go away. I want to sleep."

Azmei laughed. He was so absurd! "All right. Pleasant dreams, friend."

She went back to her camp and poked the fire back into life. Yarro might not want a cup of tea, but she could do with one.

CHAPTER FIFTEEN

Arisanat glanced over Baron Arkad's sparring ring and groaned. He had hoped he would be here alone, where he could run through his exercises and be done with it. But no, Razem and Hawk were sparring together, observed by a dozen or more soldiers, who were enthusiastically cheering any time one of the men scored a touch.

He would just sneak away and come back—

"Aris!" The prince sounded altogether too pleased to see him. Why did Razem insist upon being so friendly to him? Arisanat couldn't forgive him, not for failing to destroy the Strid, so he would rather not find Razem likeable.

Arisanat turned, hoping his face didn't show his reluctance. "My prince."

Razem waved him over, leaning against the fence and grinning at him. "I'm winded. Can't keep up with Commander Hawk here. Come chat with me while I catch my breath."

Arisanat glanced at Hawk quickly enough to see the other man make a face. Hawk couldn't possibly have the stamina Razem had. Years in prison, hobnobbing with the enemy, eating their food, wouldn't have given him much time for practice. Arisanat snorted softly but crossed the sand-and-sawdust practice ring to where Razem stood. Hawk went the other direction and began chatting with a group of soldiers.

A servant handed the prince a water skin. Razem drank deeply and shook his head. Arisanat wiped away the sweat droplets that hit his face.

"Were you looking for me, cousin?"

"I—yes, your highness." That was a better excuse for

coming down here than the truth. "I overheard Baron Arkad telling his chamberlain we would be here a week."

"We could all use a rest, couldn't we? The food will be much better than what we've had in the last few villages."

Arisanat pursed his lips. He didn't fancy the idea of staying with Arkad another week. The man made him nervous. He saw too much. Arisanat liked him well enough, but he didn't feel safe around him. Not to mention the way Arkad hung around Hawk, talking to the man as if he were an equal.

"Spit it out, Aris. I know you've got something on your mind."

"I just—wouldn't it be better if we got to Rivarden as quickly as possible?"

"Why?"

Good question, Arisanat thought. He couldn't exactly admit that he was uneasy about Arkad's perspicacity. He rolled his eyes and huffed a sigh. "Don't tell me you're enjoying this? How can you? Gods, Razem, you and I both know you don't want peace."

"My father does." Razem took another long drink. When he lowered the water skin, he was silent for a moment. "Hawk seems to believe peace would be better."

"Than winning the war?" Arisanat blurted. "Why are we the only two who realize how stupid it is to hope for peace?"

The silence stretched out between them. Arisanat glanced to either side, wondering if someone had come within earshot. But Hawk was still talking to his soldier friends, and everyone else had maintained a polite distance from the prince. Arisanat turned back to stare at his cousin. "Gods, not you too! Raz, I thought I could count on you!"

He did, too. That was the damnable thing. Arisanat had believed he could count on Razem's hatred of the Strid. He'd been fool enough to believe he and the prince were in agreement on that. He'd founded his plans on the notion that Razem would continue his intransigent position against Strid.

"Even Arkad seems to think—"

"Spare me Arkad's opinion," Arisanat broke in. "This is

dangerous. We must get you away from all of these Strid-loving peacemakers before you lose your mind entirely."

Razem managed a weak smile. "Perhaps we've all lost our minds," he mumbled. "I need to finish my exercises now that I've got my wind back. Want to join me, since you're here? Might as well take advantage of the practice ring."

Arisanat was torn between whether to fight the change of subject or to turn and leave. But that might offend Razem, now that the invitation was issued. Arisanat could argue with the prince without risking offense, but walking away... He swallowed and shrugged. "I'll need a practice sword."

Razem signaled for someone to bring them practice blades. Arisanat felt his face flush.

They sparred. Arisanat had never matched himself against Razem before, but he'd known for years that the prince must be better than he. Princes were expected to prove themselves in combat, after all, and Razem had come to the Kreyden as commander some six months after Venra's death.

Around the same time that you murdered his sister, flashed the malicious thought, and Arisanat flinched. Only a luckily-timed feint from Razem prevented him from looking like a madman. *Stop thinking,* he told himself. There was no reason for him to begin feeling guilty now.

Any guiltier than he already did, at least.

Razem beat him handily. At least the soldiers weren't shouting encouragement or cheering either of them. They'd wandered off to their own tasks, for the most part. Arisanat was uncomfortably aware of Hawk watching from the ringside, but at least he was silent until the end.

"It was well fought," Razem told Arisanat, smiling at him and holding out the water skin.

Arisanat shook his head, but he took the water. "It wasn't. I'm an engineer, not a swordsman. You don't have to spare my feelings."

Razem sighed but didn't answer.

"You pull your strokes," Hawk said. His voice was quiet, but it cut through their conversation like a blade. "Are you afraid of killing the prince? He's skilled enough to turn aside your practice blade, my lord. If you must fight, you should fight whole-heartedly."

Arisanat glared at him. "I don't recall asking for your opinion, Commander Hawk."

Razem gave him a sharp look, but his voice was mild when he said, "And what is my weakness, Hawk?"

"You signal your moves whenever you play to the left," Hawk said without hesitation. "It could cost you your life, highness."

"As a soldier," Arisanat said coldly, "your job is to make certain the prince is never in danger of that." He shoved the practice blade into Hawk's hands, ashamed at his rudeness but unable to resist. "Razem, please consider my words. Arkad's estate is in the middle of nowhere. The food might be better here than the villages, but at least let's get back to a city with real civilization."

The prince was watching him with an unpleasantly speculative expression, but he laughed at this. "I have considered them, Aris. Very well, we'll on to the Desert Jewel. Not tomorrow; Kho'll need more time to resupply his army. But the next day."

***

The night before they were to leave Baron Arkad's estate to continue to Rivarden, the baron threw Hawk a feast. He'd forgone it when they arrived, saying they were all too tired to enjoy it, and there would be time later. Hawk wasn't sure he was going to enjoy it any more now that they'd rested a few days, but he resigned himself to being shown off yet again.

He took his time dressing, amusing himself by thinking of possible excuses to miss the feast when he was the guest of honor. He could claim a sudden stomach trouble—*brought on by Arisanat's sour looks,* suggested a cynical voice in the back of his mind. Or perhaps he could contrive to fall down the steps just enough to give himself a mild concussion? But no, they would only prolong their stay while he recovered, and Arkad would likely have the feast anyway.

"Perhaps I should throw myself from the tower and be done with it," he muttered, and stalked out of his rooms to join the others.

The feast was not as painful as he had been dreading, but while Arkad managed to avoid the singing of ballads, warlike, lamenting, or otherwise, he hadn't been able to stop Razem from waxing eloquent about Hawk's courage in captivity, the stalwart faith he kept with his king and country, and what a blessing from the gods it was that Hawk had returned to them. Hawk barely managed to keep a straight face throughout the entire speech.

When they were finally free to disperse to their own amusements, Arisanat was the first to shove his chair back. He stood and turned his back on the crowd, so only Hawk and Kho could see the fury that contorted his face.

"Do not suppose the prince's pretty words means you are trusted, Commander Hawk. I am watching you, and I, at least, am not so easily fooled as my cousin. I know you for the cowardly turncoat you are, and I will see it proven."

Hawk stared at him, unable to quite cover how deeply the words cut. He swallowed and lowered his gaze to Arisanat's shoulder, trying to master himself. "I am sorry you feel so strongly, my lord," he said softly. "I will endeavor to be living proof of my loyalty."

Arisanat snorted and stalked off. To Hawk's surprise, Kho snorted too and stood, his chair scraping loudly on the marble floor of the banquet hall. His dark face was twisted in an emotion Hawk couldn't quite read. Anger? Impatience? Disgust? Kho met Hawk's inquisitive gaze with one of withering scorn and strode out of the hall.

It was too much. Hatred from Venra's brother was hurtful, but could be borne. But the treatment Hawk had been receiving at the hands of the man who had once been his dearest friend? That could no longer be tolerated. Hawk muttered a hasty excuse to the prince, who was thankfully involved in a conversation with Arkad and had missed the confrontation. Then he scrambled after Kho.

The black man had long legs. They and his temper had carried him down a long passageway and out into a long, covered portico. Hawk stopped, breathing hard, when he saw Kho standing with his head down, fists clenched at his sides.

"Emran, what is wrong?" he demanded.

Kho swung around to face him. "You," he said in disgust. "You and this sickening lack of self-worth you have been displaying from the moment you got back."

Hawk squinted, wishing the lanterns lining the portico weren't so dim. He couldn't read Kho's expression. "I...I don't understand. I am truly fortunate the prince and first lord have been so accommo—"

"Spare me the platitudes!" Kho laughed in disbelief. "Sleeping gods witness, I cannot tell if you truly believe that, or if six years in a Strid dungeon have made a wittering sycophant of you."

"It was a fairly nice room, actually. Not a dungeon at all." Hawk was surprised to find it was difficult to answer mildly. Kho thought he was being *sycophantic*?

"That isn't the point!" Kho's voice was low and furious. "Jacin, you were once in command of this whole damned district. You pointed and said *Go there* and men went there and *died* there. And what's more, they were happy to die for you. They fought for the Desert Hawk, not for Tamnen or the wealth of the mines or anything like that. The king knew it. Hells below, even the Strid knew it! You were so brilliant they could only defeat you by treachery!"

Hawk stared at him. Kho was clenching and unclenching his fists.

"Stop acting as if you are an inconsequential nobody." Kho ran out of breath and stopped talking.

Hawk cleared his throat. "I...clearly I was easily replaced. You have all been fine without me. Colonel Tropas—"

"Has been nothing more than adequate," Kho interrupted. "And I have lost a princess on my watch. Quit being such an idiot."

Hawk couldn't help himself. "I wouldn't have kept the princess had I been free," he said dryly. "As I hear it, she was in Ranarr when—"

Kho growled in frustration. "Stop. Talking."

Hawk stopped talking.

"Just—stay there." Kho stomped off back the way they had come. Hawk turned in place to watch him go. He couldn't remember ever seeing his friend so angry, in all the years they had known one another. He had always been able to count on Kho to be patient, even mild. What had happened to him?

He was still lost in thought when Kho came back, a bottle of tawny-colored liquid in one hand and two glasses in the other. "Sit down."

Hawk glanced around, saw a bench a few feet away, and sat.

"Drink this and just—just *listen* for once." Kho's voice was thick, but Hawk was beginning to grow irritated. He drank obediently, but glared at Kho over the edge. Oddly, that seemed to relax Kho just a little.

"Jacin, the point isn't whether Rivarden or the Kreyden—or even Tamnen herself—managed after your capture." He glared back at Hawk, but few people could meet Hawk's gaze for long when he let his temper show. After just a few heartbeats, Kho looked away. "So what if Tamnen managed all right? The thing is, *I didn't.*"

He choked on the words and took a long drink. "I missed you. I missed your counsel. I missed your stupid lack of humor. I missed the way I knew you would always be at my back if I needed it, just as I—" He broke off and swore, then took another gulp of his drink.

When Kho spoke again, his voice was quiet. "I failed you. We just assumed you were dead. We didn't look for you. I abandoned you and all the other wounded on the battlefield." He squeezed his eyes shut, then forced himself to look at Hawk again. "And when we learned otherwise, we were hearing it from a damned Strid emissary. Too damn late."

Hawk opened his mouth, but Kho didn't let him speak. "Shut up!"

Hawk shut up. Again. He clenched his jaw, smoldering.

"And now that we finally have you back," Kho continued, "you've turned into a man who won't stand up for himself, won't meet people's eyes. You forget what language you're supposed to be speaking. You defer to everyone. You act as if you don't deserve the mourning our nation did for you." He let out a sharp, bitter laugh. "And it's all my fault for leaving you. I should be the one who can't hold my head up."

Hawk bolted his drink and set the glass carefully on the stone bench. He stood up. "Do you know," he said quietly, "how arrogant you sound right now? The Emran Kho I once knew and loved would have laughed in your face if he could hear you."

Kho lifted his chin, staring at Hawk.

"If you had looked for me on the battlefield instead of sealing the breach in the walls, we would have lost Rivarden." Hawk fought down the urge to pace. "We would have lost Rivarden, and with her, the war. And if I had survived the battle only to lose the war, I would rather have been dead." He straightened his shoulders and made himself speak coldly. "For you to act as if you were single-handedly responsible for my captivity is the baldest arrogance I can think of. And for you to tell me that I am too humble—" He laughed. "My old friend, there isn't room for us both to be as arrogant as you."

There was a long silence as Kho stared at Hawk and Hawk gazed levelly back. Again, Kho looked away first. Hawk walked back to his bench and poured himself another glass of whiskey. He leaned against the portico railing. He took three long sips before Kho finally spoke.

"That is unfair."

Hawk arched an eyebrow at him. "Perhaps," he said. It was true that the Desert Hawk had been a rallying point, and perhaps his captivity had been a harder blow to Tamnese morale than he had realized. But it was equally true that Emran Kho was the last person he had expected to encourage him to be arrogant. "Somewhat."

Kho let out a grudging laugh and finished his own drink. "Just—stop acting as if Arisanat Burojan has the right to treat you like a traitor. You are better than that." He paused. "You're better than him."

Hawk shrugged, feeling a wash of sadness at the memory of Venra Burojan. "He lost his brother."

Kho looked away. "So did I. For six long years."

Hawk looked down into his whiskey glass. "I came back," he offered.

Kho made a choking noise and lunged at him. Alarmed, Hawk tensed, then realized his friend was hugging him. Sleeping gods, had it been so long since anyone touched him in affection that he'd forgotten what it was like? After a long moment, Hawk wrapped his free arm around Kho and awkwardly hugged him back. Kho pulled back and laughed, slapping a hand against Hawk's shoulder.

Hawk gripped Kho's forearm until Kho met his gaze. The happiness in Kho's dark eyes made Hawk's throat tighten. Perhaps their friendship would survive, after all.

"And quit with this sickening deference to Arisanat," Kho said, pulling away and going back to his drink. "He may be first lord, but he's a turd. It isn't your fault Venra died. He owes you respect."

Hawk scratched his jaw. "For his brother's sake I would be a friend to him, if he let me."

Kho looked hard at him. "He's not Venra, Jacin. Nothing like."

Hawk sighed and looked away. He felt lighter, despite the argument. He took a deep breath and looked back at Kho. "Is there any more of this whiskey?"

∗

Rivarden had changed.

Hawk supposed he shouldn't be surprised. Not only had it been six years since he'd seen it, but the city's stone defenses had had a gaping hole in them the last time he saw her, her lifeblood of soldiers pouring out of what he had feared would be Rivarden's death wound.

Since Hawk's party approached from the southeast and the breach had been on the southwest side, he didn't expect to see evidence of the repairs made to the wall; he saw something else he hadn't expected, too—a redesigned gate flanked by ominous towers. Archers were clearly visible at the tops of each tower, while a full complement of pike guards stood at attention at the base.

"I thought Salishok was the Embattled City," he remarked under his breath to Kho.

"Rivarden is still the Desert Jewel," his friend assured him. "But her masters have decided a bit more security is in order to keep the Jewel safe. This is one of only two gates into the city now. The other gates were sealed after the Push."

Hawk squinted at the walls. Rivarden had once boasted a dozen gates into the city, each named after a precious stone mined in the nearby foothills, the gates decorated with glass mosaics in the colors of said stone. The gate they were now approaching had been decorated the color of rubies and called the Gates of Fire. Now it was simple, gray-brown stone.

"I suppose the reservoir has been enclosed, too," Hawk said.

"Not yet. There was talk of it, but the citizens protested. Apparently the majority would rather take the chance that their water supply be poisoned than lose their oasis." Kho smiled. "I can't say that I blame them. Sky Lake is beautiful even after years of living near the sea."

"It's a different sort of beauty," Hawk said. "The beauty of undisturbed peace."

"As opposed to the ceaseless tides?" Kho nodded.

"Water is water," snapped Arisanat, who had ridden up beside them. "Why are we stopped here? We should get inside before they close the gates."

"The main gate of Rivarden never closes, save in utmost extremity," Hawk protested, but even as he said it, he saw Kho shaking his head.

"It does now, old friend. You have to remember, they lost a great deal in the Push. You, for one. Not to mention the countless lives of their promising young men and women. There was looting and pillaging before the last defenders of Rivarden managed to force the Strid back out through the breach." Kho looked down. "There were a lot of babes born, nine months later, with a Strid cast to their features, as well." He sighed. "Rivarden did not fare well after you left her."

"I had little enough choice in the matter," Hawk protested.

Kho shook his head again.

"I suppose you think that excuses you for your failure as a commander," Arisanat said. "But you may not find the citizens of Rivarden very forgiving."

Hawk swallowed against a sudden tightness in his throat. "That may be so, but I swore I would return, and so I have done," he said. He nudged his horse into a walk.

Hawk wondered if he had offended Arisanat, but he couldn't make himself care. After he and Emran cleared the air a few nights ago, Hawk had given long consideration to Emran's concerns. His best friend had never cared for politics, but he could see through them clearly enough. Hawk had come to agree with Emran. Lord Arisanat's hatred was not hurtful to Hawk alone; in his blind hatred, Arisanat could influence the prince to work against peace.

The guards at the gate had seen their party approaching. The main group came to attention as one of their number went inside the stone guardhouse. Hawk didn't alter his horse's slow trot, but he did shake back his robes so the guards could see that, though he was armed, he was approaching in peace, without hiding his weapons. He glanced over at Emran to see that his friend had already done the same and was gesturing for the others to do likewise.

"Halt there!" called a voice. The watch captain had come out of the guardhouse and was at the head of a mounted group. His sword was still sheathed, but the others of the group each carried a spear held at half-ready.

Hawk obeyed without protest and waited until the others had done the same before lifting his hands in a gesture of peace. "I am Jacin Hawk, former Commander of Rivarden," he said. "I am come to Rivarden to fulfill an oath that I would return. With me is Prince Razem Corrone, heir to the throne, Lord Arisanat Burojan of the First Family, and Lord-General Emran Kho of the Tamnese Army."

There was silence for several heartbeats as the watch captain conferred with the person on his left. Razem waited serenely, seemingly content for Hawk to handle the protocol. Hawk could feel Burojan's impatience, probably with the delay as much as with Hawk's presumption of speaking first. At Hawk's elbow, Emran was still and watchful. Hawk didn't look over his shoulder for confirmation, but he heard no movement from the column of soldiers behind him.

"We should have sent a messenger ahead," Hawk muttered. "Stupid of me not to think of it."

"What's done is done," Kho said. "I might have thought of it myself."

"Come forward," called the watch captain. He nudged his horse into motion as Hawk did. The person at the captain's left moved with him. When Hawk, Emran, and Burojan met up with them, Hawk saw the watch captain was actually a woman.

"I have heard of Commander Jacin Hawk," she said. Her voice was deeper than most women's, so Hawk forgave himself the mistake. "But Lieutenant Laran says he has met Lord-General Kho."

Hawk studied the man at her left—Lieutenant Laran, apparently. He was between twenty-five and thirty years of age, Hawk judged, and stringy, with short, sand-colored hair and a scraggly mustache that would never get any thicker. But his brown eyes went straight to Emran's face as he saluted, and there was respect in his gaze.

"Lieutenant Laran, yes," Emran said. "We met in Salishok...two years ago, was it?"

"Yessir, I'm honored you remember, sir."

Dear gods, Laran was keen. Hawk couldn't remember if he had ever been that young. Then again, Hawk hadn't set out to be a good soldier. He'd just been good at killing.

"I look forward to hearing what you've been doing since then, Lieutenant," Emran said. He sounded like he meant it, too. Hawk had always admired Emran's knack of being genuinely interested in people.

"Perhaps you'll allow me the honor of standing you a drink at the King's Man, sir." Laran's mustache hairs seemed to quiver with excitement at the notion.

"It would be my pleasure," Emran said. He shot Hawk a glance that said he knew exactly how amused Hawk was and didn't approve.

Hawk swallowed the smile that was fighting towards his lips. Gods, how he had missed Emran. It had been a joy to fight alongside someone who knew you so well he could anticipate your thoughts and actions. Returning to Tamnen only to have that friendship withheld had been harder than he'd expected. Perhaps their conversation at Arkad's estate had truly repaired it.

"Commander Hawk would be most welcome to join us, of course, sir."

Emran grinned. "I'm sure Commander Hawk will be most delighted, Laran. Thank you."

Burojan huffed out a loud breath. "Enough of this! The sun sinks lower in the sky and I, for one, have had a long day in the saddle. Let us to the city, where we may yet get a decent night's rest."

"Peace, Aris," Razem said. "It is well that old friends should greet one another."

The watch captain saluted the prince gravely. "You are most welcome, of course, my lord prince."

Razem opened his mouth, but Burojan bulled forward. "Who is there in Rivarden that may greet Prince Razem properly?"

She lifted her chin. "I am Watch Captain Reva Harnen,

my lord, and I greet you and welcome you to Rivarden. I am certain that Governor Tarkor would greet you himself, had he known the hour of your arrival. As it is, I hope you will allow me the honor of accompanying you to the Governor's Mansion."

"Governor Tarkor will be expected to receive the prince with all honor," Burojan told her. "Our orders, from the king himself, are that the commander's freedom is to be celebrated."

"Peace, Aris," Razem said again, his voice sharper than before. "Rivarden has lived without Commander Hawk for six years. She cannot be expected to stop what she is doing to celebrate our arrival."

Hawk smiled at the prince. "For my part, I am filled with joy merely to be back in my home city."

The watch captain spared a warm glance for Hawk, but bowed to Prince Razem. "Rivarden stands ready."

Burojan gestured for her to lead the way into the city. As soon as she turned, he shot a venomous look at Hawk. "Do not interrupt, Commander Hawk. It will not be tolerated."

Hawk met his gaze and said nothing. He was through with being bullied and intimidated by this man. Emran fell in next to Hawk as they started into the city.

"I told you to stop being so meek," he breathed, "not to deliberately provoke him."

Hawk's smile felt tight. "Lord Arisanat is going to make my life difficult no matter what I do. I might as well have it on my terms as on his." When Emran glowered at him, Hawk said, "He hates me for coming back when Venra did not. No one grieves for Venra more than I, but the lord will not see that. I fear the only way I could redeem myself in his eyes would be to die for my country as Venra did."

"What is the sense in that?" Emran muttered. "Venra was a great loss, there can be no question. But losing you would be a loss just as great." He shook his head and looked away. "It *was* a loss just as great."

"But I returned," Hawk pointed out, despite the warmth

that filled him at Emran's words, "and Venra never will, no matter how many dukes we give back to the Strid. And that is not my fault, but I can understand why he blames me."

"You are more forgiving than I would be in your place," Emran said.

Hawk snorted. "Nay, I know better than that. You are skilled in the art of war, but you are equally skilled in the art of diplomacy." His smile faded as they rode between the looming gate towers. "Emran, what you would style my forgiving nature is born more of my own guilt that I survived. I almost didn't recognize my city gate. What other changes have been wrought in the time I spent in captivity?"

Emran frowned. "Would that I could make it easier on you."

Hawk shrugged. "'Would would bring back the dead,'" he quoted. "But it is enough to be free and in Rivarden again." *And to have you speaking to me once again as a friend,* he added silently.

Once they were inside the gates, the bustle of the city surrounded them. The area surrounding the gates was devoted to meeting the needs of travelers arriving in Rivarden. Inns, shops selling general goods and trade goods, brewers, public houses, and provisioners filled the buildings nearest the gate. As the only city of its size in this part of the Kreyden District, Rivarden did brisk trade. Hawk closed his eyes and breathed deeply, drinking in the fragrance of hot flat bread, spiced nuts, mulled wine, and roasting meat.

Sweet slumbering gods, how I have missed this city, he thought. It was so good to be home.

They followed a winding path to the Governor's Mansion, the wide road curving through trade districts and rarely-visited temples to reach the top of the low hill that gave the mansion its view of the Desert Jewel. When Hawk had lived in the city, his quarters had been in the building behind the mansion, where he had equal access to the barracks on one side and the governmental center on the other.

By the time they arrived, Governor Tarkor was waiting

for them. He stood on the broad porch, dressed in robes of cream trimmed in scarlet, a wide smile on his face. Hawk didn't know Tarkor. He had replaced the governor who had died in the Push along with so many of the city's defenders. Hawk had no idea what to expect from the man.

"Welcome, welcome!" cried Tarkor. "Prince Razem! I am honored by your visit, as is the city of Rivarden. Lord Burojan, you are most welcome! And Lord-General Kho, it is good to see you again. Commander Hawk, welcome home. I am so pleased to greet you all and welcome you to Rivarden, the Desert Jewel of Tamnen!"

Hawk couldn't tell if the obsequiousness was real or feigned. Razem received it calmly enough, though his smile for Tarkor was full of real warmth. Burojan ate up the ceremony, however, preening and allowing Tarkor to bow more deeply than necessary. He clearly took the accolade as his due.

Hawk paid little attention to the words of greeting that passed between all of them until Tarkor said, "And now, for Commander Hawk! You are most welcome here. We will host a celebration in your honor, and tomorrow I myself will lead you on a tour of all the improvements we have made since your...unfortunate departure. Because you left so precipitously, you may not recognize some parts of the city. I am sure you will enjoy seeing how Rivarden has changed."

Hawk forced a smile. "I look forward to it, Governor Tarkor."

"Of course, of course. We are preparing rooms for everyone here in the mansion and I am pleased to be your host for the duration of your stay here."

Hawk let his thoughts drift away again, even as his feet followed Tarkor to his rooms. Life had once again moved on without him, and he felt adrift, nothing to anchor him. Sooner or later he had to come to rest, but he didn't have any idea when that might be.

CHAPTER SIXTEEN

Razem stared at the dusty courier, overly aware of ridiculous details, such as the man's badly mended bootlace and the hole in his tunic sleeve. Odd, that he should notice such things at a time like this, he thought. He saw the courier shifting weight from one foot to the other, biting his lip, gaze faltering. It should not be like this. But then, how should it be? "Say that again," he said faintly.

The courier gulped and glanced to Razem's left, where Arisanat was not saying anything. Razem nearly snapped at the man to spit it out, but then his temper washed away again in a wave of grief.

"Your highness, I..." the courier fumbled, "I was sent by Captain Ysdra and Lady Riman of the Second Family to find you. I...it is...I am very grieved to report to you that your father, King Marsede, has been grievously wounded. There was a surprise attack in the capital. It is feared he may not survive."

I know my father's name, Razem wanted to say. It was absurd that the courier felt the need to clarify who his father was. Razem swallowed and looked down at the floor. He was not answering the courier, and he knew he must. But what could he say? He could threaten vengeance. He could demand answers. He could weep. But what would be the point of any of those things? The courier had no answers. Razem's eyes burned fiercely with their dryness. And as for vengeance—that had not gone so well when he swore vengeance on whoever had killed his sister. Why should he think it would go any differently for his father?

Behind him, Arisanat cleared his throat. That prompted

Razem to open his mouth, if only to keep Arisanat from speaking. Gods knew what Arisanat would say, but if he said the king had got what was coming to him, Razem would draw his sword and slay him here and now.

"Tell me everything you know about what happened," Razem instructed the courier. His voice was painfully calm. He felt as if every word cut his mouth. But he didn't know what else to say.

The courier bowed. "I did not witness the attack, your highness. I was told that someone attacked the king as he was visiting the Hallowed City where your venerated mother lies. He had few attendants with him, and most of them were slain in the attack. All four of the attackers were slain. At least one of them was from the Long Coast, but I heard another was Ranarri. There is much confusion. No one has said the Strid are to blame, your highness."

He paused, perhaps fearing Razem's temper, but Razem gestured for him to continue.

"In fact, the reports are that the Ranarri gave information concerning a family in Meekin. Perslyn, it was, and he named them as being involved in the attack. Captain Ysdra dispatched soldiers to Meekin at once, but of course there was no time for them to report on it before we were sent to you.

"There is little else to tell, my lord. Your father was badly wounded, and there is fear the blade was poisoned. He has fallen into a delirium. I was dispatched immediately, along with a dozen others, to seek you and relay this news to you."

Razem stirred. "Where are the others? Were you set upon as well?"

"No, my lord. We were sent by different routes to be certain the news reached you. It was uncertain whether you would still be in Salishok, or by what route you might be returning to Tamnen City."

"Gods blind us for fools," Arisanat exclaimed. "Was the entire prisoner exchange an elaborate ruse to lure us out of the city and away from your father?"

Razem frowned, glancing away from his cousin. It

seemed a valid question, except that the exchange had taken place, and the Strid Commander had seemed genuinely grateful to have her uncle back. "What difference would my presence have made in the capital?" he asked. "I could not have saved my father from attack. He and I rarely visited my mother's grave together. My father's grief was a thing private to him." He paused. For that matter, his father's grief for Azmei had been private as well. His father, for all that Razem loved him, had rarely showed his emotions.

"And yet here we are, a fortnight's journey and more from where your father has been struck down!" Arisanat blustered. "He could even now be dead!"

Razem whirled on him. "*Do not say that*," he hissed, advancing on his cousin so suddenly that Arisanat tripped over his own feet backing away. Arisanat caught himself on a side table, opening his mouth to speak, but Razem had turned away again already, spurred into action. His cousin could wait. He strode to the door and jerked it open, startling the guard who stood outside.

"Kho!" he snapped. "Someone go for General Kho!"

When the general appeared in the door, Razem beckoned him in. "I will need a company of soldiers. Your best, for I must not be delayed in any way. We will ride at once back to Tamnen City—you, my cousin, and I. As for Hawk, I have an errand for him."

"Razem—" Arisanat began, but the prince didn't allow him to continue.

"You will accompany me, Aris. We can trust Hawk to carry out the mission I assign him, whether you like him or not." He glared at Arisanat, watching the gold flecks in his cousin's eyes flash as they seemed to bubble like liquid gold. Temper in the high houses of Tamnen always showed itself, however they attempted to mask it.

"It will be as you command, Razem."

"Good." Razem turned back to Kho, who had stuck his head out the door to issue orders. Kho tensed under Razem's hand on his shoulder, but only looked over as the prince urged him into the hall and several steps away from the guard. Razem lowered his voice. "Kho, my father has been badly wounded in an attack. I must go to him. There must be a member of the ruling family hale and visible in the capital city."

Kho's expression crumpled for a moment and then he nodded. "Well said, your highness. I have already begun arranging for your escort. Will you wait until morning, or ride through the night?"

"First light, Emran. I cannot bear the thought of trying to rest while my father needs me, but we have obligations here first." Razem's throat tightened as he spoke, but he managed to get the words out. "We must not slight Governor Tarkor after he has gone to so much trouble over the welcoming feast."

"Very good, Prince Razem. I will see that the men are ready to leave at dawn."

Razem gripped Kho's shoulder for a moment before releasing him. He watched the general stride away, once again issuing orders to his men. Now for Hawk.

Razem could hardly bear the thought of explaining everything to him. Could he send the courier? But no, the man had clearly been on his last legs. He would collapse soon, as his horse had already done. He had earned his rest. *Gods may weep*. Razem would have to do it himself.

He strode back to the sideboard, where he poured himself a stiff drink and slammed it back in a single gulp. Then he turned and went to find Hawk.

The commander was in the rooftop garden of the Governor's Mansion. Razem had to ask four guards before he learned even that much, biting the words out more viciously with each guard. His footsteps rang hard on the stone passages. Gods help him, but his temper was rising up again, just as it had so often over the past three years. He was tired of being angry! But how could he help it, when everything had gone wrong since Venra died?

He took the narrow stone steps up to the rooftop two at a time, his breath coming in explosive bursts. He wanted to find something or someone to hit. When he reached the top and came out into the sunlight once again, however, he paused and stared around him.

Everywhere he looked was a profusion of color. Roses rioted in red and gold, interspersed with orange and burgundy lilies. Date palms provided shade while fountains rippled and songbirds trilled. Razem's breathing slowed. Rivarden, the Desert Jewel. Despite his grief and anger, the beauty was a balm.

He found Hawk standing at the waist-high outer wall, looking down. Rivarden and the Sky Lake reservoir made a pretty picture from so far up. Razem wondered how pretty the streets and alleys of the city actually were. He cleared his throat.

Hawk turned, his movements relaxed enough that Razem knew the man must have heard him coming. *Of course he did, you imbecile. You were stamping about like a toddling boy in a tantrum.* He gave himself a mental shake.

"Highness, how may I be of service?"

Razem swallowed and wished he'd thought to bring a jar of wine with him. He licked his lips and said, "Hawk, my father has been attacked. It is unknown if even now he may be dead. I must return to Tamnen City."

The commander's eyes widened as Razem spoke, his mouth dropping open. "Highness—"

Razem held up a hand. He wanted to get this all out. "It was an assassination, Hawk. Not content with stealing my sister from me, our enemies have conspired to take my father as well. I will not stand for it. But I must have your help."

Hawk dropped to his knees. "Anything, highness. Just command me." He tilted his head back, staring up at Razem with an expression so warm Razem was certain he didn't deserve it. Why did this war hero care about a prince whose family could barely keep the kingdom under their control? Razem coughed to cover his emotion.

"Forgive me, Prince Razem. May I offer you drink? I brought wine with me." Still on his knees, Hawk turned to a bundle Razem hadn't seen before.

"Gods, yes," Razem said, and dropped to sit on one of the stone benches. "My thanks."

"I am grieved for your father." Hawk poured a cup of wine and held it out. "Tell me what I can do."

Razem forced himself to take only a sip of wine rather than draining the cup. "Go to Meekin."

Hawk stared at him blankly. Razem took another sip of wine.

"The courier who brought word of the attack on my father also said that the Perslyn family in Meekin was possibly involved in or behind the attack. Soldiers were dispatched from Tamnen City, but I know you, Hawk. I trust you. I want you to find the truth behind the attack. Start in Meekin. If you find nothing there, come to Tamnen City. I will make sure you are not wanting for coin."

Hawk nodded. "As you command, your highness. Shall I leave today?"

"Tomorrow." Razem drained his cup. "Gods help us, we still have a welcoming feast to get through tonight." He barked an unhappy laugh. "And you'll need time to gather your provisions. See General Kho about the details. He'll give you anything you need."

He knew Hawk wouldn't like that, but their little feud could be damned. Razem trusted both of them, and whatever problem they had with each other, they could get over it to serve him now. He turned a sharp gaze on Hawk, who lowered his head.

"As you wish, highness."

***

Hawk couldn't blame Governor Tarkor for the poor turnout at the celebration. The crown official had done everything in his power to make Hawk's welcoming ceremony more elaborate even than the one in Salishok. It was just that the people of Rivarden were tired of war.

Hawk couldn't blame the people of Rivarden. He was tired of war, too.

He sat in splendor at Prince Razem's left hand, Governor Tarkor to his left. Thankfully, Hawk was separated from Lord Burojan, who was on Razem's right. The prince sat in morose silence, his attention focused on his meal. Hawk didn't begrudge Burojan the position of honor. He was just glad he didn't have to sit next to the man.

"I really don't understand why so few have come," Tarkor said, leaning towards Hawk. "The people of this city love you, as I am certain you must know. You are honestly more of a hero to them than anyone." He leaned closer and pitched his voice to a whisper. "And certainly you should be seated at the right, but—"

Hawk shook his head. "There's no need for that, Governor. You shouldn't trouble yourself. You have been more than welcoming, and I am overjoyed to be home."

Tarkor was a pale, skinny man with a large nose and thin lips, which were pursed. His brows drew together in genuine distress. "But Commander Hawk, I had such hopes for your return. There were to have been songs and dancing and..." He trailed off and shrugged. "I had certainly planned something better than this."

Hawk smiled and looked out at the scant three score of people seated at the feast tables. "Governor Tarkor, nothing you could have planned would soothe my soul as much as being in Rivarden. I only wish my visit were not being cut short by the grave news from the capital."

Tarkor's brow smoothed, but his lips were still pursed.

"Truly, Governor," Hawk said. "Your welcome has been most expressive."

It was the truth. Tarkor had sent a tailor to Hawk's rooms to make certain he had clean, luxurious clothes to wear. There had been a bottle of wine open in Hawk's rooms beforehand, along with a bowl of fruit, and the tailor had been followed by a group of servants bearing hot water for him to bathe. It had been, on balance, a better welcome than he'd had in Salishok.

Tarkor gave Hawk a gratified smile and leaned back in his seat as the next course was served.

There were instrumentalists playing while they ate. After the meal, the singing began. There was a short set of ballads and laments, but several of the songs were traditional love songs. Hawk thought those sounded more heartfelt than the lament for his capture.

"Governor Tarkor, tell me how Rivarden has fared since my capture," Hawk said, looking over at the man. "How are the people? Are there needs to be met?"

The man sighed. "Ah, there are always needs to be met, Commander. But I do the best I can with the resources given me. The king is generous, of course, and I think there are none whose need is desperate."

Hawk nodded. "Are there many orphans?"

"Orphans, widows, crippled…" Tarkor shrugged. "We make provision for them, as we may. There are houses where the orphans may live, and meals served to the widows and crippled."

"Many of them?" Hawk pressed.

"Always too many," Tarkor said. "But any number of them is too many. No offense, Commander. You know better than anyone how Rivarden has supported the war. But it is never easy on its supporters."

"Less easy on its supporters than on its opponents, I think," Hawk agreed. "Is there anything that could be done for them if I speak to the prince?"

Tarkor considered for several moments. Hawk could see that Lord Burojan was fidgeting. He didn't seem to be actively eavesdropping on the conversation, but he was definitely annoyed at being left out of it. "I think, Commander, that the mere fact you ask this question proves that you believe the prince *will* do something."

Hawk had to content himself with that for the moment.

For now, he settled back into his chair, focusing all his attention on the singers.

After the singing was done, Tarkor gave a short speech welcoming the prince to the city and Hawk back home. His tone was thoughtful, which Hawk was quickly coming to realize was characteristic of the administrator. At least, Hawk thought, Rivarden had been in capable hands since the Push. They had had many obstacles to overcome, but Tarkor seemed to take his duties seriously.

The prince gave a short, grave speech. Hawk wondered what changes the prince had made in his speech. He said nothing of the attack on his father. He spoke only of the grave injury Rivarden had taken during the war and his admiration for the city at their determination in rebuilding.

Hawk had to stand after Razem's speech to offer his own remarks of thanks. He should have anticipated this and prepared. The speech in Salishok had been something of a surprise, but he had no such excuse here. All the same, it hadn't occurred to him.

He stood in his place, looking down at all the upturned faces. Most wore varying degrees of curiosity, some resentment, some hope, some boredom. Hawk didn't recognize many of them, though there were a few merchants he remembered seeing before the Push. Among the soldiers, there were none he recognized, but that didn't surprise him; too many of his companions had died in the Push, and of those who had survived, many had been rendered unable to continue in their duties.

After a moment, the restless shifting and quiet coughs reminded Hawk that he had been staring at them in silence when he was supposed to be speaking. He cleared his throat.

"I am not a man for speeches," he said. "I was always better at action. I feel joy at being here among you again. I am home." He paused for the brief, polite applause. He tried to smile, but the subdued mood was infecting him. "I thank you for pausing tonight to greet me. I am grateful for the chance to reacquaint myself with this jewel Rivarden, the city of my heart."

He bowed and retreated to his seat. The applause felt more genuine this time, though Hawk wasn't certain if it was for the content of his message or merely that it was over.

"That was pretty," Burojan remarked, his tone biting. "But a few pretty words will not redeem you, Hawk."

"Oh, my Lord Burojan—" Tarkor began, but Hawk waved him to silence.

"Then it is well I intend to follow them with action." He bowed deeply to the prince, and then to Burojan. That bow he made only as sharp and shallow a bow as etiquette demanded. "Prince Razem. Lord Burojan." He made his next bow, to Tarkor, no deeper but longer. "Governor. I will retire to my rooms for the night. I thank you for your generous hospitality."

Tarkor's slender hands were clasped in front of him as if he were restraining himself from reaching out to them, but he merely nodded. "Good night, Commander Hawk."

As Hawk turned to go, he saw Emran looking hard at him. He chose to ignore it. Tomorrow would bring what it brought. Tonight he was going to sleep.

***

Rivarden had a lot of refugees.

Arisanat looked around the marketplace in dismay. He had overheard Governor Tarkor and Hawk talking about the situation last night at dinner, but he hadn't understood then why Tarkor had been so noncommittal. Now he did. The refugees were an inconvenience as well as an embarrassment. Tarkor couldn't feed them all, and he couldn't house them all, so he wanted to pretend they didn't exist.

Unfortunately, pretending something didn't exist didn't make it true. Arisanat hadn't imagined the problem to be so widespread, but now that he was out in the city proper, he couldn't deny that it was.

On top of the refugees, there was an unnerving number

of mercenaries and fortune hunters in the city. The city guards were hard-pressed to control the crowds, and there were hard feelings growing in certain areas of the city. Arisanat's errand had led him through some unsavory places on his way to this marketplace. Called the Hive—presumably because of the continual buzz of activity, even at this early hour—the market was a congregating spot for those who had come to Rivarden in search of riches or escape.

Why would the refugees and the mercenaries be drawn together? Arisanat wondered as he pushed past a booth where a woman was selling repaired weapons running the gamut from a folding knife to a halberd. Perhaps some of the refugees were looking for justice that they felt could only be found at the end of a sword, though if that were the case, Arisanat would have expected them to volunteer for the army. Perhaps the mercenaries thought the refugees would be easy pickings. Not that mercenaries were all unsavory, but a fair number of them would take advantage if they found an opportunity.

That couldn't be the only reason, though. Perhaps it was just that there were cheaper meals and rooms to be had in the Hive compared to other parts of the city. Arisanat stepped out of the flow of foot traffic and leaned against a wall, folding his arms and watching the people flow past him. Some were dressed well, some were in rags, but the vast majority were at least decently clothed. The mix of people was fairly balanced between men and women, though it seemed that there were a large number of children, most of them between the ages of six and ten, compared to the number of adults.

That made sense once he considered it; the orphanages were all within a short walk of the Hive. Some of the orphans probably did some begging—or pickpocketing—in the market. Arisanat resisted the urge to slip a hand into his pocket to check that his purse was still there. He'd tucked it inside a secret pocket in his trousers, and his tunic hung nearly to his knees, disguising it. Anyway, he could feel the weight of the money against his thigh. He didn't want to draw attention to the purse by reaching for it out here in the street.

He ducked back into the endless stream of traffic and stepped into the next tavern along his route. Just inside the door, he stepped to one side and paused, letting his eyes adjust to the dim interior and enjoying the inviting smells of breakfast. This tavern was more crowded than the last two he'd looked into. A group of men and women wearing hauberks sat at a table halfway between the bar and the door. Caravan guards, he guessed. Two boys between fifteen and twenty summers sat at another table, facing each other. A motley group of at least a dozen roughly-clad people clustered around two tables they'd drawn together. In another corner, a woman wrapped in blue clothes that hid all but her face and her hands sat alone.

Arisanat glanced to his left, looking at the other half of the common dining area. Three middle-aged women sat together at a table, sharing a pitcher of coffee and laughing as they chatted together. Their conversation was the loudest in the room, and it was a mixture of Kreydeni and Tamnese. He strained his ears long enough to pick up that they were discussing the price they would get for wool that day. Shepherds, then, most likely. He passed his gaze across the room again and noticed the boy and his companion were huddled close over the table. The caravan guards were waving at the bar girl, trying to get her attention. She was looking at Arisanat, waiting to see what he would do.

He walked up to the bar, letting a smile stretch across his face. He nodded towards the table of caravan guards. "Go on and take care of them first. I'm in no hurry."

She gave him a friendly smile and grabbed her pitcher of coffee, hurrying over to the table. They greeted her with a raucous familiarity that told Arisanat they were frequenters of the establishment. She filled their mugs and returned to the bar, where she poured another mug and pushed it across the bar towards him.

"They said to add one for you," she said, grinning cheekily at him.

"Then I'm grateful," Arisanat said, lifting the mug to his

lips. He leaned on the bar. "They must be in here a lot."

"Enough that I know them," the girl replied. "Can't say the same for you."

He smiled ruefully. "Point taken. Name's Risan. I'm looking for a few warm bodies, people interested in doing work and not interested in asking many questions about it."

The girl's expression shuttered. "Are you with the Hiveguard?"

"Hiveguard? No." Arisanat frowned. He'd never heard of such an organization, though at a guess, it sounded like an organized crime group. Perhaps a citizens' watch, but he didn't think such a group would make her close down like that. "I'm actually not with anyone, really. Just asking because I have a job I need done, and the Hive seems to be full of folk looking for work."

She narrowed her eyes, studying him. "You planning to turn anyone over for questioning?"

"I'm planning on asking a few friendly questions, and maybe spend a bit of gold, that's all."

"I don't inform on folk," she said.

Arisanat sipped his coffee. It wasn't bad, despite being something a group of caravan guards could afford. "I'm not asking you to. Just asking if you know anyone who might be in need of a bit of cash. You know everyone in here?" He took another pull of his coffee and slipped a few coppers on the bar. Not enough to be a bribe, but enough to tip her for the drink. Let her see he wasn't trying to coerce her, just making an honest inquiry.

She studied him narrowly for several more seconds, then turned to refill her pitcher. Over her shoulder, she said, "Only people I don't recognize in here today are those two over there. Sound like they're northerners." She looked down at the coins on the bar, chewing her lower lip. "That group yonder," she said, jerking her chin towards the people who had pushed two tables together, "they were asking about merchants what might be hiring guards. Don't know if they'd do for you, but they might."

"Thank you." Arisanat tipped his head back and drained his mug. It wouldn't do to look ungrateful or unappreciative. Besides, the coffee was decent. He wiped his mouth and set six silvers on the bar. "This refill my mug and their pitcher?"

"And leave a bit over," she said. She licked her lips.

"Bring the pitcher over and you can keep the rest," he said. "And gods keep you."

Her lips curved up. She looked tired, but she was pretty if he looked past the shadows under her eyes and the hair escaping its knot. "My thanks, friend Risan. I hope you find someone to work for you."

Arisanat smiled and followed her over to the group of people he hoped to hire. They fell silent as he approached, but Arisanat indicated the pitcher in the barmaid's hands. "I only wish to talk for a bit," he said, "and I bring an offering."

He had addressed his remark to a grizzled man somewhere between forty and fifty. A jagged scar showed beyond the edges of a leather patch that covered one eye. But the man's good eye went to a woman who looked closer to thirty than forty. She had the light tan coloring that spoke of mixed Tamnese and Strid heritage, and there was a hard glint in her eyes.

"We'll listen and we'll drink, but I make no other promises," she said, shoving a stool out for Arisanat to sit.

"I thank you, Mistress..."

"You can call me Lail," she said. "What do I call you?"

"Risan," he answered. "I've important business to be taken care of, and unfortunately I find myself unable to do it myself. But I saw your group here and thought you all look more than capable." He smiled up at the barmaid as she refilled his tankard, then took a long sip of his coffee. "Though if I've misjudged you, I apologize."

Lail folded her arms across her chest, staring at him. Arisanat couldn't shake the feeling she saw through him, but he smiled at her anyway.

"I suppose Geritte told you we're out of work," the one-eyed man said. "Her old man gets mean when she's behind on collecting tabs, so she's jumpy about people who drink too much in here."

The barmaid flinched and hurried away from the table.

Arisanat spread his hands, offering them a guileless smile. "I just asked her who among the regulars might be up for a piece of work that involves good pay and no questions."

"What is it, then?" Lail asked. She drained her tankard and shoved it across the table at him to refill.

"There is a man who has caused me considerable trouble. My business calls me urgently to Salishok." Arisanat shrugged. "One of my ships is reported to have foundered, and I have customers awaiting shipments. I don't have the time to deal with this man personally."

"When you say 'deal with this man'..."

"I want him dead," Arisanat said baldly. "Him and any-one with him."

To his relief, Lail didn't recoil. She held his gaze for sev-eral heartbeats before giving him a slight smile. "And who is this man?"

Arisanat took a slow breath. This was the most delicate part of the operation. He couldn't lie to the woman, not if he wanted her to kill the right man. But telling her the truth risked her discovering his identity, were she overcurious.

"He goes by the name of Jacin Hawk. He'll be traveling from here to Meekin by horse. He should be alone, but I can't guarantee it."

Lail showed no sign of recognizing the name. "Why this fella? Why does he need to die?"

"Never you mind," Arisanat said. He selected several gold pieces from his purse and stacked them on the table, careful to block them with his body so no one away from this group would be able to see them. Then he withdrew a piece of paper that crackled as he unfolded it. "I am willing to pay enough that you forget your questions."

"Jae." Lail jerked her chin and a boy who looked to be fourteen or fifteen reached across the table and took the pa-per. Arisanat studied the boy while he turned the paper and squinted at it. His skin was a lighter tan than Lail's, his narrowed eyes the same green as hers; but his hair was the thick, straight black of the one-eyed man's hair. Their son, Arisanat guessed.

"It says he's got a sum on draft for us, if we complete the work. Present a sword and dagger to the holder and we'll get a thousand gold." Jae lifted his head to stare at Arisanat. "No one's got that kind of money sitting around."

"I have," Arisanat said. "And I will warn you, if you do not bring Jacin Hawk's sword and dagger, you will not receive a copper. The holder of this draft knows what names are engraved on those blades."

"This sounds like it's more than something personal," the one-eyed man said. He put a hand on Jae's shoulder. "A thousand gold is all well and good, if we're alive and well to spend it. But anyone willing to spend that kind of money on one man's death has a big reason for doing it." He exchanged a glance with Lail. "What if the Crown wants to know why we killed him?"

Arisanat let a slow smile cross his face. He'd anticipated this question. He drew out another token from his purse. It was the genuine article, though he didn't expect they would realize it. "Then you tell the Crown that you are about the Crown's business," he said, flipping the token to the one-eyed man.

"Looks good enough," the man said. "Jae, who holds the draft?"

"Vinga," the boy said.

Lail stood. "We'll take the job—provided Vinga authenticates the draft. If there are really a thousand gold waiting at Vinga's, your Jacin Hawk will be dead before the week's out."

Arisanat stood as well and extended a hand. "I'm glad to hear it."

She ignored the outstretched hand. "It'll be this crew, minus Jae. He stays in Rivarden. You change your mind in the next day, you send word to him, but you'd better send word to Vinga that we keep a day's wage out of that thousand." She gave him a smile full of teeth. "You change your mind two days from now, and it's too late."

Arisanat nodded and strode away.

When he arrived back at the Governor's Mansion, the prince's party was assembled and ready to ride out. Emran Kho was striding around snapping out terse orders. He glared at Arisanat but a moment later collected himself enough to bow.

"My Lord Burojan. The prince has been asking for you. Your servants brought out your luggage, but they didn't know where you had gone."

Arisanat held up a package that he'd purchased in the Hive on his way back. "I promised my sister I would bring her back some Kreydeni spices. I thought it would be faster if I went to purchase them and left my servants packing." He gave Kho a pleasant smile. "Which seems to have been correct. I am ready to leave at his highness' pleasure."

CHAPTER SEVENTEEN

Azmei woke with the early sun in her eyes. She stretched and sighed, and a heartbeat later she jumped to her feet and swore. She'd slept later than she had intended. Master Tanvel had the uncanny ability to decide when he wanted to wake. Azmei had always contented herself with small tricks like drinking too much water before sleeping, or lying down with her face turned to the east, but over the past year she had at last begun waking every hour or two all night.

Not last night. Perhaps it had been her midnight waking from Yarro's screams, but she had slept at least half the night without waking. She turned to the north, where Firefoot was browsing at the brushes near the spot where Yarro had camped. The boy must have been exhausted. He wasn't used to traveling all day, certainly not used to being in the saddle for such long stretches, if everything she'd observed was correct. He wouldn't have woken so early.

Azmei took a few minutes to stretch and work the life back into her muscles. She found her way to the stream she had heard last night and refilled her water flasks. She ate some dried meat and a hard biscuit while she waited for her water to heat for tea. It was enough to make her laugh, thinking of the breakfasts she had demanded when she was still a princess. How different this breakfast was to the ones she had eaten in the palace. But at some point in the past three years, she had grown to prefer this sort of breakfast.

Except for the lack of coffee. She had never realized how difficult it could be to get good coffee. She drank it in inns, but it was too much trouble to travel with it.

When the tea was brewing, she stepped lightly over to the bay horse. He put back his ears and bared his teeth at her, but she merely set out a few sweets and poured a pan of oats for him. As soon as the horse was satisfied Azmei wasn't going to try to catch him, he eased his way over to the oats and began munching on them.

Azmei found Yarro sprawled out on the ground some distance away. Apparently he hadn't seen the need to tether Firefoot, any more than he'd seen the need for a fire or a proper camp. Azmei shrugged. The horse hadn't wandered off, so perhaps there was something to the bond Yarro had claimed between them. Either way, he ought to be taught to brush the horse. She could see streaks on the horse's flanks where his sweat had dried untouched.

Shaking her head, she went back to her camp for a brush. It took her a few minutes to get close enough to Firefoot that he would let her touch him, but as soon as he felt the brush against his itchy sides, he let out a horsey groan and leaned into her touch. Azmei was still brushing him when Yarro shifted and sat up. She didn't turn to look at him, but she was aware of his movements.

"I suppose you had grooms where you grew up," she said, "but anyone who rides as well as you ought to know a horse should always be brushed dry at the end of a long day."

"Why are you following me?" he snarled. "I should eat you."

She arched an eyebrow. "Clearly you like mornings even less than I do," she remarked, and ran the brush one last time down Firefoot's neck. The horse snorted and stepped away from her, walking delicately over to rest his nose on the top of Yarro's head. It made the boy smile, which made Azmei feel a bit better about him.

"I don't think you should follow me," Yarro said. He wasn't looking at her.

"I told you last night, I'm on my way to Rivarden," Azmei lied. "This is the way to get there."

"Then why are you bothering me now?" He sat cross-legged and poked at one knee.

"Your horse was wandering around untethered and ungroomed. I thought maybe you could use some help." She tilted her head to one side, trying on a smile. "Maybe you *do* need a guide. If you're going this way, we could travel together for a while, at least. I could teach you how to brush your horse and build a campfire."

"I know how to do those things!" he flared. His gaze flickered up at her but dropped again.

She held in a sigh. How had Orya, of all people, had the patience to deal with Yarro? He looked to be about seventeen, but he acted as if he were twelve. "Very well, then I'll share the work with you. Two people traveling alone need two campfires, but two people traveling together only need one. That leaves the other person free to brush the horses while the first builds the fire and cooks. We could help each other."

"You don't even know where I'm going."

Gods above and below, now he was sulking! "No, I don't. But for the moment, at least, you seem to be going the same direction I'm going." She paused, wondering if she should appeal to his manliness. Most teenage boys would like the idea of protecting a woman. But she didn't know enough about Yarro to tell whether he would be that sort of boy or not.

He was scowling at the ground in front of his knees, rocking in place just slightly. He almost looked like he was having a conversation with himself. Azmei waited a few minutes, then shrugged. "Fine, suit yourself," she said, and went back to her camp.

She would give him some time to think about it while she took care of her own needs. She poured a cup of tea and sat near the fire to drink it. The morning was damp, the chill creeping along her skin and raising chill bumps. She held the cup under her nose and closed her eyes, trying to summon the calm required to commune with the peace god. Perhaps meditation would show Yarro that she wasn't dangerous.

God of peace, grant me your serenity, she thought. *Give me patience and grace for this boy.* She had to remember, he'd been raised in a family that appeared to be largely without love or friendship, and he was a very different sort of person than those people. If Orya had been the most loving person in his life, he must have wanted for affection a great deal.

Before she'd finished her cup of tea, she heard his footsteps crunching on the sandy ground. She opened her eyes as he stopped about ten feet away, the fire between them.

"I think I'll give you a chance," he said. "I'm not telling you where I'm going."

Azmei rested her cup on her thigh. "That's quite all right."

"And I don't think you should touch Firefoot. He doesn't like it. He might bite you."

She grinned at that. "I'm perfectly happy to leave Firefoot to you. Does that mean you want me to build the fire and cook this evening?"

He turned his head to one side, looking at her from the corner of his eye. "Maybe. First you'll have to prove you're okay to trust."

"How am I going to do that?"

He shrugged. "Don't be untrustworthy."

"I suppose that's the best way to go about it," Azmei agreed. He was a strange boy, but perhaps they could get along well enough. "Have you had breakfast?"

He appeared to think about that for a moment. "You know I haven't. You woke me up."

"You might have eaten while I was praying," she said. "Here, I have dried meat. I didn't bother with meal or porridge since it was just me, but tomorrow morning I could make a real breakfast. If you cook the meat in the porridge it tastes pretty good."

He shrugged and crouched where he was. "You don't have to give me food. I have food."

"I don't mind sharing," she said. "And maybe that way you'll also share with me in return."

"Maybe." He was silent for a minute, then moved close

enough to take the meat she had offered. "Your name is Aev-ver."

She nodded. "And yours is Yarro."

"My sister named me that. She was eight when I was born. She was my favorite person in the whole world."

Sleeping gods, how sad that was. Azmei sipped her tea to give herself a moment to steady her composure. She hadn't killed Orya, though she had damn well tried. It had been Orya's cohort, the second assassin, who had killed Orya when she failed to kill Azmei. All the same, Azmei felt somehow ridiculously responsible for Yarro's sister being dead.

She tried to kill me, she reminded herself. *And she all but succeeded.*

"She isn't your favorite person anymore?" she asked, trying to keep her voice casual.

"She died." Yarro thought about that. "She might have died. Grandfather said she died. But then Ri—someone thought she might still be alive, but hiding. I don't know. If she left me alone on purpose, then she's not my favorite person."

"That," Azmei said, "is perfectly understandable."

***

Yarro wasn't sure what he thought of the woman Aevver Balearic.

He flicked a glance at her. She was riding to his right, a comfortable distance away when the trail was wide, and falling behind him when it narrowed. She sat on her horse like the day of riding yesterday didn't trouble her at all. Perhaps it didn't. Yar had groaned aloud when he swung into the saddle. He was sore in places he hadn't even known he had.

Aevver saw his glance and smiled at him. Yar cut his gaze away again, feeling his cheeks get hot. On the one hand, she had been kind to him several times now. When they met at the horse trader's in Meekin, she had tried to protect him from what she thought was a mean horse. It wasn't her fault that she didn't know about Yar's vision of Firefoot. And last night she had woken him from a terrible nightmare wherein Orya's face was a mask of blood as she told him she was protecting him by staying dead and that the Voices were leading him to doom. And even this morning, she had fed and brushed Firefoot and then offered Yar breakfast.

On the other hand, the Voices were certain, and Yar believed them, that Aevver was lying about not following him. She was definitely following him. But why? Even the Voices weren't sure about that, and when Yar asked if they were in Rivarden, they only told him to follow. So Aevver must not be searching for them, unless she was lying about where Rivarden was.

Maybe she was. Yar had heard of a city called Rivarden, but he had never paid much attention to maps before. He'd never expected to need to. If he was going somewhere, Orya knew it already. Once Orya left, once Orya was dead, Yar never went anywhere, so it didn't matter where places were.

He'd bought a map in Meekin, but he hadn't bothered to look at it so far. He was following the Voices, and they were leading him with teasing and cajoling. Firefoot seemed almost to know where they were going, as well. He certainly didn't seem to require much guidance from Yar.

COME, LITTLE BROTHER, chuckled one of the Voices. YOU SHOULD BELIEVE MORE IN YOUR OWN SKILL. YOU KNOW WHERE YOU ARE GOING, AND YOU ARE COMMUNICATING THAT TO HIM.

How? Yar thought back at the Voice. *Does he understand me like you do?*

The Voice laughed outright, the sound booming painfully in Yar's ears and bouncing around inside his skull. He winced. NOTHING UNDERSTANDS YOU LIKE WE DO. NO ONE UNDERSTANDS YOU LIKE WE DO. BUT FIREFOOT WAS DESTINED TO BE WITH YOU, AND YOU WERE DESTINED TO COME TO US. IF HE IS TO BE YOUR COMPANION, HE MUST BE SPECIAL. Yar got the impression of the Voice licking his lips. EVEN IF

HE WOULD BE TASTY TO EAT, WE WILL NOT LET THE HUNGRY ONE EAT HIM, SINCE HE IS YOUR COMPANION.

Thank you very much, Yar thought, hoping he didn't sound as annoyed as he felt. How generous of the Voices to promise they wouldn't eat his horse!

He realized Aevver's idle stream of conversation had faltered. How long ago, he wondered. She liked to talk more than Orya did, though not as much as Tish. Had he missed something she'd said to him?

He glanced over at her. She wasn't looking at him. She was shielding her eyes against the rays of the sun, which was not quite directly overhead yet. Her golden eyes were intent upon whatever she saw in the distance. Yar turned to look that way, but he couldn't make out whatever had attracted her attention. He didn't want to ask, so he just rode in silence, straining his eyes for anything that might seem interesting or threatening to a woman who carried so many blades.

A flash of light sparkled in his vision. Yar squinted and looked up, and then white light flooded the whole world.

Thunder rumbled in his head and he saw the woman Aevver drawing her swords. A dove swooped down from the sky to seize Aevver in its talons—no, to land on her shoulder—no, to fall bleeding under her blades. Firefoot neighed a defiant or fearful challenge. A great, dark bulk rose into the sky, so tall it blocked out everything else, and so wide Yar couldn't see around it.

Something howled—was it the wind? Was it the dark bulk? Was it Yar?

A white city rose from the middle of the ocean, water splashing around the base of its walls. The sun shone on it, but dark clouds were gathering all around until a single ray of light was all that touched the white stone at the very tip of the topmost tower. Then the darkness swallowed all of it.

A great wind rose, pushing at him, buffeting him from all directions. He saw the flash of lightning and heard someone screaming. Keening. Crying.

A man with eyes like coal embers stared at him from a grief-

shadowed face. His dark hair fell into his eyes and evening shadow darkened his jaw. There were deep purple streaks under his eyes and his cheeks were hollow. The man's sharp nose made him look dangerous despite his sad eyes.

That dark bulk slammed into him, carrying off his balance as it flew past him and disappeared in the blackness of the storm.

Someone repeating his name. His name. His name.

"Yarro?"

He jerked, realizing that voice was real, not in his head.

WE ARE REAL, LITTLE BROTHER, said what he thought of as the Wise Uncle Voice. WE ARE VERY REAL. AS ARE THESE TRUTHS WE SHARE WITH YOU.

"Yarro," Aevver said again, her voice very close to him. He swung around to face her and lost his balance, tipping and sliding despite a desperate last-minute clutch at Firefoot's mane. He landed flat on his back, the world graying out as the impact drove the breath from his lungs. He tried to suck in air and failed. Tried again. Again. And finally he managed to draw breath, filling his lungs with a gasping, groaning sound.

"Siren's teeth! Are you all right?" He heard her feet thud to the ground. He closed his eyes, waving a hand feebly to ward her off. He didn't have the breath to speak yet.

It was a good thing she didn't know what he'd seen. She might have her swords drawn. Yarro shivered.

"Are you hurt?" she demanded.

"No," he croaked. He opened his eyes and found her bending over him, her eyes wide, brows drawn together.

"What happened? Did you feel ill?" She pressed a hand to his forehead.

Yarro jerked away from her touch. Even after that he could feel her fingers crawling against his skin. Why did she feel it was her right to touch him?

"Tell me what's wrong," she pressed.

"Nothing." He blinked at her.

TELL HER YOU FELL ASLEEP. That was the Sly Voice. At least it wasn't advocating eating her like it had earlier.

"Nothing? You don't fall off your horse because of nothing!"

"Sometimes you do," he muttered. He pushed himself into a sitting position. "I must have fallen asleep. You woke me up and I fell."

"Asleep?" Her voice was dubious, but she sat back on her heels, giving him more space. "I was afraid you were having some sort of fit."

He shrugged. "I fell asleep." Having found that excuse, he stuck to it.

Aevver rubbed a hand over her face. "I'm glad that's all it was. But we'll stop earlier tonight than last night, if you don't mind." When Yarro made no reply, she added, "It'll give us more time to set up camp and get a meal ready."

She kept looking at him, so finally Yarro shrugged. He didn't feel like talking any more.

Evidently that was answer enough. Aevver stood and walked back to her horse. "Feel like getting on the move again, or do you need a moment to rest?"

Instead of speaking, Yarro pushed himself to his feet and held out a hand to Firefoot. The horse sidled over to him, sniffed his hand, and allowed Yarro to wind his fingers in his mane. Yarro climbed up to the bay horse's back and looked down at Aevver.

The woman chuckled and mounted her own horse. "Very well. Let's get going."

***

Yarro and Firefoot had been traveling with Aevver for three days. Yarro was still unsure of her. She was rather abrupt at times, but she laughed easily and treated her horse well. Her daggers and sword still made him nervous, but she hadn't drawn any of them in all the time they'd been together.

That didn't mean the vision was wrong, though. Yarro was used to his visions not making sense. He didn't ever expect to actually see a dove and a serpent fighting. But in the past month his visions had been startlingly literal, and he knew it was starting to alter his perception. First there had been Firefoot and then Aevver. What had come next in the vision after the red horse and the copper-skinned warrior woman? He knew he would recognize the next thing when he saw it, but he wanted to remember it before he saw it.

I should have written them down, he thought. But he had never been much for writing anything down. He *could* write. He'd been taught at an early age along with the rest of his family. But every time he got caught up in a vision, he would rouse from it to find his pen had dripped ink splotches all over his paper and eventually dried up. He would have to clean the pen before he could ink it again. It got to be so much trouble he just didn't bother.

He glanced over at Aevver, who was riding a few paces ahead of him. Every once in a while she glanced over her shoulder to make sure she was still going the right direction, and if Yarro was looking, he would nod. But he didn't always notice. He figured she had decided if he was still going the same direction as she was, it must be right.

She wasn't looking at him now. She was relaxed in the saddle, her head turning slowly as she watched the horizon. She was always watchful. It made Yarro tired. He wondered if she even noticed the pretty pink flowers that spread low to the ground along the path they were riding. Did she notice the deep blue of the sky? Did she enjoy the feel of the cool breeze in the heat of the sun?

The vision hadn't started with Firefoot. What had it started with? The desert. Sweeping sand dunes and harsh cliffs casting shadows over the land. He closed his eyes, picturing it. To his surprise, it jumped with vivid clarity to his mind's eye. Then there had been a valley with an entrance hidden from all those who weren't worthy. And Firefoot, looking straight at him. Aevver Balearic, with her brown skin and the sword on her hip and her daggers hidden everywhere. And then—what?

A magic user. He remembered her just as her face swam into focus with her moth-green eyes and dark hair streaked with white. Her skin was unlined, her expression unhappy. She was too young for that white hair, barely older than Yarro. He didn't know why he was sure she was a mage. But he could see the power in her somehow.

He gulped and opened his eyes. Maybe he shouldn't have remembered her. He had never met anyone with magic. Orya had told him stories with magic in them. He had always wondered what it must feel like to have magic. But the actual idea of it was frightening.

And what about the vision from a few days ago? He had been seeing that man in his dreams at night, and he didn't understand why. The man hadn't been in the first visions, but he kept coming back now. He must be important for some reason. Most of Yarro's visions weren't that persistent.

Was the man someone who knew Aevver? Maybe they were friends. Maybe it was a warning of something. The man and Aevver might be planning something together. He had looked dangerous. Yarro remembered the sadness in his eyes, though.

He shivered suddenly and looked up. The sun had gone behind a cloud. That was unusual. It had been unrelentingly sunny ever since he left Meekin. Meekin got a lot of sunshine, but he knew there had been gloomy days earlier this year. But out in the dry scrub lands they were traveling through, the clouds seemed wrong.

Yar looked down at Firefoot's mane. He kept waiting for the Voices to give him new directions, but so far they seemed pleased with his progress. One impatient Voice often urged him to hurry, but Yar thought he was traveling as fast as he could, so he mostly ignored that Voice.

YOU ONLY IGNORE ME BECAUSE I ALLOW IT, the Voice said. IF I WANTED TO, I COULD SEIZE YOUR ENTIRE ATTENTION AND KEEP IT ON ME.

You'd better not, Yar told it. *If you do that, Aevver Balearic will notice something is wrong. She'll start asking questions. I don't want to tell her about you.*

SHE WOULDN'T BELIEVE YOU ANYWAY, the Voice agreed. NO ONE BELIEVES IN US ANYMORE.

ONCE WE WERE REVERED AS THE ELDEST AND WISEST. NOW WE ARE FORGOTTEN, THOUGHT OF ONLY IN HERO TALES.

I believe in you, Yarro assured it. *Not that I have much choice. But I have always believed in you.*

The Voice didn't answer in words, but Yar felt a warm humming in his mind that told him it was pleased with him. The humming was a comforting sound, lifting up to surround him, almost like an embrace. He sank into it, feeling the sway of Firefoot's walking pace but relying on the Voice's humming to hold him up.

Aevver's voice, when it broke in, was jangly and discordant. "Do you hear that?"

Yar opened his eyes, only then realizing they had drifted closed. A moment later he realized he *had* heard what she was asking about. He frowned. "Thunder?"

In answer, the sky rumbled at them. The sound sent a shiver of apprehension through him. Yar drew his cloak over his shoulders and around him.

"I think we should start watching for shelter," Aevver said. "Have you been looking at the sky?"

Yarro shook his head and looked up again. The sun was hidden by not one cloud, but several that were building in the west and had finally reached tall enough to cover the sun.

"It looks like we're in for a storm," Aevver said. "We don't want to be caught out in the open if that's the case. We should be getting close to that village marked on your map. I would think we'd start seeing houses here and there. I've noticed goats and sheep grazing in the distance."

"People?" Yar asked, his gut tightening.

"You don't like people? Meekin is full of them." She had fallen back to ride next to him. The trail they were following wasn't really wide enough for that, but she let her horse pick his way around obstacles, so it worked.

"Most people don't seem to like me much. I'm too much of a freak." He bit down on the tip of his tongue as he realized what he'd just admitted to her. He shouldn't have said that!

She would ask why he was a freak, and then he might end up blurting out something about the Voices, and—

"I don't think you're a freak," Aevver said. She tilted her head, studying him. "You're different from me, but then I'm different from myself. I'm not the same person I was five years ago. And both mes are different from my brother or my parents. That's what makes this world so interesting. People are different from each other." She smiled at him.

Tentatively, Yarro smiled back.

Thunder crashed across the sky at them, interrupting the moment. Yar ducked. Aevver's sand-colored horse shied. She got it back under control almost at once, but their brief connection was broken. Aevver swore, looking up at the sky again.

"We need to move faster," she said. "Let's trot for a while. Pay attention to the landscape around us. We'll need to find shelter somewhere. We can't sit in the middle of an open field like this while lightning strikes around us."

Yar winced. Had she noticed the way he tended to let his attention wander? "You lead the way," he said. That way she could set the pace and he could just let Firefoot keep up with her. He would look around for shelter until the Voices distracted him again.

Aevver nodded and took off in a ground-eating trot, the sand-colored horse proving his smaller size didn't mean he was slower than Firefoot. Yar squeezed his knees around Firefoot's sides, asking the bay horse to keep up, and Firefoot responded with a snort. He leapt into a gallop until he caught up to the other horse, but fell obligingly back into a trot once they did.

The thunder rumbled almost constantly now, an ominous growl that made Yar's heart pound in his chest. It was like the storm was a great beast that was chasing them, ready to pounce at any moment. He found himself leaning forward in the saddle, his gaze flitting from one rock outcropping to the next. As they topped a rise, Aevver and Yarro found themselves in the middle of a flock of sheep. The dirty-white animals scattered, baaing their distress at having two horse-men suddenly riding through them. Yar looked for shepherds, but he didn't see any.

"There should be a sheepcote somewhere!" Aevver called back to him. The wind was rising. Yar had to strain to hear her.

"Full of sheep!" he protested, but either she didn't hear him or she didn't care. Her horse picked up the pace and Firefoot accelerated to keep up. Yar didn't know what a sheepcote would look like, but he assumed it was like a house for sheep. It ought to look like a building then, right? But the faster they went, the more attention he had to give to staying on Firefoot's back. He gave up on looking for shelter and worried only about following Aevver.

YOU MUST SEEK SHELTER, boomed a Voice in Yar's mind. It was the Wise Uncle Voice, and there was a note of command there that Yar hadn't heard in some time. THE STORM RISES, LITTLE BROTHER, AND YOU ARE VULNERABLE.

"We're looking for it now," he gasped, not caring that Aevver might hear him. It seemed unlikely, anyway, between the pounding of the horse's hooves and the rumble of thunder and the ever-present shriek of the wind.

NOW, LITTLE BROTHER!

But it was too late. The skies ripped open with a flash of lightning so bright it left Yar dazzled and blinking. In the aftermath of the lightning, the clouds let loose with their burden. Not as a slow drip and drop, but as sudden and hard as if someone had upended a bucket over their heads. Yar gasped and squinted as the thunder crashed over him, rattling his teeth and shivering his bones.

"Aevver!" he screamed.

She looked back and waved her arm. Her mouth opened, but he couldn't hear what she said. The rain was too loud. He kept following as she turned her gaze ahead of them again. He leaned low over Firefoot's neck, trying to keep his hood up to shield his eyes from the rain. It was a losing battle. Every time he got the hood tugged forward, it blew down again.

It seemed like forever before they reached whatever Aevver had been aiming for. She led them inside a building, ducking as she urged her horse into a dark opening in a dry-stone-walled building. Yar followed, wondering what had possessed him to trust her so blindly. As soon as they were through the arch, he pushed his hair back from his face, blinking the rain water out of his eyes and peering around in the sudden darkness.

"Where are we?" he demanded. His voice echoed in the stone chamber.

"A sheepcote," Aevver said. "I think. It'll do for now. At least we won't be drowned in here." He heard the shuffling of her horse's hooves and then a dull thud as Aevver must have dropped out of the saddle. He reached over his head until his fingers encountered a low stone roof. He wouldn't have room to sit up on Firefoot's back. He rolled off the horse's back and leaned against him as his knees threatened to give out.

He couldn't stop shivering. How had he gotten soaked to the skin in such a short time?

"Get out of those clothes." Aevver's voice was brisk. "I'm going to get a fire lit."

Yar struggled out of his cloak. It seemed to weigh ten times more than it had when he'd swung it around his shoulders this morning.

"We need a fire first, and to get dry. Then we can dry off the horses. They won't fare well if we catch our deaths of the cold first." Aevver kept up her monologue as she built the fire. Yar mostly ignored her. His attention was taken up with forcing buttons through holes that suddenly seemed too small for them, using fingers that were stiff with cold and slippery from the rain. He didn't care what she wanted done. He just wanted to get warm.

He was shocked when hands gripped his wrists and tugged them down from where he was struggling with the top button of his shirt.

"Let me do it. You're shaking too hard." Aevver's voice

was cold. Yar let her undress him, thinking about how different this would be if it were Tish here with him instead of Aevver.

IT WOULD BE NO DIFFERENT. YOU JUST WISH IT WOULD, hissed the Sly Voice. Yar flinched. As much as he hated the thought, that was true. Tish had no time or interest for him.

"Hold still," Aevver snapped. "I'm not trying to hurt you. I just want you warm. If you don't get dry, you'll be ill. I don't suppose you want that."

Yar swallowed and held still.

Aevver's fingers were efficient as she tugged his shirt open and pushed it off his shoulders. "Can you untie your trousers yourself?" she asked. "Good. Get them off and get over by the fire. I'll get a blanket for you in a minute."

Yar did as he was told. He was huddled by the fire when a blanket settled over his shoulders. Almost at once he felt a change in the temperature as the blanket trapped the fire's heat around his body. He looked up.

Aevver was closer to naked than any woman he'd ever seen before. She was wearing some sort of cloth fastened around her bottom parts and a wrapping around her breasts, and aside from that, she was bare. With no leather armor or daggers, she seemed much less dangerous and more female. Yar stared at her.

That wasn't fair, really, he acknowledged. His sister had been dangerous and entirely female. Orya had never seemed like a man at all, so why would Aevver seem like a man simply because she was dangerous? After a while, Yarro decided that he simply hadn't thought of her as male or female because he had been so focused on her daggers. Without the sharp, pointy bits, he was able to think more about the rest of her.

"You could quit staring," she remarked. "You act like you've never seen a woman before. I didn't know boys could still be virgins when they got to be your age."

Yar gawped at her, eyes wide. It made her laugh.

"I'm teasing you, Yarro," she explained. "I don't care if

you're a virgin or not. Isn't my business. But you ought to learn that it isn't polite to stare at a woman like that if you aren't romantically involved with her."

"It isn't my fault if you're practically bare in front of me!" he protested.

She cocked her head. "Really? You're practically bare in front of me, but somehow I'm resisting the urge to stare at you."

Yar felt his face get hot, and then the heat spread through his whole body. He probably wasn't much to look at. Why would she want to look at him? He was younger than she was, though he couldn't tell what age she really was. She seemed so mature and in-control that he had assumed she was much older, but her body was taut and firm, her face unwrinkled. She probably wasn't old at all. "Sorry," he muttered.

She was actually quite pretty. He didn't suppose he ought to be thinking that at all. She probably wouldn't like anyone to think about whether she was pretty or not. But absent the sword at her hip and all the daggers that had made her seem hard-edged, she was less frightening and more approachable. Maybe, he thought, that was why she carried so many blades.

"I'm sorry," he said again.

"Well enough," she replied. "You didn't know, but now you do. A woman's body is her own, just as your body is your own. If you make no claims towards mine, I'll make no claims towards yours." She was smiling, though there was a funny curve to it that made him think she was laughing at herself as much as at him.

"Orya never talked like that," he said. "I suppose she didn't really think of me as normal, either."

Aevver went still for a moment. "Orya was your sister?" she asked finally.

Yar nodded. "She was older than me. She's the one who picked my name. Our mother died when I was born, and our father was...away." Their father had been on an assignment somewhere else. Yar didn't remember where, because wherever it was, their father had never come back from it.

"Orya and Yarro," Aevver said. She smiled at him. "She must have loved you very much, to give you a name so like her own."

He blinked hard. His eyes were stinging. If Orya had loved him so much, she shouldn't have left him. "I suppose so," he mumbled. He didn't want to talk about Orya anymore. He shivered.

"You ought to be getting warmer," Aevver said. "Scoot closer to the fire and pull your blanket tighter. I should have put water on to boil." She turned away to do that, and Yar stared at the fire, listening to the rustle of her pack and the clink of the metal pot against the stone floor. He didn't want to think about Orya, either, but now he couldn't stop. She had often called him her little boy, but Yar had always thought she was teasing him. Maybe it had been because she had named him and raised him instead of their mother doing it.

One time, when he was quite small, he had fallen in the fountain in their private courtyard. Orya had folded a paper canal boat for him and told him they would play together when she got back from her lessons. But that seemed to be forever away, so Yar had slipped out of the nursery, away from the aged cousin who nodded off more than she watched over him. He had gone to the courtyard, where he had played in the fountain before. He remembered the Voices talking to him, but he didn't remember what they said to him.

He'd climbed up on the lip of the fountain, leaning far over the water to launch the boat. Then a sparkle on the water distracted him. He had reached for it, lost his balance, and tumbled in headfirst. He remembered struggling to get his head above water, trying to cry for help, and then blackness. When he woke up, Orya was hunched over him, her face whiter than the finest bleached silk. There were tears on her cheeks and in her eyes. Yarro had reached to her, crying because she was crying. Orya had clutched him close and whispered that she thought she'd lost her little boy.

"Here, drink this," Aevver said, thrusting a hot cup into his hands. She waited until he closed his grip before letting go of it and retreating to her own side of the fire.

Yar stared down at the steaming mug of tea.

"Are you all right?" Her voice was concerned. He flicked a glance up at her. With her jaw-length hair curling wetly around her face and the compassion in her golden eyes, she looked prettier than he'd ever seen her. Yar shrugged and looked back down at the tea. "Do you want to talk about it?" she persisted.

Yar shook his head.

"All right. But if you want to, I'll listen."

He shrugged again. He didn't want to talk about Orya. Talking about Orya with a stranger meant only talking about one part of her. One of the reasons Yar had loved her so much was that other side of her. He hated the killing, hated it if she came home smelling of blood. But he loved that she could do that and then come home to kiss the top of his head and tell him stories about dragons and minstrels and boys who learned how to fly.

"I'm sleepy," he told Aevver.

"Drink your tea first. And then you can sleep if you want. We'll stay here tonight, as late in the afternoon as it is. I'll fix something to eat later, but I can wake you when it's ready."

Yarro hunched his shoulders in and sipped obediently at the tea. It was a different kind than what she'd given him every morning. This had a tang of fruit and spice in it. He took another sip and smiled just a little.

CHAPTER EIGHTEEN

Arisanat Burojan had spent the past three years trying to hate Razem Corrone, thinking it would make it easier to do what he must to seize power. In the past three weeks, he had realized he was fundamentally unable to do so. It had been a bitter truth to swallow, and sometimes, when Arisanat looked at the prince, he found himself gulping hard against the bile that rose in his throat. But his disgust was just as much for himself as it was for Razem.

I grew up loving him. It makes sense that I wouldn't find it easy to hate him, he thought.

Then again, he had also grown up loving Venra, and his little brother had been more a part of his daily life. Razem had been someone who wandered into his life occasionally, when there was a royal visit to Burojan Manor or when the First Family was in the capital. Azmei had been there almost as often as Razem, but there had been times when, as a girl, she was preoccupied with something that didn't interest the boys. Well, and there had been that time Razem visited without Azmei because Arisanat's father was attempting to interest the prince in Arisanat's sister Rija.

Gods, that had been a horrible visit.

Arisanat stared down at his hands, loosely holding the reins. How he wished for problems as simple as trying to keep his cousin and his sister from falling in love.

Venra had howled about Azmei's being left out of the visit. Looking back now, Arisanat suspected his twelve-year-old brother had already harbored a secret passion for the princess. At the time, Arisanat had thought Venra was making a fuss over nothing, but he had thrown his support behind Venra because that was his role to play.

"What do you mean, Azmei isn't coming?" Venra had demanded, staring at their father. "He's so boring. At least Az knows all the old stories and how things ought to work."

"Don't you like Razem?" their father had asked. "I've always thought you were good friends. And he will be your ruler someday, after all. You ought to know him better."

"We know him well enough," Arisanat put in. "He's pleasant and just, but he's not Azmei."

Their father had sighed impatiently. "You aren't children any longer, Aris! You, of all people, ought to realize how important it is that your sister do well for herself. It's possible her position may influence yours. We would like her and Razem to become good friends."

Arisanat had understood his father at once; he was fifteen, after all, and they were already discussing his marriage prospects. But Rija was only ten, and Razem eleven, and Arisanat's first impulse was to shout that it wasn't time yet. Azmei herself was only nine, and Arisanat wouldn't have been surprised to hear that she was betrothed; she was a princess, after all. But Rija was of the First Family—important, certainly, and fourth in line to the throne, after Razem and Azmei and Arisanat, but fourth in line meant she ought to have more time.

Looking at the situation from fifteen years' perspective, Arisanat could see that his father had been trying to protect his children, to secure a future for them. At the time, however, it had simply seemed too soon for Rija to be betrothed, even to their beloved cousin.

A deep voice broke into his memories. "My Lord Burojan," said Emran Kho, "could you spare me a moment?"

Arisanat shook himself out of his reverie and looked over at the general. He liked Kho. The black-skinned man had broad shoulders and brown eyes that seemed to be always vigilant. It was a shame, really; Kho would almost certainly side with Razem, and that made him an enemy, however much

Arisanat might wish otherwise.

"Of course, General. What do you need?"

Kho scratched at his jaw. Unlike the rest of the soldiers, he wore no headdress despite the sun. Arisanat wondered if it was because it made it too difficult to be vigilant; the man's eyes were constantly roaming the landscape. "My lord, your cousin is indisposed to an early stop this evening." He glanced away, and Arisanat followed his gaze to where Razem rode at the head of the column. "I am concerned about the men and horses both, but he insists we must carry on."

Arisanat nodded slowly. "And you believe the prince is wrong," he said. It hardly seemed possible that he could drive a wedge between the prince and his general—but he would be a fool not to try.

Kho looked down, and Arisanat wondered if a man with such deep color ever blushed. If so, Arisanat couldn't detect it. "My lord, I..." He cleared his throat. "Well, yes."

"Why come to me?"

"He'll listen to you, my lord." Arisanat stared at him, and Kho shrugged. "Well, sir, I'm just his advisor. You, he loves."

Arisanat clicked his tongue, thinking. If he helped Kho handle Razem, it might at least put the general off his guard where Arisanat was concerned. Perhaps he would believe Arisanat was trustworthy. Certainly he'd been unafraid to speak his criticism of the prince, however mild. There were some noblemen who would make a mountain out of that particular molehill.

"Very well," he said at last. "Do me a favor and find me some of that beer Razem's so fond of. The sun creates a powerful thirst." He winked at Kho and urged his horse up alongside Razem's.

His cousin was drooping in the saddle. Arisanat could easily see that Razem was taking the heat worse than most, though some of that might be his general dispiritedness. Arisanat held in a sigh. He had no right to regret it, since it was entirely his doing.

"You look tired," he said.

Razem jerked upright. "I'm fine."

"No doubt you are," Arisanat said. He made his voice as dry as possible. "And yet I wonder if you aren't expecting a bit much of yourself. We can't cover in a week the distance it took the courier two weeks to travel."

"We aren't hampered by the merchants this time," Razem snapped. "And we have fewer soldiers."

Arisanat reached into the small pouch on his belt and pulled out a cinnamon sliver. "True, but you're still trying to push us almost forty miles a day. That simply isn't sustainable, Razem. And quite frankly," he admitted ruefully, "my arse can't take it."

Razem snorted in amusement, then looked ashamed of himself. "Gods, Aris," he muttered, smiling faintly down at the pommel of his saddle. "I can't just let my father—"

"You'll do your father no favors if you collapse trying to get to him," Arisanat pointed out. "Honestly, knowing your father, he'd rather you arrive too late than make yourself ill on the way."

Razem made a choking noise. Arisanat thought it was even odds whether it was another laugh or a sob. He sighed.

"Look, Raz, let's stop for the day. Give the soldiers a chance to cook a real meal for supper and spend enough time they all get a full night's sleep, even with the watches." He reached out and touched his cousin's elbow. "You and I have had little time to talk, these last few days on the road."

Razem grunted, but Arisanat could tell he was wavering. The prince was exhausted, there was no question of that. Arisanat told himself that even a fiend probably loved his father, but that didn't make him feel any better. Razem was young, impulsive, and angry, but he was no fiend.

"Very well," Razem said finally. "Kho! Let's make camp at the next likely spot!"

General Kho rode up alongside them, not acknowledging Arisanat. "Very good, highness. The scouts say there's a small spring up ahead, perhaps another half mile. It's little more than a trickle that's been bricked around to protect it from the sand, but it'll do enough to water the animals."

"And tell the cooks they'll have time for a hearty meal."

"Yes, your highness."

Razem grunted again and waved Kho away. He and Arisanat rode in silence until they reached the campsite.

As always, the prince's tent was the first to be raised. As soon as it was ready, Razem waved Arisanat inside. Arisanat signaled Kho, who gave a discreet nod. Razem collapsed on a pile of cushions and let his head tip back until he was staring at the cloth ceiling. Arisanat swallowed. If not for the soldiers outside, he could slit Razem's throat right now.

Outside the tent, someone cleared her throat. Arisanat tried not to acknowledge the relief he felt. Of course he couldn't. He would never get away with it, not out here. "Come!" he called.

Razem lifted his head enough to give Arisanat a funny look, but Arisanat just shook his head. The tent flap pushed aside and a soldier brought in a pitcher of beer and two tankards. She managed to salute despite her full hands. "Sir. General Kho sent this with his compliments, sir."

"Very good, soldier. Thank you." Arisanat relieved her of her burden and filled the two tankards. "Have someone bring us some bread at some point." Wordlessly, she offered a cloth-wrapped half loaf, and Arisanat laughed. "I see General Kho has anticipated our drinking habits," he remarked. "My thanks again."

The soldier saluted again and left, and Arisanat handed one of the tankards over to Razem.

"You might want to sit up before you drink that," he remarked.

"You and Kho are in cahoots," Razem grumbled. "I might have known."

"Someone needed to be." Arisanat took a long sip. The beer was rich and slid smoothly down his throat. "You forget how well I know you, cousin."

Razem chuckled weakly. "I suppose I do. You always knew me better than I knew myself, Aris." The gaze he turned on Arisanat was warm over the lip of his tankard. Arisanat nearly choked on his next sip. Did the prince truly still love him, despite the coolness between them these past three years?

Arisanat was four years the prince's elder, and he had grown used to being separate from the deep friendship among Azmei, Razem, and Venra. Rija had been on the fringe of that threesome as well, but she had been viewed more as a pest than anything. Arisanat's role had been more complicated. He had been, by turns, an accomplice, an informer, an enabler, and a disciplinarian. The youngers had nearly always trusted him, but there had been once or twice, when they'd been up to one of their more dangerous stunts, that Arisanat had pulled rank and gotten them in trouble.

Could it be possible that, despite Venra and Azmei being lost to them forever, Razem still viewed Arisanat that way?

"I'll never forget when you told me I wasn't allowed to marry Rija," Razem said idly. "Do you remember that? I hadn't had the first thought about marrying her until you mentioned it. Didn't want to marry anyone, for that matter. But the moment you said I couldn't—"

"You decided I needed a black eye, and you were the one to give it me," Arisanat finished dryly. He lifted his tankard in a mock salute. "I honor your courage, if not your follow-through."

Razem laughed. "To be fair, I was only twelve, and you were nearly a man."

"You were eleven," Arisanat said. "That was the time Azmei didn't come with you. In fact, it was partly because of that I thought you needed to be forbidden my sister's hand."

"Because you wanted Azmei to marry her?" Razem joked. Then he blinked and looked sadly at his tankard.

"It was just that having Azmei left behind made me realize what Father was up to," Arisanat said. He spit out his cinnamon sliver and got a fresh one to chew on. "We had such fun when she was visiting with you, but having you come alone felt more like trouble."

"Mm." Razem took a long sip of his beer. "Do you remember that time we climbed up into the foothills above the quarries and camped out?" He smiled. "We watched the falling stars all night, reflecting in that old water-filled quarry."

"First Pond," Arisanat said. "I remember." Venra and Azmei had been so excited they'd called out a wish for each star that fell, forgetting that the superstition was you couldn't tell your wish, or it wouldn't come true.

"Azmei wished for a real horse instead of a pony," Razem said. "A stallion. She wanted to train it from a colt."

Venra had wished nothing would ever change. Arisanat looked down at his tankard for a moment and tilted his head back to drain it. When he lowered his head, he saw that Razem had done the same.

"Fill up?" Razem asked, holding out his tankard.

Arisanat obliged. He hadn't realized until tonight how lonely he had been lately. He loved his sister, but she didn't share these memories the way Razem did. She was sorry for his pain, but she didn't understand it.

"Azmei always loved the old quarries," Arisanat said. "Do you remember how we taught her to swim up at First Pond?" He smiled. "She was convinced you would actually let her drown. Hadn't she just broken something of yours? She hung around my neck so tight I thought I was going to choke."

Razem laughed. "Gods, yes, she'd snapped my bow because she left it on the ground and it got trod on. Ah, I was so furious with her. We'd been planning to hunt for our supper, do you remember? Ven said the huntmaster'd taught him to build a rabbit snare, but—"

He broke off, and only then did Arisanat realize he had dropped his tankard. He scrabbled at it, but the liquid was already soaking through his trousers. He stared down at the spreading stain for a moment. Then he put the tankard to his lips and drained it.

"Well. Get some rest, Raz. We should stay camped here until the afternoon heat is past tomorrow. Rest the horses and men."

Razem sat up, looking unhappily at Arisanat. "We'll have to ride later into the evening that way."

"They'll be up for it then." Arisanat poured himself another tankard and set the pitcher on the ground. He stood carefully. "Get some rest," he repeated.

***

Razem spent the entire journey back to Tamnen City agonizing over the words he had exchanged with his father before they parted. He should have learned from his experience with Azmei. He should have held his tongue, kept his temper in check. He should have thought first of his father and only second of himself. What must Marsede be feeling as he lay injured and in pain, without his son near? Who would sit with him and watch over him and keep him company? What if Marsede died before Razem got home?

It was probably a good thing Razem had Kho's company of soldiers with him; they forced him to stop when he would have pressed on, insisting that rest was necessary for the horses as well as the men. When Razem was particularly impatient, Arisanat had reminded him that riding a horse to death would not get him to the capital any sooner, and might delay them needlessly.

Razem found himself missing Hawk's strange introspection and odd pauses before speaking. He hadn't realized before how he had grown used to the man, despite the fact Hawk had not turned out to be quite the war hero Razem had been hoping for.

No, that wasn't right. Hawk *was* a war hero. But he wasn't...well, a hawk. He didn't seem to glory in past victories or relish the thought of new ones. He seemed to yearn more for a life of peace in Rivarden than any continued involvement with the war against the Strid. What was more, it didn't seem rooted in any love of Strid that he had acquired during his time there. Razem knew there would be some who argued Hawk had been subverted during his captivity, but that was not the impression Razem had. It was just that Hawk knew the true cost of war, and deemed it too high a price to pay.

This knowledge, combined with Razem's guilt and worry over his father's health, made the ride back to Tamnen City very uncomfortable.

What would happen when he got to the palace? Would there be people in the streets, calling for justice for their king? Would everyone blame the assassination attempt on the Strid? Razem would be inclined to, except that Strid had never claimed credit for Azmei's assassination. At first he had taken that for a realization that they had crossed a line. But as the war continued, he had realized the Strid felt no shame for Azmei's death. It had not been until recently, since meeting that Strid Commander, Elin Ayowir, and spending time with Hawk, that Razem had begun to wonder if that meant, actually, that they had not had anything to do with it.

Marsede had suggested it more than once, saying there were too many things they did not know, and too many things they might never know. But Razem had never been willing to listen. And now, he thought, gulping against a sudden wash of grief, now he might never have the chance to repent and listen to his father's opinions.

The day they reached the capital, Razem had a raging headache. He had thrashed and tossed on his cushions all night, hours of sleeplessness interspersed with snatches of sleep plagued by nightmares. After the last of these nightmares, he'd got up and paced around the inside of the tent until he heard someone calling the morning waking. He'd managed to eat half a bowl of corn porridge for breakfast, but the taste of the pork diced into it had turned his stomach.

So he rode into Tamnen City with the cowl of his robe pulled low over his eyes to shield them from the sun, his memories wandering back to the debilitating headaches Azmei had had from time to time. He missed his sister desperately.

Captain Ysdra met Razem's party before they were half-way to the palace. He saluted the prince and fell in beside him, rightly assuming the prince's bearing meant he was less interested in ceremony than in reaching the palace quietly and quickly.

"Your Highness, I am very glad to see you," the man said. "Your father's condition is unchanged, and the healers have hope that he may improve once he hears of your arrival, but..."

Razem let out a breath he hadn't known he was holding. He had assumed his father still lived, since the city wasn't draped in black. But that was a very low threshold. If his father had slipped into that permanent unconsciousness that usually ended in death, that would have been kept quiet until he drew his last breath. Then again...

"That is assuming my father is no longer angry with me," Razem murmured.

"No, my lord, he has been asking for you. He says there are things he must tell you, things he cannot tell anyone but you. Your man has been sitting by him, night and day, serving the king in your absence."

"Gendo. Bless him." Razem swallowed hard. "I wish I had been here with him. It seems every choice I make lately is the wrong one." He sighed.

"Were you successful in exchanging the prisoners, your highness?"

Razem grunted. "I did manage that much. I even threw celebrations at every step of the journey between Salishok and Rivarden, though goodness knows some of the villages had little enough to celebrate with. Not to mention it slowed your people finding me." He rubbed the bridge of his nose, wishing the throbbing would subside. "Lord-General Kho has been invaluable to me. I shall require you to continue on in the capacity you have been serving here. I need Kho with me at all times. You'll brief him when we reach the palace, and then he will report back to me."

"Very good, Your Highness."

They had reached the palace grounds. As they passed inside the palace walls, the clatter of horses' hooves on flagstones echoed off the stone walls, making Razem wince. "Gods above and below, this head will overmaster me," he grumbled.

"I'll have one of the healers prepare a tisane to ease your pain, highness," Ysdra said. "Your father is resting in his bedchamber. Shall I send the tisane to you there?"

"Yes, I'll go straight to my father. I cannot rest until I see him." Razem dismounted and threw the reins to the stable boy who was waiting. "Thank you, Ysdra. I see why Kho calls you indispensable."

Ysdra flushed with pleasure and saluted.

Razem kept his cowl pulled low as he made his way through the palace to his father's bedchamber. He was grateful for the soft soles of his boots; they let him walk softly, loosening his hips and rolling his feet to keep his brain from jarring inside his skull. As soon as he had seen his father, he promised himself, he would have a hot bath.

It was a promise that would take a long time to keep.

"The king has been asking for you, highness." Gendo's eyes had dark swathes under them, and his stubbled cheeks seemed hollower than they had a few weeks ago.

Razem abandoned propriety and embraced his manservant. Gendo, a handful of years older than Razem, froze for several heartbeats before one hand tentatively came up to touch Razem's back. With a shaky breath, Razem squeezed him more tightly and then released him, straightening. He blinked fiercely, trying to keep from falling to pieces now.

"Thank you, Gen," he whispered, and brushed past him to enter his father's bedchamber.

"His highness Prince Razem, my lord," murmured a soft-voiced healer who rose from the chair by Marsede's bed. Razem's stomach flipped at the tone. He remembered that tone from his childhood. It was a soothing voice, a voice that urged you not to excite or upset the patient. It was a voice that meant your mother was going to die. Or your father?

He swallowed and threw himself into the chair the healer had vacated. His headache was forgotten as he took in the bandages wrapped around Marsede's head and the one hand that rested atop the coverlet. He barely noticed the healer slipping out of the room.

"Father. I am so sorry. I came as quickly as I could."

Marsede opened his remaining eye and looked at him. As soon as his gaze found Razem's, his lips parted in a beatific smile.

"There you are," he said. "I have been waiting for you. There is so much I must tell you."

"Father, I love you," Razem blurted. "I'm sorry I argued with you. I've been so ungrateful—"

"No, no, never mind that." Marsede's voice strengthened. His bandage-clad hand lifted and touched Razem's clumsily. "You're here now. And I love you, son. More than you will ever know." He took a series of shallow breaths.

"What can I do, father?"

"The pain will pass. The problem is with the drugs they give me to ease it." Marsede rolled his head so he could look more directly at Razem. "I fade in and out after my dose, and I cannot afford that now that you are here."

Razem tried to smile. "What do you have to tell me that can't wait?" Sleeping gods, was his father dying? Ysdra had said the healers thought he would recover. Hadn't he?

"Much of plots, and plots upon plots." Marsede closed his eye, lines marring his forehead. "And I must ask you to forgive me, Razem, for I have done you a great wrong."

"Never—" Razem began, but Marsede opened his eye and fixed him with so stern a look that he subsided.

"Do me the courtesy of believing that I understand the magnitude of my sin, Razem," he said. "I have lied to you. To all of our people. Your sister is alive."

The wind whooshed out of Razem's lungs. If he hadn't already been sitting, he would have fallen. His jaw dropped open and he stared at his father, his brain scrabbling for words but unable to grasp any. Azmei— But— "Wha— But—" he stuttered, staring.

"You must tell no one!" Marsede's grip tightened on Razem's and he pulled his torso up from the bed. "No one, Razem! Promise me!"

"Promise," Razem repeated, more because he feared his father would hurt himself than out of any agreement. But—"I don't understand."

Marsede subsided back against the bed. "It was for her safety as well as for ours. She did nearly die. Feigning her death seemed plausible. But the Ranarri Diplomat who told me about the assassination attempt also told me that she intended to go into hiding until those behind the attempt could be uncovered."

"The Strid—"

"No," Marsede's voice was heavy. "Almost certainly not. Someone here. Someone within Tamnen." His lips curved in a smile that spoke of weary exhaustion. "You see now why I could offer you no proof, but why I was so adamant."

Razem bowed his head, eyes stinging. Azmei was alive. He was stunned, but there was an edge of joy so deep it was nearly pain. He nodded. "I see now," he whispered. "Father, what a burden for you."

"Don't pity me. I saw how it destroyed you, and I still kept it from you." Marsede's voice was even. "I knew what I was doing, Razem. I am sorry."

"I forgive you." It was easy, he found. Not only because his father might be dying, but because Azmei was alive. Because Razem had done what his father had ordered and shown Hawk honor. Because his sister had done as she promised, and protected and served her father and brother.

"There is more. The man who—protected her. Tanvel of Ranarr. He is the reason I still live." Marsede panted for a moment, his face twisted into a grimace.

"Father, can't you rest—"

"*No!*" Marsede's voice was a hoarse gasp. "I don't know how long I will have to tell you all this, Razem," he whispered. "And you must know it all."

Razem nodded. "Very well, then, Father. Tell me it all."

Marsede was silent for several long breaths. Razem almost wondered if his father had lapsed into sleep before he spoke. "You know I was in the Hallowed City when they attacked?" He opened his eye and looked at Razem, who nodded. "I had only Tzen with me. The others were at the entrance to the Hallowed City. Tzen..." He trailed off. The old manservant had been with Marsede nearly forty years. Razem had grown up loving Tzen like an uncle. He realized suddenly that the man must be dead.

"Go on," he whispered.

"Four attackers. Two were Tamnese, two from the Long Coast. I had my blade, but...When they got Tzen, I...I dropped my guard. They would have killed me outright if it hadn't been for Tanvel."

"Who was Tanvel? The Ranarri?"

"Yes. The man who trained Azmei." Marsede's smile was grim. "He is a Ranarri Diplomat, but not the sort we are used to."

"There's another sort?"

"The Shadow Diplomats. Skilled assassins." Pain lanced across Marsede's face and he lifted his bandaged hand for a cup of water.

The man who trained Azmei. Trained her in what? Razem poured the water for his father and held it to his lips, lifting his head gently with his other hand. Was Princess Azmei of Tamnen now an assassin for the Ranarri?

"So it wasn't the Strid?" Razem prompted when Marsede was done drinking.

"Tanvel and Azmei had been following the trail of her would-be killers for three years." Marsede sounded stronger. "He sent Azmei to Meekin. She went to exact justice from the Perslyn Family."

"Perslyn—that's the girl who was killed in the attack against Azmei."

"Not just the girl," Marsede corrected. "The assassin. That girl traveled with Azmei to Ranarr with the express purpose of stopping the treaty. She traveled from within our own kingdom, Razem. She was hired with Tamnese gold. Hired by someone of our people who wants no peace with Strid."

"Gods," Razem blurted. "I'm lucky you didn't think it

was me."

Marsede gave him a look that expressed how patently ridiculous the statement was. "The pool of possible suspects is far too deep, I fear. But Tanvel believed he had found proof that it was one of the major Families. He sent Azmei to Meekin partly to look for the final proof of who had hired the Perslyns."

"The messengers said Captain Ysdra sent soldiers to Meekin," Razem recalled. "Do they know—"

"No." Marsede's voice was harsh. "And they must not. She travels alone, Razem, with no protection, no—" He broke off, breathing hard. "My daughter is more capable of protecting herself than I had ever dreamed, but she must not be exposed. She will be a target. As much as you are a target." He smiled faintly. "My heir."

"Father—" Razem protested, but Marsede was shaking his head.

"I am dying, son. The healers have told me the truth, though they hide it from all the world else." He coughed. "Truly, I did not need them to tell me. I can feel the poison creeping through my body. I could not feel my toes the night after the attack. A week after, I could not feel below my knees. Last week I started pissing myself because I could not even feel my manhood." His lips twisted bitterly, then his expression smoothed out and he laughed. "The gods have a strange sense of humor, even as they sleep. Very well, then. If it is meet that a king should die pissing and mewling like a babe, so be it."

He looked up at Razem, his good eye flashing with defiance—or was that triumph? "I have my son to carry on. I have my daughter alive and well in the world. And I have faith that you will carry on my work well."

Razem took his father's hand in his, cupping it gently. "Can you feel my hand?" he whispered.

"Aye, I have that yet." Marsede smiled. "The healers expect I have some days before the poison reaches my brain. They expect it will kill me then."

Razem swallowed hard to fight back a sudden scream. It was so unfair! But then life had always been unfair. It always would. And the gods slept on, unknowing or uncaring of what happened.

"Read Tanvel's papers," Marsede mumbled. "Gendo saved them."

Razem nodded. "Do you want something for the pain, father?" His head was throbbing powerfully again, and his stomach had begun spinning slowly. He wasn't sure whether he wanted to throw up or pass out. He needed his bed.

"Yes." Marsede's hand was trembling in Razem's. "And then...will you stay until I sleep?" He sounded very young.

"I promise, father. I will stay."

***

"What is this?" Arisanat asked, staring at the nondescript man rather than the folded and sealed paper the man had handed him.

He had specified their meeting place as an alley along the path from the palace to the Hallowed City. No one would be visiting the tombs right now; Razem was beside Marsede's deathbed, and there were very few others living who had passage to the Hallowed City. It had seemed a wise choice at the time, though Arisanat suddenly wished they had met at his home in the city, where he could control the situation more.

"I think you know what it is, Lord Burojan." The man's beard was thicker than it had been when they met in the north. He was dressed in light wool and cotton now, dyed a drab, light gray designed to fit in with the city. But Arisanat remembered the man well enough, and he did know what the paper was.

But damned if I will make this easy on him, he thought grimly.

"I'm afraid I don't understand," he said.

The man bowed. "Frankly, Lord Burojan, your request has become too dangerous. My master carried out your contract, but at great cost. It has become clear there is something protecting the royal family. My people are not generally a superstitious one, but my master does not believe in willful ignorance." He inclined his head. "A portion of your payment will be refunded to you, although my master must insist on keeping a death fee for the man who was killed attempting your contract, as well as the portion specified for Marsede's death."

"Marsede is not dead."

"He will be within the week," the nondescript man replied. "The poison used on the blade has no antidote on this side of the world. It is slow-acting, but very soon it will kill him." He tipped his head to one side. "My master offers his most sincere apologies that we were unable to act against Prince Razem, but he is certain your lordship will find some other means of dealing with him."

"This is untenable." Arisanat kept his voice level. He was not an unreasonable man. He had not wished to begin on this course at all, but now that he had begun it, he would finish it. "I paid for your services, and I will have results."

The man bowed again. His unfailing politeness was irritating. "I understand you completely, my lord. However, I must point out that you *have* had results—only not as complete as you wish. My master is unwilling to risk anyone else in an attempt on the prince when security is so high. The contract, therefore, is cancelled."

Arisanat went still, studying the man. He had suspected before now that "my master" was merely a cover for the fact that this nondescript man in front of him was, rather than an in-between agent, the actual contractor known as the Problem Solver. It was tempting to draw his sword and threaten the man's life, but the Problem Solver billed himself as someone who could remove obstacles of physical, monetary, political, and human attribute; he was known primarily as a negotiator, but he would of necessity be a skilled fighter. Because he was a man who traded in treachery, he would have honed his reflexes well. Because he had come bearing bad news, he would be expecting Arisanat to react in anger, perhaps even in violence.

Violence, then, would not be the wisest reaction.

"It is most unfortunate that you feel this way," Arisanat said. He looked down at the folded paper. "I am afraid that you have disappointed me, Problem Solver."

The man neither denied nor confirmed the title Arisanat gave him. He merely watched Arisanat, muddy-colored eyes keen on his face. Arisanat's temper was bubbling up in him. That always made the gold flecks in his eyes spark. Members of the royal family—even to the cousins in the First Family—had difficulty masking their temper because of those eyes. It was inconvenient, but it could be used to your advantage, if you thought ahead.

"What do you propose to do about the fact that you have disappointed me?" he asked, drawing himself subtly up to his full height. The nondescript man stood barely as tall as Arisanat's broad shoulders. The physical threat was only implied, but it was very real.

The nondescript man looked into his face and shrugged. "Nothing, I'm afraid. I'm sorry, Lord Burojan. We will do nothing to prevent you from succeeding, but neither will we aid you. Your monies will be partially refunded. Anonymously, of course. Good day."

He bowed and walked away. Arisanat stared at his back, mouth dropping open. Before he knew what he was doing, his sword was in his hand. He lunged, half expecting the man to sense him and twist to avoid the blow. Instead, the man stumbled forward as Arisanat's blade punched through his torso. He cried out, the last note garbled with liquid. Arisanat stared down at his brown fingers, clenched tightly around the ornate but serviceable hilt of his sword. The nondescript man coughed and blood sprayed through the air.

"I don't want my money," Arisanat said.

The man turned his head, staring up at Arisanat, the whites of his eyes showing around those muddy pupils. Blood trickled from the corner of his mouth. He opened his mouth wide but said nothing.

Arisanat shoved him to his knees, facing the dingy wall of the shadowed alley. The man coughed again and blood spattered against the wall, making it filthier.

"What I want," Arisanat continued, "is the prince dead. What I want is the king dead. What I want is to take my place as the proper ruler of Tamnen." He couldn't stop staring at the red coating the corner of the man's lips. It bubbled with each of the last frantic breaths the man took. "What I want is justice."

The man actually laughed, though it came out as a choked cough. "Too—late—" he gasped. And then his head slumped down to his chest. He tilted slowly, so slowly, to one side, then crashed to the dirt like a felled tree.

Arisanat slid his sword from the man's body. "Yes," he murmured, wiping it on the man's sleeve. "Far too late."

CHAPTER NINETEEN

Arisanat walked up to the front entrance of his city home, taking care to stumble as he approached. One of his guards stepped forward to meet him.

"Lord Burojan, there you are. Captain Ysdra has been—sleeping gods, what happened?"

Arisanat glanced reflexively down at his blood-stained tunic and pitched forward, bracing himself for impact if the guard were too slow. But the guard—Kadan, he thought—leapt forward, his polearm falling with a clatter to the flagstone as he dropped it to reach out for Arisanat.

"Edrono, you idiot, go for help!" he snapped at his companion, who bolted inside. "Lord Burojan, are you badly injured? Where are you hurt?"

Arisanat shook his head and then winced. "Only superficial," he said, lifting a hand to his temple to belie the words. "But I must report—I hardly know what to report." He slumped against the guard, who faltered and then bore up under his weight.

"Here, let's get you inside, my lord. We'll worry about reporting to the palace once the healers have seen you."

"I...I killed a man," Arisanat mumbled, sounding dazed. "I... Ah! My ribs..."

The guard had put an arm around his waist, trying to support him, but he jumped back when Arisanat cried out. Arisanat reached down to show where his shirt was sliced open. A shallow cut along his ribs had blood sheeting down from it.

"My lord!" the guard gasped. "I am so sorry!"

It had hurt less than Arisanat had expected to give himself the cut on his ribs. Smacking his head against the stone wall of the alley had left him with a pounding headache and slightly blurred vision, but the sword he carried was so sharp he hadn't felt the cut right away. He'd sliced longer than he'd meant to as a result, but the effect was more convincing that way, he decided. Because it hurt less than expected, he'd given himself one more cut, on the underside of his forearm, so it would look like he'd raised his arm in self-defense.

He'd waited until it was nearly dark to come stumbling back home. It gave them time to realize he was missing. When he'd planned the meeting with the Problem Solver, he'd chosen the middle of the afternoon heat so there would be fewer witnesses and everyone would think he was resting in the cool of his room.

Footsteps heralded the arrival of Edrono the guard, leading Captain Ysdra and the household healer. His chamberlain followed on their heels.

"Lord Burojan, what has happened?" the chamberlain asked. He stopped several paces away, letting the healer begin fussing over Arisanat.

"I was beset by a man wielding a sword," Arisanat mumbled. He remembered how muddled Venra had sounded once when he'd fallen from his horse and raised a huge knot on his head. He had complained of headaches for a week after, and had dizzy spells and periods of confusion for two days. For all that Arisanat was attempting to mimic that behavior, he wasn't entirely certain he hadn't inflicted the same malady on himself by accident. He had hoped for the appearance of a concussion without the symptoms, but he had been growing more unsteady all the way back from his secluded meeting spot.

"Tell me what happened," Ysdra demanded.

"I—There was a man..." Arisanat said. Venra had never been able to tell him why he fell off the horse. Arisanat, riding a spear's throw behind, had seen the horse misstep and jolt to the side. Venra had never remembered the event. He had only known he fell because he found himself on the ground.

"Yes, a man," Ysdra repeated. "With a sword, you said."

Arisanat nodded and then regretted it. "A sword. He shouted something, I think. But I—" He lifted his off hand, pretending not to realize his arm was bleeding. "I stopped—

I—I *killed* him."

It had been shockingly easy. Perhaps the man had not been the Problem Solver after all. But even so, the idea of killing *any* man would not have occurred to the Arisanat of five years ago. Something had changed in him. Perhaps he was becoming a monster.

"You defended yourself," Ysdra said, and Arisanat felt a flash of triumph. He looked down, hoping he had hidden it well enough. By pretending to feel guilty over the man's death, he had set Ysdra up to defend him—and Ysdra had taken the bait perfectly.

"I...I suppose. But if only I had been..." He trailed off, trying to sound confused.

"Do you know what direction you just came from?" Ysdra asked. "Guards, did you see which way he came?"

Arisanat suppressed his instinctive irritation. A moment later he was glad he had, as the healer retorted, "Give him space, captain. Have you never had a concussion? He probably can't remember anything."

"Begging your pardon, Captain Ysdra," said Edrono, "but we saw him approach from the south, but where he'd been before that was anyone's guess."

Ysdra sighed. "I suppose so. All the same, I must send squads of guards out to patrol. We must make certain there are no other attackers lingering in the shadows."

"Do you remember if he said anything when he attacked, my lord?" the chamberlain asked.

Arisanat flinched. One of the healers had prodded his ribs, which woke an answering pain. "I—I—no, I'm afraid not. I am so sorry."

"Never mind," the chamberlain said. "It may not signify."

"Or it might tell us why Lord Burojan was attacked," Ysdra said. "Why would anyone wish to harm him? Are there more assassination plots afoot? There has already been one attack on the king."

Arisanat shook his head and then winced again, playing up the expression. "I...I don't understand. I have no enemies that I know of."

"Perhaps someone mistook my lord for someone else," the first guard said.

"It could be," Ysdra said dubiously.

"I...well, I have been told my cousin and I resemble one another," Arisanat said. This was the part of his plan he was least certain of. Would they believe the scenario he was trying to convince them of? "Perhaps...Does everyone know the prince has returned?"

Ysdra's head snapped up. "You think the attack on the king was part of a two-pronged strategy? It's possible. There was no secret that the prince was returning." He cupped a hand against his chin, musing aloud. "Yes. It seems entirely plausible the attack could have been meant for the prince." He looked deeply unhappy at this thought. "I must warn General Kho to have more soldiers to protect Prince Razem. Even now he could—" He broke off and shook his head. "I must return to the palace. In the meantime, we must keep Lord Burojan in the mansion, under guard, until we are certain he is safe."

Arisanat's eyes flew open. Ysdra had just turned this into a house arrest! And all without accusing Arisanat of anything—or indeed, even suspecting him, as far as Arisanat could tell. "What? Why?" he spat. He could hardly protest measures taken for his own safety, but it rankled to think of being cooped up at home. And yet...perhaps he could turn this to his advantage.

"I swore an oath, Lord Burojan." Ysdra's voice was mild, his eyes gentle as he looked at Arisanat. Arisanat blinked, watching his vision fuzz out of focus and wishing he could read the other man's expression better. "To protect every citizen of Tamnen from harm, as best I am able, lowborn or high. I can hardly fail to keep that oath when it is the king's cousin who is in danger."

Arisanat closed his eyes. "Perhaps you are right. I...I must..."

"You must rest," the healer broke in. "That's quite

enough of your interrogation, captain. You see to your duties and let me see to mine."

"Very well." Ysdra didn't sound happy. "I will be back on the morrow, Lord Burojan."

Arisanat ignored him.

***

Captain Ysdra did return the next day, bearing well wishes from Prince Razem. Arisanat had carefully remembered a few additional details for Ysdra, but he remained frustratingly vague about the most important details. He was biting back a smirk by the time Ysdra left. The captain asked competent questions, but since Arisanat had no answers, he was no further in solving the mystery of the attack when he left.

After Ysdra came Lady Talt of the Seventh Family. Arisanat had been scrupulous about avoiding Lady Talt, since she had two unmarried daughters she had been shopping around to every nobleman above the age of twelve. When the chamberlain announced Arisanat's visitor, he almost had the man turn Talt away despite his plot.

Remember the end goal, he reminded himself. *Besides, the girls aren't so objectionable—just their mother. And Talt can't live forever.* He pasted on a vague smile and gestured for the chamberlain to show her in.

"Oh, Lord Burojan!" she exclaimed as she bustled in. "The gods should smite whoever had the nerve to attack you!"

He winced at the piercing quality of her voice—his headache was, unfortunately, still quite unfeigned—but quickly repaired the smile. "Lady Talt. What a kind soul you are. I should not wish to be indelicate, but..." He coughed faintly. "I fear I myself was the gods' instrument in smiting him."

"Were you indeed?" she cooed, settling down in the chair across from his. "How brave of you. You must tell me everything!"

"Alas, I bumped my head in the struggle." He tilted his

head so she could more clearly see his bandaged temple. "I remember little of the actual attack. I know only that I was going to pay my respects to the memory of my dear cousins in the Hallowed City." He paused. "I remember him jumping at me with his blade drawn—" He shrugged, hoping his expression was modest rather than pleased. "—and nothing else until I realized I was standing over a dead man with my own sword blooded."

Talt gasped and leaned forward. "How thrilling! I am glad you were not worse hurt. But how dreadful that you were hurt at all. And how lonely you must be, that your wife is no longer here to care for you in your time of need."

And now they came to it. It had been at least a year since he saw the daughters. As far as he knew they were both still unmarried. If that were so, which of them would be preferable? Arisanat turned his lips down and bowed his head. "I confess that I have felt the lack keenly," he murmured. "Would it be unseemly, do you think, for me to consider remarrying?"

"Goodness, you've been faithful to her memory long enough," Talt said. "It must be...seven years since she died?"

"Six," Arisanat said. "Thank the gods for our boy, or I would not have had the luxury to mourn her so long. And yet..." He allowed himself to trail off.

"And yet you find you are lonely at times," Talt supplied. "Lonely for adult companionship, perhaps?"

"You understand me so well, Lady Talt."

She tittered. "Oh, Lord Burojan, I hope you aren't thinking of me! I am far too concerned with seeing my daughters settled happily."

Arisanat smiled to hide his revulsion. Talt was not a stupid woman, but she was not a pleasant one, either. He would let the Strid take him before he married Talt. "If you insist. But I am certain you must know some young woman who would be suitable. Someone who would not mind caring for my first-born and seeing him inherit rather than her own children."

Talt made a show of thinking, tipping her head to one side. "It is a hard thing to ask of a woman," she ventured. "You might want someone young, indeed. Someone with many more childbearing years ahead of her, so she could devote her attention first to raising the boy. How old is he?"

"Eight, and a clever lad," Arisanat said, letting his pride creep into his voice. "He takes after his mother in that respect, though I hope to leave him better off than I myself am."

"Do we not all hope to better our children's situations?" Talt said. "And yet you have much to offer a young lady of quality, First Family as you are."

Arisanat took in a deep breath. All pretense of concussion-induced vagueness had long since vanished. He hoped he had judged her correctly. She was desperate to marry her daughters. Having failed to catch a prince, perhaps she would settle for the man who killed said prince.

"Would that I could offer her a queenship," he lamented.

Lady Talt paused, staring at him. The silence dragged on between them. Arisanat could feel his heart thudding in his chest and wondered if she could hear it. Then Talt smiled, a small smile with teeth. "Oh, my Lord Arisanat, I am certain you can do just that."

When she left half an hour later, Arisanat had Talt's full support of his coup, including a promise to lend house guards to his own troops, provided he take the younger daughter Tarra to wife and raise her to queen beside him. It was a stretch, marrying a girl of the Seventh Family, but the last queen had been from the Fifth Family, after all, and Arisanat had bigger risks ahead of him than marrying low.

***

The king's bedchamber had become a sickroom. Razem's hair itched from nightmare sweat and travel dust. His chin prickled with a week of unshaven beard. Soon Gendo would come in and urge him to eat something, to try to rest. Razem would resist until Kho had reported, though. Last night he had agreed to rest until Kho arrived, then Gendo had refused to wake him. Razem had to know if Kho was getting anywhere with the information Azmei's assassin trainer had left behind. Marsede would ask the next time he woke, and Razem had nothing to tell him.

He raked his fingernails through his hair and bowed his head.

His whole body ached with a yearning for something—but what, he couldn't have said. What could he possibly wish for that would make this situation tenable? What miracle would return his father to vitality? What magic could send Razem back in time to stop the assassin's dagger, to prevent Azmei's ever leaving Tamnen City? Would even that be enough? Or had the gods themselves dreamt up this torture as they slept on?

Someone tapped on the door. Razem looked up, relieved to hear something besides the wet rasp of the king's breath. "Come."

Emran Kho eased into the room, the door opening just wide enough to admit him. "Highness."

Razem nodded and stood creakily. He looked down at his father. Marsede had been unconscious most of the day, rousing once to cough and once to apologize to Razem for failing to place flowers on Queen Izbel's grave before the attack. He would not miss Razem for the few minutes it would take Kho to report. With a sigh, Razem followed Kho out of the room.

Out in the antechamber, the air wasn't as thick and still. Gendo stood nearby with a meat pie and a steaming cup. As soon as Razem appeared, Gendo held them out. Razem took the meat pie and sat down.

"It's too stifling for a hot drink," he said.

"Spiced wine, highness," Gendo said. His voice was soft, his gaze on the cup rather than meeting Razem's. Razem took the cup.

"Report," he told Kho before biting into the meat pie.

Kho waved off Gendo's offer of a drink. "I have only

finished reading the first two volumes of the Ranarri's journal. It deals much with the princess. I believe your sister would best you at swords now, highness."

Razem didn't know whether to laugh or cry. He swallowed his food and followed it with a long sip of wine. His father had not wanted him to tell anyone about Azmei, but Razem didn't have the concentration to read through the man's accounts, and Kho would have discovered the fact of the princess' survival anyway. It had been a relief to see the shock and joy that spread across Kho's face when Razem told him. At least the lord-general hadn't known before him.

"Tanvel and Azmei spent long months tracking down those in Ranarr who had been part of Orya Perslyn's plot. The Ranarri Shadow Council rooted out all offshoots of the family on the White Stone. While they did that, Tanvel apprentice traveled as part of a contingent to Strid."

"What?"

"He records it as a legitimate assignment, where he was along only as a last resort. But he pursued any trace of Perslyn conspiracy while he was there, and found nothing linking Strid to the attack on the princess. I have gone no further, but I am giving you only the bare sketch. I have made extensive notes from his journal." Kho reached toward his belt as if to draw out his papers.

"Unnecessary. I'll read them later." Razem locked gazes with Kho. *Later*, Kho's dark gaze said, *when your father is dead*. And Razem's golden one, he knew, did not deny it.

"Yes, highness. There is more."

Razem took another gulp of his wine and glanced at the disheveled pile of cushions he had been attempting to sleep on for the past week. He could taste the spices that were intended to help him sleep. Perhaps they would tonight. "Go on."

"A courier has arrived from Meekin. The troops Captain Ysdra sent to arrest the Perslyns were a bit late." Kho shuffled his feet. "Someone had already slain the Perslyn Patriarch, one Karsch Perslyn. He had been slain several weeks before, and was already burned and mourned. He had four grandchildren—Rith, Kesh, Orya, and Yarro."

"Orya!" A jolt of heat blasted through Razem's body. The villainous woman who had tried to kill his sister.

Kho nodded. "Rith was slain the night after Karsch, presumably by the same person. Kesh openly admitted he was the new Patriarch when our troops arrived to arrest them. The last grandchild, Yarro, is missing, but he's said to be a half-wit. Everyone swore the boy was uninvolved in the rest of the family's mess. Our troops have secured the house and are searching the records."

"None of this is important," Razem snapped. Raising his voice drained what energy he had left. He crammed the rest of his meat pie into his mouth and lowered his gaze.

"There was no sign of Princess Azmei."

That was what Razem had dreaded hearing. The words settled on his shoulders like a heavy blanket. He nodded without looking up.

Silence fell over the antechamber. His report exhausted, Kho could have excused himself, but he stood, waiting for Razem to say something. What, Razem had no idea. What could he have to say? His father was dying. His dead sister was returned to life, but missing. The identity of his strongest foe was still a mystery to him. And his country was slowly losing a war that his sister and father had both risked their lives to end.

Razem drained his cup. "Thank you, Emran." His voice sounded as hollow as he felt.

Kho's hand settled on his shoulder and squeezed gently. They froze like that, Razem grateful for the strength Kho lent him. After a moment, Razem drew in a breath and stood. Kho's hand fell away and he withdrew.

Dusk was closing in. Through the open door to the bedchamber, Razem could see Gendo lighting a lamp by the window. Razem pushed away from the wall. When had he leaned against it? He set his empty cup on a side table and went back into the sickroom.

"You should rest, highness," Gendo murmured.

"I'll sit with him until I get sleepy." Razem was crossing the room to his chair when the king began to convulse.

Razem lunged for the bed. "Father!" Behind him, he heard Gendo calling for a healer. "Father!" He cradled Marsede's head, tipping his chin the way the healers had shown to give him more air.

The king's entire body was contorted in torment. His eyes were still closed. A ribbon of drool slipped from one corner of his mouth onto Razem's wrist.

"Father!"

The healers arrived then, easing the king out of Razem's arms, easing Razem away as they tended to their failing ruler. When they withdrew, one remained. Her eyes had a liquid shine to them as she took up a position under the lamp.

"Father?" Razem breathed.

His father's chest moved. Marsede still lived. Razem dropped limply into his chair, which was scooted up as close to the bed as it could go. The king's chin glistened with drool. He opened his eyes.

"Razem," he slurred.

"I'm here, Father," Razem choked. He moved until he was in Marsede's line of vision.

The king's gaze cleared. "Find Azmei," he mumbled. "Tell her...she is...forgiven."

Razem nodded. "I will. I promise. She's already done so much to protect us." He forced the corners of his mouth up in an attempt at a smile. "I forgive you, Father. You know that, don't you?"

Marsede didn't answer. His breathing was faster and shallower than ever. He closed his eyes. Razem leaned closer, holding his breath as if it would lend his father's laboring lungs air.

"I love you, son," Marsede whispered. He exhaled.

He did not inhale.

Razem counted thirty heartbeats, then sixty, before he realized he should cry.

He should weep and wail as the gossip said Hawk had done upon hearing the news of the attack. He should rail against the gods and scream vengeance on those who had killed his father. But instead he felt mostly tired, and just a little relieved. The past week of watching his father lose control of his bladder and bowels, seeing him unable even to lift a hand to scratch his nose, hearing his breath shudder and rasp...

No, this was best. It was a release.

Razem buried his face against his father's too-still chest and howled.

Some time later.

How much later? Razem wasn't sure.

His nose dribbled snot into his week's growth of beard. His eyes felt full of sand. His lungs kept surprising him with sobs.

"My lord. My lord." A soft voice, gentle but firm. Kho. "Majesty."

Razem took in a long breath and looked over at the general. Kho's cheeks glistened with tears.

"King Marsede is dead." Kho's throat bobbed as he swallowed. "May King Razem rule long in his stead."

Razem dragged himself to his feet. His chest felt like it had a chain wrapped around it. "Make the arrangements, Emran," he rasped. "Do...everything." He waved a hand. "Whatever is needed."

Gendo helped him, stumbling, down the passage to his own quarters, where his bed and a glass of hot whiskey awaited him. As the new king reached his bed, he heard the city's mourning bells begin to toll.

CHAPTER TWENTY

"Ow! Don't poke at it," Yarro whimpered.

Azmei rolled her eyes. "If you'd been paying attention to where you were going, you wouldn't have hurt yourself," she said. "As it is, it has to be cleaned, or the wound will go bad. That will give you a fever and we'll have to stop traveling until you recover." She rocked back on her heels. "Trust me, that's definitely worse than me poking a bit at the cut."

Yarro glowered at his leg, which was still oozing blood from the deep gash in his calf. "Fine."

"Press the cloth against it again." With a nod, Azmei stood and went back to Sandy, where her kit of medical supplies and poisons was stowed in one of the packs behind her saddle. She picked through the ointments and tisanes for the Woundclot and Feverbane. There were squares of soft cloth for cleaning and bandaging. As an afterthought, she grabbed the needle and sinew just in case. The gash didn't look deep, but it was wide. A few stitches would hold it closed and help it heal faster, if Yarro would let her sew it.

His eyes widened when he saw the needle, but Azmei had to adjust her opinion of his courage as he closed his teeth on his lower lip and visibly steeled himself. "Does it need that?" he asked, his voice hushed.

"I don't know. Maybe." Azmei knelt next to him. "Let me see it. I'll be able to say for sure once I see it without the blood."

Yarro took his cloth away. Instead of looking at the gash, he kept his eyes on Azmei's face. "I don't like blood," he muttered.

"Really? Why?" Azmei poured a bit of Feverbane on her cloth and dabbed gently at the gash. The bleeding had stopped, at least, so she could get a good look at the cut. It was wide, but the edges weren't too jagged. She thought a few stitches would be better for it.

"I cut myself once. I was little." He held out his hand, palm up, so she could see the thick scar that ran from the heel of his hand down his forearm. "Orya scolded me for being careless. She said I could have died."

"Goodness." Azmei inspected the scar, then turned her attention back to her work. "You must have been very brave."

He was silent for a moment. "I've never thought of myself as brave."

"Really?" She looked at him with exaggerated surprise. "But you left home, all by yourself. That's brave."

"Is it?" He smiled at her. "I was only brave by accident. I had to leave. I didn't think about it being brave." Then he seemed to realize he was actually looking her in the face. He ducked his head and looked back down at his scar, tracing it with one finger.

"You had to leave? Why is that?" Azmei concentrated on threading the sinew through the needle's eye. Hopefully her off-hand attitude and the distracting stitching would make him forget that she had already asked him this question once. She pinched the edges of the gash together and made the first stitch.

"Ow. Things were bad at my house. My grandfather and brothers aren't good men." He frowned. "It was fine while Orya was alive. She was my favorite person."

He paused, so Azmei said, "I remember you telling me that." She took the next stitch.

"But ever since she died, it's been worse." He sighed. "My brothers are ambitious. Not nice at all." He paused. "Well, one of them is all right. He doesn't call me a freak the way the other brother does."

"Neither of them should call you a freak," Azmei stuck the tip of her tongue between her teeth and pinched the edges closer for the third stitch. "Brothers may tease, but they should never belittle."

"Do you have a brother?"

His question, asked so innocently, made her catch her breath. She froze her needle hand, afraid it would tremble. "Yes," she whispered. She cleared her throat in an effort to speak more naturally. "Yes. And he was my dearest friend. My favorite person," she added, smiling crookedly. "But I haven't seen him in a long time."

"I'm sorry," he blurted. "You don't have to talk about him."

Azmei took a slow breath and shook her head. "I don't mind. He's older than I am, and the last time I saw him, he was going to the war. He has many duties."

"Are we going towards the war, or away from it?"

She glanced up at him in surprise. "Don't you know?" When he shook his head, she looked down and checked to be sure her hand hadn't slipped, then took the next stitch. "The war is for the Kreyden District. Rivarden is one of the cities in the Kreyden. The battle front is further south now, beyond the Salishok River, but we are heading towards the war."

"Oh." He fell silent. Azmei didn't mind, since her thoughts were tugging back towards Razem. She wondered what her brother was doing right now. Had Master Tanvel's fears proven well-founded? Perhaps Tanvel had spoken to Razem since she left Tamnen City. Perhaps he would be able to tell her how her brother was doing, if they ever met again.

If they ever met again. She took another breath and held it. She had been able to push out of her thoughts the idea that Tanvel had stayed in Tamnen City to sacrifice himself for her father. It didn't seem right, even though she knew Tanvel believed his life was worth the most if he spent it in service of someone else. Ranarri Diplomats, whether they were of the Shadow Council or those who served in the daylight, did not fear their deaths if they could serve the purpose of peace in dying.

She finished sewing Yarro's injury and then looked up at

him. He was staring blankly at the air near her left shoulder. His lower lip was caught between his teeth and his eyes seemed unfocused. As she watched, his pupils dilated and darted to stare at something to her right without focusing. He didn't move his head. Her flesh crept up in bumps at the absent quality of his gaze.

"Are you all right?" she asked.

Her words fell on deaf ears. His gaze flitted up and then back down as his breathing quickened. Azmei glanced over her shoulder, but saw nothing that would have caught his attention. She looked back at Yarro. He had squeezed his eyes shut and was shaking his head.

"Yarro," she said, raising her voice. "Are you all right?"

He jumped, eyes flying open. "No!"

She leaned back, staring at him. "Did I hurt you?"

"What?" He blinked a few times. "What? Oh." He shook his head and began rocking slightly in place, forward and backward. She wasn't sure if he knew he was doing it. "Oh."

"Yarro," she repeated, concerned.

"It's all right," he said. "I'm all right. Did you finish sewing it?" He looked down at his leg and stopped rocking.

"I did." Azmei looked down at it, too. Perhaps it was best to ignore whatever had just happened. "Let me cut the sinew. Then I'll put some Feverbane on it and bandage it. As long as you keep it clean and we keep an eye on it, I think it should heal well."

"Good." Yarro frowned, but he seemed more thoughtful than unhappy. "Aevver, do you know how to fight with all those knives?"

She blinked. All those knives? She only wore two openly, and she didn't think that quite qualified to be called "all those knives." How did he know about the others?

"I do know how to fight," she said, choosing not to comment on the number. "You shouldn't carry a blade if you don't know how to use it. Otherwise you're just asking someone to take it from you."

"Really?" He looked up at her face, startled eyes wide.

Then he dropped his gaze again. "I didn't know that."

She could almost see him filing the information away for later reflection. It made her want to smile. He was a strange boy, but she liked him. It made her angry that his brothers called him a freak. She understood why Orya had thought him special, even though she'd lied when she claimed he was all but deaf and dumb. There was something innocent about him, but he was clever, and canny enough in some ways.

"Let me finish this," she repeated, and drew her sharpest knife to neatly slice the sinew.

When she tied the bandage in place, she wiped the blood from her hands and smiled at him. "There now. Let's get some food in you, to build back some of that blood you lost. You were very brave, Yarro."

He smiled at her, and the beauty of his smile made her chest ache. How had this boy grown up in the company of hardened assassins? Orya must have cared for him as she cared for no one else, if he had somehow grown up so innocent. "Thank you, Aevver."

She patted his shoulder, then regretted it as he flinched. "Rest here. I'll get the food." He didn't like being touched, she reminded herself. She'd allowed herself to forget, since he'd let her touch him to treat the wound. But he'd had little choice in that matter. Just because he bore the necessity with dignity didn't give her leave to touch him more familiarly afterwards.

After that lecture you gave him about women's bodies belonging to themselves, you should have given him the same courtesy, she reminded herself, and decided to spend more time than necessary getting the food out of the packs. It would give him a minute alone.

∗∗∗

Yarro looked down at the neat stitches on his calf. The gash hurt, but it could have been much worse. If he'd cut himself when he was alone, he probably would have panicked and forgotten that you were supposed to press on the wound to staunch the blood flow. He had hated the sight and stench of blood since the injury he'd told Aevver about.

YOU CAN'T TRUST HER, whispered one of the Voices. He didn't recognize that one.

But I want to trust her, he thought back. *She's been kind to me, mostly. And she knows a lot.*

SHE IS USEFUL, agreed the Wise Uncle Voice. BUT SHE CARRIES SECRETS WITH HER THAT I CANNOT PENETRATE.

What does that even mean? Yarro wondered. *Doesn't everyone have secrets? Can you penetrate everyone's secrets? Or just mine? I didn't think anyone else could hear you.*

MOST CANNOT, THAT IS TRUE. NEARLY ALL ARE DEAF TO US. BUT MOST ARE NOT OPAQUE TO US AS SHE IS. USUALLY WE CAN PERCIEVE MUCH OF A HUMAN'S MIND, EVEN IF THAT MIND IS NOT AWARE OF US. YET SHE KEEPS HER SECRETS CLOSE.

What does it matter? Yarro rocked back and forth, wishing he could curl up in his blankets and not move while the Voices spoke to him. *Eventually you will figure out her secrets. Until then, she's helping me. She's nice to me.* He paused, hesitant to admit the truth to himself, let alone to the Voices. *I like her.*

The Voices rose in a clamor amongst themselves, and Yarro couldn't discern what any individual Voice was saying. He closed his eyes and rocked, taking comfort in the motion, the predictability. It was often an unconscious motion, but not always. Finally the Voices fell silent. Maybe they had reached an agreement. Maybe they had cut him off. They did that sometimes, he thought.

VERY WELL, said the Wise Uncle Voice at last. SHE IS USEFUL TO YOU. BRING HER TO US, BUT WATCH HER. BE CAREFUL OF HER UNTIL YOU KNOW HER SECRETS.

Yarro shrugged. Of course he was watching her. Just because he liked her didn't mean he trusted her. For the most part, he liked Kesh, after all, and he had never fully trusted

Kesh. Come to think of it, he had liked Orya—loved Orya—and yet she had gone away from him. He didn't trust Orya anymore, either. Aevver would be just one more person he liked but didn't trust.

"Yarro, are you all right? Does your leg hurt?" Aevver's voice was concerned, and very near.

He opened his eyes. "Not very much, but it does hurt. I was just thinking."

She crouched in front of him, her face turned towards him but her gaze not on his. It occurred to Yarro that she had realized he didn't like making eye contact with people, and she was adapting. She was trying to make him more comfortable. A surge of liking rushed through him and he had to keep from smiling. He didn't care what the Voices said. Sometimes they were wrong. They were wrong about eating Grandfather. They were wrong about other things. Sometimes.

"I hear Voices," he blurted. "I don't know who They are, but They talk to me a lot." He stopped rocking and looked at her knee instead of her face. "They say you have secrets, but that's all right. I have secrets too. I kept the Voices secret from you." He glanced up briefly, just enough to meet her gaze and flick away again. "I keep the Voices secret from everyone."

Aevver was silent for so long Yarro decided she must not believe him. He started rocking in place again, wondering if she would abandon him if she thought he was lying to her. Maybe she thought he was making fun of her. Wouldn't that be the silliest thing—if the boy who had grown up being called a freak made fun of others? But she might think he was.

"Thank you for trusting me," Aevver said finally. Her voice was very soft. "Did your sister Orya know about Them?"

Yarro nodded. He was tired of talking. At least she seemed to believe him. But he didn't want to explain about why he was following the Voices and where They were leading him.

Aevver nodded back and stood. "Now I'll know not to interrupt when They are talking," she said. "Come, let's ride a bit further today, all right? We should be in Rivarden in a couple of days. We'll get rooms at an inn and give your leg time to heal."

Without another word, she went back to her horse and started putting the medical supplies back in her pack. Yarro stood, testing his weight on the leg, and deciding it wasn't too bad. He limped over to Firefoot, who knelt to help him scramble up.

As soon as he was in the saddle, his calf began to throb. Yarro shifted in place for several minutes before Aevver realized what the problem was and called a halt.

"Of course, the blood's probably pooling in your leg, like that," she mused, studying him. "Tell you what, let's see if we can prop that leg up some. I know you won't want to ride double with me, so we'll have to get you balanced somehow."

He managed not to shudder at the idea of being pressed against her for however long they rode. It was just another reason he had never told Tish how he felt about her. The thought of touching her wasn't too bad, but the thought of her touching him didn't appeal to him at all. No one would ever want to be in love with him if they couldn't touch him. He fought down a sudden wave of despair and twisted around to watch Aevver taking her bedroll off her horse. She carried it over to him and lashed it on top of his. He didn't see what she did with the ropes and straps, but after a few minutes, she had made a prop for him to lean against while he rested his injured leg across the pommel of the saddle. It wasn't very comfortable, but it was better than letting the leg hang.

"Thank you," Yarro mumbled.

Aevver smiled up at him, her gaze open. "You're welcome, Yarro. Let's see if you can stand to ride an hour or so like that, all right? I promise we'll stop early tonight."

***

It was almost a relief to be leaving Rivarden, Hawk thought. He let his horse pick his own way through the morning crowd. He was running his gaze along the buildings and streets that he used to know. Rivarden was both painfully different and hauntingly familiar. Governor Tarkor did his best to feed the refugees and war orphans, but there were so many, and the food supply only stretched so far. Yet there were still plenty of cocky soldiers on leave, mercenaries looking for the next quick gold, and mine workers in town on rotation.

He shook his head and guided his black gelding towards the gate, the pack horse trailing them. The Diamond Gate had been fortified almost beyond recognition, but he supposed that was better than being sealed up entirely. The guards came to attention as he approached. Most of the traffic so far had been streaming into the city, and it was rare for a traveler to go north on foot. Most took a canal boat up the Kreyden Capital Canal. Hawk could tell the guards were looking forward to a chat about his business, but one look at the royal seal he carried and they went silent. They exchanged a look and the officer waved him through. Hawk gave them a polite smile. No use flaunting his status.

The first few miles went by quickly as Hawk relished his first taste of true solitude in years. Oh, he had often been alone in his cell, but that had never been under his control. It could be forced on him or ripped away at a moment's whim. And while Commander Ayowir had never been cruel, she had not always noticed what her underlings did. Even when Hawk was free again, he had almost always had someone around, either giving orders or asking something of him. Even the ever-present servants had begun to grate on his nerves.

But now, out here in the desert north of the city, Hawk and his horses were truly alone. While he was traveling at the prince's command, he took no one with him, and that was Hawk's choice, no one else's. He put his head back, sniffing at the air, and laughed.

Hawk estimated they had covered fifteen miles when he decided to stop for lunch. When he had been in fighting trim, he'd been able to ride all day and eat in the saddle, but on the ride from Salishok he had noticed that his leg ached if he pushed it too hard. Better to take a break for lunch. He loosened the black's girth and wandered around the small hollow he'd chosen. A few scrubby bushes spoke of the presence of moisture underground, while a pile of rocks twenty feet away hinted deceptively at a spring. Hawk checked and found no spring, but he had plenty of water in his skins.

He alternated bites of dried meat and figs as he paced around the hollow. There wasn't much moisture in the figs, but it tempered the salt of the meat. He would have a better supper, but he was a warrior, used to common fare. At least, he had been. *What am I now? A warrior who lost his war? A king's man who might lose his king?* He shook the thoughts aside and fished another strip of meat out of his pack.

That was when the bandits struck.

A woman with the coloration of a half-blood came at him from behind the cluster of rocks, three ragged swordsmen behind her. Hawk dropped his meat and drew Talon, spinning—but there was a one-eyed man approaching from that side, leading three more bandits. He drew Claw as well and set himself at an angle, watching them both.

"What do you want? I haven't much gold." And he didn't want to part with any of it, but if paying them would avert a fight, he would do it. Eight on one odds might have been manageable when he was at the peak of his fighting condition. It was a ridiculous notion now, with only a few weeks of honing his skills again, not to mention the bad leg.

"We've already been paid, mate," said the one-eyed man. "Someone really wants you dead." As he spoke, the woman attacked, but Hawk had been careful to split his attention. He pivoted, blocking her thrust and pushing it away. The man behind her wasn't as skilled as she was. Hawk's blade tore open his throat. He dropped his sword and clutched at the wound, gurgling. A moment later he dropped to the ground. *Dead,* Hawk tallied, and used Claw to block the woman's next attack.

Not good, Hawk realized. Someone wanted him dead.

This would be a fight to the death, whether he wanted it or not, and if he didn't get the upper hand quickly, he might as well surrender and let them execute him.

He flung Claw at the next attacker in the woman's group. It took the man in the stomach. Not where Hawk had been aiming, but it would do. The man dropped to his knees, screaming. Hawk darted away from the woman, who was coming after him again. He kicked the injured man over and stomped hard on the man's knee. He dragged the bloody dagger out of the man's gut, gratified when the man's scream rose in pitch, and spun to face the woman again. She was the greater danger, he judged, than the last of the bandits who had followed her into battle.

"Lail! Be careful!" the one-eyed man shouted. "He didn't say the bastard was an assassin!"

Hawk bared his teeth at them. "I'm not an assassin. I'm a war hero." Gods, he sounded so puffed up and ridiculous. No wonder the woman laughed.

"War Hero or mine slave, I don't care. We were paid to kill him, and we will," she retorted. "Benn! Get in here!"

Damn. Hawk had hoped the man would hang back to cut off his retreat. That was over. Hawk lunged at the last of the woman's support attackers. The man backpedaled and tripped over his own feet. He didn't go down, but it gave Hawk time to close. He punched Claw through the man's chest. The man dropped, dead and silent.

The woman swore. Hawk pivoted on his bad leg to face her. The leg didn't give, but a spike of pain shot up his thigh. It made him gasp and struggle for balance. In that instant, the woman darted in, her short sword slashing through Hawk's sleeve and into his bicep.

Hawk fell back a step. No one was blocking his retreat in that direction, but if he abandoned his horses and water skins out here, he was a dead man anyway. He raised both blades and dropped into a light crouch, transferring his weight to the balls of his feet. He'd slain two of their folk and seriously injured a third. It wouldn't be enough to make them back down, but at least it had evened the odds a bit. The one-eyed man was circling around him, his three swordsmen spreading out in a spaced line.

"We don't have to do this," Hawk said. "I don't know you. I won't seek retribution if you turn around and leave now."

The woman—Lail, the man had called her—laughed. "Retribution? That's a good one, since it's the crown that ordered you dead. Who would take revenge on the crown?"

The crown? Hawk checked his stance and footing. Why would Razem have ordered him killed by bandits? It would have been much easier to simply have him executed. They wouldn't have traded the Deranged Duke for him if they'd wanted him dead. Not Razem, then, and not Marsede.

"You've been deceived," he said. He shifted around, watching the one-eyed man as he circled.

"Maybe, but we've been paid, too," said Lail. "And we're no thieves. We took payment. Now you're going to die."

"I've already killed three of you!" Hawk snapped.

"Two at best, and you're wounded," Lail countered. "Even so, I'd make it quick if you surrender now."

"To the hells with you," Hawk said, and lunged at her.

The one-eyed man attacked at the same time, but he was slow. It was clear the woman was the leader of this group. Take her out and the others might crumble. Hawk swung at her. She managed to block, but she fell back a step. He swung again and she stood firm, but a third swing forced her back another step.

Hawk met the one-eyed man's swing with Claw and pushed him back. His bad leg twinged as he did. It might not hold much longer. He'd better make this quick.

He swung at Lail again, and her block was just a shade too slow. Talon ripped through her throat. She stared at him, reeling backwards. She managed one more swing that opened a cut on his wrist. Then she fell hard into the sand.

"Laaaaaailll!" the one-eyed man screamed. He charged at Hawk.

***

Azmei eased her gelding to a stop. "What was that?" She'd thought she heard shouting a minute ago, but now she was certain. Someone had just screamed in agony. A man.

Yarro jerked upright. "Aevver, help!"

She urged the gelding around. "Is it your leg?" He'd done all right yesterday, but she could tell it was hurting him by the time they made camp. She'd drugged him to the gills last night, and this morning she'd laced a bit of easeall into his tea. She knew he couldn't be comfortable, though.

"Yarro?"

Firefoot was still walking, Yarro sitting atop him like a lump. Azmei guided Sandy back to the bigger horse, wondering if she would have to catch Yarro. "Yarro, are you all right?" she asked. "Is it your leg?"

"Help him—help the other person," he gasped. He bent down over the pommel.

"The other—that man who shouted? Like hells! I'm trying to keep you safe, not pick fights that aren't mine!"

He lifted his head slowly. It was a gesture very unlike Yarro, and sent chills down Azmei's legs. His eyes were blank, staring past her. His mouth was slack.

He'd said these were visions, but to Azmei they looked more like fits.

She cleared her throat. He wouldn't answer her, not if he was like this. She tried to bring Sandy alongside Firefoot, but the bay stallion sidled away. Yarro turned his face towards her.

"This *is* our fight." His voice was hollow, distant. She didn't like it. "Help him, Aevver."

Azmei stared at him. He couldn't mean it. The clash of blade against blade met their ears. That was a fight, no mistaking, and if Azmei got herself involved, there would be questions asked that she couldn't afford to answer.

But he'd said they were visions. He said they told him things. What if they were telling him this?

Azmei swore and pulled Sandy around towards the shouting.

Just then another voice screamed. "Laaaaaaillll!" There was grief in that voice as well as rage. It didn't bode well for whoever Lail was—or whoever had hurt Lail. Azmei swore again and closed her legs around Sandy's sides. He leapt into a gallop.

They probably wouldn't hear her coming. Their fight would be making too much noise. But there was no sense charging straight into it without reconnoitering first. Azmei drew Sandy to a halt below a rise. The sounds of the battle were just over the rise. She slipped her hand into a pouch hanging from the pommel. Two throwing stars in hand, she lifted one leg over the pommel and slid to the ground. She landed lightly enough that the thud of her feet wouldn't carry. This close, she could hear some of what was being said.

"—killed her! I'll rip you limb from limb!" That was a tear-filled, crazed voice.

"I offered to parlay. *Twice* I offered to parlay. It's not my fault she refused." The second voice was winded, but calm. Steady. Azmei smiled, not sure why she did.

She crept up the slope, keeping low to the ground. When she saw the combatants, she lifted her right hand, one star at the ready. A skinny man in desert robes stood over a woman's body. He was tall and his black hair was just barely streaked with white. He held two blades at the ready, one long and curved, the other barely longer than a dagger. He was obviously the calm one, despite the blood that soaked his right sleeve. He favored one leg.

The other man—wait, there were more. The leader, then, of the others was a one-eyed man, bearded, with a jagged scar extending beyond the leather patch over his missing eye. He was older than the first man, much grayer, and of a heavier build. His clothing was rougher, too. Azmei took a second glance at the first man and realized that the clothing she had taken for purely practical was still practical, but much more expensive and newer than the second man's.

The other three were clad in even more ragged clothes, wearing loose turbans and cowls to shade their eyes from the sun. One carried a longsword, the other two short swords. None of them looked like they were particularly overfed.

Bandits, then. Azmei nodded and chose her first target.

Neither the lone swordsman nor the bandit leader noticed when the first man dropped, a throwing star blossoming in his throat. He fell silently and writhed in the sand for a few moments before going still. The bandit nearest him noticed and dropped into a crouch, eyes wide. Azmei's clothes were designed to camouflage her in the desert, though. She threw the second star and he never saw what killed him.

Better. One each, and even if he's wounded, he should be able to take care of the bandit leader. Azmei drew her sword as she rose to a crouch. She darted in. The lone swordsman pivoted, probably thinking she was another bandit, and he made a noise that clenched her gut with remembered pain. He stumbled, and the bandit leader took advantage of the momentary weakness.

The bandit leader charged, sword held high. He shouted as he charged. Azmei knew instinctively that the lone swordsman couldn't meet that charge. She wasn't certain she could, with as much bulk as the bandit had. But she interposed herself between them and deflected the bandit's cut. She felt like she'd been run over by a bull, but she managed to swing around and slice the back of his leg as he charged past her. He howled. More in anger than pain, she thought.

"Can you take him?" she asked the swordsman in a low voice. The last bandit wavered, eyes flicking from his enraged leader to the two of them and back. He would break, she thought. The two she'd killed weren't the first casualties. Three others lay dead, including the woman, and another bandit was curled around a gut wound that would probably end up killing him.

Gods above and below, who is this madman who takes on eight?
"Yes."

"Good." She spun around and feinted at the bandit. He

yelped and ran. Azmei could have killed him, but she preferred not to, if it wasn't necessary. She watched him go for a moment, then turned back to the rest of the fight.

The lone swordsman was engaged with the bandit leader, who didn't appear to realize he'd been abandoned. The bandit leader's strokes were obviously practiced, but they were wild with emotion. The swordsman parried each of them, though she could tell he was tiring. He'd lost a lot of blood.

Twice I offered to parlay, the lone swordsman had said. Would he offer a third time? She held her blade at the ready and advanced, letting both men see that she was ready to assist the swordsman, should he weaken.

"Surrender!" the man snapped. "I won't offer again!"

"Go fuck yourself," the bandit leader howled. He lunged at the lone swordsman. It was the sloppiest thrust Azmei had seen in years. Later she would wonder if he'd done it on purpose. In the moment, she watched as the swordsman placed himself exactly where he needed to be for the bandit leader to impale himself on the longer of his two blades.

The bandit leader groaned. The blade had punched through the right side of his chest. Probably punctured his lung, Azmei thought clinically, but not his heart. That would be slower.

The swordsman let the bandit slide off his blade. He didn't look at the man as he wiped his sword on one of the bodies. "Who sent you?" he asked, leaning in.

"—ck yourself," the bandit mumbled. Blood bubbled out of his lips. "Lail." He turned his head to look at the woman's body. Azmei felt a pang of sorrow. Whatever his crimes, he'd loved her.

The lone swordsman knelt by the bandit's shoulders. "*Who sent you?*"

The bandit sneered at him and died.

The swordsman swore and rocked back onto his heels. He tipped his head back, staring up at the sky. After a moment he flinched and dropped ungracefully to his ass in the sand.

"Are you all right?" Azmei didn't sheathe her sword as

she eased closer.

He tensed, which told her he'd forgotten about her. "I'm fine." He was breathless. Azmei listened to his panting and the groaning of the one living bandit. Perhaps that bandit would know who had sent them. She doubted it.

"Why did you help me?" the swordsman demanded.

Azmei shrugged wryly. "He said to."

"Who?"

"The boy I'm guarding."

He twisted around to stare at her. "I could have been a thief they'd caught stealing!" he exclaimed. "I could have been a murderer! I could be anyone!"

"You could be." She shrugged again. "He sees visions. I did as he said."

Hooves thumped against the sand towards them, approaching the other side of the rise. She saw the swordsman tense again, but she knew who it was. A moment later, Firefoot carried Yarro, still blank-stared, into the carnage and stopped.

Azmei glanced down at the swordsman. He was staring up at the teenager on the giant horse. Yar was breathing, but aside from that, he gave no sign of life for several heartbeats. Finally he blinked and smiled at them.

"Hello. Aevver can sew your wounded arm for you."

CHAPTER TWENTY-ONE

Razem had not been angry at his mother's funeral. She had been ill for a time and then she had been dead. He had mourned as a boy. Now, as a man, he mourned the loss of a father who had been stolen from him, and he was angry. He was furious.

But even the anger couldn't cover the pain of this loss.

He stood at the front of the great hall, draped in heavy robes in the ceremonial color of mourning—a purple so deep it was nearly black. They were thick, but somehow the hall seemed cold despite the season, and Razem was almost grateful for how heavy they were. He already felt like he had the weight of the world on his shoulders; but somehow the robes were like armor, enabling him to stand under that weight.

The room was bright, all the torches lit against the fading of light and life. Funerals were held at sunset, the time when the world slipped into darkness mirroring the slipping of life into death. Razem looked over at the clerics. The Deathtaker's high priest nodded and stepped forward.

"The sleeping gods have decreed that men shall die. In death, all become equal before the gods. But in life, not all are equal. We remember here the life of Marsede Corrone, King of Tamnen, father of Razem and Azmei, husband of Izbel of the Fifth Family. We honor him. And we commend him to the gods." He bowed his head, lifting his hands in front of him, palms outward. Everyone assembled in the great hall was silent. Even the usual rustle of cloth, normally echoed around the vaulted ceiling, was still.

Finally the Deathtaker's priest lifted his head. "Come

forth."

They came in the rank of their families, Arisanat first, placing his steps carefully. His robes were the same color as Razem's, but edged in velvet the color of old gold. His short-cropped hair showed not only the purple godsmark on his temple but the bandage tied in place over the opposite temple. A pang of guilt pierced Razem's haze. He should have called on Arisanat. He should have at least sent a personal message. He had not forgotten about the attack on his cousin. He merely hadn't cared in the face of his father's death.

Arisanat bowed deeply, his posture correct despite the careful movements. "Majesty," Arisanat murmured, "I share your grief. My cousin was a kind man and a conscientious ruler."

Razem took his cousin by the shoulders and lifted him up, embracing him. Did Arisanat truly believe what he was saying? He had argued against all of Marsede's recent peace-making. There had never been any bad blood between them before Venra's death, but before Venra's death, Marsede hadn't been attempting peace. Could Arisanat truly believe Marsede was a conscientious ruler?

"Thank you, cousin," Razem murmured aloud. "I know my father was fond of you. I hope you will stay by me as we heal the kingdom of this loss." He kissed Arisanat's cheek, pleased when he felt Arisanat's lips brush his cheek in response. Arisanat stepped back when Razem released him.

"The First Family sends its respects, King Razem," he said, meeting Razem's eyes.

"You have my thanks, Lord Burojan."

Arisanat nodded and stepped aside so Lady Riman could take his place.

Riman was older than Marsede had been, with brown skin and long silver hair that was looped in intricate braids around her head. Lines were graven deep around her eyes and mouth, and there was a profound grief in the dark eyes that met Razem's. Lady Riman and King Marsede had been friends for a very long time.

"King Razem, the Second Family sends its respects," she said, her quiet voice nevertheless carrying throughout the quiet hall. "The Second Family swears anew our old loyalty to the royal family, and mourns Marsede's death." She sank into a deep curtsy.

A rustle of whispers followed in the wake of that pronouncement. Arisanat hadn't made such an oath, because it wasn't part of the funeral ceremony. That was reserved for Razem's official coronation, which would be a month from now. Until that ceremony, the old loyalties were assumed, and there had never been any reason to doubt them.

Razem smiled at her, raising her from her curtsy and kissing her cheek. "Lady Riman, your support warms me, and the royal family's love for the Second Family is stronger than it has ever been."

Dry lips brushed his cheek. "Be careful, Razem," she whispered, and withdrew.

Razem watched her go, taking in the slope of her thin shoulders under the heavy mourning gown edged in silvery gray. She was old, and he didn't know her heir as he should. There were many things he didn't know as he should, and he suddenly felt that lack keenly.

The third to come was Lord Birona. His bulk made his mourning robes look even heavier, edged as they were in dark blue. His face seemed to droop, mouth turned down, tiny eyes nearly swallowed by downturned eyebrows. There was nevertheless a shrewd gleam in them. Razem didn't doubt the leader of the King's Council was appraising him, trying to discern how fit Razem was for kingship. He supposed he deserved it, considering the way he had behaved the last time he and Birona had met.

"The Third Family sends its respects, King Razem," Birona said. His voice was higher than expected from a man of his size, but it commanded attention throughout the kingdom. Razem hoped he hadn't lost Birona's good opinion. Birona's bow seemed fragile—he dropped as low as was correct, but he seemed to have trouble holding still until Razem stepped forward to raise him.

"My thanks, Lord Birona," he said, kissing the nobleman's cheek. "And thank you for keeping to the proper ritual," he murmured.

Birona chuckled faintly as he kissed Razem's cheek in return. "Your Majesty knows how fond I am of ritual." The brief levity made Razem feel better. All the same, the way Birona smoothed his robes in place troubled him as the man walked away.

Lady Tel of the Fourth Family was a quiet, inoffensive woman who was quietly, inoffensively pretty. Nevertheless, she held her position by right of blood and virtue both, and Razem liked her. Her husband of fifteen years had died last year of a wasting gut, and she had remained strong throughout his illness despite her clear sadness. Theirs had been an arranged marriage that developed into regard, if not true love.

She walked up the steps with a young daughter at each side, gripping her hands. If that made it difficult to climb the steps in her floor-length gown, Razem couldn't tell. The girls each carried a deep purple rose, and when Tel curtsied, the girls held out their roses.

Razem smiled and took the flowers before touching Tel's elbow for her to straighten. "The Fourth Family sends its respects, King Razem," she said. There was a quiet sorrow in her dark eyes; Razem sensed that she truly mourned with him.

"My thanks, Lady Tel," he said, leaning in to trade the ritual kiss. As Tel led her daughters away, one of them, perhaps six years old, turned to look over her shoulder at her new king. His fingers tightened around the stem of the roses.

Ilzi was next, Razem's fifteen-year-old cousin by his mother's side. Her mourning gown was edged in white, as the dead queen's nearest relation outside the royal family, and her eyes were rimmed with red. She came up the steps and he could tell she was about to throw her arms around him when she remembered and dropped into a curtsy instead. "King Razem, dear cousin, the Fifth Family sends its respects. We share your deepest sorrow." Her childish voice seemed almost that of a woman, and Razem couldn't help but mourn how quickly she was growing up.

"I thank you, Lady Ilzi, my dear cousin," he said. He drew her to her feet and kissed her cheek, allowing her to embrace him. Her slender arms around him were strong as she kissed his cheek in return. She reminded him of Azmei. With a pang, he set her gently away and watched her go.

"King Razem, the Sixth Family sends its respects," said Lord Belnat as he climbed the steps. He was a thin man in his late forties, with chestnut-colored skin and silver-streaked black hair. He was chewing his lower lip as he bowed, more deeply even than was required.

Razem felt a pang of sympathy for the man. He had come to his Family Headship—and the Council—in the past year, after his aged father's death. This ceremony must recall too much of that loss. He lifted Belnat and kissed both cheeks instead of the customary one. "I thank you, Belnat," he said for all to hear. Then, lowering his voice, he added, "I share my loss with yours."

Belnat gave him a startled look before nodding.

Lady Talt had only one daughter in tow, which was new. Usually she brought them both around whenever she thought she would see Razem. He winced inwardly at the tiresome tone of that thought. He shouldn't think ill of her. She loved her daughters and only wished to see them well settled. It was hard to fault her for that.

"The Seventh Family sends its respects, King Razem," she said, curtsying. Her daughter—the older, if Razem remembered right—curtsied along with her. He suppressed the urge to kiss the daughter's cheek and raised Talt instead.

"My thanks, Lady Talt."

Thank the gods, she left without a remark about how lonely he must be, with no wife to share his grief. It was uncharitable for him to expect such a remark, he chided himself.

Lord Restin of the Eighth Family was a tall, bluff man in his mid-forties. He strode up and bowed as he spoke the Eighth Family's respects. When Razem raised him for the kiss,

Restin remarked, "This is terribly familiar, Majesty. I pray the gods protect you." Razem's lips faltered against Restin's cheek, then he tightened his grip on the man's shoulders and drew back.

"I thank you, Lord Restin." He held Restin's gaze, but saw only sincerity there.

Finally they had reached the Ninth Family. Lord Daix was a tall, broad-shouldered man with light brown skin who usually wore a broad smile and carried a contagious laugh everywhere. Now he was solemn, his dark brown eyes sympathetic. "The Ninth Family sends its respects, King Razem," he said, his deep voice reaching across the hall. He bowed deeply.

"My thanks, Lord Daix," Razem said, and after they traded the ritual kiss, the most excruciating part of the funeral was over.

The clerics took over again after that, the servants of all five gods taking it in turn to speak of life and death and honor, though the Deathtaker's high priest presided over all. The words of the blessings and the rituals were comforting, but Razem felt it a false comfort. Would his father truly join the gods in their holy sleep? Was that all the gods were good for?

After the rituals, they made their torchlit procession to the Hallowed City, where Marsede was enshrined alongside the late Queen Izbel. To one side of their tomb was the empty tomb of Princess Azmei—the one Razem now knew she didn't need and didn't miss. Where was Azmei? What was she doing? *Please come back to me, little sister,* he thought.

The feast to end the funeral was held by the light of a hundred lamps, but Razem couldn't help seeing shadows in every corner. He sat alone at the high table, lonely but glad not to be seated with Arisanat and Riman and Birona. There was little conversation, even at the tables with more occupants. Everything was muted and reserved. Razem ate a few bites of everything that was placed in front of him despite his lack of appetite. He had no taste for it, but he must keep up his strength.

Finally he was able to dismiss everyone. He spoke a few

words of thanks and made his way to his quarters, shadowed by half a dozen guards that he pretended not to see. He was exhausted and had a headache and wanted out of the ceremonial robes.

His quarters were dim and quiet. He let Gendo remove the robes and hang them. When Gendo came back, Razem was still standing in the middle of the room, looking blankly at the carpet. Gendo brought him a glass of wine, but Razem shook his head.

"Water, please. I've had enough wine." The thick, sweet aftertaste lingered on his tongue. The water cleared it, curling coldly through his mouth. It roused him from his exhaustion a little.

He didn't want to go to bed, despite the headache. He wouldn't sleep well, and he was unwilling to drink enough to let him sleep well. He moved aimlessly around his rooms, looking at the spines of the books on his shelves, the small portraits of Izbel and Azmei that hung over the fireplace, the painting of the Governor's Palace at Rivarden reflected in Sky Lake. He drank a second glass of water.

Finally he wrapped himself in a cloak and told Gendo to go to sleep. "I will go read what Master Tanvel left us. I will not need you until morning."

***

They had chosen an unused office near Kho's office as the safest place to keep Tanvel's documents locked up. They were in a locked, reinforced wooden chest, and only Kho and Razem held the keys. The chest was hidden under a desk, and the door to the office was locked, again with keys only the two of them held. The door was locked when Razem let himself in, but he was unsurprised to find a lamp burning in the entryway. He slipped inside and shut the door behind him, turning the lock from the inside.

"Why am I not surprised to find you here?"

Emran was sitting on a cushioned bench, his lap awash

in papers. He looked up when Razem spoke. "I have to find something. Tanvel knew who was behind this. He must have."

Razem walked further into the office, trailing his fingers over dusty figurines and an inkwell that had long since gone dry. "Perhaps not. Perhaps he only knew more than we, rather than the whole."

"Whatever he knew is here," Kho said stubbornly.

Razem shook his head and sat in a leather armchair at one end of the desk. "Give me something to look through. I'll not sleep tonight. I might as well be useful."

Kho frowned down at the collection of information for a moment, finally selecting a small, yellow book. "I haven't had a chance to look at this. I thought it best to work from the beginning forward, but if you come across anything unfamiliar, I should be able to provide background."

Razem looked over the book. It was bound in tooled leather, the yellow a natural color rather than dyed. What sort of creature had once worn this skin? He flipped it open to the first page and was greeted by his sister's handwriting. His heart thumping faster, he glanced up at Kho. Had the general realized? But Kho had fallen back into his absorption with his own research. Mouth suddenly dry, Razem began to read.

Day Three — Master Tanvel came down with a fever after our first day of surveillance, but he insists on maintaining the watch. The only concessions he makes are allowing me to record the notes and taking the hot baths and hot soups and possets without complaint. He sits on the rooftop opposite the Perslyn Trading House and shivers, but he has seen four of those we have noted before. We feel this is the ideal time to remove them from the equation.

I had never been east of the mountains before. Tanvel has, but not this far north. The rain is very cold, though Tanvel says we are too far from the mountains for snow. For the sake of our operation, let us hope he is correct. Surveillance in snow would not be pleasant.

The Patriarch's man here is one Sykri Perslyn. We dare not remove him; he appears to be the grand-nephew of the Patriarch, and sends reports to Meekin almost daily. Were we to replace him, it is unavoidable that the Patriarch would get news of the loss, and we cannot afford to have him on the alert. Not yet. Master Tanvel says we must be ready to deal with the Patriarch himself before we remove Sykri.

Here his sister's handwriting ended and a thin, spiky hand took over.

Day Six - Aevver takes liberties with her notes, but she is not incorrect. We have seen four messenger birds leave Perslyn Trading House in the week we have been here. Sykri will remain, for now, but I have dispatched Aevver to deal with two of the assassins we recognize from before. She should be gone long enough for me to enter the house and search for records. I wanted her well away before I tried this—she is headstrong, and at times it is easier to go around her than through.

Razem had to suppress a smile. So Master Tanvel hadn't found his sister much easier to deal with. It was good to know that the new Azmei was no more tractable, even if she was calling herself Aevver and apprenticed to an assassin.

Day Eight — I found the missing piece of the puzzle this night. Sykri Perslyn has been receiving money from someone in Tamnen. Someone of noble blood, from the language in the letter. Based on where I found it, the letter itself won't be missed, so I have tucked it into the pages of this book. The thrust is this: Unnamed member of unnamed noble house would be happy to spend a great deal of anonymous gold to prevent the treaty between Amethir and Tamnen. While the letter is undated, it is clear Dinnsan is in the recent past, based on the reference to the massacre. My conclusion is that shortly after said massacre, this noble house decided there should be no peace.

Razem riffled the pages of the book but found no letter. He held the book spine up and shook it gently, but nothing fell out except something green. He reached down and picked it up. A dried flower—light purple, with seven petals. Rue. He twisted his lips and tucked the plant safely back into the pages. Wherever the letter had gone, it wasn't with the book.

He went back to the record. From the way Azmei had described the climate, along with Tanvel's scattered comments, he decided they must be somewhere in the Long Coast. It seemed they were far to the north, even further north than Arisanat's lands. The Long Coast wasn't really one nation so much as an alliance of city-states and fiefdoms who maintained their alliances by means both fair and foul. He had heard assassination was a guilded trade in the Long Coast, but he had never given the matter much thought. Had the Perslyn family sent some of theirs to open a guild?

He was so absorbed in the account that he looked up in surprise when the lamp started flickering. Emran looked up as well, his gaze going first to the lamp and then swinging around to meet Razem's.

"I'll fetch more oil. I have a reserve jar here." He stood and stretched.

"What time is it?" Razem said, rubbing his suddenly burning eyes.

"Based on how much oil the lamp's gone through, I'd say it isn't dawn yet, but she's closer than midnight." Kho's voice was rough. "Should I brew some coffee? There's wood by the fireplace."

Razem sighed. "Coffee. Gods bless you, yes."

Kho chuckled and brought the oil over, then set about building a small fire. "Have you found anything interesting?"

"Much that is interesting," Razem said, refilling the lamp. "But useful? I'm not sure. Some, at least. He discovered that gold was making its way from Tamnen to the Perslyn family in a Long Coast city. He didn't record which one, unless I missed it."

"Gold that originated in Tamnen, or just passed through?" Kho asked.

"A good distinction. Originated here, I'm afraid." Razem sat back, arching his back, and watched Kho strike the spark. He held his breath in sympathy until the spark caught.

"But no certainty of who spent it?"

Razem rubbed his face. What did Kho want to hear? "One of the nobility. Tanvel's sure of that much, based on the language of a letter that has been inconveniently lost. He doesn't say who it is, but at one point he made a list." He picked up the yellow book again and began flipping through the pages until he saw what he wanted.

"'It is tied to their damned war, I am certain of it,'" he

quoted. "And there's a list of those who profit from the war. House Birona is outfitting the military, and stands to lose a great deal of their trade if we make peace. House Daix is ship-builders. With the conflict spilling out onto the sea as it does, it's possible they would be affected. There's half a dozen noble houses not of the Nine who trade with the Long Coast in one form or another. Including the Perslyns, in fact, since they ship their cloth to three nations aside from ours." He read the list of houses, then added six trading houses that had lost ships to the Strid. "I would think, though," Razem added as an afterthought, "that they would be glad to have the war ended so they wouldn't lose any more ships. Profit should matter more than revenge to traders, shouldn't it?"

He stopped talking and the room fell silent aside from the crackle of the fire. Kho was staring thoughtfully at the flames. He'd placed a kettle of water on the iron pivot arm and it was hissing. Razem's brain felt swimmy. He wanted coffee.

"What do you think, Emran?"

Kho pursed his lips but didn't look away from the fire. He swallowed, his brows drawn down. What dire thoughts did he have?

Razem straightened in his seat. "Emran."

Kho sighed. "What if it is one of the Families?"

Razem stared at him. He could see Kho wasn't happy about saying it—but why suggest it at all?

"It would be treason," Kho said softly.

"I—no. No, I can't believe it. Why?"

Kho looked away from the fire finally, letting his gaze meet Razem's. He didn't speak, just looked at him until Razem felt the heat rise in his cheeks. He felt as if he were being stupid, but what did Kho mean?

"Which of them do you propose it is?" he asked, more crossly than he had intended. "You just watched all nine of them pay respects! Did you see any that you would name traitor?" Kho didn't look away. "Dragon's voice, Emran! These are my nobles you're talking about! My *cousins*!"

"I do not propose it is any of them, Majesty." Kho's voice was a tired rumble. "But it must be someone. Who would benefit most from your father's death?"

Razem had no answer for that. Too many people would benefit in some way. But none of them would benefit in a significant way, outside of treason. They fell silent. The kettle hissed and spat steam out of the spout. Kho hooked the pivot arm out of the flames and wrapped a cloth around his hand to pour the coffee in two carved wooden mugs. When they were both seated again, coffee in hand, he looked up at Razem, his gaze dark. His voice dropped almost to a whisper.

"If they have tried to kill your sister, and succeeded in killing your father, Razem, what do you think they will do next?"

CHAPTER TWENTY-TWO

Hawk kept staring at the boy. He had ridden his horse up, made that announcement about sewing his wound, and then he had dismounted and plopped on the ground. His gaze had gone blank again, staring at an empty spot in the sand. He'd said nothing since. About five minutes ago, he'd begun rocking slightly in place. The woman said the boy had visions, but even so...

As for the woman, she *was* sewing Hawk's wound. She'd brought over a kit from her saddlebags and ordered him out of his robe and shirt. She started cleaning the wound with expert hands, then she'd clucked her tongue at him and pulled out a curved needle and sinew. Hawk had been injured often enough that he knew better than to argue with her. If she said it needed sewing, it probably did.

She was awfully handy with a needle and sinew, come to that. Her head was bent over his shoulder, but he studied her as best he could. He'd already noticed she had a hard smile. This close, he could see a white line on her left cheekbone. It was obviously a scar from a dagger cut, but it had been healed well. She was obviously Tamnese and just as obviously a warrior. She was also pretty. Who was she?

The object of his study didn't look up from his wound, but she must have felt his gaze on her. "You're welcome," she said.

"Huh?"

"For saving you." She took another stitch and Hawk tried not to wince.

"Oh. Thank you."

She snorted. "That sounded sincere."

Hawk gave himself a mental shake. Just because they'd surprised him, so close on the heels of the surprise bandit attack, didn't mean he could forget himself. "I beg your pardon. I am most sincere, m'lady. I'm afraid you have me a bit off guard."

She glanced up at him with a crooked grin. It was more than a little endearing, he realized, and found himself grinning back at her. She looked down again and took another stitch.

"My name is Jacin."

She flicked a glance up. "Aevver. He's Yar."

Hawk glanced over at the boy, who was staring into space. "He...He's all right?"

"I told you, he has visions." She tugged the next stitch too hard and they both swore. "Sorry. I've gotten used to them."

He frowned down at the dark curls that swung across her cheek. "What are you two doing traveling alone in bandit territory?"

She glanced sharply at him and took another stitch. "He's going to Rivarden. I go where he goes."

Hawk nodded. They were silent for the length of time it took her to take three more stitches. "What about you?" she asked finally.

He gave her a blank stare.

"You're traveling in bandit territory entirely alone. That doesn't seem like a good plan."

Hawk shrugged with his good arm, and she hissed at him. He went still. "I have an assignment in Meekin, and have not the luxury for the canal."

"Huh." She glanced at him, appraising. He wondered suddenly if she could hear the six years of speaking Strid in his voice. Would she recognize the accent if she heard it? Did she think him a spy?

"There's your arm patched up. Try not to use it too much for the next week or so," she said. She cut the sinew and dabbed an ointment across the stitches. Then she wrapped a bandage around his arm and tied it off. When she was finished, she tied her medical kit closed and stood.

Hawk found himself blinking after her as she went to the nearest bandit body and knelt next to it. "Ah. He's died after all," she said, and he realized that was the one he'd got in the gut. "Too bad. I had some questions for him."

Sleeping gods, she was calm. He'd known plenty of women who were skilled fighters, but he wasn't sure if he'd ever met one as pretty and young as she seemed to be. "What are you doing?"

She rolled the man to one side, slipping a hand inside his belt. "Might as well see what they have. It'll be of no use to any but the jackals out here."

Hawk eased his arm back into his shirt sleeve. "Practical, if a bit gruesome."

She shrugged.

Hawk left her to it. He wanted to get his clothes back in place and clean his blades. When he felt a bit more like himself, he looked for her again. She'd made her way through half of the bodies. A stack of weapons lay to one side of the one-eyed man. As he watched, she pulled a quiver off the shoulder of one man's body. She stuck something in a pocket and moved to the next.

Hawk wasn't sure how he felt about looting the bodies. It wasn't uncommon in warfare, and certainly these bandits had attacked him, rather than the other way around. On the other hand, he'd told himself he was through with war.

That's all very well and good, but is war through with you? murmured a voice in the back of his mind. He shook himself and glanced at the boy again. Still watching something Hawk couldn't see, still rocking in place, though he'd started tapping the fingers of one hand against his thumb. He looked back at Aevver. She'd added two flasks to the stack of weapons and was staring down at a folded piece of paper. It crackled as she unfolded it. She could read, he saw, as she studied the paper. Her eyes narrowed as she read it. She glanced up at Hawk, and he found himself tensing. Her body language had suddenly become less friendly. She was standing over the woman. Lail, the one-eyed man had called her. Their leader.

"These aren't bandits," she said.

"What?"

She folded the letter into her pocket and stood. She gestured around. "Their clothes are better than they look. The top layer is ragged, all right, but the shirts and trousers aren't. They have shoes, all of them, and good ones. Weapons that have seen fighting *and* care." She took a few steps closer to him, one hand dropping to the hilt of her sword. She didn't draw the blade, but Hawk knew she would in a moment if he moved wrong. He held very still as she stared narrowly at him. "Not to mention they've been paid a hefty sum to kill someone. Who are you?" she demanded.

Hawk stared at her for a moment before transferring his stare to the bodies. She was right, now that he looked more closely at them. He hoped he would have seen it himself if she hadn't been here to point it out. Mercenaries, then. That wasn't a good sign. There weren't many people who could afford to send a band of mercenaries after him.

Did Arisanat Burojan hate him so much he would pay to have him killed? But why?

***

Yarro had begun to think he would never find the Voices when he heard the shouting. The Voices seized on it, shrieking in his head that he must save the man. So Yarro sent Aevver to save him. The Voices ripped his mind back to them as soon as he told her, and he saw the fight as it happened. A lone swordsman, fighting off bandits in ragged clothes. He wasn't aware of Aevver riding away from him, but he saw her when she arrived at the battle. She killed so efficiently, letting nothing stop her as she came to the man's defense.

Who was this man? Why was he important to the Voices?

YOU WILL NEED HIM. HE TASTES OF THE DESERT JEWEL. HE WILL AID YOU.

When Firefoot carried him to the edge of the finished battle, Yarro struggled away from the Voices, and they let him go for a moment. He saw the man with his own eyes, saw the blood dripping from his right arm, the exhaustion in the man's stance, the wariness in his eyes. He liked the man, so he smiled.

"Hello. Aevver can sew your wounded arm for you."

Then, as quick as he'd slid from Firefoot's back, the Voices swept him back up, swirling around him, their words caressing his cheeks, teasing his hair, pulling at his clothes. He felt his body sit, then he was lost.

SMELL THE BLOOD! LICK IT UP. EAT THE BODIES. WHY WASTE THE DEAD?

Yarro's mind shuddered in revulsion, though he couldn't tell if his body did, too. *We don't eat people. Maybe you do, but I don't. Humans don't.*

The slithery Voice cackled. HOW DO YOU KNOW? HAVE YOU EVER CROSSED THE SOUTHERN WASTES TO THE VERY TIP OF SLARDA?

Stop it! Yarro commanded, wishing he could lift his hands to his ears and blot them out. It wouldn't work. It never worked.

HUSH, said the Wise Uncle Voice. LEAVE HIM BE. HE IS DOING OUR BIDDING, AND HE IS DOING WELL. YOU ARE CLOSE, LITTLE BROTHER. DID THESE HUMANS ATTACK TO STOP YOU? WE FEEL YOUR APPROACH.

I don't know why they attacked. They didn't attack us, they attacked that man. The one you told me to save. Why did you tell me to save him?

The darkness clouding his vision cleared slowly, as if he were coming through a dense fog. He saw storm clouds building, so dark they were purple-black at the center. Vast wings flapped overhead, the sound buffeting his ears. Yarro felt like he blinked tears from his eyes, and in that blink, he was standing high over a city, watching people fighting in the streets, breaking a heavy wooden door to get into a huge building. A palace? There were dead bodies on the street. Angry shouts filled his head.

He was watching the fighting, but he could hear something building, some deep noise building, groaning. The sound of sand and stone shifting against itself. Something immense and old turning in its sleep. The world shuddered.

A hawk stooped from the middle of the storm clouds. Its talons were wet with blood. Yarro watched its descent until it came to circle his head. It screamed and landed on Aevver's outstretched hand. She smiled at the hawk.

WE KNOW HER NOW. YOU MUST BRING THEM BOTH.

He woke from his vision and found himself staring at the man. They were inspecting the bodies, he and Aevver both. Neither of them looked happy, but the man looked tentative, while Aevver looked accusing. She was trying to protect Yarro, he realized in a rush of love. She didn't know he didn't need to be protected from this man.

"Hawk," he said.

The man turned, his mouth dropping open when he saw Yar looking at him. Yar smiled.

"Come with us."

***

Azmei jerked her head up at hearing Yar speak. He called the man Hawk? And Jacin responded. Why did that tickle at her memory? It seemed... She had heard it, long ago.

Then she realized what Yar had just done.

"No! He can't!" She didn't trust any man with a thousand gold riding on his death. Especially when she didn't know why, or who it was that wanted him dead. He'd gone very quiet when she confronted him about it. He seemed sad, but he didn't answer her questions, either. He had too many secrets.

There was a certain irony in that, she knew. After all, she had her own secrets, and plenty of them, yet she'd convinced Yar to take her with him. Then again, he had those Voices.

Had they told him her secrets? Perhaps she only thought she had secrets from him. Perhaps he was just kind enough to let her pretend.

"I appreciate the offer," Jacin was saying, "but I cannot. I gave my word I would investigate what happened in Meekin."

Azmei stiffened. What happened in Meekin? Did that mean what she had done? How had word of that traveled so far and so quickly? No messages from Meekin had overtaken them, she was sure of it. The canal boats were too slow, and she and Yarro were on the most direct path to the city that she knew of.

"We came from there," Yarro said. "What do you mean, what happened in Meekin?"

She saw the hesitation before Jacin answered. He didn't quite glance over his shoulder at her, but she realized suddenly that he was caught between her and Yarro, and it was making him uncomfortable. Good. Perhaps he would tell the truth, then.

"There was an attack," Jacin said finally. "My...my commander learned that a family in Meekin was responsible." He turned, trying to see both of them. "I am to learn the details."

"What?" Yarro had gone still. It was frightening how *present* he could be. It was just as powerful in its way as the times when he was so completely gone. He looked at Azmei, meeting her gaze without flinching. "It was my family, wasn't it?"

She couldn't lie to him. She held his gaze, letting him read the truth there. Tanvel must have interfered in the attack he said was coming, the attack on her father. He was going to give her father all the information they had gathered over the past three years, but he had been waiting for the attack. She felt a pang in her stomach. Was Tanvel dead, then?

She looked from Yarro to Jacin. "The Perslyn Family?"

Jacin was silent. He had turned to look at her, so he couldn't see the distress creeping across Yarro's expression. The boy's normally pleasant face became distraught as he realized they were talking about his family.

"Aevver, what did Grandfather do?" His expression twisted through apprehension into rage, his lips drawing back. Aevver felt a chill run down her arms. "We should have eaten him!" he hissed. "We should have swallowed him whole!"

She realized now that it was the Voices speaking through him when this happened. That made it no less unsettling. Who *were* these Voices they were going to find? Or more to the point, *what* were they? She licked her lips and held Yarro's gaze. "Your grandfather tried to kill the king." She glanced at Jacin. "Am I right?"

Jacin stared at her, but he kept twitching a look back at Yarro. Azmei moved to her left, letting him shift his angle so he could see them both. It would be more than unsettling to have Yarro at your back, after what he'd just said.

"And you were sent," Azmei went on, "because someone caught the Perslyns finally."

"My lady." Jacin looked unhappy, though whether he was unhappy about being caught out or unhappy about how much she knew, Azmei couldn't tell. He was working very hard not to reach for his sword hilt. After a moment, Azmei deliberately dropped her hand to her side. It worked to relax him somewhat. "I was not—I may not speak of it." He paused again.

Azmei fought her rising impatience. Why was he lying to her? Who was this man, who had been sent to investigate Meekin? She tried not to show her impatience, but she must have twitched. Jacin bowed his head.

"I am on an errand for the Crown, Aevver. I cannot say more than that."

The last piece clicked into place. "Oh gods, I'm an idiot!" Azmei exclaimed. She looked at Yarro's confused face and realized the Voices must not have told him everything. She looked back at Jacin. "Prince Razem must have sent you. You're Jacin Hawk—the Hawk. Commander Hawk." He had been with her brother. How long ago? Would he be able to tell her about Razem? But how could she ask? "And this is the welcome you get?" Her lips twisted wryly. Poor man.

"Welcome to the peace process."

Hawk grew more tense the longer she spoke. Yes, she could see the warrior commander in him now that she knew. She'd not seen him more than a few times, and it had been another lifetime—for both of them, it seemed. She had been a spoiled princess of sixteen or seventeen, and he had been the Kreyden Commander, resplendent in armor and a scarlet cape, his stride confident, his stature strong, muscular, and authoritative. His years in captivity had changed him. *As my years in the peace god's service have changed me.*

"I don't know how you know all this," he began, "but you know I cannot—"

Azmei smiled. How fate must laugh at them as they scrambled to make their own way. "Will it help if I tell you I have already dealt with the Perslyns? Yar's grandfather is dead." She flicked a glance at Yarro as she said it. He flinched, but then a reptilian smile flickered across his face. He licked his lips and ducked his head, not meeting her gaze.

Hawk stared at her, then turned to stare at the boy who was staring at the ground. "Yar's—"

"Yarro Perslyn," Azmei said. "He is the last worthy scion of that family." Yarro's head jerked up and he stared at her, his smile growing more human, more vulnerable. "His sister died a few years ago, and he finally got away from them after that." She sighed. "I promise, Hawk, your time would be better spent with us than in Meekin."

Yar's face was a joy to behold. It was as if no one had ever said nice things about him before. She couldn't understand—Orya had clearly been devoted to him, and he to Orya. She must have said nice things to him all the time. Then again, Orya had been gone more than three years. What kindness had he heard since then? Only the distant kindness of Tish and the intermittent kindness of Kesh. Neither of them had the strength that Orya had, and neither of them stood up to the Patriarch as Orya apparently had.

Hawk was shaking his head. "I cannot countermand the prince," he said quietly. He was looking at Azmei intently. She almost thought he was waiting for something from her. She knew what it was he wanted, and she knew what it would mean. If she did this, her life as Aevver Balearic was as good as over. But Yarro had told her to save Hawk, and Yarro had invited Hawk to join them, and Hawk had been with Razem. There was nothing for it.

"I can," she said quietly.

His gaze sharpened as he held hers. She let him hold her gaze, let him search it as Yarro had searched it only minutes before. But Hawk was seeking some other truth, and she knew he would find it. She hadn't changed so much that someone who had met her in that other life would fail to recognize her. Not when he had reason to suspect her true identity. She had recognized him, she had named him, and she had claimed the authority to alter the prince's orders. There could be only one woman in the world who had that authority.

She saw him understand. She saw the shock in his eyes as his mouth dropped open, the sudden shift in his stance as he prepared to bow. His gaze flickered down to the blade at her hip. She could tell he was registering the way she had fought, the fact that the princess of Tamnen had sewed his wound for him, had seen him shirtless, had touched his bare skin. She saw his throat bob as he swallowed. He began to bow.

"Princess Azmei—"

"Was killed by Orya Perslyn three years ago and more," she broke in, hoping her voice didn't sound as desperate as she felt. Couldn't it stay unspoken between them? Couldn't they just ignore this truth for now? She didn't want to go back to being the princess. She liked Aevver. She was a real person when she was Aevver. "Do you understand, Hawk?"

Hawk was silent, watching her. She wasn't certain if he did understand, but she could see he was trying to. He tipped his head to one side, almost looking like his namesake for a moment, an ember flaring in his charcoal eyes. His mouth was a straight line, giving her no hints as to his thoughts. After a long moment, he dropped his gaze, his lips turning down.

What was he thinking?

"Princess Azmei?" Yarro's voice was small. When she looked at him, the boy was tapping his fingers against his thumb as he stared at her. His expression was as open as Hawk's was closed. He was shocked, he was hurt... He was angry.

Azmei held very still. She didn't want this. She had come to care for Yarro over the course of their travels. She knew she couldn't take his sister's place, but she had hoped she could be *like* a sister to him. She had wanted to believe in him, to show him that life didn't have to be like it had been in the Perslyn House. He had just begun to trust her, to smile at her and meet her gaze and tell her things. And now—

"*You're* Princess Azmei!" He was standing with fists clenched in front of his stomach. She couldn't tell whether he wanted to hit her or be sick. "You told me your name is Aevver! You *lied* to me! You were the reason my sister died!"

His face twisted with rage and his eyes glinted orange. Azmei's throat tightened. She had never tested the extent of what he could do. What powers did those visions give him? What if those Voices were demons, slowly taking control of his mind? Could they take control of his body as well?

You know they can, whispered a voice in the back of her mind. *Remember the bodies of those two thieves in Meekin.*

She tensed, hoping she wouldn't have to run from him.

"You killed my sister! You—You—" He threw his head back and screamed. "I'll kill you!" Then he dropped to his knees, staring at her, tears running openly down his face. The orange glint had faded from his eyes, the rage twisted into fright and fear.

Azmei looked sadly back at him. "Darling, I'm already dead."

CHAPTER TWENTY-THREE

Razem rubbed his eyes. It had been a long night, and the coming of dawn had made him no happier. He poured himself another cup of coffee and watched dully as the stream dried up before the cup was full. Damn.

"We're out of coffee," he told Kho.

The lord-general looked up. There were dark smudges under his eyes, but he looked alert. Two hours ago, he'd left and returned with a tray of meat pies and pastries, along with a fresh-brewed pot of coffee. They'd brewed another pot of it since.

After a moment, Kho sighed. "Majesty, I know you don't want to hear this—"

"Then don't say it!" Razem snapped. The general's expression didn't change, but shame washed over Razem. "No, I'm sorry, Emran. Go on."

Kho nodded. "The more we learn about the assassinations, the clearer this becomes." He sat forward in his chair, setting aside the documents in his lap. "I know the Nine are your cousins, but I cannot overlook this if I am to protect you."

Razem rubbed his face again. "Not Ilzi," he murmured.

"No." The quiet, certain dismissal comforted Razem. Kho wouldn't deny her involvement unless he were sure. He was more a strategist than Razem, and he wouldn't be blinded by love.

"You think you know who it is," Razem said. It wasn't a question.

Kho was silent. His brows were drawn together as he

looked at Razem, but his lips were pressed together as if he were judging what to say.

"Emran, you've earned the right to speak freely to me. I promise not to snap at you again."

Kho shook his head. "Majesty. You know it must be Burojan." His voice was quiet.

Razem wasn't ready to hear it. But then, when would anyone be ready to hear that a man he grew up with was prepared to kill him—had already killed his father and tried to kill his sister? How could any man prepare for such news?

He dropped his head into his hands. Kho didn't speak. Razem thought of the way Venra had always looked at his brother, like Arisanat had all the answers, like he could do anything. It was the way Azmei had looked at Razem for so many years. Arisanat had changed after losing Venra, there was no denying that. Had he changed enough to try to kill people? Who could say?

I've changed since losing Azmei, he admitted to himself. *What would I be capable of, if I had the person I blamed in front of me?*

But no, Razem had never resorted to assassination. It was not the way things were done. War was terrible, but it was the proper way of settling things, once diplomacy had failed. *And diplomacy failed us the moment Azmei pretended to die.*

Finally, Razem lifted his head. "You know we need proof, Emran."

Kho hummed an agreement. "Captain Ysdra has been investigating the attack on Lord Burojan."

"That wasn't someone trying to get to me," Razem said. "It was a decoy. Aris and I look enough alike that no one would question it, and it gave him the perfect alibi."

Kho nodded. "While Ysdra's investigation has probably been in vain, he has made some interesting observations. I confess that, in the absence of other instructions, he has been artificially prolonging his investigation to give him reason to revisit Burojan's home."

Razem nodded. "Bring him to me. I'll want to hear everything. And commend him for his initiative, I suppose." He paused, looking around the dusty office. He couldn't even re-member whose office this had been. Perhaps Emran had been friends with the person who used it. The figurines of the desert foxes wouldn't have been left behind if the person had lived. Not unless... Hawk, he realized. They were meeting in Hawk's office, kept ready for him in case he ever returned from captivity. "I don't suppose there's been any word from Hawk."

"It's too early, Majesty." His gaze, too, was on the desert foxes.

"This was his office," Razem said.

Kho nodded.

"Of course." He stood. "Well. We'd better make this of-ficial. I'll go back to my apartments for the midday meal. You and Ysdra will join me. No one else."

Kho saluted and left.

Razem stared down at the figurines. They were carved stone, their faces rendered in loving detail, the tails and ears disproportionately large. It seemed odd that the man wouldn't have hawks. But perhaps these had been a gift from someone.

He sighed and turned away from the desk. He knew so little about Hawk, and instead of bringing him to the capital with him, he had sent him away. He had put him to use when he should have known the man needed more time to adjust to his freedom. What was he becoming? Was this how kings acted, or despots?

He rubbed his face and left the office, locking it carefully behind him. He encountered a few servants and minor cour-tiers in the passageways, but no one did more than bow and leave him alone. Thank the gods for that. He couldn't handle having to make small talk with anyone right now. The king-dom would run itself for a day.

Gendo was inclined to fuss when he reached his rooms. His manservant was neatly dressed but still managed to appear harried.

"My lo—majesty, you weren't here when they brought breakfast. I—"

"Don't worry, Gen. I ate breakfast with Lord-General Kho. In fact, I'll be eating lunch with him, as well. He and Captain Ysdra will be joining us here. I would like a full meal brought."

Gendo bowed, but before he could leave, Razem put a hand on his arm.

"Gen, I don't know if I've properly thanked you for all that you have done." He held Gendo's gaze, hoping his sincerity was obvious. "Your service to me, sitting with my father, saving Master Tanvel's work..." He shook his head. "There is no way I could ever repay you for that."

Gendo's gaze dropped to the floor. "My lord. I'm happy to serve."

Razem squeezed his arm and let go. "And I am grateful."

Gendo bowed again and left, his rapid steps cut off by the closing of the door to the main passage. Razem sighed and looked around his rooms. They had been his rooms since he left the children's nursery at eight, but they felt alien all of a sudden. He went to a cabinet and poured himself a generous glass of wine. He carried it out to his private balcony and stopped, gazing out across the city.

Tamnen City had dressed herself in mourning. Deep purple banners flew from the palace and all the royal buildings. The harbor was draped in mourning purple. The gates were hung in purple. The city would wear mourning clothes for a month, when Razem ascended to the throne.

He took a mouthful of wine and swished it around, relishing the bitter edge of it. He had planned to be a good king. In his childhood, whenever he thought of kingship, it had been a glory of wealth and valor. His childish mind had somehow ignored the notion that his father would have to die, so he had imagined himself as a glorious young king. His reign would be a prosperous time when young King Razem performed feats of strength and won renown.

That had been before the Strid war, of course. After the attack on the Kelischad Mines, which had come when he was six, his dreams of kingship had expanded to winning the war, and maybe conquering all of Strid. It had been years before he understood that conquest was not, at least for the Tamnese, an objective of that war.

He sighed and took another sip of wine. He had come to his kingship too young, but by all the sleeping gods, he felt old and tired. He turned his back on the city and slid down the balcony wall to sit on the stone bench there.

Until recently, his dreams for his kingship had included the defeat of Strid. Now that he knew they had not murdered his sister and father, he would settle for a cessation of hostilities in the Kreyden. But how to achieve that? Would he live long enough to see it?

He set the glass aside and buried his face in his hands. He wanted Azmei here. He missed her strength and even her unasked-for advice. They could share the throne if she would return. There was precedent. Some three hundred years ago, the sisters Sylene and Sala had ruled together, their children raised as siblings instead of cousins. The throne had passed peacefully to the eldest of Sylene's daughters. When she died heirless ten years later, Sala's son had inherited.

"We could have made it work," he whispered. Then he shook himself. "We can. There is still time." He reached for his glass and drained it. "Gods listen, let there be time."

Footsteps inside the apartments brought him to his feet, one hand dropping to the dagger at his belt. It was probably Gendo, but he shouldn't lower his guard. Not now, not when they knew someone—*Arisanat*—was trying to kill him.

It was Gendo. He stopped at the doorway to the balcony and bowed his head. "Majesty, General Kho and Captain Ysdra are here. I have spread lunch in your receiving room, where they await you. I took the liberty of serving them drinks."

Razem smiled wanly and held out his empty glass. "Good. Fetch me another, would you? I promise not to over-indulge, but I needed something to counter all the coffee."

Gen gave him a reproving look, but took the glass and led the way back to the table.

Once the greetings were done, Razem and his guests settled at the table. Gen served the first course and withdrew. Razem weighed the idea of eating first, then decided against it.

"We know there is business to discuss. Well enough, let's get to it."

Kho nodded to Ysdra, who swallowed the bite he had been chewing. "Majesty, I have been much at Lord Burojan's home this week. He has had many guests. I confess, some of them have...surprised me."

Razem slowly lowered his spoon. "Is that so."

"I thought you should hear it, Majesty," Kho put in.

Razem nodded and gestured for Ysdra to go on. He continued eating as Ysdra spoke, but found his appetite waning as the list went on. Finally he shoved his bowl away and sat back. Gendo took that for his cue to appear with the main course. Razem waited until the plates of meat and bread were set out, then gripped Gendo's wrist.

"Stay and hear this. Ysdra, what are your thoughts on each of Arisanat's visitors?"

Ysdra cleared his throat. "Majesty, Lady Talt is too cordial. She is often, ah, overenthusiastic, but this goes beyond that. She has brought her younger daughter Tarra with her on more than one occasion. Lord Burojan is rather...familiar with the girl."

So Arisanat had finally decided to remarry, Razem thought. And he couldn't have picked more unwisely, in Razem's opinion. He nodded to Ysdra.

"Lord Birona has visited three times."

"Three?" Razem pushed down his sorrow at the words. He had respected Birona. He'd never been quite sure if he liked the man, but he knew him for a shrewd thinker, and Birona had a firm hand with the Council. He knew his father had liked Birona, though they clashed on the matter of the war.

"He does have legitimate cause to visit Lord Burojan, Majesty. Lord Birona may simply be settling Council business with him."

Razem nodded and gestured for Ysdra to continue.

"I have only seen Lord Belnat once, and that time he was unhappy. I could have missed him, of course—I cannot spend all day at Lord Burojan's home." He licked his lips. "Lady Riman has not called. Lady Tel has not called. I cannot say who Lord Burojan has visited while he is away from home. His movements here in the palace can be accounted for, but aside from that..."

He trailed off. The silence stretched. Gendo shifted on his feet and Razem lifted a hand to gesture that he could go. He would ask Gendo's thoughts later. His manservant was shy of speaking up in front of others, and Razem didn't want to make him uncomfortable.

What now? he wondered as they ate in silence. *These are chancy reports, but Ysdra has been one man alone, making observations of his own initiative. And this is not proof. There is still no proof.* He almost didn't want to find proof. But a lack of proof wouldn't prevent Aris from plotting. He couldn't afford to ignore this.

"Very well," he said finally. "Ysdra, I want a watch on Arisanat. Who visits and how often. Where he goes. Everything. Detail a handful of your most trusted men. Tell them they're guarding Aris from further attack, if you think it will help. But leave nothing out." He sighed. "Birona, too. Let us not regret later the safeguards we failed to take."

Ysdra nodded.

"Do you have suggestions, either of you?" Razem looked from one to the other. Ysdra's thin, solemn face was thoughtful. Kho was studying his wine glass.

"We must prepare to defend the palace," Kho said finally.

There was a long silence. Razem thought of how it would look, if people saw the palace bristling with guards. Then he realized the palace guard postings had been doubled since he returned. Of course. People would merely think it a natural reaction to the assassination of King Marsede. He shook his head faintly, ashamed of his slow thinking.

"I don't like it. I don't like suspecting the worst from Aris. And I'm not sure there will be an attack on the palace, not the sort you're thinking."

Kho shrugged. "Better safeguards than regrets," he reminded Razem.

"Yes," he murmured. "But quietly, Emran. And for now, let the guard believe they are protecting against assassins. If they are watching for people creeping in the corners, they shouldn't be taken by surprise by the army that might march against the palace."

CHAPTER TWENTY-FOUR

Dinner had been a quiet affair. Arisanat's cook had outdone himself tonight. The meat had been tender, the pastries flaky, and the bread soft with a crunchy crust. Arisanat had ordered his servants to keep the wine flowing freely, but even that had not lifted the mood of this assembly. Finally he signaled to his servers to bring the dessert wine out.

As soon as his cup was filled, he stood. The guests around his table all raised their gazes to him. He looked around, smiling at Tarra on his left, at Lady Talt to her left, and then Lord Belnat. Tarra had been shy to the point of timidity all night, though her mother's smugness had more than made up for that. Belnat, on the other hand... Arisanat was worried about Belnat. The man still seemed to waver, despite his initial interest in the conspiracy.

Arisanat let his gaze travel further around the table, to Colonel Urval, head of the city guard, seated across from Lord Belnat. Lissa Daix, the head of the merchant guild, sat between Urval and Lord Birona, who sat opposite Tarra at Arisanat's right hand. Arisanat hoped fervently that this was the right group of people. Of the Nine, he had only four—but he had the First, the Third, the Sixth, and the Seventh. There had never been any hope he would get the Second and Fifth, and if he were honest, even the Seventh was less important. The Eighth and Ninth Families were furthest removed from court; he expected they would care little about a regime change, so long as their houses weren't impacted. Lissa Daix was technically a scion of the Ninth Family, but she had no rank within the family.

"My friends. I thank you for being with me tonight as we finalize our plans to return Tamnen to her former glory." Arisanat smiled. "I can think of no others I would rather have with me."

"That's good, since you haven't any others," Birona remarked lazily.

"Yes," Belnat interjected. "I thought you had more than three of the Nine, Arisanat."

Arisanat raised an eyebrow. "Who says that I do not? Belnat, I have invited my closest supporters, not all of them." He smiled benignly. "Besides, have you forgotten how to count? I myself am one of the Nine. I have four present here tonight."

Birona's small eyes were focused on Belnat. "You had better hope we are your closest," he said.

Lady Talt tittered. "Of course Arisanat knows he can trust us all. We have thrown our lot in with his, haven't we?" She smiled and placed a hand on her daughter's. "Haven't we, my dear?"

Tarra looked unhappy about having the attention of the room on her. "Yes, mother," she murmured. She gave Arisanat a shy smile, but he could tell she was troubled. That would require a careful touch. He lifted his glass.

"A toast to our glorious future," he said, and waited until the others murmured a response before drinking. "Come. Let us repair to the sitting room. We will have to do without music. I am afraid I have found no bards for our revolution."

Birona, Talt, and Colonel Urval laughed, as they were supposed to. The others did not. Arisanat led the way to the sitting room, where he flicked a gesture at his servants to keep the wine circulating. He waited until everyone had settled into a spot, then drifted over to Tarra's elbow.

"My dear, you look lovely this evening," he murmured. "I hope nothing is troubling you."

She startled and Arisanat winced internally. He hadn't meant to make her more uncomfortable. She was a good deal younger than he, no more than twenty, and he wasn't displeased with her. He wondered whether Tarra were displeased with him.

"All these plots," she said after a moment. Her voice was faint. "I..." She trailed off, looking at him in confusion.

"You know, I hope," he ventured, "how much I dislike what I must do." He set down his wine glass and took one of her hands in both of his. She was lovely, with her warm brown skin and the red undertones in her black hair. He couldn't help but remember that Talt had tried to snare Razem with her daughters.

"I have always liked Prince Razem, my lord," she said hesitantly. She looked down at their hands, a blush rising to her cheeks. "It is very hard."

"I understand, Tarra," he said quickly. "I love my cousin. We grew up together, and I have always loved him." Gods help him, it was the truth, too. "But he is weak. The best quality of a king is not whether you *like* him, but if he can rule."

Arisanat ducked his head, trying to catch her gaze. She let him, tilting her head up to meet his eyes. After a moment, her expression cleared and she nodded slowly. "I...see."

He squeezed her hand gently. "Your mother has chosen the proper side for you. She is a long-sighted woman. She wishes the best for you." He ventured a smile. "As do I."

"Yes." She smiled faintly.

Arisanat smiled back and kissed her forehead. "Good girl. You'll see. With you by my side, we will be able to make Tamnen what she once was."

Belnat drifted over, a full glass of wine in one hand. "I cannot pretend I didn't overhear what you just said." He darted a glance at Tarra, but she had withdrawn into herself and didn't respond. "Is it true you still love your cousin, Arisanat?"

Arisanat sighed and raised his voice so everyone could hear. "How can anyone doubt that I love my cousin?" he demanded. "I loved Azmei when I sent her to her death, after all. She might have wedded my little brother, had he returned from the war. But instead she forgot him as soon as he was dead. She went to chase a false hope of peace with a nation entirely unlike ours. She was abandoning us. She could not be permitted to continue." He shook his head. "I loved her, but I could not allow it."

"So that was you, too." Birona's voice was sardonic. "I had wondered."

"And how has your trade fared, my Lord Birona, since the princess died?"

Birona's eyes flashed. "Better than it had since the Push, Arisanat. I am sure you will not be surprised."

Arisanat nodded. "And Marsede gave the Strid back their Deranged Duke instead of punishing him for his crimes!" he continued, letting his gaze travel from Birona to Belnat. "How does that help the kingdom? He will send the Strid back to their ravening ways."

Belnat wrinkled his forehead. "Duke Oler was dying. He won't be going back to war."

"You don't think he would train someone to take up his mantle?" Arisanat demanded, and the venom he felt crept into his voice. "Fool!" He turned his back, trying to regain his composure. "No," he said more quietly. "No, Belnat, Marsede did us no favors by sending Oler home to die."

Colonel Urval cleared his throat. "My lord Burojan, I thought this was all arranged."

Arisanat took a long sip of his drink, giving himself a moment to gather his words. "Indeed, Colonel. We are here to finalize our plans, not justify them. Belnat, if you are not with us—"

"I am," Belnat broke in quickly. His mustache trembled as he pursed his lips. "I only hope we are in the right."

Arisanat held his gaze, putting every ounce of conviction into his expression. "We are."

There was a pause. Arisanat needed time to breathe, and he suspected everyone else did. He'd been a fool not to find some bard he could bribe to play without listening to their conversation. If nothing else, he could have found someone who wouldn't be missed if they were held captive in the pantry for a few days. He took a long drink of his wine and sighed.

The Colonel cleared his throat again. "We have nearly everything ready, Lord Burojan." He stepped closer, his expression hesitant. "I still think we should wait until they've calmed down a bit at the palace. Everyone's a little jumpy still from the assassination. If we only gave it a few more—"

"We've been over this, Colonel," Arisanat broke in, his voice warm. "If we wait too long, they'll be preparing for the coronation. It is *vital* that we strike before that." He paused and glanced around at the nobles. "None of us have taken any oaths to Razem yet."

Birona smirked. "Except lady Riman."

Arisanat made a dismissive gesture. He'd never expected Riman on his side. She was too closely tied to Marsede. There had been talk, about five years ago, that the king was thinking of taking her as his second wife. Though nothing had come of those rumors, they did underscore the deep regard between the two of them. It would have been foolish to go to Riman.

Colonel Urval sounded exasperated when he spoke next. "Very well. The odds will be somewhat against us, at least in numbers. We'll have surprise on our side, though, and that's important."

"I think our numbers will be fine," Birona said. He gave the Colonel an indulgent smile. "I am placing my soldiers at your disposal, Colonel. They won't be in my colors, but they will follow your orders." He seemed to register that Belnat and Talt were staring at him and shrugged. "What? I prefer to bet only on a sure thing." His smile widened. "It's how I've kept my fortune."

The Colonel nodded approvingly. "Aye, that'll help even things up. With your troops and my Lord Burojan's, we should outnumber the palace guard. We'll have to make sure General Kho hasn't brought in more of the regular army."

"We're safe on that front," Birona said. "In council yesterday, we ordered the general to station troops a day's ride east of the capital. We wouldn't want to be surprised by an attack from Meekin, would we?" He grinned mirthlessly at

Colonel Urval.

"Well done, my lord," Urval replied.

"Lady Talt should be able to spare her soldiers for the attack," Arisanat said, directing a hard look at Talt.

It was unnecessary. She beamed at him. "Of course, my dear Arisanat. I'll rely on you to handle that after I relay the orders to my captain."

The Colonel was nodding. "That gives us the numbers easily, then. The main thing is that we seize the palace quickly. Once we have the palace closed from the inside, I believe we can hold it indefinitely. By the time reinforcements arrive, we'll have dealt with the prince and my Lord Burojan will be king."

"How do you know the army will listen?" Belnat asked. He was such a mousy fellow. Arisanat suppressed a moue of distaste.

"Once my cousin is dead," he said, "who else do you suppose would the army expect to lead the kingdom?"

Belnat gaped at him. "You're going to *kill* him?"

There was a moment of silence and then Lady Talt laughed shrilly. "My dear Belnat, what did you think we would do? Depose him and leave him a dungeon somewhere? That's just asking for someone to rescue him and place him back on the throne."

Belnat gasped, staring at Talt in fuddlement. Arisanat didn't break the silence. What was there to say? He'd already made his decision, and it was clear his allies stood behind him—except, perhaps, Belnat, and he could be dealt with, if necessary. There were poisons that would incapacitate him long enough for the coup to go forward. Once Arisanat was king, Belnat would fall in line. He was too ambivalent to do anything else.

Belnat drew in a long, shuddering breath. "Gods forgive us for what we plot," he whispered.

Arisanat smiled. Belnat had said 'we.' "I am less concerned with the gods and more concerned with the other Families." He made his voice harsh. "Belnat, your wife was a

Restin. I'll expect you to bring them in hand afterwards. Birona. You deal with Tel and Daix; you have nephews in those families, yes?"

Birona nodded. "And Lissa will be able to help." He raised his glass at the head of the merchant guild, who lifted her glass in response. "The real difficulties will be Riman and Ilzi," he added.

"Oh, Ilzi!" Talt exclaimed. "She's a child!"

"Not so much younger than Tarra here," Belnat remarked. "Four years? Five?"

Arisanat didn't miss the apprehension on Tarra's face. She was a kind girl who hadn't much chance to think for herself. Arisanat hoped she wouldn't falter. "Well," he said, "perhaps Tarra will become friendly with Ilzi and help her understand this is for the best."

After a moment, Tarra met his gaze and smiled tremulously.

Colonel Urval coughed. "You shouldn't meet like this again before the attack. People might notice, and we are relying heavily on the element of surprise."

Arisanat nodded. "As you say, Colonel." He looked around at everyone. "Thank you all. When next we meet, our kingdom will be a different place." *And me at the head of it,* he didn't add. It seemed gauche. And besides, it wasn't as if he'd wanted to be king. He just wanted to see Tamnen win the war against Strid without any further compromises.

Urval was the last to leave. He paused just before walking through the door. "Good luck, my lord. I'll send word when we're ready to move."

***

After the dinner broke up, Arisanat couldn't settle down to anything. He finally poured himself another glass of wine and wandered to the library. Most of the books here were Venra's—books of tactics and strategies, campaign histories, drilling exercises, and adventure tales. A few of them had been

Arisanat's, but most of those were up at the estate, where he needed them. Here in Tamnen City, he had retreated to this room to remember his brother. The tactics and campaign books held no interest for him personally, but they were a part of Venra that he still had.

He sank into his favorite chair, an oversized, cushioned chair covered in leather. His brother had smelled of leather and cloves. Venra had been fond of tea spiced with cloves and nutmeg and carhash seeds. Arisanat closed his eyes, breathing in the scent of leather and thinking of Venra.

The age difference between them had never mattered unless Razem and Azmei were around. When it was just the two brothers, Arisanat was Venra's protector but also his conspirator. He had gone along with Venra's harebrained schemes partly for fun and partly to keep him safe. They had laughed together and teased each other. And fought, yes, as any brothers did, but they had always made up, and no one had supported Arisanat more than Venra.

Arisanat had never really minded being outside their threesome when they were together, though. He'd seen how devoted Razem was to Venra and had approved. And Azmei adored both boys, looking up to them and imitating them. Razem had found her annoying, as any little sister might be, but Venra had worshiped the ground she walked on. When they were young, it was innocent friendship, but as they grew up, Arisanat had seen the way Venra's feelings for her deepened, and he had worried.

The hoped-for agreement between Rija Burojan and Razem had never come about. Razem might have been willing, but Rija hadn't. She had fallen in love with the eldest son of their quarry foreman, and though the man was a commoner, he was clever and industrious. Arisanat had seen his father's disappointment when Rija confessed the truth, but by then her talent with the stone was showing itself. Their father had seen the sense in keeping her at the quarries to assist Arisanat, and he had blessed Rija's marriage.

Perhaps their father had also seen Venra's feelings for

Azmei, though Arisanat never found out one way or the other. Their father had died before they had a chance to test it.

He realized suddenly that his glass was empty. With a sigh, he went to the wine cabinet and poured himself another. Why not? He would likely have few chances to indulge in the coming months. He carried the bottle back to the chair along with his glass.

Venra had finally confided in Arisanat a few days before he left to begin his first assignment in the Kreyden. He'd been home on leave, saying his farewells and making arrangements for his things to be sent to Rivarden after him.

"I know Father isn't happy about Razem and Rija," Venra had said. He was lazing on his bed, head hanging upside down from the edge. It was a warm day at the beginning of summer, and Arisanat had slipped away from his duties and his wife to spend the afternoon with his brother. He'd been half dozing when Venra spoke. He sat up and looked over at his little brother, but Venra's eyes were closed. "She wouldn't have been happy in the palace, though. I'm glad Father realized it."

Arisanat nodded. "She's happier with Fenla. She couldn't have had the freedom to sculpt if she'd become queen."

Venra was quiet for a few heartbeats. "Do you think..." He trailed off, and Arisanat realized his brother was blushing. Or perhaps that was simply the blood rushing to his head from hanging upside down. "That is...Would Father still be happy to tie our family to the Corrone, do you think?"

Arisanat had known this day would come. He'd half dreaded it, even though he wanted his little brother to be happy. He'd seen the way Venra watched Azmei when they were together. These past few years, it had changed. It was pure devotion, and it was sweet and true, but Arisanat had no idea what the king planned for Azmei. Royal children were for treaties—but then, King Marsede had fallen madly in love with Lady Izbel from the Fifth Family, all those years ago when he made her his queen. Everyone knew the stories. Perhaps Marsede would be sympathetic to young love.

"Why wouldn't Father like it?" Arisanat said aloud. No need for Venra to know about his doubts. Not yet. At least Venra had been spared an arranged marriage. Arisanat had done his duty, and he'd grown to care for his wife. Just last week she had announced that he was going to be a father. It took the pressure off of Venra.

Still, Arisanat was sure of Venra's feelings, but he wasn't sure of Azmei's. He'd never seen her look at Venra with anything but love...but it was love for a friend, love for a cousin, as far as Arisanat could tell. He'd never pressed her on the matter. He didn't feel it was his business. And he would never in a million years have asked Razem about it. Azmei was a sweet girl, but she was young, and she still seemed to think there should be quests and romance in life. What if she refused Venra's suit because she was still too childish to see the value in it?

Venra sighed. "I just wondered."

"I don't know, Ven. I think it would please Father." He paused and licked his lips. "Have you spoken to Azmei about this?"

Venra was definitely blushing. He sat up, turning his face away from Arisanat. "No. I don't think she's ready to hear it. She...she's still so absorbed in her books. I think she lives half her life in her imagination." He laughed awkwardly and shrugged. "I don't mind."

Arisanat sat back against the wall, relieved. At least Venra didn't have any unrealistic expectations. Arisanat should have realized he wouldn't. Ven was a smart young man, able to keep the end goal in mind while dealing with the plans along the way.

"I'd thought I would wait until I've done my first year in the desert." Venra was fidgeting with something. "I want to see what it's like. Make sure she would like it. I—I've heard Rivarden is pretty."

Arisanat smiled. "The Desert Jewel, they call it." His heart ached for his brother. He deserved every good thing. "You...Marriage isn't easy, Ven. It's good, I mean. But...well, you know you don't have to marry, right?"

Venra was staring at him. "You're so happy. I know you and Janira didn't choose each other, but you love each other now. And...And I love Azmei, Aris. I don't know if I could stand to see her wed some other man. Gods—imagine if they tried to arrange a treaty through Anderlin! It would kill me."

Arisanat nodded, throat tight. He wanted to hug his brother. "I know. I mean, I thought you loved her. I just— wanted to be sure you know it isn't your duty."

Venra shook his head. "How could Azmei ever be a duty?" he breathed.

Arisanat came back to the present and realized his cheeks were wet, though he was smiling. So much devotion, all for Azmei.

"And as soon as Venra was buried, she let them sell her to Amethir," he snarled. Gods, it had hurt to sign the Perslyn contract. He'd loved her so much, for his own sake as well as his brother's. But she had failed them. Just like Marsede. Just like Razem.

"Tomorrow, Venra," Arisanat whispered. "Tomorrow we will end this charade."

PART THREE RE-BELLION

CHAPTER TWENTY-FIVE

Hawk sat with his back to the fire, gazing out into the darkness. The heat was a pleasant wall against his back, allowing him to enjoy the coolness of the desert night on his face. He could hear the other two moving around behind him, but he didn't want to ruin his night vision by turning to watch them. He had nothing to fear from either of them, anyway. He was more worried about another attack. What if more than one mercenary band had been hired to kill him? What would they do if they realized he was in the company of the princess?

He shook his head. Of all the bizarre things that had happened in his life, this had to be the most bizarre. To leave the prince on an errand for the crown only to discover a princess who was supposed to be three years dead—it almost defied belief. But that was fate for you. The gods were laughing in their sleep.

A rustle beside him made him look up. Princess Azmei crouched next to him, holding out a clay mug with thick walls. "Mulled wine," she said. "With something to take the edge off the pain. I've seen you favoring the arm."

"I don't want my senses dulled," he said, not reaching for it.

Her brows pulled together. She didn't withdraw the mug. "Have some faith, Hawk. I have spent the past three years training with the Shadow Diplomats. Do you think we want our senses dulled as we try to complete a peace mission?"

He narrowed his eyes but accepted the mug. "Shadow Diplomats? I've not heard of them." For that matter, she hadn't been very forthcoming about *how* she was alive when she was supposed to be three years dead.

She gave him that crooked smile that had charmed him before. "Very few have. I probably ought to swear you to secrecy before I tell you, but..." She shrugged and sat on the ground next to him. "We have a few minutes before the meat is ready."

He sniffed the wine, but there was nothing out of the ordinary. He took a tentative sip. A few moments later, he felt the muscles of his back relax as the throbbing in his arm and head eased. He felt her watching him, but to her credit, the princess didn't tease him about being wrong.

"When Orya Perslyn attacked me," she began, her voice low, "I was badly injured. There's no denying that I nearly died. But there are healers in Ranarr who put ours to shame. They saved my life, but we hadn't eliminated the threat to my life. Or, worse, to my brother's life. I thought it best to play dead until we got to the source of the contract on my life. But I couldn't stand to be idle, so I asked the Shadow Diplomat who saved my life to take me as his apprentice." She lifted a mug to her lips and took a tiny sip. "Master Tanvel was the best assassin sworn to the Shadow Council. The Shadow Diplomats serve the peace god, just like all Ranarri. But they serve him in a somewhat more direct way."

Her gaze was on the darkness, so Hawk allowed himself to watch her more closely. There was strength in the lines of her face, and sadness. He wished he could somehow have spared her from the sadness, but he knew the strength must have been born of that sadness.

"Master Tanvel agreed to take me as his apprentice, and so for the past three years I have learned the art of killing while we try to find out who hired the assassins to kill me."

Hawk swallowed. "I...Princess, I told you there had been an attack. I didn't tell you that it was on—"

"My father?" She looked up at him and smiled, her lips curving wistfully. "I know, Hawk. Master Tanvel anticipated it. He stayed behind in Tamnen City to prevent it while he sent me to Meekin to deal with the Perslyns." She bowed her head, black hair swinging forward to hide her eyes. "He stayed in Tamnen City to die while I went to Meekin to earn my own mastery."

"What?"

"You needn't censure me. I tried to argue with him, and I failed. I assure you I have censured myself far more than anyone else could." She shook her head and tilted her face back to look up at the stars. Hawk saw the glitter of tears at the corner of her eyes. "Tanvel saved my life and taught me so much, and the only way I could repay him was to follow his orders and let him die." She sighed. "We knew it was someone in Tamnen. Strid wasn't responsible for my assassination. But we didn't know who."

"Someone in Tamnen," Hawk repeated. He'd forgotten his wine, but Azmei reached over and lifted his mug for him. He took an obedient sip. "You think it was one of the noble families?"

"It seems likely." Her voice was weary. "I'm certain it's one of the Nine. Not Ilzi, of course. She wouldn't. And Lady Riman is above reproach. But..." She trailed off and lowered her head. When she spoke again, her voice was very soft. "But I fear very much that it's Aris, and that will break my brother's heart."

"Aris?" Hawk demanded. "Arisanat Burojan?"

She lifted her head to look at him. "You know him."

"He was with us." Hawk blinked. "He came to Salishok with your brother, and rode with us to Rivarden. He blamed me for his brother's death. I—I served under Lord Venra, before I was captured."

"How could it be your fault Venra died?" Hawk didn't miss the way her voice caught on Venra's name. "You were already in Strid. You were captured in the Push, weren't you? That was...two years at least, before Venra died."

"Three." Hawk sipped his wine again. It was cooling quickly. "I misspoke. He didn't blame me for Venra's death, exactly. But he blamed me for living when Venra did not."

She bowed her head again. They were silent for a long time. "Do you think Arisanat is capable of hiring assassins?"

Hawk swallowed. "Your highness, that is just the question I asked myself when you asked me who wanted me dead."

There was nothing else to say after that. They sat in

silence until he finished his wine. Then Princess Azmei took his mug from him, cool fingers grazing his and sending a flash of heat up his arm. She rose and went back to tend the fire.

"The meat is done," she said. "Yarro, are you awake?"

He heard her shaking the boy. He'd been in a stupor most of the afternoon, though he'd roused once to tell them to go around Rivarden and again when they stopped for the evening. Hawk supposed that great beast Yarro rode must be more docile than he looked, or else he must love the boy more than anything else. He hadn't misplaced a foot all afternoon.

With a sigh, Hawk stood. His arm had subsided to a dull ache, he realized. Whatever she had given him, it was effective, but he didn't feel dizzy or drowsy the way he was used to with painkillers.

When he sat down by the fire, Azmei handed him a plate. "Thank you for the hare," she said. "It'll make our supplies last longer."

He took the plate, nodding. He began eating as she turned to shake Yarro once more before giving up. She set the boy's plate near him and came back to sit a few feet from Hawk at the fire.

"Why are we going this way? Won't we run into trade from the mines? They're southeast of Rivarden somewhere, according to my map."

"We shouldn't." Hawk smiled. "You may have maps, Princess, but this is where I grew up. There are mines all along the foothills here, south and southeast and east of the city, but I know paths that are seldom used by the miners. There are a few villages up in the hills to the east of here."

"And south?"

He stiffened. "Not south." To the south was the Shrouded Vale, and he'd grown up with nightmares about the tales of that valley. People didn't go that way. Those who did never returned. Hawk forced himself to relax. "The route around the city is longer to the southeast, but we'll have more game if we stick to the foothills." He took a bite of the hare and reflected how odd it was that a princess should be able to dress and roast her own game. "More water, too," he added.

Azmei lapsed into silence as they ate. When they had reached the stage where they were picking shreds off the bones and licking their fingers, Hawk ventured a question. "I thought you said his business was in Rivarden. Why did he tell us to take you around?"

She glanced over at Yarro, who still hadn't roused from his trance. He was rocking slightly in place, and if Hawk watched long enough, he realized the boy must be rocking in time with his heartbeat. Or perhaps the heartbeat of whatever sent those visions of his.

Azmei sighed. "I might as well tell you what I know. I don't think he'll fully wake up until we get there."

"Get where?"

"Listen. You know he has visions. He left Meekin to get away from his family, but he was following those visions. I think he's trying to find them. Whoever sends those visions."

Hawk looked down at his empty mug and reached for a water skin. "This doesn't seem like the wisest path, Princess. Are you sure—"

"Stop calling me that," she said tightly. "I'd rather you just call me Aevver and forget what I told you completely."

"How do you propose I forget that you are my dead liege, returned to us after years of mourning?"

"You weren't even in Tamnen," she snapped. Hawk fell silent. He shouldn't have argued with her. She might be a skilled warrior and capable of dressing out her own game, but she was still a princess. No matter what she said, he could never forget that fact, and he shouldn't.

"I'm sorry," she said after a moment. "That was unkind."

Hawk shrugged. "It was the truth."

Azmei smiled wryly at him. "I've met very few kind truths. I'm sorry, Hawk."

"My lady." He held her gaze, hoping she would see that he took no offense.

They lapsed into a companionable silence. After a while, Azmei refilled his mug. She didn't speak, but he could see it was another dose of the painkiller. He didn't think he needed it. When he glanced over at her, she was looking past him. He turned and saw that Yarro's eyes were open.

"Where are we?" the boy asked.

Azmei crawled over to him and held out the mug. "East of Rivarden. You told us to go around." She pressed the mug into his hands without touching him. "Drink this. It'll help your leg."

"It doesn't hurt as much. We can't stop, Aevver—" He broke off, his face twisting. He didn't refuse the mug, but he pulled away from her and closed his eyes.

Azmei sighed and withdrew. Hawk wondered why it hurt her so much that the boy was angry. How long had they been together, these two? It couldn't have been too long, if she'd been in Tamnen City with Master Tanvel just a short time ago. Gods, what a convoluted mess this all was.

Yarro drank the wine without speaking to either of them. Hawk turned his back to the fire again, relishing the warmth and letting his vision readjust to the night. He heard Yarro eating. The horses shifted drowsily where they were tethered. Somewhere in the darkness a desert fox yipped. Hawk smiled. He'd always been fond of the big-eared foxes. They were shy and had been known to raid the fowl villagers bred, but there was something fierce and endearing about their loyalty to their families.

"We have enough food and water for another week. Two if we drink sparingly," Azmei said. She came over to sit next to him again. "I'd planned to resupply in Rivarden. I just...I don't like to upset him."

Hawk glanced sidelong at her. "Too late for that, I think."

She rubbed her forehead. "I don't need to make it worse."

***

The Voices wouldn't leave Yar alone. They were always

in his head now, sometimes as a whisper, sometimes as a rumble, sometimes as a hiss. They didn't always speak with words, but he had to concentrate to filter out the singing of their Voices in order to hear anything Azmei and Hawk said to him. That was all right, though. Yar didn't want to hear anything Azmei said.

Azmei—the princess. The woman who had his sister killed. Why had she lied to him?

NEVER MIND THAT, LITTLE BROTHER. HURRY. TIME RUNS TOO FAST FOR YOUR LITTLE LIVES. COME TO US. FOLLOW OUR CALL.

He rubbed at his forehead. Their Voices were always in his head, but they weren't as enveloping as they used to be. He could feel his body, could see where he was going. He could hear Azmei and Hawk talking, faintly. Yar wasn't sure if this was better or worse than having them take over his entire consciousness. At least this way he might know if there was some danger. He might not hurt himself again like he had his calf.

But he couldn't ignore the nagging headache, either.

"Do you think there's a storm coming? The sky's so much darker to the south," Azmei said. Hawk answered, but Yar didn't hear his reply; it was blotted out by a flash of rage. How dare she lie to him?

Laughter boomed through his head. WE TOLD YOU, LITTLE BROTHER. TOLD YOU SHE HAD SECRETS. YOU DIDN'T CARE.

DIDN'T CARE, snickered the Slithery Voice.

DIDN'T CARE, echoed half a dozen other Voices.

Well, I do now, Yar thought at all of them. He stared down at his hands, folded on the pommel of his saddle. Firefoot's steps were smooth, making a comforting thump on the sandy rock underfoot.

SILLY MORTALS, one of the Voices teased. NEVER LET ANYTHING GO DESPITE YOUR SHORT LIVES.

SHE LOVES YOU AS ORYA DID, said the Wise Uncle Voice. WE SEE THAT NOW.

She killed *Orya!* Yar thought, furious.

NO. SHE CAME SEEKING YOU. ASK HER.

Yar shook his head and clapped his hands over his ears. For all the good it did him. He could still feel their laughter. He could still hear the singing. His head throbbed.

"Yar? Are you all right?" Azmei had dropped back alongside him. He could feel her watching him, but he scrunched his eyes closed. He knew he was acting like a child. He didn't care. He wanted to hate her. She'd made him love her, made him trust her, and then she betrayed him.

SILLY MORTALS, said Wise Uncle Voice.

Yar glared at her. "Why didn't you tell me?"

She sighed. "I'm supposed to be dead. I had to be sure I could trust you." She tugged her hood up to shade her forehead better.

Yar looked away from her. They were in the foothills. Everything was brown and ochre and tan. The sky was hot and blue overhead. In front of them, behind the tallest hills, loomed a darkness that beckoned him. He shifted in the saddle and wished Azmei would leave him alone.

"You didn't tell me about your Voices right away," she pointed out.

"That's different!" he snapped. The Slithery Voice snickered in his head.

"Is it?" Azmei finally looked away from him. She scanned their surroundings and turned to face forward. Yar didn't answer her. He didn't have an answer. It *felt* different, but maybe it wasn't. He didn't care.

YOU SHOULD CARE. YOU MUST KNOW YOURSELF, LITTLE BROTHER, BEFORE YOU REACH US. YOU MUST SEE INSIDE YOURSELF.

"They're talking to you more now, aren't they?" Azmei asked softly.

Yar glanced ahead to see if Hawk was listening. "We're close. I think...it's like they don't have to reach as far to me." He saw her nod out of the corner of his eye.

"You're the princess," he burst out. "My sister was

supposed to kill you. Why don't you hate me?"

Azmei shrugged. "*You* didn't try to kill me. I'm sorry she left you."

He glanced sidelong at her. "You're not sorry she's dead," he accused.

"Not really. You can't attack the princess and escape punishment. But I am sorry you lost your sister."

He looked away again.

SHE SPEAKS TRUE, LITTLE BROTHER. WE KNOW. WE CAN TELL.

How is it you could never tell before? Yar demanded.

WE AREN'T TRYING TO REACH AS FAR TO HER NOW. The Voice snickered in his head. Yar rolled his eyes and looked back down. He ran his fingers through Firefoot's mane.

"I don't like the look of that sky," Hawk called back. "We're going to turn west for a bit. Let's see if it clears up down that way."

Yar glanced up in time to see Hawk turn his horse. Azmei waited until Firefoot turned before she, too, turned west. At the change in directions, Yar's head squeezed. He whimpered, lifting a hand to press at the pain behind his brow.

"Yar?" Azmei murmured.

"No. South, Hawk. South," he whimpered. "We're going the wrong way." With every step Firefoot took, the throbbing in his head grew worse. He clutched at his head. Hoof beats moved away from him. Azmei had caught up to Hawk.

The singing subsided as the pain increased. It meant Yar could hear their conversation without straining.

"How accurate are those visions of his?" Hawk asked. He sounded like he'd tried to lower his voice, but Yar didn't care.

"I don't know." Azmei paused for three ever-more-painful steps. "He knew your name."

Hawk was silent.

"What's so bad about this Shrouded Vale, anyway?" Azmei asked.

"Besides the fact that the mouth of the vale is always wrapped in a wall of mist or fog or...something?" Hawk's voice was sardonic.

"All right," Azmei said after a moment, "besides that."

Hawk snorted. "I've never been there. I've never met anyone who has. I've never even met anyone who claims to have been anywhere near it. People don't go there."

"How do you know? Maybe they go there and it's so nice they just stay."

Hawk snorted again.

"What do you think is there?"

"Who knows." Hawk cleared his throat. "Maybe a clan of magic users. Maybe man-eating monsters. Maybe it's where the gods sleep."

The Voices chuckled in Yar's head. He shivered. Gods? He hoped not. He couldn't believe the gods would be like his Voices. What god would be the Slithery Voice? And anyway, weren't there too many Voices to be the five gods?

"Let's go closer tonight," Azmei said. She lowered her voice, but the pain subsided briefly so Yar heard her. "Maybe he'll change his mind tomorrow."

He wouldn't. But let her think that, if it got them to ride south. Yar lifted both hands to squeeze his head, trying to change the pressure inside his skull.

Firefoot shifted under him and the pain in Yar's head faded until all that remained was pressure with no discomfort. Firefoot had turned south. Yar opened his eyes to make certain Hawk and Azmei had, too.

Hawk's shoulders were set, his back very straight. Yarro wondered if he were angry at Yar or at Azmei. Yar didn't want Hawk to be angry with him. He didn't know why, but he liked Hawk right off. He wanted Hawk to think he was right.

Then one of the Voices snickered in his head again and Yar was swept into the song.

***

Azmei frowned at the haze in the southern sky. Over her right shoulder, the sun had faded into a diffuse golden-tan light. Everything she could see, including Hawk, the dun, and herself, was golden-tan. Even Yarro's cloak blended in. Only Firefoot stood out, his bright bay head held high despite the rising wind.

Yar hadn't spoken since before midday. Azmei couldn't tell if he were still angry at her, or if he had just decided to go put up with her until they got to wherever the Voices were leading him. Once or twice she had seen his shoulders jerk, but that could just be the sand flies.

Sandy's hooves rang faintly against the rocky trail. Azmei hoped his shoes held out. She'd planned to have them checked in Rivarden. Then again, she'd planned to do a lot of things in Rivarden. She had *not* planned to find the legendary commander who had just barely been released from captivity, and she'd certainly not planned to skip Rivarden entirely. She sighed and shielded her eyes to look ahead to where Hawk led them. Was the haze to the south thicker? Maybe it only looked that way because the sun was lower in the sky. She glanced to the right again and frowned. The sun had slipped behind a bank of dark clouds.

Was that a storm? She hadn't thought there would be much rain this close to the desert. Just because they'd left the sand dunes behind them two days ago didn't mean the country here was much more forgiving. The wind gusted her hood back off her head. Sandy nickered.

"Yarro?" she called over her shoulder. She looked back. He was riding with his head down, swaying slightly with every step Firefoot took. He'd fallen into a stupor again. Damn those Voices, anyway. Who were they? What did they want from him? He was such a bright boy, despite his naiveté. If he could just escape the clutches of these tyrannical visions, he could make something of himself, now that he was away from his family.

Azmei sighed and urged Sandy into a trot. As she pulled abreast of Hawk, he glanced over at her and her stomach jumped. He was handsome, despite the sadness carved in every line of his body. She wondered what he had hoped for when he learned he would be free again. Did he have a family awaiting his return? Had he expected to take up his position in the army again?

What did you think of first, when you learned you were coming home? she asked herself, and almost smiled. That was easy. The coffee and the doves and the spices. Maybe that was what Hawk had thought of, too.

She realized he was watching her, a quizzical half smile on his face. Her cheeks burned as she straightened in the saddle. "Do you know the weather out here?"

He raised an eyebrow and looked to the south. "That's not weather," he said. "That's the Shrouded Vale."

"Maybe that is, but what about the wind? Look," she said, pointing. The wind was blowing her hair across her face. She squinted, trying to see.

Hawk swore. "That doesn't look good."

The bank of clouds was building, rising into towering cliffs that ranged in color from dark brown to purple. Azmei swallowed and looked from the cloud bank to the southern haze. Neither direction looked appealing, but she could tell from the way the wind was picking up that turning around would do them no good.

"What do we do?" she asked.

"We should find shelter," Yarro said. Azmei jumped. He'd come up quietly enough that she hadn't heard Firefoot's hoof beats above the rising wind.

Hawk raised his voice to be heard. "Our best bet is to ride for the hills. There might be a dry cave or a tumble of rocks we can shelter in. We should—Yarro!"

Firefoot had broken into a trot. Azmei swore and nudged Sandy. "We can't lose him!" she called back.

After a few minutes at that pace, Azmei found herself leaning forward, wanting to urge the dun faster. The wind was whipping her clothes around; she could feel the lash of sand against her cheeks. She squinted, concentrating on keeping her eyes on Yar.

She'd never seen him so confident. He shouted for them to follow and cut off uphill at an angle across the wind. Azmei screamed at him but he didn't look back. Against her better judgment, she turned Sandy after him. A few moments later, Hawk's black outpaced her. After only half a minute, Azmei felt the wind drop as they entered some hidden windbreak. Behind her, the building storm seemed to howl like a beast that had been denied its prey, but ahead of her, she saw Yarro let Firefoot slow his trot.

Hawk caught up with him first. She heard the sharp tone he used, but not the words. To her surprise, Yarro snapped back, and that she did hear.

"Shelter!" He slowed Firefoot again so Azmei caught up. When he looked over at her, she caught her breath. His gaze was vacant, but he was somehow completely alert. "There's a cave. Not big, but enough for us—all of us." He paused. "Horses too."

"How do you know?" Azmei demanded, but he was already urging Firefoot ahead.

She didn't have the breath to question him further. She exchanged a wary look with Hawk, and they followed in silence. The dun trotted on without hesitation, and Azmei decided she had faith in her horse, even if she doubted Yarro's voices.

To her astonishment, it was barely a handful of minutes before Yar was guiding Firefoot to a gaping cave mouth in the cliff wall. When he reached it, he dismounted and beckoned to them. She halted the dun beside Firefoot and Hawk's black and slid down, her feet sinking into soft sand. How could Yarro have known this cave was here? The Voices had to have told him.

As soon as they got under cover of the rocks, the howl of the wind dropped to a low moan, rising and falling in pitch but almost quiet enough to ignore. Sandy shook himself violently, pelting Azmei with sand. She let go of his lead, confident he had no desire to go back out into the storm.

For several heartbeats they stood in the near dark, letting their eyes adjust and—in Azmei's case, at least—digging sand out of ears.

"Do you have a torch?" Yarro's voice echoed back to her.

"Just a moment," Hawk rumbled. Azmei stood still until she saw a spark flare ahead of her. A few moments later, shadows loomed around them. The light was comforting. There was a cozy intimacy to their shelter from the storm. The back of the cave wasn't visible in the flickering light, but it didn't matter somehow.

"I'll build a fire and brew some tea," Hawk said, "if my lady will care for the horses." Azmei gave him a pleased look and did as she was told. He'd finally begun treating her like a person instead of a princess. She could only hope it would continue.

Finally she could shake out her bedroll and sit in front of the fire. She leaned against her pack and took the steaming mug Hawk handed to her. "How did you know about this place, Yar?" she asked.

His complacent expression shadowed, his eyes hooded. "They told me. They know we're close."

"Who are these beings, Yar?" Hawk's head was bent to stare into his mug, his face half in shadow.

Yarro didn't answer for a long time. Azmei listened to the howl of the wind and the crackle of the fire. Finally Yar said, "That's what I'm going to find out."

"How do you know they're not luring us into a trap?" Hawk asked.

This time, Yar didn't answer. When Azmei peered through the darkness at him, she saw that he'd lapsed into a trance, his eyelids lowered until only the gleam of the firelight told her his eyes were open. He wasn't rocking in place, but he didn't speak again.

Azmei glanced at Hawk and found him watching her. She told herself the sudden warmth was from the fire, but she suspected she was blushing. What was it about those charcoal eyes that made her feel so strange? She took a hasty sip of her tea but didn't look away. After a moment, Hawk smiled slowly.

"Why do you follow him, my lady?" he murmured. "Half the time he seems a halfwit, though I can tell there's more to him than that. But how did you come to know him? He seems convinced you killed his sister."

Azmei cupped her hands around her mug and breathed in the scent of the tea. "In a way, it's my fault she's dead. But mostly it's her own fault. Orya traveled with me to Ranarr when I went to meet Prince Vistaren. The Ranarri Diplomats had arranged a treaty between us and Amethir, if Vistaren and I would agree to marry. I agreed to meet him, and someone—" *Arisanat?* "—objected to that." She sighed. "I didn't realize at the time that Orya was an assassin. We became friends on the ship. It was nice to have someone near my age to talk to." She smiled wryly. "Until she tried to kill me."

CHAPTER TWENTY-SIX

Razem was learning that kings could not afford to be late risers. He'd been up since dawn and was on his third cup of coffee, and he was trying valiantly to ignore his desire to crawl back into the feathery softness of his bed. There was too much to be done, and too little time in which to do it.

He and Kho had compiled a list of offenses they could prove against the Tamnese nobleman who plotted against the throne. Despite Razem's unhappiness over the situation, he had also compiled a list of reasons it was likely Arisanat. Ysdra's watchers had reported on a dinner hosted at Arisanat's home; Talt, Belnat, and Birona had been in attendance, along with the head of the merchant guild. She was an offshoot of the Daix family, which deepened Razem's unhappiness. Was Daix involved in the plot? He could find no other connection, but that unfortunately didn't prove anything.

Kho shoved his chair back from the table and turned to face Razem directly. "Majesty, I do not think we can wait any longer. We must apprehend at least Lord Burojan. He must be the ringleader of the insurrection. If we bring him to the palace under our control, perhaps we can still forestall an all-out civil war."

Razem rubbed his forehead. What would his father have done in this situation? More than ever, he missed his father's level temper and sound advice. "Soon," he promised.

"We've finished going through Tanvel's documents," Kho argued. "We won't be able to prove that it's Burojan until we arrest him and seize his own records. Not unless you wish to send someone into the house secretly to gather that information."

"No," Razem said sharply. "I will not become King Harkai, cringing at the center of a web of informants and backstabbers. We are not like that."

Kho opened his mouth, but before he could speak, someone tapped on the door and Gendo looked in. "Majesty, you have a visitor. Lady Tarra Talt is here to see you, and she begs an audience."

Razem raised an eyebrow. Tarra Talt—who had not been in attendance with her mother and sister at Marsede's funeral. Why would Tarra be coming to see him? Under any other circumstances, he might have cringed, but the situation being what it was, it intrigued him. "Show her in, Gendo. And bring more coffee."

"Majesty, this interruption—"

"Might be important, Emran. You said Talt was at Aris' dinner. Perhaps Tarra can shed some light on that." He leaned back in his seat and watched the door expectantly.

Tarra was wearing a dress of muted purple-brown. It didn't flatter her coloring, but she had a quiet self-possession that made it unimportant. Her hair was pulled into a simple hairstyle and the only jewelry she wore was a necklace of twisted gold. The moment she was inside the room, she sank into a deep curtsy and held it.

"Good morning, Lady Tarra," Razem said. "You may approach."

She rose and walked sedately to him, pausing before sinking into a curtsy once more. "Majesty. I thank you for taking the time to see me."

"His majesty is very busy," Kho began, but Tarra cut him off with a glance.

"I am aware of how many demands there are on your time," she said directly to Razem. "My king, I am here alone, in defiance of my mother and the man I have been betrothed to. I am here to tell you of a threat and to beg you for mercy."

"In that case, you'd better stand up," Razem said. "Join us at the table and explain yourself."

She hesitated before choosing a seat equidistant from Razem and Kho. "My mother is not an evil woman, but she is ambitious and desperate. You cannot be unaware of her attempts to secure husbands for my sister and me. Last week she promised me to Arisanat Burojan, in exchange for her support." She folded her hands on the table and met Razem's eyes. "Your cousin plots your overthrow, King Razem. My mother has agreed to provide troops and loyalty if he agrees to make me his queen."

The coffee Razem had already drunk gurgled in his stomach. He straightened. "You have proof of this?"

"I witnessed it myself. Arisanat invited us to dinner with his co-conspirators. Lord Birona and Lord Belnat are chief among them. He also has the support of the merchants guild and the city guard."

"The city guard?" Razem repeated. Gods save them, Arisanat was shrewder than he'd expected. The rivalry between palace and city guard was long-running. Usually it was a friendly one, but there had been moments when it had spilled into more than posturing and boasts.

Kho was at attention in his seat. "Lady Tarra, we will need all the details."

Razem listened in rising horror as Tarra outlined what she knew of Arisanat's plot to take the throne. When she had finished, Razem swallowed and looked at Kho.

"We were too slow," the general said. He was staring at the tabletop, shaking his head.

"No," Razem said. Kho couldn't give up on him. Razem wouldn't make it through this without Kho. "There's still time, and thanks to Lady Tarra, we know enough to strike now." He licked his lips. "We can prevent this, if we act quickly."

"Emran. Send Captain Ysdra to arrest Arisanat, Belnat, Birona, and Talt. *Quietly.* We cannot have any gossip. Bring them to the palace, where we will deal with them accordingly. After they have been brought to me, have Guild Leader Lissa Daix arrested. Once that is done, and only then, issue an invitation for City Guard Commander Urval to join us here. I will be most interested in hearing what he has to say to these allegations."

"Majesty," Tarra began.

"You have done us a great service, Lady Tarra. I suggest you stay here so we may protect you."

She straightened in her seat. "Am I a prisoner?" she asked stiffly.

Razem made his expression softer. He probably should make her his prisoner. She had been involved in the plotting. But she had chosen to stop it, at great personal expense. "No," he said. "But do you honestly believe you will be safe anywhere else? Where would you go? Home? How will your mother react when she learns you came to me?"

Tarra was silent. She folded her hands in her lap and bowed her head.

"No one will hinder you if you choose to leave. But I will have rooms prepared for you, in the event you should choose to accept our hospitality." Razem stood. "Kho, send Ysdra now. Have him report back as quickly as possible."

Kho bowed and went. Razem looked at Tarra. He hoped she would stay. "Lady Tarra, you have shown great courage in coming to me. You have my thanks."

"Tezira and I always knew you had no desire to marry either of us," she said softly. "But you were always polite to us and kind to Mother. It is a kindness I wished to repay somehow."

He swallowed. Gods, he'd thought—he'd hoped—he had been more subtle than that. Before Azmei left, he'd always sent his sister to cut them off before Talt could flaunt her daughters before him. "It is not a matter of desire, my lady, but of...necessity. I never expected to have any choice in the matter of my marriage, and so I have tried to avoid any...complications." He hadn't wanted to fall in love at all. Harmless flirtations were one thing, but his father's marriage had been made purely for love, and while it had been a happy marriage, it had not strengthened Tamnen's standing with other nations. Razem had always expected to be married in a treaty, much as

Azmei had.

Tarra smiled. "As you say," she said. Razem had a feeling she could see right through him.

There was a tap at the door and Kho reappeared. "Ysdra has gone," he said. "I instructed him to be subtle."

"Let us hope he will return swiftly," Razem said. Then all that was left was for them to wait.

***

Arisanat was eating breakfast when they came to arrest him. He'd always had a weakness for sweet pastries, and he was enjoying the cinnamon and sugar crust while reading a cryptic note from the commander of the City Guard. He had managed to pick out the fact that Urval would be ready to attack tomorrow at dawn. Arisanat had just indulged in the thought that, since Razem was such a late riser, the revolution could probably wait until the eighth hour, when his chamberlain flung open the door and scrambled into the room without warning, shoving it closed behind him.

"My Lord Arisanat, I apologize—I couldn't stop—" The door slammed open again, shoving into the chamberlain. He stumbled aside with a cry. Captain Ysdra stepped inside, his thin, solemn face drawn into lines of terrible resolve.

"Captain Ysdra," Arisanat said, injecting surprise into his voice while he fumbled for any explanation but the most obvious for the interruption. "Have you discovered who attacked me?"

Ysdra ignored the question. "Lord Arisanat Burojan, Head of the First Family, you are under arrest for treason, for conspiracy against His Majesty King Razem, for committing murder upon His Majesty King Marsede, for attempting murder on Her Highness Princess Azmei, and for attempting the overthrow of the gods-ordained throne."

Arisanat took another bite of pastry and washed it down with a sip of coffee. *Be calm,* he told himself. *Do not give yourself away.* "That is an impressive list of charges," he said mildly, "but the only thing I am currently engaged in is breakfast. Perhaps you will sit and join me."

Who had betrayed him? Or had he betrayed himself somehow? What had Ysdra meant, "attempting murder" on Azmei? The princess had been mourned and memorialized. His informants from the Amethirian court had reported that Prince Vistaren went into mourning himself for six months. He was so close! How could this all unravel now?

"Surrender peacefully, Lord Burojan," Ysdra said. "The king may yet be inclined to clemency." He approached the table, drawing his sword.

"Clemency?" Arisanat repeated, slipping one hand down to the knife at his belt. He curled his fingers around the knife and his fingernails dug into his palm. "*Clemency?* The king did not show clemency when he refused to pay the Strid back for their murder of my brother." He gathered his legs under him, tensing his muscles to spring. "The king showed more clemency to the *Deranged Duke* than he showed his own people. I am not interested in the king's *clemency*."

He jumped to his feet, shoving the chair over with a crash. Ysdra was expecting it. He raised his blade to fend off Arisanat's attack, but the chamberlain leapt on his back, locking his arms around the captain's shoulders and pinning his arms. Ysdra shouted, thrashing enough to break the chamberlain's hold. Arisanat swung his knife again and Ysdra blocked it again.

Several crown soldiers burst through the door, spreading out on either side of the table. The chamberlain hooked his foot around Ysdra's ankle, yanking him off balance. Even then, Ysdra seemed reluctant to hurt the unarmed servant. He shoved him back with an elbow in his stomach, but it had succeeded in distracting him. Arisanat lunged, thrusting his knife deep into Ysdra's gut.

The captain groaned and fell back. He managed to slice Arisanat's forearm as he fell. One of the crown soldiers leapt forward.

"Guards!" Arisanat shouted. "To me! Protect your lord!"

The door behind him opened and his guards, belatedly alerted to the threat, boiled into the room behind him.

Arisanat slashed at the next soldier in line, who automatically blocked the attack. It opened the soldier to a cut from one of Arisanat's guards, and soldier's sword clattered to the ground, hand still gripping the hilt. The soldier screamed and bashed his shield at the guard, but Arisanat didn't stay to watch the rest of the fight. He gripped his chamberlain's arm and yanked him out of the dining hall, slamming the door behind him.

The chamberlain was disheveled, hair askew across his forehead, but his gaze was alert on Arisanat's face. "You're unhurt?"

Arisanat nodded. "And you?"

"That doesn't matter, my lord."

It did, but there was nothing Arisanat could do either way. "Send word to Urval. We can't wait until dawn. We must attack. Get word to Urval first, then get word to our allies. We attack *now*."

CHAPTER TWENTY-SEVEN

Yarro woke suddenly and completely. He was propped up against something soft. It was almost all dark around him, except for the glow of embers off to his left. Behind him he could hear the breathing of horses. One of them shifted its feet.

He rolled to his knees and looked around, squinting through the dimness. Azmei was lying down, rolled into her cloak. Hawk was sitting up, but the way his head had drooped to one said he was asleep too. Besides the horses, Yarro couldn't hear anything. What had woken him?

LITTLE BROTHER. YOU ARE HERE.

Oh. Yarro's face didn't know whether to frown or smile. He peered through the darkness. *Here? In this cave?*

IN OUR VALLEY.

His mind was seized with a vision of huge golden eyes staring down at him from the darkness. Somehow he knew it wasn't real, but he could feel the tug in his gut.

COME, LITTLE BROTHER.

The golden eyes turned from him and the darkness fell away like panes of glass. The sun was shining down on him, baking his shoulders, heating his head. He was standing in front of a massive stone structure, half palace and half cave. It had a huge, arching entry that made him feel like an ant. The stone hall was massive and ancient, the weight of untold years bearing down on those stone arches.

I CALL YOU, LITTLE BROTHER. COME. I, DAR-IXU, CALL YOU. COME. BE OUR VOICE. SPEAK FOR US. COME.

Yarro stood. He could no more disobey that call than he could fly. His heart thudded in his chest, making his breath come faster. He picked his way over to the horses, where he found Firefoot by touch. The horse breathed on him but made no noise as Yarro leaned against him. He didn't know where they were going, but he knew they had to.

Side by side, Yarro and Firefoot walked away from the embers, deeper into the cave. Firefoot's hooves rang against the stone floor.

Behind him, Yarro heard someone move.

He wound his fingers in Firefoot's mane and swung up onto his back. They would try to stop him, but he couldn't allow that. He had to follow the Voices.

"Yarro?" It was Hawk's sleepy voice. One of the horses nickered and Yarro heard cloth rustle. "Yarro, where are you going?" Hawk's voice was sharper. He was alert now.

COME, LITTLE BROTHER.

Yarro looked over his shoulder as the fire flared back to life behind him. He smiled. "I am Called," he said, and urged Firefoot into motion.

Behind him, he heard Azmei and Hawk calling after him, but their words no longer mattered. He was going to his Voices. He had been Called.

YOU ARE JUST AS WE HAVE SEEN YOU, Darixu told him. COURAGEOUS AND STRONG, UNSTOPPA-BLE AND UNKNOWABLE. YOU ARE OUR LITTLE BROTHER. YOU ARE OUR VOICE.

I'm coming, Yar said in his mind. *I can hear you so much clearer now.*

YOU HAVE DONE WELL, LITTLE BROTHER. YARRAX, OUR VOICE. COME. YOUR COMPANIONS WILL FOLLOW.

They'll be safe, won't they? he asked, suddenly anxious, but the booming laughter of Darixu reassured him.

THEY HAVE GUIDED AND PROTECTED YOU. WE WOULD NEVER HARM THEM.

And you won't eat Firefoot. The horse was carrying him

trustingly through the darkness. Perhaps he saw better than Yar did, or perhaps he was just placing one foot in front of the next, knowing Yar needed to go. Either way, Yar didn't want his horse ending up as a meal. He squeezed his eyes shut.

BUT SUCH HEART, whispered the Slithery Voice. THERE WOULD BE SUCH FIRE IN HIS BLOOD. HE WOULD MAKE A MEAL FOR KINGS.

XELLAX! There was a reproving note in Darixu's Voice. YOU MAY TEASE OUR LITTLE BROTHER, BUT YOU MUST NEVER THREATEN HIM.

Yar felt Xellax's sigh as a gust of breeze against his face. He flinched, then laughed. Was he that close? Somehow he wasn't even afraid of Xellax anymore. He had finally arrived.

Firefoot stopped moving and whinnied, the sound shrill and interested. Yar opened his eyes and lifted a hand to block the sudden glare of light. He squinted his eyes almost closed as they teared up. There had been no warning, no gradual lightening of the tunnel. It was completely dark and then it simply...was light.

Yar sat up straight, ignoring the tears on his cheeks as he stared around him. They were standing on a hillside in bright sunshine. There was no storm. When he looked behind him, there was no tunnel. His heart thumped once in his chest and then he turned to look forward again. The tunnel had been there. It would be there again, if he needed it.

Firefoot was on high alert, his ears pricked forward, nostrils flared, but he was not afraid. He lifted onto his back feet slightly, then dropped to all fours and snorted, shaking his mane. Yarro laughed.

"It's beautiful!" he said aloud.

Behind him was an impenetrably high wall of mountain. Spreading out around him was a lush green vale filled with date palms. A sparkling river ran along the lowest point of the valley, tributaries wandering down the slopes to join with it. A herd of deer grazed about a hundred yards from where he and Firefoot stood. They were unconcerned with his presence. A bird darted past him, spiraling past. Yar followed its flight, smiling at its joyful abandon...

...and gasped.

Far up, deep in the sky, other shapes swooped and swirled. They, too, flew with joyful abandon, but they were larger forms, huge and graceful. Blue and red, golden and white, they rode air currents and threw their leathery wings wide to catch the wind. They dove and danced, singing all the while.

Dragons.

COME, LITTLE BROTHER! called a chorus of Voices. COME TO US!

When he lowered his gaze to the land again, he saw that some of the crags at the far end of the valley were occupied by dragons, perched and watching him.

At last he understood. No wonder they could call to him from so far away. They were magnificent. They were powerful. And they were isolated here. They had called to him from their loneliness, from their need. They could speak to him, and he could speak to others.

COME, YARRAX! JOIN US!

Whooping with excitement, Yar nudged Firefoot into a gallop.

***

Hawk swore and punched his thigh. He could kick himself for nodding off while on watch. What had possessed Yarro to go running off? And more importantly, where had he gone? Hawk had explored the cave thoroughly after they took shelter from the storm. It hadn't been a deep cave, and there had been no surprises.

"Don't blame yourself," Azmei said. She had prodded the fire into life and was kneeling next to it, trying to light a torch. "Yar is following a call that's stronger than anything we have. It took hold of him while we were running from the storm."

Hawk sighed and rubbed at his thigh. That was going to

bruise. "I shouldn't have fallen asleep," he muttered.

"No, but you did. Maybe these Voices are strong enough to put us to sleep against our will. Maybe you were just too tired to stay awake." She gave him a crooked smile. "Does it matter? What matters is finding Yarro."

He scowled at her. "You think they'll let us?"

"Let's see what's at the back of the cave." She held out a torch. Hawk took it, trying to ignore the way the graceful brush of her fingers against his sent a flame up his arm that had nothing to do with the torch.

"Nothing," he told her, clinging to his temper. "There's nothing there. I checked it myself."

"I know. But Yar went that way, and he's gone. So something's changed."

"That's not even possible."

"A lot of things that aren't considered possible are happening to us. Including someone hearing things that aren't there." Azmei's smile taunted him. He looked away. She was strong and beautiful, and she was a princess, so far above him he shouldn't even gaze on her.

You told her brother you'd never been in love, whispered a voice. *Don't make an idiot of yourself now.*

He shoved aside the voice and the longings and stormed away from the fire, ducking to keep from hitting his head on the cavern roof...

...that abruptly wasn't there.

"What—" He broke off, staring. The roof of the cavern was suddenly at least two armspans above his head, and the walls were too far apart for him to touch. When he had checked it before, the cavern tapered to an end that was barely big enough for a cat to have denned in.

"There's a tunnel," Azmei said, her voice strange.

Hawk looked again, and there it was—a tunnel wide enough for two horses to walk abreast, and tall enough for the humans to ride. "By all the gods," he whispered. "What power are we dealing with?"

Azmei cast a glance at him. "We're going to find out. I'll

put the fire out while you saddle the horses."

Five minutes later they were in the tunnel, their horses walking as placidly as if they were in the open desert once again. Hawk watched the walls and ceiling, trying to spot anything that would explain how this had happened. All he got out of it was a lightheaded feeling and the vague sense that someone was laughing at him. It didn't do anything for his mood.

"Are you all right?" Azmei was watching him instead of their surroundings. He wanted to snap that of course he wasn't all right, but he just gave a curt nod. "I know you've seen a lot of horrible things," she said softly. "I know war is terrible. But there was never any magic in the war with Strid, was there?"

Hawk shook his head. No magic, but a lot of suffering.

"I've seen some things in my life that I can't explain," she said. "I've met one of the Amethirian stormwitches and talked to someone who's seen the great stormsingers who taught humans magic. I've survived wounds that should have killed me, thanks to the peace god's followers, who have healing skills we can't imagine in Tamnen. I won't pretend to understand what's happening, but I'm not going to reject it just because I don't understand it." She was silent for a moment. Hawk glanced over at her, only to find her smiling hopefully at him. "Hawk, can you trust me long enough for us to find Yar?"

Damn it. Hawk pressed his lips together and met her gaze. She must have realized it was an affirmative, because her smile widened. "Thank you."

He didn't think that required a response. They rode in silence for several minutes, the ring of hoof beats against stone gradually changing in tone. When he looked down, he realized they were riding on packed earth now, rather than stone. He lifted his gaze to the tunnel ahead and the world changed all over again.

The horses stopped walking. They were standing in a broad valley, green grass fluttering against the horses' hocks. The sun gleamed against Azmei's dark curls. She squinted, lifting one hand to shade her eyes. Hawk tore his gaze away from her and looked out over the vast sea of grass.

Walls of craggy gray stone rose around them, shutting them into a private world without closing them away from the sun. He glanced over his shoulder; the tunnel was gone. The sunshine was warm on his shoulders. Hawk loosened Talon in its scabbard.

"Where is this?" he muttered.

Azmei turned and looked soberly at him. "I think perhaps we know why nobody ever goes to the Shrouded Vale," she said.

He turned his horse in a slow circle, taking in the craggy walls of this natural fortress, the river rushing and tumbling downhill to spread out lazily in the middle of the valley. He had almost completed his circle when Azmei screamed. He whipped around to look at her. She was throwing herself towards him, off her horse's back. She dragged at his elbow, throwing him off balance. A shadow fell across them and he looked up, and then he screamed, too.

Huge leathery wings snapped open above them with a noise like thunder. Gleaming talons, spread wide for catching, snapped closed overhead. A great wind rushed over them, whipping Hawk's clothes around and making him choke as his cloak swirled out away from him. The ground shook as a ponderous weight dropped in front of them. Then someone laughed, clear and high, and Yarro tumbled from the dragon's back to the ground in front of them.

Azmei lunged forward and hugged him, while he squirmed to get away from her. Hawk bared Talon and moved to stand between the two of them and the dragon, his heart pounding against his chest so hard he thought it would push its way through.

"Leggo." Yar sounded like any other teenaged boy who was being hugged against his will. He half laughed as he spoke, but he didn't relax until he managed to extricate himself from the princess' arms. "What are you doing?"

"I thought we'd lost you," Azmei said. "Why did you run

off?"

"I was Called."

Booming laughter rolled over them with the force of a great hand pushing them down. It echoed against the mountains and rumbled back to them. To Hawk it sounded like thunder building, ready to avalanche down on them.

Yarro laughed too. "Darixu greets you," he said. "This is the Shrouded Vale. The Valley of Dragons."

Hawk saw Azmei tear her gaze away from the boy. She stared up at the great golden dragon looming over them. It met her gaze, expression ineffable. Azmei twitched and then dropped into a deep curtsy. Hawk wondered if he should bow, but opted against it. He would rather be disrespectful than let the dragon bite off her head without a fight.

"I thought the dragons were all gone," Azmei whispered. "They're so..." She trailed off, shaking her head.

The dragon made no move to bite her head off. It sank back on its back legs, looking as if it were waiting for something.

"So did I." Hawk tightened his grip on Talon's hilt.

"I have to go," Yarro said. "I've been Called. Now that I'm here, there's..." He paused. "I have to...I have to Become."

Azmei jerked her gaze away from the dragon and looked at Yar again. "Become?"

Yarro made a helpless gesture. He seemed more alive, more present, than Hawk had ever seen him. "Their word. I think..." He paused for so long Hawk wasn't sure if the boy were going to speak again. Maybe he'd been caught in another vision. But the dragon lowered its head and Yar finally said, "I think it's a joining somehow. Maybe..." He trailed off again.

"An initiation?" Hawk offered, suddenly understanding.

"Yes." Yar gave him a relieved look. "It's all right. I'm safe. They...well, they don't *need* me. But they want me." He smiled. "They won't hurt me."

"Or us?" Azmei said sharply.

Yar's laughter was the infectious giggle of a boy half his age. "Or you," he said, still giggling. "They welcome Princess

Azmei and her Champion Hawk. They thank you for guiding their Voice to them, and invite you to stay in their home this night." He gestured over his shoulder towards the far end of the valley. Hawk followed the gesture and could see a huge stone structure there, though he wasn't certain, at this distance, if it was natural or built.

"I'm not sure..." Azmei began, but Yar touched her shoulder. She stopped talking as he met her gaze. Princess and boy stared at each other for several heartbeats. Hawk didn't dare interrupt. He looked up at the dragon instead, hoping he didn't look as terrified of it as he felt. It watched him with all the contemplation of a bored cat.

"All right," Azmei said finally. She sounded unhappy. "But please be careful, Yar. If you don't like it, tell us."

He gave her a brilliant smile and went to the dragon. It lowered one shoulder for him to climb up. As they watched the boy settle into place on the dragon's back, Hawk felt Azmei's hand creep into his. She squeezed tightly as the dragon flew away, taking Yarro with it.

When it was nothing more than a speck in the distance, Hawk glanced around again. One of the mountain crags seemed to move and he realized it was a golden-brown dragon, stirring in its sleep. Another dragon, its scales a brilliant pearlescent white, was crouched about a quarter of a mile away from them, its head turned to watch them. He tightened his grip on Azmei's hand.

That seemed to jar her out of some reverie. "Well," she said, and tugged away from him. "I suppose we might as well explore."

Hawk told himself he wasn't disappointed she had pulled away. "I suppose so." He sheathed his sword and looked over his shoulder at the horses. They were standing at attention, clearly aware that they were in the presence of something dangerous, but only wary rather than frightened. Hawk sighed and shook himself.

"There's some sort of structure down at the far end of the valley," he said. "We might as well go that way."

"Do you think there are any other people here?"

He paused. "I think the dragons *are* the people here."

"Humans, I mean."

"Why would they need humans?"

"To eat?" she muttered darkly.

Hawk snorted in amusement. "You were the one who said you'd seen magic things wild and strange. If they were going to eat us, wouldn't they have done it right away?"

"Dragons." She shook her head. "Gods wake and save us. All right. Let's see what's in that structure."

They rode at a leisurely pace down the slope to the river. Once their passage startled a herd of deer that were browsing among the date palms. Hawk's black shied as the deer took flight, but quickly settled down again when he realized it was nothing scary.

Hawk had to fight to keep from relaxing. Azmei was looking around, her head up and her shoulders loose. The valley's beauty was disarming, and she wasn't fighting it for some reason. Hawk couldn't help but feel as though they were surrounded by hidden dangers, though. The princess might not be worried, but he wasn't going to lower his guard.

The sunshine felt good. It wasn't the searing heat of the desert, but the wholesome warmth of being outside after an illness. The breeze was vaguely scented with jasmine and some other flower he couldn't identify. It lifted his hair away from his forehead and teased at his cloak, doing its best to lull him into carelessness. It was like the whole valley was alive somehow.

"It feels different here," Azmei said. "Welcoming."

Hawk glanced over at her. She wasn't looking at him, but her body was angled towards him; she'd been talking to him.

"Maybe," he said.

Though they didn't hurry, they grew closer to the structure more quickly than he'd expected. As they drew near, the grass thinned out until they were riding across what looked like a limestone courtyard—except that it had never seen the touch of human hands. It was like the land had been trained somehow and grew to the will of its masters. His mouth went dry. How powerful were these dragons, if they could make the earth itself do their bidding?

A petite hand covered his and he jumped. Azmei was looking up at him. "Hawk? Are you well?"

He frowned at her. "You say you feel welcomed here." He swallowed. "I feel nothing but dread."

She looked at him in understanding. "I trust Yar. He said we were welcome here. I...I can tell there is some great power here, but it hasn't hurt us, has it? Confused us, but not hurt us. And we have done nothing to give offense. I think that as long as we are respectful, the dragons will respect us. Because we came with Yar."

Hawk tilted his head in assent, but he was unable to fully relax until they reached the dragons' palace. There was no other word for it. The smooth rock face stretched up at least seventy feet above them, round pillars supporting wide archways that gave access on three levels. Of course there would be openings at the top as well as the bottom, he thought. Dragons could fly. Why would the architecture not support that?

As the horses came to a halt, a sound echoed from inside the palace. It was a whinny—Firefoot? Hawk's horse called a response, ears perked up.

"Sounds like there's stabling within," Azmei said, grinning at Hawk. He swallowed and followed her as she urged her dun through the center arch.

Firefoot had been comfortably stabled in a vast stall. Everything was stone, but the floor was covered in thick straw, with a tall pile of hay and a deep basin full of water. There were dozens of stalls, so Hawk and Azmei settled their horses next to Firefoot. Azmei frowned at the hay.

"I had to teach Yar how to take care of horses, but we never had any hay," she said. "I wonder how he thought to give Firefoot hay." She lifted her head and glanced around. "Hello?" she called. Her voice echoed through the stone passages, but no reply came.

"You think there's someone else here?" Hawk asked.

"I suppose not." Azmei lifted her pack and slung it over one shoulder. "Let's explore. If there's stabling for horses no dragons need, there might be beds for humans no dragons need."

Hawk smiled and gestured for her to lead the way. They reached the end of the row of stalls and came to a stairway up. Upon climbing to the next floor, they entered what looked like a receiving hall. It was wide and punctuated by columns, the ceiling soaring overhead in graceful arches.

"This place could hold a thousand people," Hawk murmured.

"And probably half as many dragons," Azmei agreed. "But where are they all? Even if the dragon—what was its name? Darixu?—anyway, even if the dragon who called Yar had to leave, would all of them go? And go where? Why not have their joining thing here?"

"Maybe there's some sacred spot they have to visit," Hawk suggested. "Who knows what's sacred to a dragon?"

"Mm." Azmei peered around a corner. "There's a passageway here leading further in. Come on."

Hawk followed her through empty stone passageways and empty stone studies and empty stone dining halls, both of them growing more and more perplexed as they continued. It was as if the palace had been full of life one moment and abandoned the next.

"But there's no dust anywhere," Azmei protested. "And there are dining halls, but where are the kitchens?"

"The whole palace is made of stone," Hawk said. "They could have the kitchens on the same levels as the stables with no danger of fire."

"Maybe."

They climbed another set of stairs that wound around and up at least thirty steps. When they got to the top, Azmei stopped so abruptly that Hawk ran into her. The resistance made him flail to keep from falling back down the stairs. Azmei grabbed his arm and tugged him forward.

"Look," she breathed, turning away from him quickly enough that she probably didn't notice the flush on his cheeks. "It's magnificent!"

It was. This was clearly a throne room, but it was a throne room for beings on a grander scale than humans. Instead of an actual throne, there was a raised dais that had a large platform at the center. A gallery up the walls on three sides had square stone bays, almost miniature rooms, except that the walls dividing them were only three or four feet high. The ceiling was at least fifty feet above them and inlaid with some sort of black stone that had pale pink bands running through it. As Hawk turned, staring up at it, sparkles winked at him from the depths of the stone.

"Maybe we shouldn't be in here," he murmured.

"There's no one here," Azmei said. She flashed a smile at him and tugged his hand so he followed her to the back of the room. "Look—there's a staircase built for dragons!"

"Why would dragons need stairs?" Hawk said, but he could see she was right. The steps were wider and deeper than normal steps.

"Baby dragons?" Azmei guessed. "Oh, baby *dragons*!" She looked delighted at the thought. Hawk thought the idea was a recipe for fiery disaster. But maybe newborn dragons couldn't breathe fire. For that matter, they hadn't seen any indication that these dragons breathed fire. But all the stories said they did.

"I think we should look for a place where we can build a fire and cook supper," he suggested. He was feeling uneasy again.

"Let's go up one more level. There are people-sized—human-sized—stairs over there." Azmei pointed. "What if there are bedrooms and baths up on the top floor? Dear gods, what I wouldn't give for a hot bath!" She ran up the stairs.

Hawk followed more slowly, listening to her footsteps. His leg was beginning to ache, and he had to admit, the thought of a hot bath was a tempting one.

"Hawk, come look!" Azmei sounded pleased, rather than

alarmed, but he hastened his steps all the same. When he reached the top of the steps, he found her standing at a waist-high stone wall, looking out across a small plaza. "Fountains! And I'm willing to bet the rooms behind them are baths."

Hawk hummed. "Let's see."

There were, though he was afraid *hot* baths were too much to hope for. There he was in for a pleasant surprise. The water cisterns had been in the sun all day, so when Hawk pulled the lever that let water sluice down into the basin, it was sun-heated. He grinned at Azmei. "There's your hot bath."

She grinned back. "Merciful dream of a merciful god." She dropped her pack. "There was another bath chamber beyond this one."

Hawk took the hint. "I don't think we should let ourselves be separated," he said. "I'll leave the door open so we can hear each other." Azmei nodded and he went on to his own soak.

The tub was far too big for a human, but he supposed even dragons might like baths. He was afraid to fill the tub too full. He climbed in while it was filling and let the hot water splash down over his thigh, warming away the ache. It felt so good he leaned back against the polished stone side, letting his eyes fall half closed. He could hear the princess splashing in the next chamber. She was humming, the tune breaking up when she ducked under the water and splashed back up. He didn't recognize the tune, but it had a soothing quality.

Water splashed against his chest. Hawk shook himself and sat up, opening his eyes. He must have dozed off. The water was at least a foot deep and the tap was still gushing water at him. He pushed the lever to stop the flow and reached for the cake of soap he'd dug out of his pack.

When he was clean and dry, he stared down at the water. He hadn't noticed a mechanism for draining it, but he could hear gurgling from the next room. He dug out his spare clothes and dressed, shaking his damp hair back from his face. He felt like a new man.

"Azmei," he called softly. "Is there a way to empty the basin?"

"I'll show you," she replied. "That is—are you decent?"

"I'm dressed. I'm not sure if I'm ever decent."

She laughed and came in. "There's another lever on the side of the tub," she said, showing him. "And now that I'm clean, my stomach has decided I'll expire if I don't eat something."

Hawk smiled. "Then we should remedy that."

"I wish the dragons had let Yar stay one more night to show us around before they whisked him off." She sobered, looking at the floor. "Oh. I hadn't thought about him for a while. I was so excited about the bath. I hope he's all right." She glanced up at him from behind the wavy curtain of her chin-length hair.

"He seemed confident he would be," Hawk said. "Come, let's find a good spot to make supper."

***

They ended up back on the stable level. Hawk pointed out, correctly, that with a stable built of stone, there was little danger from a campfire. They found a clean stall near the horses and spread their bedrolls. Hawk offered to go for water.

Azmei waited until Hawk's footsteps had retreated before she sank onto the bed and buried her face in her hands. She'd lost Yarro to a dragon and then forgot about him at the seductive song of the baths. Some protector she was turning out to be. But Yarro had seemed confident and happy when he came back to them. He'd found his Voices. Maybe he didn't need her anymore.

She rubbed her face and pushed her hair behind her ears. She'd been letting it grow out for the past year, though she wasn't sure why. Assassins were better off with short hair.

Dismissing the thought, she knelt and went back to feeding kindling into the fire. A few minutes later, she heard

Hawk's footsteps approaching again. He wasn't limping, she realized. The bath must have helped.

"What do you suppose the dragons need Yarro for?" she asked as he poured water into a kettle and set it next to her.

"I don't know. The stories don't say anything about them needing people."

"They don't say anything about the dragons having re-treated to a Shrouded Vale in the middle of the desert, either," Azmei said. She paused. "We always thought the war with Strid was about the mines. Do you suppose they were actually looking for dragons?"

Hawk sat cross-legged on the floor near her. "I'd never thought about it." He began rooting around in his pack, his tone turning dark. "The first place they attacked was the mines, though. That seems like a good clue that it was about the mines."

Azmei nodded, wondering if she'd upset him. He wasn't looking up at her. He'd grown up in the Kreyden, hadn't he? He looked to be about thirty, though she wasn't the best judge of age. He might remember the start of the war.

"Tea?" he said, without looking at her.

"I'll make some." She found the leather pouch that held the most expensive of her teas. This was a spicy tea that tasted best when brewed with milk added, but was still sweet and spicy without it. She hadn't had any since leaving Meekin, but she needed something comforting tonight.

The conversation dwindled as they focused on their tasks. Azmei measured out the tea and got the water heating. Hawk toasted bread over the flames, letting cheese melt over it. By the time supper was ready, evening had fallen outside. A cricket was chirping somewhere in the stable. Aside from that, the only sounds were rustling straw and the breathing of horses.

"You grew up in the desert, didn't you?" Azmei asked softly.

Hawk nodded and swallowed the food he was chewing. "A town called Hedron. Three hundred or so souls, Tamnese,

Strid, and mixed." He looked down at his toast. "I've been in the desert most of my life, except when I went to Tamnen City."

"Even Strid?" Azmei asked. She'd never been to Strid; it had been the one place Master Tanvel had refused to take her with him. Too much at stake, he'd said at the time. She swallowed hard and poured the tea. It must be brewed by now.

"The part they held me in, yes," Hawk said. His voice was soft. "I've heard further south it's more fertile and green."

"What are the Strid like?" She poured a second cup of tea and set it on the floor by his knee.

He shrugged. "People, mostly. Some good, some not so good. It wasn't too awful. They did heal me."

"The leg?" she asked. She'd wondered about that. She was glad it hadn't been torture. She didn't like to think of someone hurting Hawk like that.

He looked away from her. "I was left for dead on the field after the Push. Someone recognized me, thought I'd make a good hostage." He paused. "I suppose eventually I did."

Azmei shivered. There had never been prisoner exchanges before, that she could recall. If her father hadn't pursued this one, she might never have met Hawk. "How was my brother when you left him?" she asked.

He cleared his throat. "Anxious for your father's sake. The reports said the king was badly injured in the attack."

When Azmei looked over at him, he was frowning down at his cup. "Tanvel meant to protect Father," she said. "He thought he'd worked out..." She trailed off. If her father had been injured, Tanvel must be dead. She swallowed hard. "Something must have gone wrong. Is the tea all right?"

He looked up, eyes wide. "Yes, it's nice. Different from what we've been drinking."

She fought not to smile at him. She had smiled a lot at him today. He would start to think she was silly.

"Prince Razem didn't know you're still alive," he said, studying her face.

"He might now. He'll have reached the palace by now, won't he? Tanvel told my father right after the attack on me. Maybe Father will tell him now." Azmei brushed her hair back behind one ear. "Oh, gods, I hope I made the right decision." Tanvel had thought it best, and he had carried the word to her father. He had reported later that her father agreed, but what if he'd said that to make her feel better?

"What else could you have done?" Hawk said. "I'm sure your brother will agree."

Azmei didn't answer. She sipped her tea and stared at the fire. With the sun down, its warmth was pleasant. She suddenly felt very tired.

"What will you do now?" Hawk asked after a time. Azmei looked up from the fire, staring in his direction as her eyes cleared from the dazzlement. She didn't know what he was asking.

"Will you come back and be the princess again?" he said, when it was clear she wasn't going to speak.

Azmei had no answer to that. She cupped both hands around her mug of tea and looked back at the fire. "You think it's Aris, don't you? My cousin Arisanat."

He didn't protest her changing the subject. "My lady, he's the only one who could have sent those mercenaries after me. I'm not important enough, in myself, so the only reason anyone could want me dead is to protect whatever was in Meekin."

She huffed in frustration. "But I didn't find anything there!"

He was silent for so long she thought he wasn't going to answer. When she glanced over at him, he was watching her, the firelight flickering in those charcoal eyes. "You found Yarro."

"Oh, gods save the foolish." She jumped up and scrabbled at her pack. "I *did* find something, and I'd forgotten about it until just now."

Hawk had risen to his knees. "What?"

"Before I killed the Patriarch. There was a packet of

papers in a hidden drawer. I took it with me to look at later, but then I was searching for Yarro, and I completely forgot about it." Her fingers closed on the smooth parchment. She drew it out and cut the string with a dagger.

"Kesh, the last of Yar's family, said it was one of the Nine who commissioned my death. A man, but that was all he knew." She knelt next to Hawk and opened the packet of papers.

The first was a contract for an assassination in the Long Coast. Azmei turned to the next page, which was a shipping schedule—canal boats traveling between Meekin and Tamnen City. The third was a letter. As Azmei stared at it, her hand began to shake. Her eyes fuzzed with tears. She scrubbed impatiently at them.

"It's Arisanat's handwriting," she whispered. Even after four years, she would know it. He'd always done that funny corner with his capital letters.

Hawk leaned in closer, his hand closing around hers and holding the paper so they could both read it. She closed her eyes and focused on the warmth of his skin instead of the ache at Arisinat's betrayal.

"Patriarch," Hawk read aloud. "I wish to commission your family's services. I will not discuss the particulars except in person, but I assure you the contract will be worth a princess' ransom. My messenger will tell you the meeting I propose. Send your reply with the messenger. With all due respect, A Prospective Customer."

Azmei dragged in a ragged breath. "You were right," she whispered.

Hawk's arm slipped around her shoulders. "For once, I wish I weren't."

***

Yarro had often wondered what it would be like to fly. He had watched the swallows swooping over rooftops in Meekin and had imagined himself darting like a dragonfly. He had never believed he would experience it one day for himself. It was better than he could ever have imagined, and for a wonder, his mind was his own the entire time Darixu carried him to the mountaintop.

The ponderous wings beat slowly and steadily, carrying them forward so quickly the ground blurred under them. The wind blew Yar's hair back from his face and made his eyes stream with tears, but he turned his face up to the sun and laughed. Under his legs, he felt Darixu rumble with laughter, too, and the great golden dragon folded his wings, plummeting for several heart-tumbling moments before snapping them wide and coming out of the dive.

Yar shrieked, clutching at the thick, craggy scales, but he didn't stop grinning. Orya had made him feel loved, and Azmei had made him feel accepted, but Darixu made Yar feel whole for the first time in his life. It was like his mind had been divided all his life until now, and the pieces of himself were finally coming together.

Darixu let out a long bellow. Then they were climbing, the wings beating powerfully so they began gaining altitude. Yar leaned forward over the great shoulders, inhaling the crisp smoke and sulfur of Darixu's scales, and wept.

Another being pressed gently against his awareness. It was a light touch, but it slithered warmly against his thoughts. DISTRESS?

"No," he whispered, not knowing if the Slithery Voice heard him. But the gentle pressure withdrew, so it must have.

Then Darixu soared down, all four legs outstretched to touch down more gracefully than seemed possible. They were not quite at the mountain's peak, but a huge ring of stones indicated that this was their destination. On each of the blocky menhirs perched another dragon.

A slender, serpentine dragon with scales the color of new grass stretched its neck out, flickering a tongue at Yar. LITTLE BROTHER, WELCOME, she said, and he recognized the Slithery Voice. She was beautiful, something he hadn't anticipated from hearing her in his head. Her eyes were a deep, swirly silver, her leathery wings edged with a feathery fringe along the primary bone. I AM XELLAX.

Yar slid down Darixu's front leg and tumbled into a deep bow. "Greetings, elder brothers and elder sisters," he said. "I am Yarro Perslyn."

There was a murmur of laughter, but it was Azmei's sort of laughter, not the kind of laughter Yar had received from Rith and Kesh. Gentle, warm. Enveloping.

NO, LITTLE BROTHER. YOU *WERE* YARRO PERSLYN. NOW YOU ARE YARRAX, VOICE OF DRAGONS.

He staggered upright, staring around at them. Voice of Dragons? What did that mean?

A deep blue dragon lifted his head and sang out his name—VETTERIX. Yar recognized his voice as a kind one that liked warm sunshine and listened to Yar's daydreams. A red dragon with black-edged scales—REXIEL, he roared—was a voice that had come during his nightmares and whispered that all would be well. Xerin was a bulky midnight green dragon with a ridge of spines down his back who had given Yar dreams of heroes. Inlux was a delicate bronze creature, only twice the size of a horse, with wings that looked almost lacy in the scarlet sunset.

WELCOME, LITTLE BROTHER. Xellax leapt into the air and dropped lightly to the ground in front of him. IT FILLS US WITH JOY TO SEE YOU IN THE FLESH AFTER SO MANY YEARS OF WATCHING FROM AFAR.

Yar took a deep breath, bending backwards and craning his neck so he could see all of Xellax. His heart was pounding so quickly he felt light-headed. "You are all...so much more than I ever dreamed," he breathed.

WE TRIED TO SHOW OURSELVES TO YOU, BUT THE DISTANCE WAS TOO GREAT, said Darixu. Yar turned to stare up at him. Dizzied by the height of the dragon towering above him, he swayed. Darixu lowered his head. AND YOU WERE UNPREPARED. YOUR MIND COULD NOT TAKE US IN.

Something smooth, like a marble sculpture, pressed against Yar's back. It was cool when the bare skin of his forearm brushed against it. Yar peered over his shoulder to see that Xellax had delicately placed one talon where it would support him. His heart twisted and he smiled painfully at her.

IT WAS DARIXU WHO TOLD US TO CALL YOU, she crooned in his mind. HE IS OUR LEADER, THE ELDEST OF US AND—USUALLY—THE WISEST.

Yar couldn't help laughing. He was relieved when he felt laughter from the golden dragon, too.

TRUE, BUT XELLAX IS THE DRAGON WHO FELT YOU FIRST. SHE SAW YOUR POTENTIAL, SHE CALLED YOU WHEN YOU WERE YET A BABE. Darixu lowered his head until his snout glittered just a few feet from Yar's face. His breath smelled like a blacksmith's furnace. His teeth were easily as long as Yar's arms. XELLAX WATCHED YOU GROW. SHE TRIED TO HARDEN YOU, TO PREPARE YOU FOR US.

A warm, dry wind ruffled Yar's hair, blowing it over his forehead, and he realized Xellax had sighed. WE DID NOT ANTICIPATE HOW OUR CALL WOULD CHANGE YOU.

Yar looked down at the ground. *Freak,* whispered a voice that sounded like his brother's. *Lackwit. Idiot. Monster.* "I hated being different."

Xellax's nose brushed his hair. IT WAS NOT WHAT WE WISHED FOR YOU. WE MEANT TO BRING YOU STRENGTH, NOT TO DIVIDE YOUR MIND FROM ITSELF. Yar could feel the deep sorrow in her words. He sighed.

IT HAD BEEN TOO LONG SINCE WE HAD A VOICE, said Darixu, lifting his head and backing several steps. WE HAD FORGOTTEN.

Yar glared up at them. "It didn't help that you told me to eat my grandfather." *You filled me with all these thoughts and urges I didn't understand,* he wanted to shout at them. *You ruined me!* But they resonated sorrow and regret, and somehow he didn't have it in him to wound them.

HE WAS WICKED, Xellax said simply.

Yar straightened, standing away from her support. "He's dead. Azmei killed him." He folded his arms across his chest. He still wasn't sure how he felt about that, either, but he couldn't change it, and now at least he was free of the Patriarch.

Rexiel bugled, stretching his scarlet head to the sky. AZMEI OF TAMNEN HAS SERVED YOU WELL.

Yar scowled, turning to face him. "She's a princess. Probably I ought to be serving her," he said. Though he didn't think most princesses would care one way or the other about a strange young man from a textile family—or even a family of assassins. Then again, Azmei didn't seem much like a princess at all.

NAY. WHEN THE VOICE OF DRAGONS SPEAKS, THE WORLD SHOULD LISTEN. That was Darixu's Wise Uncle Voice, the one that quelled arguments and spoke the law.

Yar was thirsty. He looked around and found a rock that would make a comfortable enough seat. "Dragons aren't exactly revered. For that matter, you're only even remembered as stories. No one sits around wondering what dragons think about this or that."

Xellax gave a dry, whispery chuckle like the rasps of scales against stone. NO ONE MUCH REMEMBERS WE EXIST. BUT WE WILL REMIND THEM. Her tongue flickered out and licked her scaly lips.

Yar sat up straight. "Are you going to take over the world?"

Laughter rumbled around the circle of dragons. TOO MUCH TROUBLE, said Vetterix, letting herself drape down over her menhir.

BUT WE KNOW THINGS, added Darixu. IMPORTANT THINGS. YOU MUST SPEAK FOR US, VOICE OF DRAGONS.

Yar stared at him, but the dragon sat calmly, his metallic eyes reflecting light back at him. The other dragons all looked serious as well. Yar spread his hands to either side. "How?"

YOU WILL FIND A WAY, Xellax assured him.

FIRST THERE MUST BE THE JOINING. Darixu stood, spreading his wings so they stretched like a canopy over Yar's head. YOU WILL KNOW US MORE FULLY ONCE WE ARE JOINED. WE WILL NOT OVERWHELM YOU AS MUCH THEN.

Yar wanted to cover his face and hide. He wanted to curl up inside his cloak and pretend the world didn't exist. But where would he retreat to escape from the dragons? They had been in his head all his life. Where would he go?

Did he even have a choice? What if he refused, would they kill him? Make him a prisoner? Would they hurt Azmei and Firefoot and Hawk?

Xellax lowered her head, meeting his gaze. Her smoke-silver eyes were full of sorrow, hope, and love. Yar had never felt that love when she was whispering to him of bloody things and revolution, but facing her now, he couldn't doubt it. He sighed and looked down.

"All right. What do I do?"

BLOOD AND FIRE. The words slid into his thoughts. He jerked his gaze up to Xellax again. She was watching him. She said nothing else.

"B-blood?" His calf throbbed at the thought. But they said he wouldn't be overwhelmed by them if he did this. Wasn't that worth a little blood? "How?"

BLOOD, Xellax whispered again, AND FIRE.

"Fine!" he shouted. He drew his dagger from his belt and sliced it across the inside of his left forearm before he could think about it. The knife was a good one—even the freaks of the assassin family knew how to care for their weapons. The pain took several heartbeats to register. Xellax's head thrust forward, her tongue darting out. It licked across his arm, fire dancing along her tongue and searing the wound.

Yar screamed. The touch held him immobilized, his blood boiling in his veins and searing through his skull. He squeezed his eyes shut. It felt like he was being turned inside out like a dirty shirt. Then something shifted inside him, something clicked into place, and the agony was past. His forearm pulsed where the dragon's tongue had scorched it, but when he pried one eyelid open and looked, only a white welt remained, its edges turning red. There was no blood.

Yar stood panting and staring down at the arm. Now he had a scar on each arm, one from his childhood and one from the dragons. He looked up at Xellax again. He drew in a long breath.

"I don't feel any different."

"You will," Xellax replied. Her voice didn't hiss and echo around in the corners of his mind anymore. He could hear that quality about it, but he didn't want to cringe from the ill-fitting corners that used to poke his thoughts. "Rest, Yar. The dawn will come soon enough." She settled down on the ground, her serpentine body curling like a cat. She stretched out her wings and looked at him with open invitation.

Yar crawled under her wings, snuggled against her side, and slept.

CHAPTER TWENTY-EIGHT

Azmei woke only once in the night. She could hear Hawk breathing. She rolled onto her side, staring across the dark stall to where he sat, propped against a bale of hay. Was he standing watch? She didn't bother to fight the warm fondness that rose inside her at the thought. She nestled deeper into her blanket and let the sweet fragrance of the hay lull her back into sleep.

She was up before dawn. She'd slept deeply and peacefully, but at the first thump of horses rattling their wooden feed buckets, she was fully awake. Hawk was no longer in his place. Azmei stood and stretched. The stable was dim, the first hints of light not yet reaching in as far as the stall they had chosen for their sleep. She wouldn't be able to get back to sleep. She buckled on her sword belt and went to find her companion.

Hawk was out in front of the huge stone palace. He was stripped to the waist, going through a series of stretches that almost looked like combat forms. Azmei licked dry lips, wondering if that was something he'd learned in Strid, or a routine he'd devised himself. The rays of the rising sun limned his figure with gold. He was too skinny, probably from all the years spent in prison, but she couldn't ignore the lean strength of his body. Except for the slight limp, he was grace incarnate, and even that was a badge of honor, something he had earned in service to his kingdom.

He must have caught sight of her during one of his turns. He stopped moving and straightened. Azmei jerked her gaze away, feeling her face get hot. She hadn't meant to interrupt, and now she had been caught.

"Azmei. I didn't mean to wake you." His words were hesitant. She glanced at him, wondering if he felt as awkward as she did.

"You didn't. I think it was one of the horses. But I'm ready to be awake. I slept well." She smiled. She wished she knew how to thank him for standing watch last night without making things even more awkward. "Can you teach me what you're doing?"

He raised his eyebrows. "You must have your own practice routine."

"Yes, but I like learning new things." She smiled. "And then perhaps we could spar against each other."

"You are almost certainly more skilled with the blade than I."

She stepped across the paved yard to join him. "I doubt it. I am good at killing in controlled environments, and I am good at creating those environments. But you survived years on the battlefield, which I have not done."

"You've also been honing your skills for several years, where mine have been rusting," Hawk countered, half-smiling at her. "But very well." He fell into a loose stance, his weight distributed on the balls of his feet, and stretched his arms over his head. "Mirror my poses. We'll go slowly at first."

Azmei did as she was told. At first she had to focus on following his movements, but soon he looped around to the beginning and she realized everything he did was based on half a dozen stances. He varied where his arms were held, or the combination of poses, but once she had learned those stances, she found the routine almost meditative. Hawk's poses were like the stretches she had learned, but with more purpose; his could be turned into martial movements with little adaptation.

It was a mixed blessing, she discovered. With her body occupied by the routine, her mind wandered back to the situation in which she found herself. Stuck in a hidden valley with one companion taken by dragons. Her brother and father threatened by assassins, certainly sent by one of the Nine

Families, possibly by her cousin. What was happening in Tamnen City right now? Was Tanvel still alive, or had he been killed? Was her father still alive?

"You aren't concentrating anymore." Hawk's voice was neutral, his gaze observant on her but not condemning.

"I'm sorry," she said anyway. "I'm afraid my mind keeps wandering."

He just nodded. "Perhaps the swords, then. That should keep your mind from wandering."

Azmei laughed. "I hope so! I don't have a practice blade with me."

"We'll be careful." He glanced over at her, waiting until she nodded slightly. It wasn't usual to practice with live steel; the purpose of practice was to make the motions instinctive, and if you pulled your strokes in practice, your instinct would be to do so in a real fight. But this once, it wouldn't be a problem.

She drew her sword and waited while he walked to where his shirt and sword belt were draped over a stone. She fell into a ready position and watched as he drew his sword and worked his shoulders.

He attacked without warning. Azmei had been watching, but his muscles hadn't betrayed his intent. He simply struck. She parried and countered, but he blocked her own attack easily. After a few traded blows, she found herself smiling. It was a joy to match herself against him. It had been months since she'd last sparred with Tanvel, and he had been the last opponent who outmatched her. As she and Hawk tested each other, she realized that he, too, outmatched her, both with strength and with cunning. She was in better condition, but only just. Her biggest advantage was that she had been trained in the fighting styles of three nations, and Hawk had only one.

Still, he pressed her hard. Soon she was sweating, grateful for how it cooled her in the dry air. It gratified her to see that Hawk was breathing hard, the same fierce joy on his face that she felt on her own. Their feet scuffed sand against the stone yard, the clang of blade against blade and their panting and grunts the only other sounds. She had to admit it was a relief when Hawk's blade finally darted in to stop a few inches from her throat. "Check," Hawk gasped, and Azmei replied, "Yield."

They lowered their blades, grinning at one another. The happiness in his eyes pleased her. Until then she hadn't realized just how sad he looked most of the time. She was proud to have brought him such pleasure. She wondered, as he stared at her, if he was feeling much the same.

"Thank you," she said. She wiped her blade against her trousers and slid it into its sheath. Later she would check it for nicks, but now she slid into a stretch, making sure her muscles would stay loose.

"You are skilled, indeed," he said, following her example.

"But not as skilled as you." She smiled. "You will continue to improve as you rebuild your stamina. I'll have to work hard to keep up with you."

There was a brief pause. She wondered if he'd caught what she'd let slip—that she wanted to try to keep up with him. It wasn't possible. He would have duties when she returned him to her brother. And she would have duties of a very different sort. But for now, hidden away in the Shrouded Vale, waiting for Yar to return with his dragons, Azmei could dream.

"You're capable of it," Hawk said finally, and twisted at the waist. He bent over, working at his thigh. She'd seen him favoring it some during the fight, but it didn't hinder him. He knew how to fight through the pain.

"We should eat," she replied. "There's a little meat and bread left."

He nodded and followed her back to their stall, where she handed him the food pack. She grabbed the kettle and filled it with water while they returned back to the yard. Hawk portioned out the food while she built a fire and began heating water. When the coffee was ready, they ate. They didn't speak much, but Azmei felt more relaxed with him than she had anyone except Tanvel and, longer ago, Razem and Guira and

Venra.

"Hawk?" she ventured, as they lingered over their coffee. He looked over at her, his charcoal eyes curious and open. It made her hesitate, but she couldn't forget what they'd discovered about Arisanat. She licked her lips. "Tell me again how Aris reacted when you first met."

He frowned, the curiosity fading from his eyes, though the openness remained. At last he shrugged. "He was tense. Cold. I saw hatred in his eyes, but I thought it was for me alone. I lived while his brother did not."

She frowned too. For Hawk alone? But it wasn't, was it? There was no reason Arisanat would have ordered her death without having any involvement in the attack on Marsede. Something nagged at her memory. There had been something about what Hawk said that caught at her. What was it? "What did he say to you? Exactly, if you remember?"

"He said a prisoner exchange does not bring peace." Hawk's gaze turned sad. He sipped his coffee, letting his gaze drop to it instead of Azmei's face.

She sighed. "He must have been more destroyed by Venra's death than I realized." She shook her head. She missed Venra, too, but he had been dead four years, and she had lost others she loved since then. Time had not erased the grief, but it had dulled it. "I loved Venra myself. I...I think he meant to ask my father about an alliance between us. But I was still very young when he went to war."

"Did you..." Hawk trailed off, looking awkward. Perhaps he had realized the question he started to ask wasn't the sort of question a warrior ought to ask a princess. But Azmei didn't mind.

"He was my dearest friend after Razem," she said. "But no. I could have learned to love him, I know. But it was not to be." She smiled sadly at Hawk, who looked soberly back at her.

"His love for you is not shared by his brother," he said.

"It was once. Aris looked after us all. We got into all sorts of mischief, the three of us—my brother, Venra, and I—but

Aris tried to keep us out of the worst trouble. He worked to keep us safe." She laughed. "It was like he was a herd dog, and we his sheep. We caused him no end of headache and worry, but we were devoted to him, and he to us." She bowed her head. "Perhaps it was my agreeing to the treaty with Amethir that drove Aris to hatred."

"A man is responsible for his own actions, Azmei." Hawk's words were quick and low. "If Arisanat chose hatred, it was *his* choice, not yours."

Azmei shook her head, not denying it, but unable to accept it, either. "He must be very lonely."

They were silent for a time. Azmei poured herself a second cup of coffee. Hawk set down his cup and drew his sword, going over it for any blemish. The breeze picked up Azmei's hair and ruffled it. She looked away, down the length of the Shrouded Vale, and wondered if she saw dragons flying in the distance.

"Was it difficult to be away from your father and brother for so long?" Hawk asked finally.

Azmei glanced over at him. "As difficult as it probably was for you." She smiled. "But I have only been dead for three years. You were a captive for...what? Five years? Six? I've lost track."

"Ah. Six." Hawk didn't look up from his blade, which he worked carefully with a whetstone. "But I have no family."

"There were still people you loved, surely," Azmei murmured. "You must have missed them."

He lifted a shoulder. "Emran Kho was a friend. Your cousin Lord Venra was, as well. It grieved me deeply to learn of his death."

She sat forward, watching his face. "You knew Venra?"

"He was my commander in Rivarden. I liked him."

"Was he well-loved?" Azmei had exchanged letters with Venra, but he had always been humble. He had felt drawn to right the wrongs in the Kreyden, to attempt to rule the district as peacefully as possible while protecting the citizens from the Strid. But he had never claimed to be a popular leader or a visionary. She had always wondered what he left out of his letters.

"Aye, and respected." Hawk's lips curved up as he spoke of his commander. "He had a keen mind for strategy, but he was always willing to listen to advice or opinions. He knew he had been well educated, but he acknowledged that experience often tops education. He never stood on rank." Hawk's hands went still, his eyes unfocused. "He was generous."

Azmei smiled. "I can tell you loved him. It was churlish of Aris not to be kind to you. He should value anything you can tell him of his brother."

Hawk's eyes focused and turned cold. "I must beg your pardon, my lady. I call him worse than churl. I call him traitor."

Pain stabbed through Azmei's stomach. She clenched her muscles against it and drew in a long breath. "I know." She bowed her head, staring down at her hands, folded tightly in her lap. "Aris tried to have me killed." Hawk was silent. "He tried to have my father killed. He will likely try to have my brother killed." Still Hawk made no answer.

Azmei sighed and lifted her gaze to meet his. "He plans rebellion."

Hawk nodded silently. His sorrowful gaze was steady on hers. Azmei swallowed. There didn't seem to be anything else to say after that. They had to get to Tamnen City and stop this. She didn't know how they would accomplish it, but it was her duty, now that she'd brought Yarro to his goal.

Hawk looked away first. "My lady—" He broke off, pointing down the valley.

Azmei followed the line of his arm, not bothering to remind him to call her Azmei. Approaching them, far enough that they were still out of earshot, was a phalanx of dragons. At this distance, she couldn't make out their colors, just the shapes. But she could tell that the lead dragon carried a human figure on its back.

"Yarro," she said.

"Let's hope so." Hawk's voice was grim.

"There's no reason for them to have lured us here and then harmed us. It makes no sense."

He glanced over at her. "Do dragons make sense?"

Her lips quirked at that. She rested a hand on her sword hilt and waited.

Soon they could hear the ponderous beat of dragon wings. As they drew closer, Azmei saw it wasn't the golden dragon in the lead, but a sinuous green dragon. To its left flew the golden dragon, and to its right was another green. She wondered if their colors signified anything, or if they were just like kittens, born several different colors from the same mother sometimes. She wondered if she would ever have the chance to learn.

All too soon, the dragons were overhead, their wings raising a wind that swirled Azmei's hair around her face and tugged at her clothes. She narrowed her eyes to protect them from the flying sand and lifted a hand in greeting. Through the cloud of debris, she saw Yar lift his hand in return. The green dragon settled down in front of them. The others winged backwards until they could land in a semicircle behind the green.

"I'm back," Yar said. He slid down the green's shoulder and rested a hand on her neck as he walked forward. "I have much to tell you."

That would be weird, Azmei thought. It wasn't as if Yar was given to much speech. But he stepped up to her and looked down into her face, meeting her gaze deliberately. She stared up at him. His eyes were silver now, a swirly silver that—she gulped—matched the swirly silver of the green dragon's eyes.

"I am no longer Yarro Perslyn," he told her. "I am Yar-rax, Voice of Dragons."

"What does that mean?" she whispered.

To her relief, he gave her a wry grin, and it was the same grin she had seen on his face on a few occasions. "I don't know," he said simply. "But I guess I'm going to learn."

"What did they do to you?" She was surprised at how

fierce her voice was. She gripped her sword hilt.

"Nothing I didn't choose," he said. "I could have refused the Joining. They would have let me. But it would have made Xellax sad, and I..." he faltered, then looked back at the green dragon, who had pressed her nose against his back. "I find that I don't wish to make Xellax sad."

Azmei looked beyond him to the green dragon. It was watching her. She had a feeling it had noted her hand on her sword, and it was amused, but approved. She deliberated a moment, then removed her hand from her sword and bowed. "Greetings, Xellax," she said, trying to pronounce the name with the same hissy, throaty sound that Yar used. "I am Princess Azmei of Tamnen, sometime known as Aevver Balearic of the Shadow Diplomats. I am honored to meet you."

She felt a pressure in her head, a sort of soundless laughter, and Yar said, "She says, of course you are. But she is also pleased to behold you in the flesh, Azmei of Tamnen. There is great work in store for you."

Azmei heard Hawk shift behind her. He must not like the suggestion that the dragons had some use for Azmei. She wasn't sure what to make of it herself, but she would at least hear them out.

"For me?" She raised her eyebrows and met the dragon's eyes again, then transferred that look to Yar. "I suppose you'd better fill me in."

The pressure in her head came again, and Yar tilted his head to one side, his gaze going unfocused for several long heartbeats. His bearing was both like and unlike the way he had been when taken by a vision. It was as if it didn't engulf him as fully as it used to, but also that he was understanding it better, more clearly perhaps. Azmei watched his face, counting on Hawk to keep his eyes on the dragon—Xellax.

"There have been...rumblings," Yar said at last, and from the continued pressure in her head, Azmei could tell that Xellax was still speaking and Yar's hesitations were from translating as the dragon spoke. "We have suspected for...for some time...that the gods are waking. We now know this is true." He ignored Azmei's gasp and Hawk's muttered oath. "They stir in their slumber....it becomes more restless..."

He closed his eyes and went silent for several heartbeats, but though Azmei wanted to blurt out questions, she suddenly couldn't think of which to start with. She waited for him to speak again.

"Something has gone wrong to our west. Amethir...Amethir can affect this somehow..." Yar opened his eyes again. "You, with your ties to Amethir, Azmei, you can speak to...Vistaren?" He glanced at the dragon, then turned his gaze back to Azmei's. It was unnerving, after so many months of his trying not to meet her gaze, for him to look so directly at her, and with such strange eyes.

"Prince Vistaren is my betrothed," Azmei whispered. She felt Hawk go still next to her.

"Yes...He may be able to change things..."

"To keep the *gods from waking*?" Azmei's voice cracked on the question.

The dragon swung its head around Yar to look closely at Azmei. Its breath ghosted across her face, hot but surprisingly dry. She winced at the sudden pressure in her head.

"Xellax...is frustrated that she can't speak directly to you." Yar's voice was strained. "She knows you feel her, but you just can't understand."

"No. But you can, Yar." Azmei rounded on him. "Explain to me. Make me understand."

He didn't withdraw from her as he once might have. "The dragons don't know what Vistaren may do. But they know he's the only one who might be able to...to have some effect. I...I don't know whether it's to...to mollify the gods, or to..." He shook his head and shrugged. "I don't know. They don't know. But Vistaren is key. You and Vistaren."

Oh, gods. It came back to her marriage, didn't it? As her stomach rolled over inside her, Azmei realized how much she had been hoping that, despite her regard for Vistaren, she would be able to negotiate some new treaty, some way that she could be free to live her own life.

But this is my life, she thought. And then she remembered her father and brother.

She folded her arms across her chest. She lifted her chin and met the dragon's gaze, gambling that the dragon could understand her, even if she couldn't understand it. "This is indeed an important message. But now that I have fulfilled my duty to Yarro, I have other duties that demand my attention."

The dragon's head drew back, its gaze steady on her. Another dragon, the golden one, trumpeted. Azmei couldn't help wincing at the pain in her head. She wished they would stop trying to make her understand. But maybe they couldn't help it. Yar didn't wince when they spoke. Perhaps that was why he had to be their Voice.

"No duties can be as important as this," Yar translated. "That is Darixu who says it."

"My cousin plots treason," Azmei snapped. "My father and brother are in danger. I must save them."

There was a pause. Darixu paced closer, and Xellax lowered her head. Yar gasped, then said, "Your father is beyond danger." He broke the stiff mask of his translation and gazed at her in anguish. "Oh, Azmei, your father is dead."

Azmei hunched over, staring down at the sandy stone underfoot. It didn't matter that she had been half prepared to hear it. It didn't matter that she hadn't seen him for more than three years. There was no way to be ready for the news that you would never see your father again. She heard two steps crunch towards her and Hawk's hand settled gently on her shoulder. She sucked in a breath, fighting not to sob. "And...and Tanvel?" she whispered.

Yar cleared his throat. She could hear the regret in his voice as he said, "There is no time to mourn. You must tell Prince Vistaren that the gods begin to wake."

"My father is dead!" Azmei burst out. "My brother is in danger! My cousin has committed treason! I must save my brother."

Darixu stepped so close that his shadow fell across them. He was taller and broader than Xellax, but even in her grief,

Azmei saw that Xellax didn't retreat from him, and was glad. "You must warn the world," Yar said.

Hawk's hand tightened slightly on her shoulder. Azmei straightened and lifted her chin in defiance. "How can I do that, if my life is in danger and my brother is taken from the throne? How can I carry any message if I am pursued by my enemies, who would see my entire family dead so they can wrest the throne for themselves?"

"A petty mortal concern—" Yar began, and then broke off as Xellax turned her head and snapped her teeth together at Darixu. Azmei didn't need a translation to tell her that the green dragon was angry at the golden one.

"Wait," Yar said, tilting his head. "No, Darixu, it is logical. Princess Azmei is more useful than Azmei of no kingdom. As sister to the king, she will have a louder voice." He lowered his face. "Have we not seen how humans act?"

There was a moment of silence, and the pressure bled away. Azmei's head throbbed in the absence of the dragon speech.

"Besides," Yar said, and he turned his back on her, facing the two dragons. He was speaking for himself now. "Azmei helped me. She's the one who brought me to you. I wouldn't have made it here without her. I want to help her." He paused. "I need to help her."

There was a long silence then. The dragons were looking at each other, and Azmei had the sense they were communicating with each other, but she didn't feel the same pressure she did when they were trying to communicate with her. Did they have some other method? Why did they even care that the gods were waking? Why did they want to warn the humans, if they lived so far away in their hidden valley and thought the deposing of kings was a mortal concern?

And if they thought of humans as petty mortals, how long did dragons live?

"What is your request?" Yar said, and she was jolted out of her thoughts. He had turned to face her again. Azmei stared at him. She didn't have a request. She hadn't even considered...

She should have. Kicking herself for being so unprepared, she lifted her chin and straightened her shoulders, trying to remember how she had stood when she was a princess and not a mere assassin. "My condition is this," she said, choosing her words carefully. "Come out of your valley. Fly with us to Tamnen City. Help me show the world that my brother has powerful allies."

There was only a moment of silence before the air around them erupted into bellows and snorts, trumpeting and roaring. Each of the half-dozen or more dragons that had flown with Yar exploded into sound. One blue dragon leapt into the air, screaming shrilly, and settled back to earth with a shuddering crash. Azmei shifted her feet to give her better balance, but she didn't withdraw the challenge.

She realized one of the dragons hadn't moved. Xellax was still watching her, swirly silver eyes focused on her in an unnerving analysis. The elegant green head lowered until her eyes, each bigger than Azmei's fist, were even with Azmei's. There was appreciation in those eyes, and respect, Azmei thought. Xellax seemed to be Yar's dragon, the one he was most closely bonded with, somehow. Azmei hoped that any fondness Yar had for her was shared now by his dragon.

"You don't know what you are asking," Yar said quietly. "They have been hidden here for..." His gaze flickered as he searched for words. "For centuries. For...longer, maybe. It has been ages since the dragons revealed themselves openly to humans."

"We have stories of dragons," Azmei argued. "Not all of those stories are that old." She looked back at Xellax. "You know it's true. Maybe dragons as a—as a nation haven't revealed themselves. But some of you have. Some of you have fought with humans, or tricked humans, or been tricked by us. But I know there's more to you than that."

Yar sighed. "Your brother may already be deposed," he whispered.

"What?" Azmei whirled on him. "What did you see?"

He closed his eyes. "There is fighting. Between buildings.

In streets. The buildings are white and made of stone." He licked his lips and swallowed. "I see statues carved of people, white statues, and...and tombs. There is...one of them is new. It isn't finished. And when I look up, lift my gaze beyond the statues, I see smoke coming from the white towers."

Azmei uttered a cry of disbelief before she could stop herself. Then she swallowed it and pushed her shoulders back. Hawk's hand fell away from her. "Those are my terms, regardless," she said, and her voice rang out through the fray. The dragons fell silent, all of them watching her.

"Come to our aid, or I will not serve you," she said. "Even to save the world."

Darixu bellowed, and for just an instant, Azmei understood him. SHE CANNOT BE SO STUBBORN! She didn't need Yar's whispered translation. But Xellax's silvery gaze was amused as she watched Azmei, and she did not try to make Azmei hear her.

"Oh," Yar said. "I believe she can."

***

An hour later, the dragons were still arguing. Azmei, Yar, and Hawk had retreated to the fire, where Hawk had brewed another kettle of coffee. Yar was staring down at the fire, his shoulders relaxed, his silvery eyes half closed. He was eavesdropping casually on the dragons, but he knew they would give in.

"Is it well?" Azmei seemed to accept the changes in him, but he could tell she was concerned. He didn't know what Hawk was thinking, but he decided he would worry about that later.

Yar looked over at her. "I am content, if that's what you mean," he said. "I understand them better now. And because of the Joining, they won't—they won't have to take over my mind entirely. They'll be able to reach me better. At least, Xellax will, and the dragons can reach each other no matter how far they are, unless they deliberately cut each other off."

Azmei nodded. "What will the dragons do?" she asked.

He shrugged. "They'll give in. They'll have to. They can't carry the message themselves. You've seen how hard it is for them to communicate. They can't make people understand them. Most people."

"But you can carry the message," Azmei pointed out.

Yar grinned at her. "But I won't, unless they agree to your terms. I said I wanted to help you. You're my first friend, really." Orya didn't count, because Orya was his family, and now Orya was dead. He pushed down the tiny reminder that Azmei was there when Orya died. Orya had chosen her path, and if he wanted to blame someone, he ought to blame himself. Orya had chosen the path she did to protect him, after all.

The relief and gratitude on Azmei's face made him uncomfortable. He looked back down at the fire. "And I don't want your brother to die. You and Hawk like him, and that means he's worth liking."

"Thank you." Hawk's voice was quiet and Yar couldn't read any emotion in it. Hawk was scary, even though Yar liked him.

"What will you do?" Azmei said.

Yar shrugged. "I think I'd better come with you. And Xellax will. And Rexiel wants to come, though he won't say why. They'll come whether or not any of the others do. But they will. She'll talk them around."

Azmei nodded and went still. Yar looked up and realized the dragons had approached. Xellax led them, but Vetterix, Xerin, Rexiel, and Inlux came too. Darixu brought up the rear, and his wings were folded tightly against his back. Yar wasn't sure how he knew, but Darixu had been overruled, and he didn't like it. But he accepted it, and that was all Yar needed.

"Very well," he translated as Darixu spoke into his head. "Six dragons will accompany you. These five, and another who has volunteered. I will remain here to guard the Shrouded Vale. Should you tell anyone where we hide, it will go ill."

"I wouldn't tell anyone," Azmei said. "Why would I wish you ill? You have agreed to help me."

Darixu lowered his head and didn't reply.

"You won't be able to take the horses," Inlux told Yar. "They won't allow us to carry them. It would fright them to death."

Xellax looked slyly at Yar. "We could eat them."

Yar glared at her. "Not funny," he said, and then realized from the puzzled expressions on Hawk and Azmei's faces that he hadn't translated. "We can't take the horses," he said. "What do we do?"

Hawk deliberated. "Turn them loose here in the Vale. They have plenty of grass, water, and shelter. They'll be fine until we can return for them, whenever that may be."

"They will be safe here," Xellax assured Yar. "Why would anyone eat horse when there is venison aplenty?" The lofty tone of her voice in his head denied that she had ever suggested eating Firefoot.

Yar gulped. He hadn't thought about leaving Firefoot behind. "I'll have to say goodbye to Firefoot," he mumbled.

"Very well," Xellax told him. "Say your farewells. When the sun is full overhead, we fly."

CHAPTER TWENTY-NINE

Razem stared down at the map of the city, wanting to weep for each red stone that marked spots where fighting had broken out. "Father, I've let you down," he whispered.

A red stone at each of the city gates, because the city guard had barred the gates from the inside and out. They barred entry and exit, and Razem could only pray that his cousin Lady Ilzi had already left the city. If none of the rest of them survived this, at least she could be safe. But then, if Arisanat won, Razem knew he would execute Ilzi and all her family. He wouldn't be able to let any blood relatives of the Corrone live, not after this.

A red stone at the docks, also held by the city guard. That had to be Razem's next objective. If he could free the docks and send a ship to Salishok for aid—but that was a big if. And who could tell if there would be any loyal ship captains left? Arisanat would be a fool if he hadn't secured the docks for himself, and Arisanat was anything but a fool.

Then again, whispered a little voice, *Venra was the strategist, not Arisanat.* That gave him some hope. Not much, because Birona was shrewd enough to make up for Arisanat's lack. But at least it gave Razem a chance.

"What does it say about a king, that his nobles rebel against him less than a week into his reign?" he muttered to himself.

There was another red stone marking the family homes of Burojan, Birona, Belnat, and Talt. Razem didn't know for certain that there was fighting at all of them, but certainly there had been fighting at Arisanat's home. The guards who managed to escape after the arrest went wrong reported that he had slain several guards and taken Ysdra captive, wounding him in the process. Razem had been watching Kho carefully since that announcement; there had been no ransom demand for Ysdra, and Razem feared there wouldn't be. Insurrectionists couldn't afford to allow for ransoms.

Footsteps rang on the floor behind him. "Add a red stone to the guild section," Kho said. "Burojan's troops have taken it handily. And still no word of Ysdra." He stared down at the map, his brown face haggard. "I fear for him, my lord," he murmured.

"As do I." Razem rubbed his forehead, trying to dispel the headache that had nagged at him since Aris' rebellion. "Lady Tarra's warning may not have come in time." He couldn't help resenting her for keeping her silence for so long before coming to him. He understood why, and he wasn't petty enough to punish her for it, but he still wished she had told him about the rebellion sooner.

"We'll have to make the best of it," Kho said.

Razem nodded. His whole body ached for sleep. He wanted the tiny luxury of sitting on his balcony with a glass of wine at sunset, and then a full night to spend asleep in his bed. Instead, he knew he faced another night of pacing around the war room, eating on his feet and stealing snatches of sleep in his chair. He must be available to Kho at all times.

"Any response to the messages we sent to Lord Daix and Lady Riman?" The nobles who were in the royal palace when Arisanat attacked had been required to stay, both for their own protection and to prevent them from joining the insurrection. Razem had not seen any way to keep the news from them, nor had he seen any benefit to hiding the news from them.

Lady Tel and her daughters and sons were all within the royal palace; they had closed their house in the city after Lord Tel's death, removing to their estate except when Lady Tel was needed for Council. Razem had offered them apartments in the palace for Marsede's funeral and they had planned to remain through Razem's coronation.

Lord Restin was also within, as was Lord Daix's wife and heir. No one knew where Lord Daix and his younger son and daughter were, however, and Razem feared the worst.

"Only that Lady Riman will aid us," Kho replied. "Nothing from Daix. I have a report that there are archers in the area near the homes of lesser nobles."

"Damn." As one of the Nine, Daix was entitled to one of the mansions in the Family District, but they had only risen to Ninth a handful of generations ago, and they had never moved the household. Razem wondered now if that was because they lacked ambition, or because they preferred the privacy and distance from the other Families.

"Just so, majesty."

"What about Ilzi? Is it still unknown whether her retinue made it outside the city?"

"No one knows. I will keep my men searching." Kho was standing very straight. Razem could tell he was ashamed of his failure, but Razem had no time for recriminations.

"I must see for myself," he said, his impatience finally boiling over. "Let us inspect the walls. I can't stand to stay pent up in here, Emran."

Kho's expression said he understood, but didn't like it. "Majesty, if they should test the palace walls again—"

"They inevitably will," Razem interrupted. "And I will be there if they do. I would encourage my soldiers, and thank them for their service."

Kho sighed and bowed.

As they made their way through the palace, Razem was all too aware of the healers bustling along passages, carrying bandages and healing unguents in preparation for receiving the wounded. In the passage to the chapel, he saw families gathered, waiting for comfort from the clerics. Razem couldn't ignore the fear singing silently through the hallways. He summoned a page and gave orders that the evening meal in the great hall should be open to all who were sheltering within the palace walls. The page nodded smartly and trotted off to convey the orders.

When they reached the defenses, the soldiers lining the wall cheered him. It was all Razem could do not to stare. Why did they revere him? Why did they care at all? What had he done to inspire loyalty? He'd been a poor prince, the past three years. He'd stomped around in a temper, drinking too much and fighting too much, and frankly, as much as Aris' betrayal hurt, he wasn't sure he could even blame him.

It should have been Azmei here in front of them, he thought. *She at least deserved their loyalty. She could command their love.*

"But I'm all they have," he whispered, and straightened his shoulders, looking at the soldiers with pride on his face and in his bearing.

"My loyal soldiers!" he cried. "We are being tested, but I swear I shall stand with you and fight beside you. We will pass this test!"

They cheered again, but they were restless, and he knew he must find something else to say. "I know you are angry," he said, pitching his voice to carry. "I, too, am angry. I know you are hurt at this betrayal." He looked around at them and saw nodding heads. "I, too, am hurt at this betrayal." What now? How could he inspire them? He licked his lips. "But I tell you now: I would rather have no other men and women to fight beside me than you! This palace guard is made up of the most valiant fighters, the most loyal soldiers, the bravest men and women that we could find! I am proud to call you my companions!"

This time the cheer went on and on, and Razem smiled at them, holding out his hands, arms spread wide as if he would embrace them all. They pressed forward, each of them wanting to meet his eyes, to touch his hand. He obliged as many as he could, giving a smile to everyone, nodding his head, allowing them to tug at his sleeve and pat his shoulder. It felt almost as if they were sucking energy away from him, but it was worth it, if it gave them new heart.

Finally the press thinned and Razem and Kho were standing alone on a parapet overlooking the city to the north.

In the street below, a makeshift barricade stretched from building to building. It was made of boards and cobbles torn up from the street and packing crates that had been torn apart. In one spot, a fruit vendor's cart, still half-full of produce, had been rolled into place to fill a gap, and rubble had been piled against it on either side. The barricade was bristling with pikes and spears and halberds. Razem stared at it, feeling as if someone had punched him in the gut.

"Majesty." Kho's voice was quiet. "You have given them courage. It was well done. But I beg you, return to the palace."

Razem shook his head.

"At least take shelter inside one of the guard towers," Kho urged.

"When dark falls, perhaps," Razem said. "But for now, I must be here, with them." He squinted. "What is that smoke there?"

Kho strained in the direction Razem had pointed. His shoulders slumped. "It looks like a warehouse is on fire, majesty. I believe Lady Riman owns that block of buildings."

Razem had opened his mouth to speak when a ruckus below caught his attention. He looked down and saw that a small force of armed men was attacking the barricade. "The king!" shouted the attackers. "The king!"

Whether they meant to fight for him, or whether they were calling for his blood, Razem wasn't sure. He peered down. "Is that Ilzi's standard?" His heart jumped and he coughed against the tightness in his chest.

"A white dove, majesty." Kho's voice was grim.

Razem swallowed against a rush of bile. She was sixteen. Sixteen and not even betrothed yet. "Order a sally," he whispered. "The palace guard will ride out to assist her."

"It could be a ruse," Kho began, but Razem cut him off.

"I will not abandon my cousin to them!" he snapped.

Kho saluted smartly and ran to shout orders. Razem leaned on the parapet, bent forward so his chest rested against the sun-warmed stone. He couldn't tell at first if he was being obeyed, and then he saw the gates swing slowly open, just enough to let out a column of soldiers, two riders abreast. As soon as the horses were out, pikemen on foot went out to defend the retreat, and the gates crashed shut again.

Despite his fear, Razem had a sudden wish to be out there with them, wielding his sword in his own defense instead of relying on men and women he had probably never met. He strained to see what was happening, until he heard a whizzing noise. He jerked back and a crossbow bolt shattered against the stone near where his hand had been pressed.

"I beg you, do not make yourself a target!" Kho hissed, dragging him back from the parapet and into a crouch. "We will need you when this is over, my lord."

"Tell me what is happening," Razem said, then shook his head as Kho began to stand. "No, wait—don't make yourself a target either, Emran. I can't win this without you."

Kho rocked back on his heels and regarded him. "I believe you would, Majesty. You have already begun to grow into your title. Your anger has gone."

"Not gone," Razem corrected tiredly. "It is still there, my friend. But I am angry for the right reasons now, I hope. And angry at the right people." He sighed and rested his head back against the stone. "All the same, I would far rather have your counsel than not."

Kho nodded and crouched there for a moment more, then lifted his head. "You there, sergeant! What is happening?"

The woman he had hailed peeked over the wall, then dashed to them. "The Lady Ilzi and her soldiers are winning through, sir!" She stuck her head out again and ducked back. "The barricade has been breached in one spot. She will carry it!"

They could hear cheers from the soldiers on the ground, and a few minutes later, someone shouted up from inside the wall. "General! May we open to admit Lady Ilzi and the sally?"

"Open!" Kho bellowed, and the gates creaked open again. Ilzi's troops and those of the palace guard who had come to her aid pounded into the courtyard, washed on the cheers of the victorious. Kho jumped to his feet and looked over the wall, then helped Razem stand.

"Look, my lord," he urged.

Razem peered down through the lengthening shadows to see the barricade shattered, one part of it smoldering from an overturned brazier. Dead soldiers littered the ground on either side of it. Razem closed his eyes and breathed out a long sigh. He was grateful beyond measure that his young cousin was well, and that his side had won the skirmish. But he couldn't help mourning for the treacherous dead as well as the loyal. They had been misled, and though they might well have been executed anyway, he was grieved at their deaths.

He started down the steps to meet the new troops. The mounted warriors in the courtyard circled their horses around a slight figure in half-plate armor, a wimple wrapped around her head and a circlet helm over it rather than a full helm. She grinned up at Razem as he leaned over the stairs. Her face was smudged and she looked very young and very alive.

"Cousin!" she called up, "I bring you succor! We have few enough soldiers, but they are yours, as is my sword!"

Tears rushed into Razem's eyes so he had to wipe them away before he negotiated the rest of the stairs. When he reached the bottom, Ilzi was off her horse, straightening the split skirt of her tunic. Razem caught her in his arms, armor and all, and swung her in a circle. Ilzi shrieked with laughter, then remembered her dignity and struggled to be set down.

"Lady Ilzi, the gods bless you and your family," he said, grinning down at her. He had never wanted to see it come to this, but he couldn't deny that he was grateful she had come to his aid.

Feet pounded towards them from across the courtyard. "Majesty! They are attacking the wall to the west of here!"

Kho gave Razem a pleading look. "Majesty," he whispered, "please let me deal with this. Take yourself to safety, have supper brought for you and the lady, and be safe."

Razem lowered his voice and leaned in. "Only if you swear to be safe yourself, Emran," he murmured. Then he raised his voice so everyone could hear. "Cousin, come with me to the war room," he told Ilzi. "Bring your captain. General Kho, see to this new threat, then return to us there."

Kho bowed and dashed off while Ilzi and an armed man who looked to be closer to twenty than thirty followed Razem back into the palace. "This is Captain Rone, your majesty," she said. "He is captain of my personal and household guard, who I have brought to your defense. One hundred and eleven men in all, cousin."

"That many?" Razem said in wonder. It hadn't looked like so large a group, but he knew fear made the enemy's numbers larger and your allies' numbers smaller. "You have my thanks, Ilzi."

The smile she gave him was grave, her initial excitement fading. "We lost nearly twenty in the assault. Some of my troops are not very experienced, I must admit. But they all love you, cousin, and to a man, they volunteered to come with me."

Razem looked over to Captain Rone, who hung on Ilzi's words as if he couldn't get enough of her voice. He flushed when he saw the king looking at him, but Razem only smiled. "Captain Rone, well met. You have my thanks."

"Majesty," the man choked, and snapped out a salute. Fighting a smile, Razem answered it with one of his own. Thank the gods for Ilzi and Rone. He had needed some show of support, and they had given more than a show. They had broken through the barricade and demonstrated it could be done.

When they reached the war room, he found Lady Tarra waiting in the hall outside under the watchful eyes of the guards. Razem surveyed her and then gestured her to follow them inside. Gendo was within, laying out a tray of cold meats and cheeses.

"Thank you, Gendo. Bring wine and bread, and then you may retire."

Gendo bowed wordlessly, but Razem knew his manservant would wait up until he saw Razem asleep in a chair, just as he had done last night.

"Lady Tarra, I do not know if you have met my cousin, Lady Ilzi." It was likely they had met, but Razem didn't have the patience for protocol tonight, just as he didn't care to take time for the proper mode of introductions. "Ilzi, Lady of the Fifth Family, this is Tarra, younger daughter of the Seventh."

The two young woman made grave curtsies to each other, as was proper, but they both seemed to realize Razem was uninterested in formalities. Ilzi smiled at Tarra and then turned back to Razem.

"Before we attacked, I had Rone send spies through the western quarter of the city. We were nearly to the Dockside Gate when the fighting broke out. It took us some time to figure out what was happening, and by that time the gate was closed to us. We fought our way free to an alley we could hold and regroup."

"I thank the gods you are safe," Razem said. "Can you tell me the situation near the docks?"

"Better." Ilzi strode over to the table and stabbed her finger at the map. "The red stones are rebel strong points? What are the blue?"

"Unknown loyalty, but significant targets," Razem replied. "The docks office and levy house, there, and the royal bank, there." He pointed as he named them.

"What color for loyalist?" Ilzi demanded.

"Gold, of course."

She snorted and scooped up two of the gold stones. "The levy house is besieged, but my scouts report at least three score men inside, and they're holding their own. I wanted to try to take it, but Rone insisted on getting me to safety first."

"As well he should," Razem agreed. "But do you think the levy house could be relieved?" he added, looking over at Rone.

"Yes, majesty." The man's voice sounded strangled, but he cleared his throat and came to attention. "I don't delude myself that I'm the man to do it, but I would be happy to place my soldiers at the command of one of your men."

Razem nodded. "As soon as Kho returns, he'll assign you somewhere. I want the levy house relieved. For that matter, I want control of the docks. We need to get a ship out to sea as soon as possible. I want word sent to Salishok, to transfer troops back to the capital at once."

Ilzi cleared her throat. "I wasn't finished with my report, cousin," she said. "In addition to the levy house, I believe we could liberate the docks entirely. There was fighting down at one end, but it looked to me as if the sailors were fighting against the rebels."

"Well done, Ilzi!" Razem cried. "I am very pleased with you. Come, let us sup together. Have you eaten?"

"Not since noon," she said, "and not much to speak of then." She followed Razem over to the table and settled into a chair.

"Join us, Lady Tarra. Captain Rone." Razem smiled as Gendo reappeared, carrying two bottles of wine. "We will not stand on ceremony just now."

Gendo poured the wine, and for a few minutes they ate in silence. Finally Ilzi cleared her throat. "Cousin, is it true what I heard, that Lord Arisanat leads the rebellion?"

Razem closed his eyes, but to his relief, Tarra answered.

"It is true, Lady Ilzi. My mother is allied with him. He signed a betrothal agreement and said he would make me queen, but I have no wish to be queen."

Razem opened his eyes to see his cousin staring at Tarra. "Did you inform on Burojan?" Tarra only lowered her gaze, but Ilzi recognized it for agreement. "Well done, Tarra! For my cousin's sake, you and I shall be friends."

Tarra gave a little laugh that sounded as much sad as happy. "And how Lord Burojan would twist to hear that," she said softly. "He wished me to befriend you and turn you to his cause."

"As if that would happen," Ilzi said scornfully. "But come, we aren't so different in age, are we?"

"I am nineteen, Lady Ilzi."

"And I am rising seventeen," Ilzi replied, which was a

considerable exaggeration, since she had only turned sixteen at the Spring Evener, but Razem didn't bother to correct her. "We shall be very good friends, Lady Tarra, and I must introduce you to some of my other friends. I think they shall all approve of you."

Near the end of dinner, Kho returned, sweaty and moving stiffly. Razem stood. "Emran. Are you injured?"

"It is nothing, majesty. I stepped wrong and twisted my knee."

"Still, we will have it seen to. Gendo, fetch a healer." As his manservant bowed and left, Razem gestured Kho to a chair. "Sit. I will pour for you." He carried a plate of food and a cup of wine to Kho, whose dark eyes gleamed with warmth as the king served him.

Razem made himself wait a full five minutes while Kho took his refreshment, but finally he could hold back the questions no longer. "What happened?"

"It was an all-out assault on the palace walls, majesty. Birona's troops led, with Burojan's and the city guard in support." Kho drained his cup. "We repelled them, but not easily. I don't think they'll attack under cover of darkness, but we are heating pitch just in case."

"Gods forbid we have to use it," Razem murmured. He sighed.

"What are we going to do, Razem?" Ilzi whispered. When he looked over at her, the high spirits of earlier had fled entirely, and she looked at him with wide eyes. Razem was unable to dredge up even the hint of a smile, though he wished to reassure her.

"Keep fighting. I am king, and I cannot compromise with a traitor." His voice broke. "Even if I love him," he added in a whisper. *Gods, Aris, what drove you to this? What could I have done differently to keep you from this betrayal?*

Ilzi slipped her hand into his and squeezed it gently.

***

Arisanat knew, somehow, when his chamberlain showed Lady Talt into his study alone, that his bride-to-be had betrayed him. Why else would Talt be here without Tarra, when this was the safest possible place for them to be? He had planned to send for a cleric as soon as Tarra arrived. He had even considered sending for the cleric beforehand and having him waiting. He felt a sudden twinge of relief that he had decided against it. At least this way he would look less a fool.

He steepled his hands in front of him and gave Talt a hard look. "Lady Talt, where is my betrothed?"

He was surprised by the woman's red-rimmed eyes. "She...she has defied me, Arisanat." Talt faltered, then held out a folded and crumpled paper. "She left a letter for her sister." The woman's voice broke. Was she so distraught that her daughter had not confided in her?

Well, she should be.

Arisanat snatched the letter from her hand and unfolded it. He didn't want to read it. He stared at Talt, his gaze hard, until she looked away. She had read it, then. She knew what it said, and that he wouldn't like it.

My dear sister, I am writing to you because I know I cannot confide in Mother. I beg you, keep this letter from her as long as possible. I don't know what she and my lord betrothed will do when they learn what I have done. But first, let me tell you that I love you. I know the past years have been a trial for you, the way Mother has pursued any match that might seem advantageous—

Arisanat skipped ahead. He wasn't interested in sisterly affection. He wanted to know what Tarra had done—though some part of him knew already.

That he is so much older does not bother me. It was always a possibility, that my husband would not be my age, that my marriage would not be a love match. And once I would have believed a marriage to Arisanat Burojan the best thing that could happen to me. He is handsome, certainly. But...I see no kindness in him. I could forgive him if he was not entirely sane. But there is no question—he chose this path with his eyes open. He plots against the king, Tezira, and I cannot be part of it. I know Mother will never forgive me, but I pray you will.

Talt clasped her hands in front of her when Arisanat looked up at her. "Tezira did not bring this to me until our attack had begun." Her voice was stiff. "I have failed you, my lord."

Arisanat wished he could pretend it didn't hurt. His first marriage had not been a love match either, but he and Janira had learned to love one another. He had looked forward to training Tarra to his likes and dislikes and learning hers. He had thought her shy and virginal rather than sly and conniving. What a disappointment that she had deceived him so thoroughly.

"Well." He considered his next words carefully. Talt *had* failed him, and he could not have her fail him again. He could not let her think it was of no consequence. But she was properly repentant, and he could hardly blame her for Tarra having a mind of her own. It was something he admired, after all—a woman who thought for herself. Azmei had been just such a woman.

Then again, Azmei had chosen peace over Venra's memory.

He clenched his fist around the letter and looked at Talt. "Birona has just returned from an assault on the palace. Unsuccessful, but he swears that he will do better next time. Belnat is not here, but I expect him soon."

Arisanat saw her moue of distaste at the mention of Birona, but he didn't care. The man had been a more valuable ally than Talt, after all, and had actually commanded the assault. He had not fought, there was no question of that, but he had at least been willing to show himself standing against the prince—the king, Arisanat reminded himself. Razem was king now.

No matter. Soon Razem would be dead and Arisanat would be king.

"Go wait with Birona in the drawing room," he ordered. "I will join you both presently."

He watched her leave the room, her head bowed, and let the smile fade from his face. He couldn't deny that Tarra's betrayal hurt. He knew he was pursuing the proper course. He was going to stop Razem from destroying this kingdom. But how could Tarra have so badly underestimated him? He would have been kind to her. He would have made it a point to please her, in the bedroom and out of it. Why could she not see that he had offered her everything?

He had planned this so carefully, and still everything was spiraling out of control. What would Venra do at this juncture? Venra had ever been the better strategist. He would surely have seen some use for Tarra. Arisanat had an heir, it was true, but wouldn't it look good for him to have a queen, someone young and beautiful and agreeable to temper public sentiment about the coup?

Arisanat rubbed his forehead, staring at the dancing figurines on his desk. They were made by desert artisans, little glass sculptures of horses. They had been a gift from Venra. What to do? What to do?

Birona had said he could take the walls with one more push, but Arisanat wasn't sure. Tarra's betrayal had given Razem time to prepare his defenses.

Someone tapped at the door and he snapped, "Enter!"

His chamberlain came in. "My lord. I believe Lady Talt and Lord Birona plot against you."

Arisanat clenched his fist and followed his chamberlain into the secret room between his study and the drawing room.

"—she is a better judge of character than you, Talt." That was Birona's voice, indulgent and superior. Arisanat found suddenly that he hated the man, hated his smug superiority and his calm confidence. Why had he chosen this man for an ally? His shrewdness had seemed advantageous, but now it was like a dagger pointed at Arisanat's back. "How embarrassing for you."

"And are you so certain, Lord Birona, that Belnat remains true to us?" Talt's voice was tart, defensive.

Birona was pacing. Arisanat heard the slow, plodding footsteps. "He has no way out now. We know he betrayed the king, and he cannot use the same ploy that Tarra has already taken. No, he will stay true."

"Then where is he?"

A good question, Arisanat admitted to himself. Where *was* Belnat? He should have been here half an hour past.

"He was overseeing the evacuation of his family."

Talt laughed bitterly. "Are you certain he won't simply evacuate with them? I should have done so."

Birona hissed at her. "Be silent, Talt! Do you think his servants are deaf?" He lowered his voice, and Arisanat could tell he had drawn closer to the woman. He wanted to laugh aloud. They had more to worry about from his spy holes than from the servants.

"I am frightened," Talt whispered. "The palace was prepared for your attack. Can you truly take the walls with another try?"

"Perhaps. But it doesn't matter so much. If we hold the entire city and the king has only the palace, who is truly in command?" Birona grunted. "Burojan fancies himself as king. I don't care whether he's king or not, as long as I can keep this war with Strid from ending."

"Will you protect me and my daughter?" Talt asked.

Birona laughed. "Tarra?"

"Tezira, you fool! My older daughter. My heir."

Arisanat narrowed his eyes. He had known, of course, that Birona was in this for himself. But he had thought Talt a more devoted parent. She didn't care for Tarra—nor, probably, for Tezira. She cared for herself, for her fortunes and her possessions—her heir. Arisanat was doing this as much for his son Varidan as for his brother Venra.

"Enough," he hissed, and went back to his study. His sword was there. He strapped it around his waist and stalked to the drawing room. Talt and Birona were huddled close together in the corner furthest from the door. They jumped apart as he walked in, but while Birona managed to feign nonchalance, Talt was unable to hide her guilt.

Arisanat strode across the room as Birona backed hastily away from Talt. Arisanat's sword was in his hand, and though he hadn't planned it, he suddenly found it good. He thrust the blade through her torso, enjoying the way her eyes widened and she gasped like a fish on a hook. Arisanat jerked his blade back, feeling it rip through her flesh.

"Thus do we deal with traitors and failures," he hissed.

Birona was staring at him. "My dear Arisanat—" he began, but Arisanat didn't give him a chance to finish.

"Are you turning on me, too? May I remind you that I had the reach to kill Azmei in Ranarr and Marsede here, though I was leagues away in the desert? I will not brook disobedience, Birona." He liked how he felt when he was glaring hard at his ally. He liked even more the feeling that his ally feared him. Birona, of all people—Birona of the Third Family, who wielded so much power in the king's Council—Birona feared him.

Arisanat smiled.

There was a long pause. He could see Birona weighing his options. Arisanat would not be able to trust Birona much longer. Clearly the man would have to die, but how soon? How much longer could he still be useful to Arisanat?

Birona drew himself up, his considerable girth making him seem even taller. "I am in your full support, Lord Arisanat. I am hurt that you could doubt me."

Arisanat snorted, but made no reply. The chamberlain tapped politely at the drawing room door. He stepped inside, his gaze never flickering from Arisanat's face. It was as if there was no woman bleeding her life out on the floor.

"My lord, Lord Belnat is here. He seeks audience with you."

Arisanat didn't miss the way Birona's eyes flickered at the word 'audience.' He didn't care. Birona would have to learn sooner or later, or he would have to be slain. This way was tidier, at least for now.

"Show him in." Arisanat wiped his sword on Talt's dress, ignoring for the moment the disgusted noise Birona made.

When Belnat came into the room, his expression was already unhappy. When he saw Talt sprawled on the floor, her sightless gaze on the ceiling, he blanched. "Sleeping gods, Arisanat! I leave to get my wife and children out of the city and return to find you've turned on us? I should—"

Birona gestured sharply at the man, and Belnat fell silent. Arisanat chuckled.

"Should what, Belnat?" He liked how ominous his tone was. For so many years, he had been the simple stone mason. He had been only the king's cousin. Now, he was someone important. It felt good.

Belnat cleared his throat. "I should reaffirm that I am your servant, my lord."

Arisanat studied Belnat through narrowed eyes. The man was a coward, with a painful desire to do whatever made him most popular. But at least he was weak. He would not defy Arisanat, not yet.

"Very good. Birona, Lady Talt offends me. Remove her to the dining hall. We will have supper served in here." Neither of them said anything, but Birona moved hesitantly closer to the body. Arisanat smiled and paced back to his favorite chair. "Chamberlain! Bring me whiskey."

CHAPTER THIRTY

Azmei had never imagined seeing her home like this. She stared down at the ground as it rushed past. Seeing the desert they had spent weeks crossing spread out, seemingly endless, before her...it cut at her heart. It was so wild, so beautiful. So vast.

One of the dragons bellowed and as one, the two dragons in the lead—the defiant red that Azmei rode and Yar's green—angled to the left, flapping their wings to gain altitude. Looking over her shoulder, Azmei could see that the other four followed. Their formation was breathtaking, it was so seamless and precise. She imagined how the dragons must fly together for hours, dancing through the wind and around each other's wings and tails.

Her head was pounding. The red dragon, Rexiel, had warned her through Yar that travel like this might make her sick from the motion or the pounding of the wind. Neither of those bothered her, though. A dragon in the air moved nothing like a horse, but at least she could transfer those same skills to moving in concert with Rexiel's flight. The wind drove tears from her eyes, but her carefully wrapped clothes kept the worst of it from touching her.

She was certain it was the voices of the dragons, talking to each other and to Yar, that had given her such a headache. Something about them was too big for a human's mind to comprehend or contain. Something in Yar was different enough that he could manage it, and now that he had Joined with the dragons, he was even more changed. Azmei didn't envy him that.

Her back ached from the strain of holding on with her thighs and calves. She didn't have to; the dragons had suffered them to wrap makeshift harnesses to give the humans handholds. Still, she couldn't get over the instinct that said she should ride like a horse. The tight muscles of her back and shoulders had to be making her head pound worse. She jerked upright and realized she had been slumping again, her head drooping.

"Azmei!" It was Yar, and she could tell he was repeating himself. "You can sleep. Rexiel says to rest. He won't let you fall."

She wanted to believe him, but what if the dragon didn't notice her starting to slip until it was too late? She craned her neck to stare at Hawk. He was slumped over against the blue dragon's neck, one arm slipped through the hand strap. She couldn't see his eyes to see if he were asleep, but if not, he was at least relaxed. How could he be so comfortable?

She looked back to her left, where Yar was watching her, a mixture of amusement and frustration on his face. "You can trust him!" he shouted over the wind.

Azmei nodded. "I know!" she shouted back, but she couldn't deny the flicker of fear, like the taste of copper and salt water at the back of her throat. With a sigh, she shoved her arm through the hand strap, pushing until she could crook her elbow around it. That put her at an awkward angle, so she shifted her hip around and leaned forward. It wasn't completely comfortable, but it was much better than she'd expected, and to her surprise, Rexiel's movements felt almost like the rocking of a ship.

Azmei smiled, picturing a ship in full sail across the sky. What would the desert people think of that, if they saw it? A quick, lithe schooner like the *Dawn Star*, the ship Prince Vistaren and his friend Arama had sailed, cutting through the air above the sand. It made her chuckle. She slipped easily into a sleep laden with dreams of ships and whispers.

When she woke again, they were still flying, but not as swiftly. The powerful wing beats had turned into a glide. She slipped her arm out of the hand strap and sat up, yawning. Rexiel rumbled at her, so low she didn't hear it, but felt it vibrate under her and inside her head both. "Where are we?" she asked, knowing he would understand her, even if he couldn't answer.

There was a squeezing in her head, which revived the throb that had settled during her sleep. Azmei winced, but then Xellax and Yar slipped in above them. Yar leaned over, grinning at her.

"Sleep well? We flew through the night, and Xellax tells me we are near the capital city. She says much has changed since she last came this way."

"When was that?" Azmei asked. How long did dragons live?

Yar shrugged. "Many lives ago."

She peered down through the morning light. They were higher than they had been, so high the canal underneath them looked like painted glass instead of water, except for the little boxes that must be canal boats. She wondered if anyone on the boats had looked up and seen the dragons. Would they recognize them, or just think them eagles, flying higher than human could reach?

"Is that the Tamlikin Canal?"

"I don't know what that is," Yar said.

"It's the canal that stretches from Tamnen City through Lishan and all the way to Meekin." She looked up at him. "It's how I got to Meekin when I came to you."

His expression brightened. "Yes, Xellax said she remembered Lishan—but she said it had grown since she saw it last." He grinned. "Grown from a handful of houses and a town hall, she said. That must have been forever ago."

Azmei's eyes widened. Many lives ago, indeed. Lishan was not as large as Tamnen City, or even Meekin, but it was a city in its own right, and boasted a university and a dozen or more guild halls. She eyed Xellax with respect that was trying to edge into awe. How could a being so vast and ancient care about humans? Even one special human boy who could talk to her?

To distract herself, she looked ahead of them and stiffened. On the horizon, she could see a dark smudge in the sky. Tamnen City? Was the capital in flames? What had happened?

"Where's Hawk?" she shouted.

"Here, my lady."

Hawk's voice was nearer than she'd expected, and she realized that Rexiel was flying above the blue dragon who carried Hawk. She twisted to peer down at him. "Do you see—"

"I do. I've been watching a group of riders and wains. Look there." He pointed to the southwest. She followed his gesture and realized there was a caravan riding at haste away from the capital. "There are refugees, it seems, but the fighting hasn't spread this far."

Azmei wasn't sure if that was a comfort or not. She yawned again and fumbled at the pack strapped to her back. What she wouldn't give for coffee—but a sip of water would have to do. The leather of the water skin crackled as she squeezed it; frost rimmed the mouthpiece. Thankfully the water itself wasn't frozen, so she was able to wet her throat.

"We should go lower," she called to Yarro. "I need to see what's happening."

There was no signal, but as one the dragons began spiraling into a slow descent, turning and turning so she could keep the caravan in sight. When at last they were low enough that she could discern the symbol on the standard, she sucked in a breath. "Belnat! Thank the gods."

Hawk's gaze was steady on her face. "You feared it would be your brother."

"Has the palace ever been defended before?"

"Twice, both times successfully. Prince—King Razem has General Kho with him. They will be well." Hawk's quiet confidence gave her courage.

"Let them see us!" she shouted to the dragons. "Let everyone know that dragons fly with Azmei to Razem's aid!"

Rexiel, at least, was pleased by the suggestion. He bellowed so loudly it shook her. Below them, the caravan burst into confusion as horses whinnied and shied and people stared up and screamed. Xellax joined in, her voice higher and more melodious than Rexiel's, and at that, the other four added their voices, a strangely harmonious battle cry.

Azmei laughed, raising one fist in defiance. Arisanat may have been fool enough to defy the crown, but Razem was cunning enough to keep it, and Azmei brought allies to his side. The dragons flew to Razem's aid. Not at his bidding, no, but at least in his defense.

As they pulled away from the caravan, the dragons swung around wide to the west. Azmei was blinded by the glitter of the sea. She shielded her eyes until they adjusted, then she stared hungrily at the city where she was born.

Tamnen City was in agony. There was no fighting at the outer city walls, but there was fighting in the streets. From this vantage point, Azmei could see barricades at several key intersections. The city guard looked to have control, but somehow that didn't look like a good thing. Rexiel drove up in a steep climb, spiraling as he did. Azmei saw a ship putting out to sea. The docks flew Razem's standard.

And so did the palace.

"To the palace!" she screamed, leaning closer along Rexiel's neck. "My brother will be there, and he will welcome you!"

Rexiel trumpeted his agreement and banked to the right, bearing for the tallest tower of the palace. As they broke over the outer palace walls, a flurry of arrows hissed up at them, disappearing into smoke as Rexiel exhaled a flame just large enough to destroy them.

Azmei laughed in delight as Rexiel settled on the parapet. She shouldn't enjoy frightening her brother's soldiers, but she was glad to know they made an imposing sight.

"Cease your attack!" she called. "I am Azmei Corrone! I come in support of my brother, King Razem!"

***

Razem was leaning over the map in the war room, consulting with Kho, Ilzi, and Tarra, when a sharp rap on the door interrupted their discussion. The captain of the tower guard was standing there, sweaty and out of breath as if he'd run through the palace from the towers. "Majesty, General," he said, snapping out a salute, "you're going to want to see this. We've, ah...the situation has changed."

Razem made sure his sword was still belted on and dashed after Kho as he followed the captain. Behind him, he heard Ilzi and Tarra's steps ringing on the stone in pursuit, but he didn't waste time telling them to wait. Ilzi was as strong-willed as a desert tortoise, and Tarra had made it clear how personally she took Razem's survival, now that she had betrayed her blood to warn him. Let them come—they had proven better allies than the head of the First Family, after all.

To his surprise, when they reached the stairs, the captain went up rather than down. So at least it wasn't a breach of the palace wall—but why climb inside the palace? He didn't have the breath to voice the question, though, and Kho trusted the man, so Razem would follow blindly for the moment. As it turned out, when they reached the top of the tower, he had no need to ask his question.

He reached the flat roof of the tower and stopped so abruptly Ilzi ran into him, her armor bruising his elbow. Then she gasped and clutched at his arm. Razem's mouth dropped open and he stared, his heart racing and his lungs unable to draw breath for a long moment.

A vast crimson dragon stood, neck arched, wings spread, surveying them with glowing golden eyes that were currently half-closed. Circling overhead were half a dozen more dragons of all colors. Two of them had human figures on their backs—and at that, he brought his gaze back down to the crimson dragon. Astride its back was a slight figure in off-white robes, her hood down so dark curls could spill around her face. Her golden eyes and tawny-skinned face were alight with triumph.

"Brother!" she cried. "I brought you allies!"

Razem found he could move again. He sprinted towards the dragon, shouting, "Azmei!" His sister slid down the dragon's shoulder and tumbled into Razem's arms. They were squeezing each other so tightly he couldn't catch his breath again, and he didn't care. She was so strong and slender in his arms, and he had thought he would never see his sister again, and suddenly, despite everything that was wrong in the world, Razem found he could feel nothing but joy.

Finally he kissed the top of her head and let her lean back, though he kept his hands on her shoulders. "Thank all the gods," he choked. "Azmei."

She grinned up at him, and he could see there were faint lines at the corners at her eyes that had never been there, but she had the same crooked, impish grin, and if her hands were more calloused from the hilt of a sword than his, what did it matter? She had survived, beyond all hope, and Razem was not alone in the world after all.

"You'd better reassure your troops that we're really here to help. The tower guard recognized me, thank the gods, but dragons are a bit...mm, unnerving, after all." Her eyes danced with mirth at the understatement. "We were lucky they agreed to send for you—though I don't think they could actually have hurt the dragons."

Razem lifted a hand and waved, and he heard Kho shout for the troops to stand down. "Do you think all six can land here?"

"All six don't need to, but we'd better have Xellax and Vetterix come in." Azmei turned to indicate the red dragon behind her, and Razem's brain froze as he realized how close he was to the massive being. At this distance, he could see the crimson scales were edged in black, the golden eyes flecked with red. He swallowed and offered a bow from one monarch to another. He could sense the dragon's amusement, somehow, but the creature made no movement other than to lower its head.

"This is Rexiel," Azmei said. "Rexiel, this is my brother, King Razem of Tamnen."

She turned back to look up at Razem. "I'm sorry I stayed hidden from you all these years."

Razem considered his words before speaking. "I...can't pretend it doesn't hurt," he admitted, "but I'll have time later to be upset. For now, we have a few obstacles in our way."

Azmei grinned again. "Opportunities, you mean. This is your chance to show everyone what a strong and cunning king you are. Look at the mighty allies you've brought to your side."

Razem sobered. "Do you know who's leading this insurrection?"

The tower trembled and Razem glanced over to see that a blue dragon had landed. Its rider slid down and limped stiffly towards them—Razem gaped, then tried to rearrange his face into something more kingly. It was Hawk! Hadn't he gone to Meekin? Not that Razem was sorry to see him, all things considered, but...how did Hawk end up coming back with Azmei and *dragons*?

Azmei turned to watch Hawk's approach. Her voice was sad. "It's Arisanat leading them. He tried to have Hawk killed just outside Rivarden, which is how we met."

Hawk reached them and knelt with difficulty. "I beg your majesty's pardon—"

"Enough of that, Hawk," Azmei interrupted. "Razem, I revealed my identity to Hawk and countermanded your order to keep him from wasting time." She straightened her shoulders. "I'm the one who took care of the Perslyn Patriarch in Meekin."

Razem was reminded forcibly of the accounts he'd read in Tanvel's diaries. He wondered how Azmei would feel if she knew how much he knew about her past three years. He merely nodded. "You were right to do so. And Hawk, get up," he added, holding out a hand to help the man to his feet. "I know how impossible it can be to resist my sister. She's like a force of nature."

Azmei snorted and rolled her eyes, and so she missed the way Hawk looked at her. But Razem didn't. *Oh, gods,* he thought, with a sudden pang. *That's...* The tower shook again, distracting him, as a sinuous green dragon landed.

"*Dragons,* Az. By all the gods, *how?*"

Azmei made a wry face at him and looked back at the green dragon. Its rider was slipping down more gracefully than

Azmei had, and he strode over to join them. Razem was surprised to see he was only a boy on the cusp of manhood.

"Razem," Azmei said, "I present to you Yarrax, Voice of Dragons, first human in centuries to be so called. I was honored to travel with him for some time, and I believe in his mission." She smiled at the young man, who—despite his outward show of confidence—colored faintly. "Yarrax speaks for the dragons, and they share their wisdom and vision with him."

There was nothing in the protocol books for greeting dragons or the Voice of Dragons. Razem decided on another bow as deep as one monarch to another. "Yarrax, welcome."

The boy opened his mouth to speak, but a clamor rose from below, hundreds of voices raised in fear and anger and confusion, and Razem held up a hand. "Wait. General Kho, send someone down to reassure our troops, as well as the people below. The dragons are come as allies to the royal throne, and not to harm."

Kho nodded and hurried off. Razem looked back at Yarrax with a smile.

"I apologize. You have had time to get used to dragons. My people have not."

Yarrax had a grin that transformed his face from a too-thin, anxious expression into a friendly, confident young man. "If you want the truth, they've been in my head nearly all my life, but I only met them in person a few days ago." He glanced over his shoulder at the green dragon, and Razem felt a surge of admiration at the love and respect on the boy's face. When Yarrax looked back at him, Razem realized the boy's silvery eyes matched those of his dragon.

"The dragons have a dire message for the whole world, your majesty, but Azmei elicited their assistance here in exchange for helping me carry the message. I suggest we deal with your situation first."

Razem nodded. "We have a map in the war room, but I would not wish to be discourteous to our new allies..."

Yarrax shook his head. "They don't rely on sound to

communicate. I will be able to convey our conversation to them, and theirs to us." He paused, his silver eyes going unfocused for a moment. "Rexiel offered to transform himself, but Xellax says that would take too much of his energy. I—" He paused. "I think they can be shaped like us, if they wish, but it's not easy."

"Shaped like us?" Startled, Razem turned to look at the crimson dragon. The golden eyes widened, and just for a moment, Razem's head squeezed painfully as a booming Voice echoed through his head. HOW ELSE COULD WE HAVE OUR STAKE IN THE ROYAL LINE?

"Royal—" Razem broke off.

"You understood that?" Yarrax whispered.

Razem stared at the golden eyes, seeing in them a reflection of the golden eyes that had only ever been passed down in the Corrone line for a score of generations. Arisanat's mother had been a Corrone, and Aris and Venra had the golden flecks that flashed in their temper, but nowhere else had he seen golden eyes. "Dragon blood?" he whispered.

Rexiel didn't speak again. The pressure on Razem's head subsided, though he was left with a throbbing headache. "Gods," he muttered. "Let's get down to the war room."

***

Ilzi helped Azmei into a suit of gold-washed armor as the impromptu war council finalized their plans. Yar and Xellax would stay with Razem and Kho to quell the fighting at the palace. Xellax, along with two other dragons, would breathe fire and look menacing while the palace guard sallied from the gate as if they had only been waiting for the dragons' arrival. Azmei couldn't help worrying that three dragons wouldn't be enough to intimidate the insurrectionists, but Razem laughed at her when she ventured the opinion aloud.

"Trust me, sister, *one* dragon would probably be enough. Especially when word comes back that you've seized the rebel leaders."

That was Azmei's part—to take Hawk, Rexiel, Vetterix, and Xerin and clear a path through the streets for a mixed group of soldiers belonging to Ilzi and to the crown. Ilzi's Captain Rone would lead them, and their only task was to take captive the four leaders of the rebellion. Tarra had pleaded for her mother's life, but Razem, his voice grim but gentle, had stated it was death to be part of treason against the crown, and Tarra had accepted his judgment without tears.

Ilzi tugged the last strap tight and slapped Azmei's shoulder. "Ouch!" she said, shaking her hand, and kissed Azmei's cheek. "I wish I were going with you, cousin. To fly on the back of a dragon and finish the rebellion!"

Azmei shook her head. "Be glad you don't have to. I am grateful beyond measure that you came to our aid, but I hate that you had to fight when you're still so young."

"You aren't that much older," Ilzi protested, but Azmei lifted a hand, laughing.

"Eight years isn't that much older? And I didn't have my first real fight until three years ago. Have patience, Ilzi. There are such storms coming as shall shake the very foundations of the earth. You will see your share of fighting."

The sorrow in her voice sobered Ilzi, but before her cousin could grow truly frightened, Azmei grinned at her and kissed her forehead. "Now go make sure my brother doesn't do something reckless like get on a dragon's back himself."

Azmei and Hawk climbed the tower steps alone and in silence. Azmei wondered what he was thinking. Arisanat had tried to kill them both. Did Hawk hate him for that? Did she? But she felt no hatred as she climbed the steps. She felt mostly sad. There had been so much promise when they were all young together. Where had that promise gone so wrong?

As they climbed, she felt the pressure in her head increasing. Had Rexiel really meant that the Corrone family had a dragon as one of their ancestors? Razem believed it, if his whispered comment to her on their way to the war room was any indication. It might explain how she had understood the dragons once, and how their attempts to communicate with her almost broke through. She wondered if they had wanted a ruler with dragon blood so they wouldn't have to search for a Voice of Dragons. With effort, she thrust the thoughts from her mind. It was time for her to concentrate on the task at hand.

God of peace, she thought guiltily, *I have been remiss in my meditation. Grant us success, I pray you. There will be no peace as long as my cousin has rebellion and hatred in his heart. Help us defeat him. Guide my hand in the service of peace.* Even as she prayed it, she felt a fraud. What if peace meant Razem losing? She wouldn't allow that. She was not, in her heart of hearts, serving peace. She was serving her brother.

When they reached the top of the tower, Rexiel was stamping impatiently. He trumpeted at her as soon as he saw her, and Azmei broke into a jog. Had their steps lagged as they climbed? She watched Hawk running to Vetterix and realized he was favoring his leg. She had automatically matched her pace to his.

"All right," she said, climbing up Rexiel's front leg. It was more awkward in a breastplate and chain than it had been in linen and silk. "We're here now. Let's go."

With a sky-shattering bellow, Rexiel lifted into the air. For a moment, Azmei was flattened against his back, held in place by the weight of the wind. Then they were swooping down over the palace walls into the square they had agreed on. The fighting was lightest there, and true to Kho's expectations, the rebels broke as soon as they saw the two dragons bearing down on them.

It wouldn't last, Azmei knew. Sooner or later they would find their courage and make a stand. But as she watched Captain Rone and his soldiers securing the street below, she found it in her heart to hope it wouldn't happen until they reached Arisanat's home.

As it turned out, she had underestimated the sheer terror factor of dragons. Exposure through Yar, who could speak to them, had inured her, making her forget her initial fear. The further they flew, the dragons blasting fire harmlessly into the air and bellowing in false rage, the less resistance they encountered. When they reached the only intersection with barricades, it was completely unmanned, the square behind the barricade littered with dropped weapons.

The crown soldiers slowed as they tried to clamber up the barricade. Azmei shouted, "Wait! Fall back from it!" She didn't need to explain to Rexiel. As soon as the soldiers were a safe distance away, he circled around and flew at the barricade, loosing a blast of flame that engulfed it. In a matter of minutes, the barricade was smoking rubble and ash. It was the perfect opportunity to demonstrate the sheer might of the dragons. Hopefully word of this would travel swiftly to the other rebels and steal the heart out of them.

Across the square, Arisanat's house stood shuttered and locked tight. Azmei had no doubt they were watching from within, so she simply nudged Rexiel to settle down in the middle of the square. Vetterix and Xerin would circle around behind the buildings in the square, clearing a path for the soldiers to fan out and surround Arisanat's house. Azmei didn't watch them. She merely sat astride Rexiel and waited. She could burn the house down around them, stone or no stone. The fact that she didn't meant she was willing to talk. They would come out. Curiosity would get the better of them sooner or later. She could wait.

It didn't take as long as she had anticipated. The door cracked open and Lord Birona lumbered outside, his bulky figure squeezed into armor as it probably hadn't been in twenty years. Azmei didn't dismount as the crafty head of the Third Family crossed the yard to stand in front of her. She had to admire his courage, despite her dislike. There couldn't be many men who would willingly come out to face a dragon.

Birona stopped some distance away, perhaps hoping he was out of range of the dragon's teeth. He studied Azmei for a long moment. She had forgone a helmet for just this reason—she wanted everyone to recognize her and see she was back from the dead.

"So. Princess Azmei Corrone." Birona made a face of

disappointment. "Another of Burojan's failures, I see."

She arched an eyebrow. "So you know your ally attempted my murder three years ago."

Birona lifted a hand, palm up, in lieu of a shrug. "As he succeeded in murdering your father three weeks ago," he replied. "When I allied myself with him, I thought he was sane and in control. He intended to carry the war with Strid to a victorious conclusion, rather than letting it drag on for another twenty years. I intended to profit from that."

"That doesn't seem to be working out quite as you'd hoped," Azmei replied. "What is your plan now, Birona? I know you too well to think you don't have one."

"Come down from there. It's ridiculous to shout up at you while you're sitting on the back of that beast." His tone was one of arrogant annoyance, as if she were his daughter caught out stealing sweets from the pantry. Azmei suppressed a flash of rage, but she would not let that stand. Her hand whipped out and a moment later Birona was staring down at a dagger buried hilt-deep in the packed dirt at his feet.

"You will not speak to me in that fashion," Azmei said coldly. "You have nothing with which to bargain, Birona. Speak respectfully, or be silent and send my cousin out to speak."

He snorted. "Do you think he'll be more respectful?" he asked, but his stance was wary now. Good. He must learn he was not dealing with a naïve, young princess anymore.

"What is your proposal?" she snapped.

Birona bowed. "Lord Belnat and I are prepared to surrender Burojan to you without a struggle. We will also surrender ourselves peacefully, if you will guarantee our safety."

Faced with the princess he had thought dead and her dragon allies, and Birona still thought only to bargain for his own safety. *Ah, Birona, you are shrewd, but I fear you are short-sighted,* Azmei thought. Then again, his willingness to participate in a rebellion purely for profit proved that. She sighed.

"Bring Arisanat out to face me," she ordered. "And Belnat as well." When Birona hesitated, she shouted, "Go!"

Rexiel shifted under her, and that last was too much even for Birona's stubborn pride. He turned and all but ran for the door.

Arisanat was not dressed for war. He wore rich purple robes edged in gold and a heavy ceremonial chain around his neck, from which hung his family symbol of a block of marble with a crossed chisel and hammer. Birona had come to her as the warleader of a rebellion; Arisanat came to her as a monarch waiting to be crowned—or a man deep in mourning. Azmei swallowed her sudden grief at the thought of Venra and made her face hard. Her cousin wore no armor, but he did wear his sword.

"Cousin." Arisanat came much closer than Birona had. He peered up into her face, hope and disappointment warring in his expression. "Part of me is glad to learn I failed," he admitted. "Venra loved you so much. How amazed he would be to see you now."

Despite her resolve, Azmei shook her head. "Oh, Aris. You have been such a fool." Her voice was softer than she'd meant it to be. "Do you really think this is what Venra would have wanted?"

Arisanat bowed his head. "He isn't here to want anything, is he? Strid killed him, and so I will see Strid destroyed. Every last one of them." His voice was so calm it chilled Azmei. He had chosen his path deliberately, not in madness. And still he was unrepentant.

"At what cost?" Azmei demanded. "That of destroying Tamnen's royal family along with Strid's? That of destabilizing the throne? That of murdering and betraying those who only ever loved you?"

Arisanat lifted his chin. "A crown isn't stable if it's on the head of a weak, unworthy king." He faltered. "Love or no love."

His treachery *was* taking its toll on him, she realized. He had been an honorable man once, an intelligent, somewhat priggish elder brother, exasperated and plagued by their childish tricks, but loyal. Some part of him must hate what he had become. If only she could appeal to that part and persuade him to repent. It wouldn't save him, but it would make this easier on Razem.

"Arisanat, I must demand your surrender," she said, her voice clear and pitched to carry to Lords Birona and Belnat, who hovered nervously at a safe distance. "My brother cannot now be merciful, but unless you submit yourself willingly to his rule, he will be forced to eradicate House Burojan entirely as punishment for your sins and to destroy any remaining element of sedition. Does your son deserve to die for his father's sins?"

Arisanat's resolve broke into astonishment. "He's only a boy!" he protested.

Azmei let herself go very still, her face hard. She said, coldly, "So is Prince Kaiden of Strid."

"You will not harm Variden!" Arisanat shouted. Lord Belnat ran towards Arisanat. Perhaps he meant to calm him, but Arisanat heard the footsteps approaching and whirled, drawing his sword. Belnat wasn't expecting it. He flailed to a stop, fumbling out his own sword. Captain Rone's soldiers, not yet in place, raced to intervene, but they were slow. Belnat was bleeding heavily from one arm by the time they took Arisanat and Belnat into custody.

Azmei frowned. Where had Birona gone? He had been standing back by the house just a moment ago...

Someone cried out as Vetterix landed next to Rexiel. When she turned to look, she saw Hawk begin to slip from Vetterix's back. He caught himself on the strap, but he was grimacing, and she could see his bad leg was twisted awkwardly.

"Hawk!" She slid down Rexiel's back and drew her dagger. "Here, lean on me." She got a shoulder under his arm to support him and then cut the strap.

Hawk grunted and stumbled against her, his free hand resting on Vetterix's flank.

"Are you hurt?" she breathed.

He shook his head and looked up, his face flushed.

"Embarrassed. Vetterix turned too sharply and I wrenched my bad leg." He coughed and glanced behind her. "I'm afraid we have an audience."

She gave him a crooked smile. "Three years of not being a princess have taken their toll," she said. "I've forgotten how to act regal."

"No, you haven't," he murmured. He straightened and pulled away from her.

Trying not to regret the new distance between them, Azmei strode forward, her gaze on Arisanat. She would look him in the face before he was taken to stand before her brother. Arisanat's eyes had shadows under them, and there were new lines by his eyes and mouth. He met her gaze for only a moment before his faltered.

"Aris," she whispered. "I could almost forgive you for myself. But I will never forgive you for murdering my father." And Tanvel. She swallowed. "Shame on you. Shame on your whole house."

As she turned away, Arisanat recoiled. The guards holding him shouted, and she heard Hawk scream her name. She spun to face whatever threat was approaching.

"Birona!" she spat, eyes widening as the man charged her, light flashing from his upraised sword. His fleshy face was contorted with hatred.

Azmei grabbed at her sword hilt, but before she could draw, a gaping red maw shoved between her and the charging third lord. Her hair whipped across her face in the wind of Rexiel's movement as the dragon's jaws chomped shut on Birona's head and shoulder with an audible crunch.

Azmei stumbled back, shuddering at the snap of bones between Rexiel's teeth. What remained of Birona's body crumpled, gushing blood across the courtyard. Then Hawk was there, one hand on her elbow, guiding her away from the dragon. Rexiel snorted and turned golden eyes to Azmei. She heard the dragon remark, XELLAX WILL BE SO DISAP-POINTED.

She turned back to face Captain Rone's soldiers, who

were suddenly twenty feet further away from the dragon. Arisanat, held between two of them, opened his mouth, staring at her wordlessly. Azmei met his gaze, then looked beyond him to where Lord Belnat huddled against the side of the house.

"Lord Belnat, I trust you will put up no resistance."

When Captain Rone strode forward, another dozen men behind him, and put Belnat and Arisanat in shackles, Azmei sighed and let her shoulders relax. Hawk limped up next to her.

"Azmei, I promised Emran Kho that I would look for his Captain Ysdra. He was last seen here, when they attempted to arrest your cousin."

Azmei nodded tiredly. "I will come with you." He opened his mouth, whether to thank her or protest, she didn't know, but he closed it again without speaking and nodded.

Hawk went in first, then Azmei, a dozen soldiers shadowing them. The front hall was empty, so they pressed further into the house. In the dining hall, a man she recognized as Arisanat's chamberlain leapt at Hawk. It couldn't have been any more than a suicide; Hawk's sword flashed out and sliced the man's throat. Only afterwards did they see the man had been unarmed. Lady Talt's body was sprawled under the table. She had been dead at least a day.

They found Ysdra next to the fireplace in the kitchens. He was alive, and there was a surprisingly small amount of blood on his uniform. He didn't wake when Hawk knelt next to him and rested two fingers against his neck. His skin was beaded with sweat, his hair plastered to his forehead.

"His pulse is thready and fast," Hawk murmured. "Fever's set in. The wound may not have gone bad yet, but..." He pressed his fingers against Ysdra's stomach and the man groaned faintly. "His stomach's hard and swollen. That's not a good sign."

He frowned down at Ysdra's stomach, lips working as if he were chewing the inside of them. Finally he shook his head. "Better if we don't wake him yet, I guess. He's been here three days, and if it hasn't killed him yet, he'll probably wait until a healer gets here."

Azmei swallowed. His voice sounded hopeful, as if he thought Ysdra could hear him. His eyes, meeting hers, were grim.

She nodded. "The king would have only the best for Captain Ysdra," she said aloud. "Soldier! Fetch a healer!"

"We should report to your brother," Hawk said.

"You can't leave Ysdra to make the report," she said, "and I will not leave without you. So we will wait until the healer arrives." She leaned down and stroked the man's hot forehead. "I will find some cool water to wash his face."

He wouldn't live, she thought. Gut wounds were bad, and there were too many ways for them to fester. The best they could hope for was to ease his pain and give him a quick death. But at least she would make certain the man was in the palace and knew his king loved him when he died.

CHAPTER THIRTY-ONE

Razem had never realized how uncomfortable his father's throne was. He braced his elbows on the elaborate gold arms and steepled his fingers together as he surveyed the room. He had gathered as many members of the Nine Families as he could find inside the palace. He would not have it said he dealt with the traitors in secret. There would be discontent after this; there always was after the king had to deal harshly with his council—or after the council forced the king's hand. But he would do whatever he could to mitigate it.

Belnat looked as though he were choking on regret. Razem could well imagine he were. To be tested so sorely while he was newly come to his headship—Belnat had made a poor decision, and would not be remembered kindly in his family histories. Razem let his gaze move on. Arisanat—

Arisanat mostly looked tired.

There was no rage or hatred in his eyes as he looked up at Razem. There was, he fancied, some despair, and perhaps some relief. How could one man feel so many things? Then again, Razem felt much of those same emotions. He sighed.

"I am deeply disappointed," he said finally. "Lord Belnat, you have acted foolishly. Many transgressions may be forgiven. Treason, however, may not. You will await your trials in our dungeon."

"Trial?" Belnat blurted.

Razem arched an eyebrow. "Yes, Lord Belnat. You will be given a fair trial. We will permit you to call witnesses to your defense, if you can think of any that will truly aid your case. There has been a great deal too much killing already. I will not summarily put a man to death without a trial first."

Razem gestured and the guards jerked the chains that bound him. Belnat was conveyed out of the audience chamber without further comment.

"As for you, Arisanat..." Razem shook his head, staring at the face he had loved and looked up to for so long, the face that looked so much like his own, so much like Venra's. "What shall I do with the cousin who so generously and lovingly guarded me in my youth?" he asked sadly. "What shall I do to reconcile that man with the man who tried to kill me and my sister, who *did* kill my father?"

Arisanat looked calmly back at him. Those gold-flecked brown eyes were clear of madness or hatred, though there was plenty of grief. "You will kill him, Razem. It is what you must do." His voice was steady. "Just as I did what I must."

Razem stared at him, aching to assault him with a barrage of questions. But how many questions would it take to cut to the heart of this? Arisanat could never make him understand how he could betray him, and that was the only thing Razem really wanted to know.

Arisanat's shoulders heaved as he sighed. "Life without Venra was...not. He was so much cleverer than I. He would have had a solution." He shook his head. "I acted as I did to avenge Venra, but also to secure a greater inheritance for my son." He smiled bleakly at Razem. "The quarry is flooding. Variden will have nothing." He bowed his head. "Not even, now, a father."

Razem bowed his head as well. He heard the shuffling of feet as one of the spectators shifted. Near the back of the chamber, someone coughed. When he looked up again, a ray of sunshine angling in through a stained glass window caught his eye. Motes of dust danced and wavered in that ray, as they would tomorrow and the next day. What did sunlight care for kings?

"Yes," Razem said finally. "I will have to execute you. But I will take Variden into my household and raise him with all the love you showed me as a boy. I will tell him stories of his uncle and will help him come to terms with being the son of a traitor."

"He knew nothing of my plans," Arisanat said. "He's just a boy. Be kind to him, Razem." Razem nodded. "Nor did my sister. I told only Venra—only Venra's grave." His calm exterior crumbled and a sob escaped. "I am sorry, Razem. But Venra should have lived."

"He should have," Razem agreed. "But so should my father." He gestured, and the remaining guards led his weeping cousin away. He would be housed in a room in the tower, inaccessible but full of sunlight and fresh air, because Razem wanted to give his cousin that much comfort until his death.

When Arisanat was gone, the assembled crowd was ushered out. Razem waited until the room was nearly empty before he slumped and buried his face in his hands. The heavy double doors boomed shut, enclosing him with his most trusted friends.

Small, strong hands rested on his shoulder. "You've had so much to deal with alone," Azmei whispered. "Razem, I'm so sorry."

He sighed and lifted his head. "I'm not alone now, am I?" He managed a smile for her, though he knew it wasn't very convincing. "Let's have a meal sent to my private chambers. I will have everyone here with me."

When the meal was spread, he glanced around at the group before offering a generic toast to allies and friends. Everyone drank to that, though Lady Tarra looked uncertain whether she truly belonged. Razem sipped his wine, considering. He would have to do something about her, but he still didn't know what. She could have made herself queen, but she'd given it up for loyalty to him. That deserved a reward. But what reward would be best? Would she agree to be queen if he offered it to her honestly? Did he want her to be his queen? Would that be the wisest alliance for him to make, or should he wait to see if he could open negotiations with Strid?

He shook his head. "Emran."

Kho looked away from his murmured conversation with Hawk. "Majesty?"

"I will need you to pick your most loyal soldiers to root out the rest of the rebels. I cannot have the disloyal members of the city guard still in positions of authority. For that matter, there will have to be a change in how we have done things. I do not like that Arisanat was able to exploit the rivalry between the city guard and the palace. There should be rotations—every man or woman will be a member of the *royal* guard, and they will serve the king in the palace and in the city both. There will be no division, because there will be only one guard."

Kho nodded. "A wise solution. I fear we'll be a bit thin for a while."

Razem took a long breath. His next idea might not be a popular one, at least outside of this room. "I want you to find the most troublesome of them and remove them from the guard entirely. Keep them separate from one another and assign them to units posted in the Kreyden. Perhaps it is time Dinnsan was rebuilt. We will need a large number of soldiers there to accomplish it."

Kho nodded again, offering no opinion.

"As for the merchants guild..." Razem shook his head. "I will think on that. They are neither nobility nor military, but civilian citizens. We must deal carefully but fairly with them. I will consider and welcome advice on that matter—tomorrow."

Kho sipped his wine and nodded again.

"How is Captain Ysdra?"

Kho set his wine glass down and looked away. "It...doesn't look good for him, majesty. The healers say they'll know more if he lives through the night."

Razem rubbed his eyes. "I will visit him before I sleep. He did us great service."

"Thank you," Kho whispered.

A somber silence fell over the group. Razem almost regretted having asked about Ysdra, though he knew it was proper, and he'd hoped...well, he'd hoped for some good news. Dinner was nearly finished when Tarra spoke.

"Your majesty, what about me?"

Razem looked at her, uncomprehending, for several seconds. "You are free, Lady Tarra," he said finally. What about her? What would he do to thank her? Perhaps Azmei would have some idea. "I give you my condolences for your mother's death."

When dinner was finished, five of them stayed around the fire, drinking mulled wine and staring into the shadows. Razem wondered if Hawk would ever feel comfortable talking about his years in Strid. He wondered if he had the right to ask the man. Perhaps if he assured Hawk that he earnestly desired peace, Hawk would be willing to help.

Yarrax was sitting to Azmei's right, furthest from the rest of them and a little apart even from Azmei. Razem had noticed during dinner that the young man didn't seem to like being touched. He didn't meet people's eyes or speak very often, though he seemed to be, for the most part, listening to the conversation around him. He occasionally blanked and stared into space as if he were talking to the dragons. Xellax and Rexiel were resting on the tower in the last of the fading light of day. The other dragons had flown away, though Yarrax had assured Razem they weren't going far.

Ilzi spent a lot of time darting glances at Yarrax when she didn't think anyone was watching. He couldn't be much above a year or two older than she, and while he looked a bit underfed, he wasn't bad looking. He supposed it was natural for her to look at someone with admiration. Of course, he also hadn't missed the way Hawk darted those same sort of glances at Azmei from time to time.

He cleared his throat. "Yarrax, you said the dragons had a dire message for us. Now that we have dealt with the insurrection, may we hear it?"

Yarrax jerked back to attention. He stared at Razem for a moment, then flickered a glance at Azmei and licked his lips. "The main of it is this, your majesty: The gods are waking, and they are not happy."

Razem felt as if the palace trembled, but this time he knew it wasn't a dragon landing. The gods were waking. Why now, after a sleep of centuries? Why would the dragons care? And—

"That's what you meant," Ilzi said, her voice soft. She was looking at Azmei. Azmei nodded. Clearly she had heard the message already.

"What—well, what do they—the dragons—want *us* to do about it?" Razem asked. He wondered if he sounded as young and helpless as he suddenly felt.

"They say Vistaren must be told," Azmei said. "It was my half of the bargain, if they agreed to help you."

"Why Vistaren?" Razem asked.

"I don't know," Yarrax put in. "Xellax will be able to discern more when we meet him."

Razem sat back in his chair, staring at his sister in consternation. "So...you're leaving me again, just after I got you back. You're going to Amethir."

Azmei nodded. It was little balm that she looked unhappy about it.

"Are you going to marry him?" he asked softly. Yarrax and Hawk both startled at the question, but Hawk's surprise faded into unhappy acceptance, while Yarrax just kept staring at Azmei.

She looked crossly at her brother. "I'll ford that stream when I reach it."

Gods, what a mess. Razem nodded slowly, thinking. "You can't go alone," he said after a moment.

"I'll go with her," Hawk blurted. He turned to face Azmei directly. "I'll go with you. If you'll allow me."

Azmei didn't look as happy about it as Razem had expected. Perhaps she realized it would further complicate things. But she smiled at Hawk. "I wouldn't ask it of you," she said softly. "But...it pleases me that you wish to."

Razem pretended not to notice as Hawk took her hand. "So it is settled. I will send word to Destar Thorne. The *Victorious* took no damage in the fighting; they were at sea until we'd already retaken the docks." He grinned briefly. "Thorne was furious that he missed it."

Azmei laughed, though it sounded choked. "Thank you," she said.

"Will you come back, as you are able?" Razem asked. He wasn't sure he wanted to hear her answer. But she smiled, and it looked genuine.

"As I am able," she said. Then she glanced at Hawk and amended, "As we are able."

EPILOGUE

In the scrubby shale lands south of the Shokanda River delta, a cave had been formed on the banks of one of the river's nameless tributaries. Any number of things washed up on the rocky shore in front of the cave, from fishing nets to rusted-out buckets to driftwood to seaglass. A man lived in the cave, scratching out what living he could gather from the river's bounty.

People from the nearby village called him crazy, but they also took things to him to be mended, if no one else could manage it. He cobbled together equipment for fishing and the meager farming that was done, and in return, the villagers gave him bread and salt fish.

The man thought of himself only as The Scavenger, and he spent his days muttering prayers to the maker god while he used glue rendered from fish to stick things together. He did not expect to get any answer from the sleeping god; it was just a habit he'd formed, mostly to hear a human voice, even if it was his own.

One night, when The Scavenger was at least five decades old, he slept more deeply and dreamed more vividly than he could remember ever doing. When he woke, he remembered little of his dreams, but he knew he had a task.

He gathered a kit of his making supplies and collected every last bit of seaglass he owned. One piece in particular was nearly round and a gorgeous wintry blue-white. He'd always liked it, and he'd always wanted to use it in something, but he'd never found any project worthy of it.

"Find her," he mumbled to himself, repeating the command that had boomed through his mind at the moment of his waking. "Find her. Fix her."

The Scavenger struck out along the shore, the voice of his maker god echoing in his head.

ABOUT THE AUTHOR

Stephanie A. Cain writes epic and urban fantasy for fun, and a history blog for work. She lives in Indiana. She graduated from Purdue University before the turn of the (21st) century with a Bachelor of Arts in History and Creative Writing, with a Medieval Studies minor. She enjoys hiking, reading, birdwatching, and general geekery. A proud crazy cat lady, Stephanie is happily owned by Eowyn, Strider, and Eustace Clarence Scrubb.

In her free time, Stephanie enjoys hiking (except for the spiders), bird-watching, visiting wineries, and collecting anything with owls on it. She likes to unwind by playing World of Warcraft and Skyrim. She enjoys organizing things, is overly fond of 3-ring binders, and visits office supply stores for fun. She owns way more movie scores and fountain pens than she can actually afford. She can be found online at www.stephaniecainonline.com.

AUTHOR'S NOTE

Thanks for reading my novel. If you enjoyed this, would you please take a moment to leave a review of my book at Amazon or Goodreads? Writing just two or three honest sentences is one of the best things you can do to support any author.

Thank you!

Stephanie

www.ingramcontent.com/pod-product-compliance
Lightning Source LLC
Chambersburg PA
CBHW070733120726

47910CB00001B/88